J.R. Ward lives in the South with her incredibly supportive husband and her beloved golden retriever. After graduating from law school, she began working in health care in Boston and spent many years as chief of staff for one of the premier academic medical centres in the nation.

Visit her at: www.jrward.com | www.facebook.com/JRWardBooks

RAPTURE

J. R. WARD

piatkus

PIATKUS

First published in the United States in 2012 by New American Library,
A Division of Penguin Group (USA) Inc., New York
First published in Great Britain as a paperback original in 2012 by Piatkus

A CIP catalogue record for this book
is available from the British Library

ISBN 978-0-7499-5700-1

Printed and bound in Great Britain by
CPI Group (UK) Ltd, Croydon, CR0 4YY

Papers used by Piatkus are from well-managed forests
and other responsible sources.

MIX
Paper from
responsible sources
FSC® C104740

Piatkus
An imprint of
Little, Brown Book Group
100 Victoria Embankment
London EC4Y 0DY

An Hachette UK Company
www.hachette.co.uk

www.piatkus.co.uk

For our Rachel,
who not only puts the "heart" in Heartland,
but introduced me to the real live Fi-Fi.

>———————————<

Acknowledgments

With great thanks to the readers!

And as always with love to Team Waud, you know who you are, and so many thanks to Steve Axelrod, Kara Welsh, Leslie Gelbman, and Claire Zion.

None of this would be possible without my family, both those of blood and adoption.

Oh, and of course, WriterDog.

RAPTURE

Chapter One

Grave.

And not as in serious. As in headstone and freshly disturbed earth, as in a body down under, as in ashes to ashes, dust to dust.

Matthias was naked on a grave. In the middle of a cemetery that stretched out as far as he could see.

First thing he thought of was the back tats he'd made his men get, the ones of the Grim Reaper standing in a field of marble and granite slabs.

Fucking ironic, really—and maybe he was going to get sliced and diced by a sycthe at any second.

Try saying that three times fast.

Blinking to clear what little vision he had, he gathered his limbs closer to his torso to preserve warmth, and waited for the scene to shift back to his reality. When nothing changed, he wondered where the wall that he'd been trapped in for an eternity had gone.

Had he finally gotten free of the cloying, crowded torture pit?

Was he out of Hell?

With a groan, he tried to push himself up, but it was hard enough to just lift his head. Then again, finding out firsthand that those religious nuts had been right about a lot of things kind of made a guy want to take a nap: In fact, sinners did go down under, and not to Australia, and once you were there, the suffering made all the stuff you'd bitched about aboveground look like Universal Studios on a free pass.

There was a Devil.

And her living room sucked.

Although the Holy Rollers hadn't gotten everything straight. Turned out Satan didn't have horns, or a tail; no pitchfork or cloven hooves, either. She was a bitch and a half, however, and she did wear red a lot. Then again, brunettes looked good in that color—at least, that's what she told herself.

With his left eye, the one that worked, he blinked again, bracing himself for a return to the dense, hot blackness, with the screams of the damned ringing in his ears, and his own pain ripping up his throat and exploding out his cracked lips. . . .

Nope. Still on a grave. In a cemetery.

Buck-ass naked.

Taking it all in, he got an eyeball full of white marble tombs, and family plots marked with angels, and ghostly statues of the Virgin Mary—although the low-to-the-ground headstones were far more common, as if the runts of the litter had taken over the place. Pine trees and maples threw shadows across scruffy spring grass and wrought-iron benches. Streetlamps glowed peach at their tops like candles on a birthday cake, and the winding lanes might have been romantic in another place.

Here they weren't. Not in this context of death—

From out of nowhere, scenes from his life passed by his eyes, making him wonder if he wasn't enjoying a second shot at dying. Or a third, as was the case.

There was no happy-happy in the retrospective. No loving wife or beautiful children, no white picket anything. Just dead bodies, dozens of them, hundreds of them, all ones he had killed, or had ordered killed.

He had done evil, true evil, during his lifetime.

Forcing himself to sit up off the loose dirt, his body was a jigsaw that didn't fit right, its bits and pieces jammed into sockets and joints that were sloppy in some places, too tight in others. But that's what happened when you Humpty Dumpty'd yourself, and the medical profession and your limited healing powers were all you had to put things back together.

Shifting his eye over to the face of the grave marker, he frowned. James Heron.

Jesus Christ, James Heron . . .

Ignoring the fact that his hand was shaking, he traced the deeply engraved letters, his fingertips sinking into what had been carved into the polished gray grantite.

A ragged breath left his chest, as if the pain he suddenly felt behind his ribs had bullied the oxygen out of his lungs.

He'd had no idea that there was an eternal reward, that your deeds were in fact counted and weighed, that there was a judgment that came on the heels of your heart's final beat. That wasn't what the pain was about, however. It was the knowledge that even if he'd known what waited for him, he wouldn't have been able to do anything differently.

"I'm sorry," he said, wondering exactly who he was talking to. "I'm so fucking sorry. . . ."

No answer.

He looked up at the sky. "I'm sorry!"

Still no reply, and that was okay. His regrets were jamming up his head so there wasn't a lot of room for third-party input anyway.

As he struggled to get up on his feet, his lower body buckled and sagged and he had to rely on the headstone for balance. God, he was a mess, his thighs pockmarked with scars, his belly riddled with keloids, one calf nearly stripped off the bone. The doctors had worked relative miracles with their bolts and rods, but compared to what he had been born like, he was a broken toy repaired with duct tape and Super Glue.

Then again, suicide was supposed to work. And Jim Heron was the reason he'd survived for another two years. Then death had found him and claimed him, and proved that the earth just borrowed souls. What was on the other side were the true owners.

Out of habit, he looked around for his cane, but then concentrated on what he was more likely to find: shadows coming for him, either those oily creatures from down below, or the human variety.

Either way he was fucked: As the former head of XOps, he had more enemies than a third-world dictator, and all of them had guns or guns for hire. And as a reject from the devil's playground, it went without saying that he hadn't gotten out of jail for free.

Sooner or later, someone was going to come after him, and even though he had nothing to live for, ego alone demanded that he put up a fight.

Or at least make a halfway decent target out of himself.

He started off with a limp, and continued on with the grace of a scarecrow, his body jerking in a series of spasms that culminated in a messy gait that hurt like hell. To conserve warmth, he tried to wrap his arms around himself, but that didn't last. He needed them to compensate for the lurching.

With his zombie shuffle and his scrambled, what-the-fuck head, he walked on, crossing the scratchy grass, passing the graves, feeling the brush of the chilly, damp air across his skin. He had no idea how he'd gotten out. Where he was headed. What day, month, or year it was.

Clothes. Shelter. Food. Weaponry.

Once he had secured the basics, he would worry about the rest of it. Assuming something didn't take him out first—after all, a wounded predator became prey fast. It was the law of the wild.

When he came up to a boxy stone building with wrought-iron fringe, he assumed it was just another tomb. But the Pine Grove Cemetery name across its pediment, and the shiny Master Lock on the front door suggested it was a grounds crew facility.

Fortunately, someone had left one of the windows open a crack in the back.

Naturally, the thing stuck like glue to its position.

Picking up a fallen branch, he wedged it in the crack, and heaved until the wood bowed and his arms clenched up tight.

The window budged and let out a high-pitched screech.

Matthias froze.

Panic, unfamiliar but hard learned, had him twisting around and searching the shadows. He knew that sound. It was the noise the demon's minions made when they came for you—

Nada.

Just graves and gaslights that, no matter how much his adrenal gland suggested otherwise, didn't turn into anything else.

Cursing, he threw himself back into the effort, using the branch as a winch until he had enough space to squeeze through. Getting his sorry ass up off the ground was a production, but once he had his shoulders inside, he let gravity do the rest of the work. The concrete floor he landed on felt as if it had refrigerator coils in it, and he had to take a TO, his breath dragging down his throat, his gut going into a twist as pain sizzled in too many places to count—

Overhead, fluorescent lights flickered in the ceiling, and then glowed steady and sure, blinding him.

Goddamn motion sensors. The upside was that as soon as his eye adjusted, he had a clear shot at all kinds of mowers, weeders, and wheelbarrows. The downside? He was a diamond in a jewelry case, ready for the grabbing.

Over on the wall, hanging from pegs like the skins of dead animals, sets of waterproof overalls were a wardrobe waiting to happen, and he threw a bottom and a top on. The things were built to hang loose, but on him they flapped like boat sails.

Better. Better with the clothes, even though they smelled like fertilizer, and chafing was going to fast become an issue. A baseball hat on the counter had the Boston Red Sox logo on it, and he pulled the thing on to conserve body heat; then he looked around for anything he could use as a cane. The long-handled spades were going to weigh too much to be efficient, and it wasn't like any of the rakes were going to help.

Screw it. His immediate mission critical was getting away from all the overhead light raining on his gimpy little parade.

He exited the way he'd come in, forcing himself through the open window again and landing hard on the ground. No time to bitch and complain at the impact; he had to get moving.

Before he'd died and gone to Hell, as it were, he'd been the pursuer. Shit, his whole life he'd been the hunter, the one who stalked and cornered and destroyed. Now, as he returned to the darkness of the graves, all the intangibles of the night were dangerous until proven otherwise.

He hoped he was back in Caldwell.

If he was, all he had to do was stay under the radar and gun for New York City, where he had a stash of supplies.

Yeah, he prayed this was Caldwell. Forty-five minutes south on the highway was all it would take, and he'd already broken and entered. Hot-wiring an older-generation car was a skill he could also resurrect.

A lifetime later, or at least it seemed that way, he came up to the wrought-iron fence that rimmed all the RIP acreage. The thing was ten feet high, and top-hatted with spikes that in an earlier life had probably been daggers.

Facing off at the bars that kept him on the side of the dead, he gripped them with his hands and felt the cold of the metal grab back. Looking upward, he focused on the heavens. The stars overhead actually twinkled.

Funny, he'd always thought that was just a saying.

Inhaling, he drew clean, fresh air into his lungs, and realized he'd grown used to the stench in Hell. In the beginning, it had been what he'd hated most, that nauseating, rotten-egg stink in the sinuses that invaded the back of his throat and traveled down to poison his gut: More than a bad smell, it had been an infection that had entered his nose and taken over from there, turning everything that he was into territory it owned.

But he had become inured to it.

Over time, and in the midst of suffering, he had acclimatized to the horror, the despair, the pain.

His bad eye, the one he couldn't see out of, watered up.

He was never going to make it up there to the stars.

And this respite was probably just a way to heighten the torture. After all, there was nothing like a period of relief to revitalize a nightmare: When you returned to the shithole, the contrast sharpened everything up, wiping clean the acclimatization, the illusory Ctrl-Alt-Del resetting things to the initial shock he'd felt.

They would be coming again for him. It was, after all, exactly what he'd earned.

But for however long he had, he was going to fight the inevitable—not with hope of evasion, not for the possibility of a reprieve, but simply as an autonomic function of his hard wiring.

He fought for the same reason he'd done evil.

It was just what he did.

Pulling himself up off the ground, he wedged the better of his two feet into the bars and shoved his weight higher. Again. Again. The top seemed miles away, and its distance just made him focus more tightly on his goal.

After a lifetime, his palm locked on one of the spikes and then he linked his arm around the vicious point.

Blood was drawn a moment later as he swung his leg up and over the fence's head and shoulders, one of those sharp-and-pointies biting into his calf and taking a hunk out of it.

There was no going back, though. He'd committed himself, and one way or the other gravity was going to win and take him down to earth—so better it be on the outside than the inside.

As he went into a free fall, he focused on the stars. Even reached a hand up to them.

The fact that they just got farther and farther away seemed apt.

Chapter Two

Mels Carmichael was alone in the newsroom. Again.

Nine o'clock at night and the *Caldwell Courier Journal*'s maze of cubicles was all office equipment, no people, tomorrow's issue put to bed from a reporting standpoint, the printers now doing their work on the far side of the great wall behind her.

As she leaned back in her chair, the hinges let out a squeak, and she turned the thing into an instrument, playing a happy little ditty she'd composed after too many nights like this. The title was "Going Nowhere Fast," and she whistled the soprano part.

"Still here, Carmichael?"

Mels straightened up and crossed her arms over her chest. "Hey, Dick."

As her boss oiled his way into what little space she had, his overcoat was draped across his arm, and his tie was loose at his fleshy neck from yet another postgame wrap-up at Charlie's.

"Working late again?" His eyes went to the buttons down the

front of her shirt, like he was hoping the whiskey he'd sucked back had given him telekinetic powers. "I gotta tell you, you're too pretty for this. Don't you have a boyfriend?"

"You know me, all about the job."

"Well . . . I could give you something to work on."

Mels stared up at him, nice and steady. "Thanks, but I'm busy right now. Doing research on the prevalence of sexual harassment in previously male-dominated industries such as the airlines, sports . . . newspapers."

Dick frowned as if his ears hadn't heard what they'd been hoping for. Which was nuts. Her response to this act had been the same since day one.

Well over two years of shutting him down. God, had it been that long already?

"It's illuminating." She reached forward and gave her mouse a push, clearing the screen saver. "Lots of statistics. Could be my first national story. Gender issues in postfeminist America are a hot topic—course, I could just put it on my blog. Maybe you'd give me a quote for it?"

Dick shifted his raincoat around. "I didn't assign that to you."

"I'm a self-starter."

His head lifted as if he were looking for someone else to harass. "I only read what I assign."

"You might find it valuable."

The guy went to loosen his tie like he needed some air, but surprise! It was already open. "You're wasting your time, Carmichael. I'll see you tomorrow."

As he walked off, he pulled on that Walter Cronkite raincoat of his, the one with the seventies lapels, and the belt that hung loose from loops like part of his intestine was not where it should be. He'd probably had the thing since the decade of Watergate, the work of Woodward and Bernstein inspiring his twenty-year-old self to his own paper chase . . . that had culminated at the top of a medium city's masthead.

Not a bad job at all. Just not a bureau chief for *The New York Times* or *The Wall Street Journal*.

That seemed to bother him.

So, yeah, it didn't take a genius to ascribe his inappropriateness to the ennui of a balding former coxswain, the bitterness from a lifetime of not-quite-there intersecting with the almost-out-of-time of a man about to hump sixty.

Then again, maybe he was just a prick.

What she was clear on was that with a jawline more ham sandwich than Jon Hamm, the man had no objective reason to believe the answer to any woman's problems was in his pants.

As the double doors clamped shut behind him, she took a deep breath and entertained a fantasy that a Caldwell Transit Authority bus ran tire tracks up the back of that anachronistic coat. Thanks to budget cuts, though, the CTA didn't run the Trade Street route after nine o'clock at night, and it was now . . . yup, seventeen minutes after the hour.

Staring at her computer screen, she knew she probably should go home.

Her self-starter article wasn't actually on leering bosses who made female subordinates think fondly of public transportation as a murder weapon. It was on missing persons. The hundreds of missing persons in the city of Caldwell.

Caldie, home of the twin bridges, was leading the nation in disappearances. Over the previous year, the city of some two million had had three times the number of reported cases in Manhattan's five boroughs, and Chicago—combined. And the total for the last decade topped the entire Eastern seaboard's figures. Stranger still, the sheer numbers weren't the only issue: People weren't just disappearing temporarily. These folks never came back and were never found. No bodies, no traces, and no relocation to other jurisdictions.

Like they had been sucked into another world.

After all her research, she had the sense that the horrific mass slaughter at a farmhouse the month before had something to do with the glut in get-gones . . .

All those young men lined up in rows, torn apart.

Preliminary data suggested that many of those identified had been reported missing at one point or another in their lives. A lot of them were juvie cases or had drug records. But none of that mattered to their families—nor should it.

You didn't have to be a saint in order to be a victim.

The gruesome scene out in Caldwell's rural edges had made the national news, with every station sending their best men into town, from Brian Williams to Anderson Cooper. The papers had done the same. And yet even with all the attention, and the pressure from politicians, and the exclamations from rightfully distraught communities, the real story had yet to emerge: The CPD was trying to tie the deaths to someone, anyone, but they'd come up with nothing—even though they were working on the case day and night.

There had to be an answer. There was always an answer.

And she was determined to find out the whys—for the victims' sakes, and their families'.

It was also time to distinguish herself. She'd come here at the age of twenty-seven, transferring out of Manhattan because it was expensive to live in NYC, and she hadn't been getting anywhere fast enough at the *New York Post*. The plan had been to transplant for about six months, get some savings under her belt by living with her mother, and focus on the big boys: *The New York Times*, *The Wall Street Journal*, maybe even a network reporting job at CNN.

Not how things had worked out.

Refocusing on her screen, she traced the columns she knew by heart, searching for the pattern she wasn't seeing . . . ready to find the key that unlocked the door not just to the story, but her own life.

Time was passing her by, and God knew she wasn't immortal. . . .

When Mels left the newsroom around nine thirty, those lines of data reappeared every time she blinked, like a video game she'd played for too long.

Her car, Josephine, was a twelve-year-old silver Honda Civic with nearly two hundred thousand miles on it—and Fi-Fi was used to waiting at night in the cold for her. Getting in, she started the sewing machine engine and took off, leaving a dead-end job. To go to her mother's house. At the age of thirty.

What a player. And she thought she was magically going to wake up tomorrow morning and be all Diane Sawyer without the hair spray?

Taking Trade Street out of downtown, she left the office buildings behind, went past the clubs, and then hit the lock-your-doors stretch of abandoned walk-ups. On the far side of all those boarded-up windows, things got better when she entered the outskirts of residential world, home of the raised ranch and streets named after trees—

"Shiiiiiiit!"

Ripping the wheel to the right, she tried to avoid the man who lurched into the road, but it was too late. She nailed him square on, bouncing him up off the pavement with her front bumper so that he rolled over the hood and plowed right into the windshield, the safety glass shattering in a brilliant burst of light.

Turned out that was just the first of three impacts.

Airborne meant only one thing, and she had a terrifying impression of him hitting the pavement hard. And then she had her own problems. Trajectory carried her off course, her car popping the curb, the brakes slowing her momentum, but not fast enough—and then not at all as her sedan was briefly airborne itself.

The oak tree spotlit in her headlights caused her brain to do a split-second calculation: She was going to hit the goddamn thing, and it was going to hurt.

The collision was part crunch, part thud, a dull sound that she didn't pay a lot of attention to—she was too busy catching the air bag solidly in the face, her lack of a seat belt coming back to bite her on the ass. Or the puss, as the case was.

Snapping forward and ricocheting back, powder from the SRS got into her eyes, nose, and lungs, stinging and making her choke. Then everything went quiet.

In the aftermath, all she could do was stay where she'd ended up, much like poor, old Fi-Fi. Curled over the deflating air bag, she coughed weakly—

Someone was whistling. . . .

No, it was the engine, releasing steam from something that should have been sealed.

She turned her head carefully and looked out the driver's-side window. The man was down in the middle of the street, lying so still, too still.

"Oh . . . God—"

The car radio flared to life, scratchy at first, then gaining electrical traction from whatever short had occurred. A song . . . what was it?

From out of nowhere, light flared in the center of the road, illuminating the pile of rags that she knew to be a human being. Blinking, she wondered if this was the moment where she learned the answers about the afterlife.

Not exactly the scoop she'd been looking for, but she'd take it—

It wasn't some kind of holy arrival. Just headlights—

The sedan screeched to a halt and two people jumped out from the front, the man going to the victim, the woman jogging over to her. Mels's Good Samaritan had to fight to wrench open the door, but after a couple of pulls, fresh air replaced the sharp, plasticky smell of the air bags.

"Are you okay?"

The woman was in her forties and looked rich, her hair done up in a thing on her head, her gold earrings flashing, her sleek, co-ordinated clothes not matching an accident scene in the slightest.

She held up an iPhone. "I've called nine-one-one—no, no, don't move. You could have a neck injury."

Mels yielded to the subtle pressure on her shoulder, staying draped over the steering wheel. "Is he okay? I didn't see him at all—came from out of nowhere."

At least, that was what she'd meant to say. What her ears heard were mumbles that made no sense.

Screw a neck injury; she was worried about her brain.

"My husband's a doctor," the woman said. "He knows what to do with the man. You just worry about yourself—"

"Didn't see him. Didn't see him." Oh, good, that came out more clearly. "Coming home from work. Didn't . . ."

"Of course you didn't." The woman knelt down. Yeah, she looked like a doctor's wife—had the expensive smell of one, too. "You just stay still. The paramedics are coming—"

"Is he even alive?" Tears rushed to Mels's eyes, replacing one sting with another. "Oh, my God, did I kill him?"

As she began to shake, she realized what song was playing. "*Blinded by the Light . . .*"

"Why is my radio still working?" she mumbled through tears.

"I'm sorry?" the woman said. "What radio?"

"Can't you hear it?"

The reassuring pat that followed was somehow alarming. "You just breathe easy, and stay with me."

"My radio is playing. . . ."

Chapter Three

"Is it hot in here? I mean, do you think it's hot in here?"

As the demon crossed and recrossed her mile-long, Gisele Bünd-chen legs, she pulled at the low neckline of her dress.

"No, Devina, I don't." The therapist across the way was just like the cozy couch she was sitting on, heavily padded and comfortable-looking. Even her face was a chintz throw pillow, the features all stuffed in tight and slipcovered with concern and compassion. "But I can crack a window if it would make you feel more comfortable?"

Devina shook her head and shoved her hand back into her Prada bag. In addition to her wallet, some spearmint gum, a bottle of smartwater, and a bar of Green & Black's Organic dark, there was a shitload of YSL *Rouge pur Couture* lipstick. At least . . . there should have been.

As she dug around, she tried to make casual, like maybe she was double-checking that she hadn't lost her keys.

In reality, she was counting to make sure there were still thirteen tubes of that lipstick: Starting from the left in the bottom of the bag, she moved each one to the right. Thirteen was the correct number. One, two, three—

"Devina?"

—four, five, six—

"Devina."

As she lost count, she closed her eyes and fought the temptation to strangle the interrupter—

Her therapist cleared her throat. Coughed. Made a choking noise.

Devina popped her lids and found the woman with her hands around her own neck, looking like she'd swallowed a Happy Meal in a bad way. The pain and the confusion were good to see, a little hit off the pipe that had Devina curling her toes for more.

But the fun couldn't go any further. If this therapist bit it, what was she going to do? They were making progress, and finding another one she clicked with could take time she didn't have.

With a curse, the demon called back her mental dogs, relinquishing the invisible hold she hadn't been aware she'd thrown out.

The therapist took a deep, relieved breath and looked around. "I . . . ah, I think I will open that window."

As the woman did the honors, she was unaware that her shrink skills had just saved her life. The two of them had been meeting five times a week for the past couple of months, talking for fifty minutes at the cost of one hundred seventy-five dollars each time. Thanks to the sessions of emoting and crap, Devina's OCD symptoms were getting slightly easier to bear—and considering how things were going in the war with that angel Jim Heron, counseling was so going to be needed for this next round.

She couldn't believe she was losing.

In the final contest for supremacy over the earth, that angel had won twice, and she just once. There were only four more souls to battle over. If she lost two more? There was going to be nothing left of her or all her collections: Everything would disappear, those precious objects that she had gathered over the millennia, each an invaluable memento of her work, gone, gone, gone. And that wasn't the worst part. Her children, those glorious, tortured souls trapped in her wall, would be subsumed by the good, the beatific, the untainted.

The mere thought of it was enough to make her sick.

And on top of that bad news? She'd just been penalized by the Maker.

The therapist resettled on her cushions, back from the fresh-air hunt. "So, Devina, tell me what's on your mind."

"I . . . ah . . ." As anxiety rose, she lifted up her bag, inspected the bottom for holes, found none. "It's been hard. . . ."

None of the lipsticks could have fallen out, she told herself. And she'd checked the number before she had left her lair. Thirteen, a perfect thirteen. So logically, they were all there. Had to be.

But . . . oh, God, maybe she had put the bag down sideways, and one had escaped because she forgot to zip it closed—

"Devina," the therapist said, "you seem really upset. Can you please tell me what's going on?"

Talk, she told herself. It was the only way out of this. Even though counting and ordering and checking and rechecking felt like the solution, she'd spent aeons on this earth getting nowhere doing that. And this new way was working. Kind of.

"That new coworker I told you about." She wrapped her arms around her bag, holding everything in it close to the body she assumed when she walked among the monkeys. "He's a liar. A total liar. He double-crossed me—and I was the one who got accused of foul play."

Ever since she had started therapy, she had couched the war

with that fallen angel Heron in terms a human of the early twenty-first century could understand: She and her nemesis were coworkers at a consulting firm, vying for the Vice Presidency. Each soul they battled over was a client. The Maker was their CEO, and they had only a limited number of attempts to impress Him. Whatever, whatever, whatever. The metaphor wasn't perfect, but it was better than her doing a full reveal and having the woman either lose her own mind or think Devina was not just compulsive but certifiable.

"Can you be more specific?"

"The CEO sent both of us out to talk to a prospective client. In the end, the man gave us his business and wanted to work with me. Everything was fine. I'm happy, the client was . . ." Well, not happy, no. Matthias had not been happy at all, which was just another reason she'd been satisfied with the victory: The more suffering, the merrier. "The client was being taken care of, and it was all settled, the contract for service signed, the matter closed. And then I get dragged into a bullshit meeting and told that we both have to reapproach the man."

"You and your coworker, you mean."

"Yes." She threw up her hands. "I mean, come on. It's done. The business is secured—it's over. And now we're stuck with a redo? What the hell is that about? And then the CEO says to me, 'Well, you'll still retain your commission for the contract.' Like that makes it all okay?"

"Better than your losing it."

Devina shook her head. The woman just didn't understand. Once something was hers, letting it go, or having it taken away from her, was like a part of her true body being removed: Matthias had been ripped out of her wall and placed once again upon the earth.

Frankly, the power of the Maker was about the only thing that frightened her.

Aside from the compulsions.

Unable to stand the anxiety, she cranked open her bag again and started counting—

"Devina, you work well with the client, right."

She paused. "Yes."

"And you have a relationship with him or her."

"Him. I do."

"So you're in a stronger position than your coworker, right?" The therapist made a gesture with her hands, a physical representation of "no problem."

"I hadn't thought of that." She'd been too pissed off.

"You should. Although I will say, there is something I'm a little confused about. Why did the CEO feel the need to intercede? Especially if the client is not only under contract with the company, but satisfied?"

"He didn't approve of some of the . . . methods . . . used to secure the business."

"Yours?"

As Devina hesitated, the woman's eyes made a quick dip downward in the décolleté direction.

"Mine, yes," the demon said. "But come on, I got the client, and no one can fault my work ethic—I'm on the job all the time. Literally. I have no life except for my work."

"Do you approve of the tactics you used?"

"Absolutely. I got the client—that's all that matters."

The silence that followed suggested the therapist didn't agree with the whole ends-justify-the-means thing. But whatever, that was her problem—and probably the reason why she was shaped like a sofa and spent her days listening to people bitch about their lives.

Instead of ruling the underworld and looking hot as fuck in Louboutins—

As the anxiety spiked again, Devina started a re-count, shifting the lipsticks one after another from left to right. One, two, three—

"Devina, what are you doing."

For a split second she nearly attacked for real. But logic and a reality check kicked in: The compulsions were on the verge of taking her over. And you couldn't be effective against an enemy like Jim Heron if you were trapped in a closed circuit of numbering or touching objects that you knew perfectly well hadn't been lost, moved, or fingered by someone else.

"Lipstick. I'm just making sure I have my lipstick."

"Okay, well, I want you to stop."

Devina looked up with true despair. "I . . . can't."

"Yes, you can. Remember, it's not about the things. It's about managing your fear in a way that is more effective and permanent than giving into the compulsions. You know that the split second of relief you get at the end of a ritual never, ever lasts—and it doesn't get to the root problem. The fact of the matter is, the more you comply with the compulsions, the stronger a hold they have on you. The only way to get better is to learn to bear the anxiety and reframe those impulses as something you have power over—not the other way around." The therapist leaned in, all earnest cruel-to-be-kind. "I want you to throw one of them out."

"*What.*"

"Throw one of the lipsticks out." The therapist eased to the side and picked up a wastepaper basket the color of Caucasian skin. "Right now."

"No! God, are you crazy?" Panic threatened on the periphery of her body, her palms breaking out in a sweat, her ears beginning to ring, her feet going numb. Soon enough, the tide would close in, her stomach doing flip-flops, her breath getting short, her heart flickering in her chest. She'd been through it for an eternity. "I can't possibly—"

"You can, and what's more, you have to. Pick your least-favorite shade out of them, and put it in the bin."

"There is no least-favorite color—they're all the same red. 1 Le Rouge."

"Then any of them will do."

"I can't. . . ." Tears threatened. "I can't—"

"Little steps, Devina. This is the linchpin of cognitive behavioral therapy. We have to stretch you past your comfort zone, expose you to the fear, and then get you through it so you learn that you can come out on the other side in one piece. Do that enough times and you begin to loosen OCD's grip on your thoughts and decision-making. For example, what do you think is going to happen if you throw one of them out?"

"I'm going to have a panic attack. Especially when I get home and it's not with me."

"And then what."

"I'll buy another to replace it, but it won't be the one that I threw away so it's not going to help. I'll just get more compulsive—"

"But you haven't died."

Of course not, she was immortal. Provided she could win against Jim Heron. "No, but—"

"And the world hasn't ended."

Well, not under the lipstick scenario, no. "But it feels like it."

"Emotions come and go. They are not forever." The woman jiggled the little bin. "Come on, Devina. Let's try it. If it's too much for you to handle, you can take the lipstick back. But we need to start focusing on this."

Sure enough, an anxiety attack bloomed on her, but ironically, fear was what got her through it: fear that she was going to get hobbled by this problem she couldn't control; fear that Jim was going to win not because he was the superior player in the Maker's game, but because she cracked under the pressure; fear that she was never going to be able to change. . . .

Devina shoved her hand into the bag and grabbed the first lipstick that hit her palm. Then she ditched it. Just let the thing go into the wastepaper basket.

The dull sound as it hit the Kleenex balls of previous clients was like the jaws of Hell shutting on her.

"Good job," the therapist said. As if Devina were a five-year-old who'd done the alphabet right. "How do you feel?"

"Like I'm going to throw up." Eyeing the bin, the only thing that kept her from vomiting was the fact that she'd have to lose it *on* the lipstick.

"Can you rate your anxiety on a scale of one to ten?"

When Devina threw out a ten, the therapist went on a roll about breathing through the panic, blah blah blah—

The woman leaned in again, like she knew she wasn't getting through. "It is not about the lipstick, Devina. And the anxiety you feel now is not going to last forever. We won't push you too hard, and you'll be amazed at the progress. The human mind can be re-wired, new pathways of experience forged. Exposure therapy works—it is just as powerful as the compulsions. You need to believe this, Devina."

With a shaking hand, the demon wiped the sweat from her brow. Then, gathering herself inside her fitted overalls of human flesh, she nodded.

The couchlike woman was right. What Devina had been doing up to this point was not working. She was getting worse, and the stakes were only getting higher.

After all, not only was she losing . . . she was also in love with the enemy.

Not that she liked to remind herself of it.

"You don't have to believe that this is going to work, Devina. You just have to believe in the results. This is hard, but you can do it. I have faith in you."

Devina locked onto the human's eyes and envied the therapist's conviction. Hell, with that kind of confidence, you were either delusional . . . or standing on the concrete floor of experience and training.

There had been a time when Devina had been that sure of herself.

She needed that to come back.

Jim Heron had proven to be so much more than a worthy opponent and a good fuck. And she couldn't let him keep this upperhand thing going. Losing wasn't an option, and as soon as this session was over, she had to return to work with a clear head uncluttered by any bullshit.

Closing her eyes, she leaned back into the soft chair, put her hands on the padded arms, and dug her nails into the velvety fabric.

"How are you feeling?" the therapist asked.

"Like one way or another I'm going to beat this."

Chapter Four

"Just tell me if he's alive."

As Mels spoke up, the ER nurse at her bedside gave that one a total pass. Sticking out a pen, the woman said, "If you'll sign these discharge papers, I'll give you your prescriptions—"

Screw the Bic routine. "I need to know if the man lived."

"I can't divulge anyone's condition. HIPAA. Sign this so you can be discharged."

Subtext: *Get off my back, wouldja. I got work to do.*

Cursing quietly, Mels scribbled on the line, took the two slips of paper and the copy that was hers, and then Nurse Ratched went on to terrorize the next patient.

What a night. The good news was at least the police had called it an accident, recognizing that she hadn't been negligent or under the influence. But there were still problems . . .

Glancing down at her ticket to leave, she scanned the notes. Mild concussion. Neck strain. Follow up with her primary care in a week, or earlier if double vision, nausea, dizziness, worsening headache presented.

Her car was probably totaled.

There was no way that man was alive.

With a groan, she sat up from the pillows, and her bandaged head registered the vertical shift with a ballerina spin. As she gave things time to settle, she eyed her clothes on the orange plastic chair across the way. She'd gotten to keep her camisole, bra and her slacks on during her examinations. Blouse, jacket, and coat were just waiting to be put back into service.

She hadn't called her mother.

The family had already been through one automobile accident— and in that case, the person who hadn't lived through things had been her father.

So, yeah, she'd just texted and said she was going out with friends and would be home late. The last thing she needed was her mother upset and insisting on picking her up, especially given what she wanted to do now.

Mels took the whole getting-dressed effort slowly, although the foot drag wasn't just about being a good little patient. Evidently her shot at being a crash-test dummy wasn't the kind of thing you could brush off. She felt ancient and decrepit—and oddly terrified.

To have killed someone was . . . unfathomable.

Shoving the paperwork into her pocketbook, she pushed aside the pea green curtain and faced off at a crapload of managed chaos: People in scrubs and white coats were ping-ponging around, jumping into rooms, jumping out of them, giving orders, taking them.

Considering she'd already been in one collision tonight, she was careful not to get in anyone's way as she headed for the exit.

Which she didn't use.

The waiting room out in front was filled with various versions of the halt and lame, including one guy with a black eye and a badly bandaged hand that was bleeding. Looking up at her, he nodded, like they were bonding over the fact that she'd gotten into a bar fight, too.

Yeah, you shoulda seen what that oak tree looked like after I was done with him. Word.

At the front desk, she propped herself at the counter and waited to get noticed. When a man came over, she smiled like nothing was a big deal. "Can you tell me what room the John Doe from that car accident is in?"

"Hey, I know you. You're a reporter."

"Yeah." She dug into her bag, got out her laminated press pass, and flashed the thing like it was an FBI badge. "Can you help me?"

"Sure." He started tapping on the keyboard. "He's been moved to an inpatient room. Six sixty-six. Take the elevators over there, and follow the signs."

"Thanks." She knocked on the counter: He was still breathing, at least. "I appreciate it."

"You know, you don't look so hot," the nurse said, making a circle around one of his eyes.

"Rough night."

"Clearly."

The ride up to the sixth floor was an exercise in data processing that her brain flunked badly. Unsteady to begin with, the ascent gave her middle ear a workout that left her hanging on the rail that went around at hip level. Good idea to put one there; then again, they'd probably had a lot of woozy people on this thing. And the fact that the panels were matte gray metal was another bene. She hadn't seen what she looked like, but given her reception down in Reception, the air bag she'd tried to eat hadn't done her complexion any good.

The ding was Disney-cheerful, but the doors opened slowly, as if they were exhausted.

Doing as she'd been told, she followed the signs and found the right place, entering a long, broad hall that was marked by countless oversized doors. Things were quieter up here, although no one looked over from the nursing station as she approached. Just as well—she didn't want to run the risk of someone asking questions, not liking the answers, and shutting her down.

The room was nearly at the end of the corridor, and she half-expected there to be a cop sitting outside of it. There was nothing and nobody. Just another door with a buff-colored number plate on its jamb, and a laminated face that approximated pine.

Pushing on the toggle, she leaned inside. In the dim light, she could see the foot of the bed, a window on the far wall, and a TV mounted by the ceiling. Beeping sounds and the smell of Lysol proved it wasn't a hotel room—not that she needed help on that one.

She cleared her throat. "Hello?"

When there was no reply, she stepped in and left the door slightly ajar. Walking past the bathroom, she stopped when she got a full view of the patient.

Bringing her hands up, she covered her mouth as her jaw dropped. "Oh . . . dear God."

Up above the utility garage, in the cramped studio apartment he'd been renting, Jim Heron couldn't sleep.

Everyone else around him was out like a light: Dog was at the foot of the cramped twin bed, paws twitching as he dreamed of bunnies or gophers . . . or maybe black shadows that had teeth. Adrian was propped up around the corner, his back against the crawl space, big body tense even though his breathing was even. And Eddie? Well, the guy was dead, so it wasn't like he was up pacing the floor.

Desperate for a cigarette, Jim got out of bed on the wrong side to avoid disturbing Dog, and grabbed his pack of Marlboros. Before he left, he went over and checked on Adrian.

Yup. Asleep sitting up.

With a crystal dagger in his hand, in case someone came after his boy.

Poor damn bastard. Eddie's loss had been a crippler for the team . . . but particularly for the pierced and tatted wild card who had been on vigil ever since it had happened.

Why did a strong man showing grief in a tough way seem so much sadder than any kind of histrionic weeping and wailing?

And P.S., it was fucking weird to have partners.

Back when Jim had been an assassin in XOps, he'd been a strict solo operator. Now, so much had changed, from his boss to his job description to his weapons of choice—and Eddie Blackhawk had been the one to show him the way, teaching him what he needed to know, calming him and Adrian down when they were throwing punches at each other, being the voice of reason in situations where there seemed to be no logic whatsoever . . . like when you were standing over your own corpse. Or fighting a demon who had a penchant for Prada and a thing for men who didn't like her. Or bearing on your shoulders the future of all the good souls and the bad ones that ever had been or would be.

Kind of made a guy want to flip burgers for a living.

With a curse, he went over to the couch, snagged a leather coat, and draped it over Adrian's lower legs. The other angel grunted and shifted on the floor, but stayed under the coat. Good thing—the goal was to keep the guy warm, not talk to him.

Jim didn't feel like talking to anybody.

No newsflash there, at least.

Stepping out onto the top landing of the stairs, the cold air clawed into the bare skin of his chest. Before he had a roommate and a dog, he'd always slept in the nude. Now he wore sweats. Helped with the fact that in April, Caldwell was still pretty chilly at night.

Not that he did much sleeping.

The fresh pack of Marlboros was still wrapped in cellophane, and he smacked it on the heel of his hand as he shut the door quietly. One of the advantages of being both immortal and corporeal was that you didn't have to worry about cancer, but nicotine still had an effect on your nervous system.

You also didn't have to pat your pockets for a lighter.

Ripping the flip top open, he took out a coffin nail, put it between his lips, and brought up his hand. As his forefinger glowed on command, he thought of Eddie again—and felt like murdering Devina, as usual.

At least overall, the good guys were still ahead two to one in the war. If he could just squeak out two more wins, he'd have done it: snatched the Earth out of the jaws of damnation, kept his mother safe in the Manse of Souls . . . and gotten his Sissy out of Hell.

Not that she was his.

Exhaling, he wasn't one hundred on that last one, but that had to be the way it worked, right? If the angels won, and Devina didn't exist anymore, he had to be able to go down and get that poor, innocent girl free of that prison. Hell would be his to do with what he chose.

Right?

On that note, he wondered who the next soul in play was.

Thinking about his new boss, he heard the Englishman's voice in his head, Nigel's smooth, haughty tones echoing around, getting on his nerves: *You will recognize him as an old friend and an old foe who you have seen of late. The path could not be more obvious if it were spotlit.*

"Thanks, " he muttered, the smoke leaving his lips along with his breath. "Big help there, pal."

How the hell was it fair that his enemy knew the target and he did not?

Fucked. Up.

Last round, he'd tricked Devina into giving him the intel, and she wasn't going to fall for anything like that again—say what you would about that demon, she was not a dumb blonde on so many levels. And that meant that here he was again, stuck in neutral, as the opposition no doubt got a head start.

Which was precisely the problem he'd had in the battle over his former boss's soul. The whole time, he'd assumed the one on deck was someone else's, but it had turned out to be Matthias's all the way.

Too little, too late, and the SOB had made the wrong choice.

Win: Devina.

At this rate, the game was set up to be unfair—as long as Devina continued to interact directly with the souls. According to the rules, Jim was the only one who should be doing that, but in practice, she was as much a part of the ground action as he was. Naturally, Nigel, chief Boy Scout in charge, was convinced she was going to get shanked for this kind of coloring outside the lines—and maybe she would. But who knew the when of that?

In the meantime, Jim had no choice but to stay sharp and hope he didn't fuck up again.

He had to win. For his mother . . . and for Sissy.

As he took another drag and let it out, he watched the milky white smoke curl up into the cold air and rise until it disappeared. Between one blink and the next, he saw Sissy Barten, that beautiful young girl, hanging upside down in a white porcelain tub, her bright red blood staining her light blond hair, her skin marked with symbols he'd never seen before, but that Eddie had understood all too well—

A subtle scratching interrupted his train of thought, and he reached behind and opened the studio's door. Dog limped out, his shaggy hair all discombobulated—although that was the stuff's SOP, not because he'd fallen asleep in a weird position.

"Hey, big man," Jim said softly as he reclosed things. "You need to go out?"

The poor old thing had a hard time with the stairs, so Jim usually carried him down to the ground. As he bent down to oblige, though, Dog just lowered his butt onto the landing—which was his way of saying he wanted to be picked up and held.

"Roger that."

The animal, who Jim knew damn well was so much more than just a random stray, weighed next to nothing in his arm, and was warm as a Bunsen burner.

"I told her to think of you," Jim said as he held his cigarette downwind of the dog—just in case he was wrong about the something-else. "I told Sissy to picture you chewing on my socks. I want her to imagine you playing in the bright green grass when things get . . ."

He couldn't finish the thought aloud.

In his lifetime, he'd done ugly things, hideous things, to ugly, hideous people—which meant he had been long hardened to his emotions—

Well, actually, that had happened when he was still a teenager, hadn't it. On that day when everything had changed forever.

On the day his mother had been murdered.

Whatever. Water under the bridge.

The fact of the matter was, the idea of Sissy in the demon's Well of Souls was enough to make even a battle-hardened soldier like him lose his mind.

"I told her . . . to think of you, when she felt like she couldn't hold on any longer."

Dog's stumpy tail wagged back and forth, like Jim had done the right thing.

Yeah, hopefully she was using Dog down there to sustain her. Shit knew there was nothing else.

"I gotta find the next soul," Jim muttered before taking another hit of the cigarette. "Gotta find out who's on deck next. We gotta win this, Dog."

As that cold, wet nose gave him a nuzzle, he was careful to exhale over his shoulder.

The fact that Nigel maintained he knew the soul at bat told him absolutely nothing. He'd known a shitload of people during his life.

He could only pray it was someone he could bring around.

Chapter Five

Matthias knew the moment he was no longer alone: The light around him intensified, which meant a door had been opened, and that didn't happen for no reason.

His right hand curled in on a reflex, as if there should have been a gun against his palm. But that was all he could do. His body was immobile from pain, sure as if he were chained to whatever he was lying on—a bed. He was in a bed . . . and the ambient beeping told him what kind. A hospital. He was still in the hospital.

Was he never going to get over—

His thought processes ground to a halt at that point.

Nothing but a black hole.

No idea what had gotten him here. No clue why his body hurt so much. No . . . Jesus, he knew his first name was Matthias and that was it.

Panic opened his eyes fully—

There was a horrified woman standing at his bedside, her hands up to her face, her expression one of shock. One of her eyes was bruised and there was a bandage on her forehead. Darkish hair was pulled back. Pretty eyes. Tall . . . she was tall—

Beautiful eyes, actually.

"I'm so sorry," she said hoarsely.

Huh? "About . . ." His voice was rough, his throat raw. And one of his eyes wasn't working right—

No, the thing wasn't working at all. He had lost half of his vision a while ago. That was right, back when he was . . .

He frowned as his thoughts fell off that cliff again.

"I hit you with my car. I'm so sorry—I didn't see you coming. It was so dark out, and you came into the road before I could stop."

He tried to reach out a hand, a compulsion to calm her overriding his pain and confusion. "Not your fault. No . . . no tears. Come . . ."

On some level, he couldn't believe anyone would cry over him, now or ever. He was not the type of man who inspired that kind of reaction.

Not him, no. Why that was true, though, he didn't know. . . .

The woman came a little closer, and he watched with his one eye as she extended her soft, warm hand . . . and slid it against his palm.

The contact made him feel warm all over, like he'd been submerged in a bath.

Funny, he hadn't been aware of being cold until she touched him.

"I'm squeezing," he said in his broken voice. "In case you can't tell."

She was tactful and didn't comment on the fact that she clearly hadn't had a clue he was putting any effort into the contact. But he was. And as their eyes held, for some reason he wanted to point out that he hadn't always been broken. Once, not long ago, he had been able to stand proud, run far, lift much. Now he was a mattress with a heartbeat.

Not because she'd hit him with her car, though. No, he'd been broken for a while.

Maybe his memory was coming back?

"I'm so sorry," she said again.

"Is that how you . . ." He motioned up to his own face, but the gesture just made her focus on him—and her wince suggested it was tough for her to look at how ugly he was. "You were hurt, too."

"Oh, I'm fine. Have the police come and talked to you yet?"

"Just woke up. Don't know."

She took her hand from his and rummaged around in a bag the size of a small duffel. "Here. This is my card. They spoke with me while I was getting treated, and I told them I accept all responsibility."

She turned the thing to face him, except his vision refused to focus.

And he didn't want to look anywhere but into her eyes.

"What's your name?"

"Mels Carmichael. Well, Melissa." She touched her own chest. "I go by Mels."

As she put the card on the little rolling table, he frowned, even though it made his head pound. "How were you hurt?"

"Call me if you need anything? I don't have a lot of money, but I—"

"You weren't wearing a seat belt, were you."

The woman looked around like maybe she'd gotten that from the police earlier. "Ah . . ."

"You should wear a seat belt—"

The door burst open, and the nurse who strode in was all business, making like she owned the place.

"I'm right here," she announced, as she marched over to the machinery behind the bed. "I heard the alarm."

His immediate impression was of a lot of breasts. Tiny little waist. Long brunette hair thick as a duvet, shiny as a china plate.

And yet she made his skin crawl. To the point where he tried to sit up, so he could get the hell away from—

"Shh . . . it's okay." As the nurse smiled, she all but shoved Mels Carmichael away. "I'm here to help."

Black eyes. Black eyes that reminded him of something else, somewhere else—a prison where you were choked by darkness, incapable of getting free—

The nurse leaned down, bringing them closer together. "I'm going to take care of you."

"No," he said strongly. "No, you will not. . . ."

"Oh, yes, I will."

Warnings shifted around the edges of his consciousness, things he couldn't quite capture sending up alarms like smoke trails before bombs exploded. He got nowhere with any specifics. His memories were like camouflaged bunkers in a landscape viewed with night goggles; he knew his enemy had set up fortifications, but damned if he could visualize them in any detail.

"If you don't mind," his nurse said to Mels, "I need to take care of my patient."

"Oh, yeah. Of course. I'll just . . . yeah, I'll go." Mels leaned around the other woman to glance at him. "I guess . . . I'll talk to you later."

Matthias had to look around the nurse as well, his stomach muscles clenching as he shifted his weight—

The nurse blocked the view. "Close the door behind you, will you. That'd be great. Thanks."

And then they were alone.

The nurse smiled at him and leaned her hip on the edge of the bed. "How about we clean you up."

Not a question. And, man, he suddenly felt naked—and not in a good way.

"I'm not dirty," he said.

"Yes, you are." She put her hand on his forearm, right where the IV lines went into his vein. "You are filthy."

From out of nowhere, strength began to funnel into him, the energy burrowing in and inflating his flesh with health, sure as if he had had good nights of sleep and days filled with rest and plenty of food.

It was coming from her, he realized. Except . . . how was that possible?

"What are you doing to me?"

"Nothing." The nurse smiled. "Do you feel different?"

Staring into her eyes, the dense, cloying black seemed as irresistible as it was repulsive—and he didn't know how long they stood there like that, linked by her hand, that one-way exchange like a miracle drug.

"I know you," he thought out loud.

"Funny when you feel that way about a stranger."

The power entering him felt evil, and very familiar. "I don't want—"

"Don't want what, Matthias? Don't want to feel better, be stronger, live forever?" She eased down even closer. "Are you telling me you don't want to be a man again?"

His lips started to move, but nothing came out, a sluggishness coming over him as she retracted her touch. Hazy and confused, he tried to rouse himself, but it was as if, in the aftermath, he'd been drugged.

"I'm going to wash you now," she said, her lids lowering, her smile speaking of blow jobs, instead of bedpans.

As she went over to the equivalent of a bar sink, Matthias inhaled, his ribs expanding without pain, his exhale even and smooth. All the aching had gone away, giving him a sense that it had been years since he'd inhabited his body without difficulty. Centuries?

"What date is it?" he mumbled as she ran water into a basin.

The nurse glanced over her shoulder. "That's right. You have amnesia."

A moment later she reapproached the bed, bringing the rolling table with her. As she pulled the sheets down to his hips and loosened the ties on his johnny, he lifted his heavy head and stared at himself. The top half wasn't so bad, just a scar here and there. Lower half was a mess.

The washcloth was soft and warm.

As the nurse stroked his chest, her skin was so smooth and glowing, it was like it had been airbrushed, and her hair was impossibly thick and luscious. She even had lips like a piece of fruit, glossy, with the promise of sweetness.

I don't want her, he thought.

But he couldn't seem to move.

"You need to put some weight on," she commented, drawing the washcloth over his pecs. "Too thin."

That stretch of terry went ever lower, lingering across his abdominals, more lover than health care provider. And with sudden clarity, he knew there had been a time when she would have been impressed—those women he'd contracted with for sexual exercise had always been struck by his body back in the day—

Wait, was this really happening?

When she went to push the covers down further, he stopped her. "No, don't."

"Yes, definitely."

With her eyes locked on his, she removed his hand from her wrist and wrenched everything off. The violence in the act made him stir somewhere deep—why, he didn't know.

"Did I strike a chord," she said, even though she knew she had. Somehow . . . she knew he'd liked things dangerous. "Did I. Matthias."

"Maybe." His voice was stronger all of a sudden. Deeper. . . .

"How about now?"

She touched him on that place that defined his gender, the cloth rasping over his cock.

As she licked her lips like she was enticed, he had to laugh out loud. For whatever inexplicable reason she was breaking all kinds of protocol, she was about to get a whole lot of going-nowhere—and that was going to solve the problem of his not wanting this: It didn't matter if she got herself good and naked and did jumping jacks on top of him; that flaccid stretch of flesh wasn't going to stand up and notice.

Even with the amnesia, he knew that like he knew he couldn't see out of one eye. It was fact; not a recollection.

"My memory isn't the only thing I've lost," he said dryly.

"Really."

When she stroked where she shouldn't, he jumped. But then, impotence didn't mean you had no feeling. Just meant you couldn't do anything about—

That river of power tunneled into him again, this time stronger. And with a moan, he arched back, automatically rolling his hips up to the source.

"That's right," she said, her voice warping. "Feel me. I'm in you."

That long-missed sexual surge rocketed through him; the aggression and the need to penetrate something he knew he hadn't felt for so long. God, the reminder that he was in fact male, not some broken, androgynous—

Ah, shit, this was good. Fuck . . . so good.

"Look at me," she commanded him as she worked his cock. "*Look* at me."

He'd been so distracted by the novelty, he'd forgotten who was doing him, and the sight of her drained the sensation out of him, his emotions going impotent even as his body went to town. She was beautiful, but she was . . . as lush as poison ivy.

"Don't you like this, Matthias?"

No, he did not. He didn't like this at all. "Not in the slightest."

"Liar. And we need to finish what we started, you and I. Yes, we do."

Devina entered the Saks Fifth Avenue at The Caldwell Galleria Mall at close to five a.m. Stepping through the glass and into a storefront display of mannequins in pastel dresses, she posed with them for a moment, arching her back and feeling her breasts stretch the seams of her blouse under her coat.

Spring was in full swing, and that was good news for her thighs.

Maybe while she was here, she'd pick up a few things off the racks.

With a shopping tingle sparkling in her veins, she popped around the side of the backsplash and disabled the motion detectors with a wave of her hand. For a second, she thought she'd let the video surveillance cameras stay on—just for shits and giggles.

Nothing more fun than being watched—even if it was just by a paunchy human sitting behind a security desk at the tail end of a night shift he'd probably slept through half of.

She was here for a serious reason, however.

Her stilettos made a clipping sound over the polished marble floor, and she liked the echoing noise, walking harder so her dominion over the emptiness reached out in every direction. God, she loved the smell in the air: floor polish and perfume and cologne . . . and wealth.

Passing by the handbag boutiques that were set against the wall, she checked out Prada, Miu Miu, and Chanel. The merch looked great even in the dim glow of the security lighting, and she cracked when she got to Gucci. Slipping through the chain-link security gate, she nabbed a python bag in dark green, and then kept going.

Man, short of sex, high-end department stores were the best high there was: Thousands and thousands of square feet full of things, all of which were well-ordered, tagged, and cataloged. And protected.

A total OCD-gasm.

So she had to watch herself. She could feel the bonding happening, and if this kept up, she would be in danger of grafting a sense of ownership onto all these precious things. And that wasn't good for anyone. She'd have to kill the humans who came in to buy them, and that was exhausting.

But it did make her think that she should get her Lenovo on and go digital with her own collections.

Next virgin that she slaughtered to protect her mirror? She was going to have to reanimate them and get them to geek-out her things.

After all, there were a lot of computer programmers out there who couldn't figure out how to get their boney asses laid.

Cutting into the center of the first floor, she found the makeup counters clustered together, the Chanel its trademark black and glossy, the Lancôme all glass cases . . . and the Yves Saint Laurent, which had a lot of gold around its stand-up displays.

Flickering in behind the counter, she sprang the lock on the cupboard that was down by the floor, and as she lowered herself onto her haunches, her palm lit the way, illuminating the tiny labels on the butt ends of the packaging.

1 *Le Rouge* was easy to find, and she took one from the careful arrangement, flipped open the box, and slid out the shiny metal tube.

Lovely, so lovely, all unscratched, never been touched. She nearly trembled as she twisted and exposed the perfectly formed column of lipstick.

The smell, flowery and delicate, made her eyes roll back.

The therapist was right: The panic attack hadn't lasted forever in that office, and as Devina had gone about her work afterward, the separation anxiety from that tube she'd tossed had gotten plowed over with her focusing on other things. The anxiety had resurfaced, however, when she'd gone back to her private space and sat in front of her mirror, ready to go down to her wall and enjoy some private time with her children.

Cue the trouble.

Her thoughts had quickly spun out of control, images of all manner of trash compaction and oozing Dumpsters and overcrowded, stinking landfills making her want to cry.

She could have gone back for the specific tube, but she wanted to honor at least part of the therapist's religion: It would have been very much part of her cycle to become obsessed with getting that one particular lipstick back, and execute that plan no matter what got in her way.

Except she couldn't keep going down that road—and so she was here and not at that office, and she had this fresh, pretty new tube to replace the one that she had sacrificed in the name of self-improvement.

There were five more in her color, all stacked one on top of another in the cutest little tower. Reaching forward, she wanted to take them all as backup for her backups, but she stopped herself. Closed the cabinet. Flickered out of range.

She was proud of herself as she walked away.

Enough with the break; time to get back to work.

Returning to the window display she'd come in through, she stopped in front of one of the mannequins. The thing had a straight blond wig on and had been dressed in a flowery creation Devina wouldn't have been caught dead in—

It was galling to wonder what Jim Heron would think of her in it.

No doubt it was right up his alley, feminine, pretty, not too revealing. Modest.

That fucker. That lying double-crosser.

Naturally, the fact that he'd played her so well in the last round only made him more attractive. . . .

Devina frowned as the therapist's voice came back to her. Cognitive behavioral therapy . . . a rewiring of the brain through experience.

The demon leaned in and fingered the fake hair, the long, straight fake hair that was the color of a canary diamond.

Sissy Barten, Jim's precious darling, had had hair just like this. Would have loved a dress like this. Would have stood in the back and waited for Jim to approach, never forward, ever fucking virginal.

It was enough to make her want to kill them both—and with that stupid little girl, that would be an "again" thing as she'd already sliced the kid's throat open over that tub—

Devina began to smile. Then laugh.

With a quick jerk, she yanked off the wig, stripping the plastic model bald . . . and headed out through the glass.

Chapter Six

It had to be a dream, right?

Adrian *had* to be dreaming. Except, damn, this felt real, everything from the velvet couch under his ass to the cold beer in his hand to the heat in the club visceral and authentic.

He was afraid to turn his head. Terrified to discover that he was alone here in this noisy, desperate place filled with hollow people who were just like him.

If he were alone, Eddie really was dead.

Taking a swig of the longneck, he braced himself, and pivoted—

Adrian slowly lowered the bottle, exhaling all the oxygen out of his lungs. "Hey, buddy," he whispered.

Eddie's red eyes swung around. "Ah . . . hello." The guy shifted in his seat. "Listen, are you okay?"

"Yeah, just . . ."

"Why are you staring at me like that?"

"I've missed you," Ad said in a low voice. "I didn't think I would ever see you again."

"Just because I went to the bathroom?" Eddie smiled. "Usually I do come back."

Ad reached out a hand, knowing touch would prove which side they were walking on—

Eddie frowned and eased out of range, looking like Ad had grown a horn in the middle of his forehead. "What up with you?"

That face was exactly right, the darkly tanned skin sporting a beard shadow, those reddish eyes open to the world, neither suspicious nor naive, that heavy braid down a thick, muscled back.

"I don't"—Ad rubbed his face—"know."

"You want to leave?"

"God, no."

"Okay." Those red eyes shifted back to the crowd. "So are you going to force me to have sex again?"

Ad laughed loudly. "Right. That's happened. Suuuuure."

"Throwing women at me—"

"I've never thrown—"

"Picking ones you know I'll like—"

"Well, I have done that—"

"Ruining my virtue."

As the guy took another swig, Ad got serious. "No one could do that."

"Yeah, you're right. Before I was an angel, I was a vestal virgin and it stuck."

"Which would explain all the hair."

"Nah, that's because it makes me look hot."

Ad laughed again and leaned back, a sudden surge of energy coming over him. The sense that life had returned to normal, that tragedy hadn't occurred, that everything was reset back to the way it should be, was a relief so tremendous he was flying even as he was sitting down. In a rush of optimism, his eyes went to the crowd, his fuck filter slipping into place, a rare happiness turning the slutty candidates into beauty queens.

"See anything we like?" Eddie said dryly.

"If it weren't for me, you'd never get laid."

"You know, I'd like to argue with that."

"You're too honest."

"Damn it."

Ah, yes, that redhead would do, Ad thought. And she was with a black-haired—

He frowned, stiffening. There was someone on the periphery, over in the far corner in the shadows, watching them.

"It's time," Eddie said. "Either we do what we're going to do, or we have to order another round. Ad? Hello?"

Adrian shook himself. "Yeah . . . sure."

His best friend gave him the hairy eyeball again. "What's wrong with you, man?"

Good question, he thought as he got to his feet. "Just gimme a minute to reel something in."

"Take your time—and make it quick."

"Isn't that a contradiction?"

"Not when it comes to you."

Easy laughter. And then he was all about the two ladies. As he closed in on the red and black, their giggled responses were predictable, and not nearly as satisfying as the orgasms they were all going to have.

"My name's Adrian," he said, as he came up to them. His slow smile got the females blinking fast, and doing little rearrangements of their stances—breasts up, bellies tucked in, legs out more in front so thighs showed.

"I like your perfume," he said, leaning into the neck of the redhead.

In actuality, he hadn't smelled it yet, and he didn't care what it was—

Breathing in, he froze. That scent. That . . .

"I'm glad," she said, her hands roaming around his back and settling on his ass. "I wore it just for someone like you."

Adrian moved away, his brain hurting. Or maybe that was his chest. "Yeah. Good."

He glanced over his shoulder. Eddie was over on the couch, sprawled out, but focused intently, as if he were ready for the sex.

Just like normal.

Ad nodded in the direction of his buddy. "I come with a friend. How 'bout you?"

"She has a BF," the redhead muttered, like that was a character defect.

"Sorry," the other woman said.

Like it mattered. "Okay, just you then, provided you can handle two?"

When the chippie nodded like she'd won the lottery, he took her hand, and that perfume of hers followed them, making him wish the black haired one had been single and willing, and that Jessica Rabbit with the Goth makeover had been the chick with the boyfriend. No going back, though—it was just too much like work to find another recruit, and besides, this was nothing permanent. None of them had ever been permanent.

Goddamn flowery smell, though. It gave him the creeps.

When he got to the couch and sat down, the redhead made like a throw blanket, covering both his and Eddie's legs, and, as she happened to be facing in the other angel's direction, Eddie got to work kissing the hell out of her.

For a guy with no game, he'd always had a hearty appetite.

As Ad watched, and did some stroking of the hip and breast variety, he thought it was amazing how much power a nightmare could have over you. It was like all that imagined shit about Eddie had actually happened: that harpy sweeping in from out of nowhere and nailing the angel with a blade, taking the I-M out of *immortal*. Then the death, in the lobby of that bank that was not far from here. Then the suffering afterward, the sense that the purpose had gone out of the world for him . . .

Adrian frowned and wondered why he was talking to himself like it had actually gone down—

The redhead arched and parted her legs, clearly inviting him to play in her sandbox. And as he complied, Eddie took over working on her breasts, pulling down the top of her black shredded something-or-other, being more aggressive than usual as he exposed a pair that were considerably smaller than they'd looked.

Just as Adrian was slipping a hand in deep, the waitress showed up with some fresh bottles, and she obviously was used to the kind of business that was being conducted: she didn't bat an eye as she put the beers down.

"I got it," Ad said, squeezing his wallet out of his back pocket and popping her a twenty. As she left, he glanced at the beer, and then shot a glare over at Eddie. "Coors Light? What the hell?"

The other angel disengaged from the lip lock and shrugged. "Watching my weight."

Ad rolled his eyes and got back in touch with touching the meal that was about to be consumed. Moving his hands upward under the short skirt, he discovered to his surprise a pair of underwear with all the holding power of steel girders—and the sprawl of an army tent. What the fuck? Then again, he supposed Spanx was cheaper than lipo—

That perfume flooded back into his nose, suggesting that maybe it hadn't been the woman's after all.

Glancing around, he could see nothing unusual—

"I think you should do her first," Eddie said, playing with those breasts . . . that now seemed rather flabby.

And that hair. Once thick and wavy, it now looked kind of frizzy.

The woman smiled, revealing teeth that were crooked.

"Go on, Adrian . . . do her." Eddie's eyes were all but sparkling in the darkness. "I want to watch you."

The woman took Ad's hand and moved it back between her legs, rubbing herself against his palm and fingers—

From out of the crowd, a figure stepped into view, a tall, proud figure dressed in a white robe. As it arrived, the scent of the flowers grew so strong, it overpowered everything—

Eddie.

It was the real Eddie, standing true and real, unbowed and whole in the midst of a crowd of walking dead.

"Oh, for fuck's sake. Just when things were getting interesting."

Ad's head shot around. Devina was beside him on the other end of the couch, for once wearing her true guise: She was a corpse animated, her flesh in a perpetual free fall from her gray bones, her grotesque rotting palms on the breasts of the almost-pretty woman. The demon's expression was one of annoyance, her loose lips and sagging jawline as clenched as they could get.

Adrian shouted and went to jump up, but the redhead held his hand in place—and as he struggled against her astronomical strength, she morphed into what she really was: a decrepit has-been, the illusion of loveliness gone as if it were no longer sustainable.

As he tried to pull free, a black stain began to creep up his arm, starting at his fingers, riding up his wrist, staking claim to his elbow.

Screaming loud, he jerked violently, but he was a fly stuck on paper, a mouse in a trap, a—

Eddie, the real one, the dead one, broke the connection with a simple touch, not on Ad but the redhead: Suddenly appearing beside them all, he just leaned in and put his forefinger to the harpy's shoulder, and poof! it was gone.

As Devina cursed the angel, Adrian ripped free of the hold, his body falling backward off the couch, his eyes only for Eddie as his heart shattered, the loss that had really occurred coming home to rest yet again.

"Fuck you," Devina spat at the angel.

Eddie's wonderful face, that kind, smart, handsome face, showed no reaction to the insult. He just nodded over at the Coors Light and drawled, "In your condition, I'd be worried about a hell of a lot more than my figure."

Vile epithets were hurled from the couch, but Devina did nothing more—to the point where you had to wonder what exactly Eddie had done with that ET-finger-move thing.

The other angel looked at Ad for what seemed like the longest time, as if the dead missed the living even more. "I'm never far," Eddie said in a cracking voice.

"Ah, shit . . . don't go," Ad moaned. "Just stay here—"

"So fucking touching." Devina's black eyes were livid. "You two want to make out before he leaves?"

Eddie began to recede like he was a statue on a rolling platform, his still body drawn backward through the milling crowd, that smell of a fresh meadow going with him.

"Eddie!" As Ad reached forward, the stain on his arm was nearly to his shoulder.

"I'm in you," Devina said with satisfaction. "And it's too late for you to do anything about it. Too damn late."

Adrian screamed at the top of his lungs—

Chapter Seven

Matthias woke up because sunlight was shining on his face. He wasn't sure when that nurse with the wandering hands had left, but he'd intended to take off right after she had. No go. An unnatural sleep had rolled over him, sucking him under in a way that made him feel owned.

Frankly, he was surprised to have come out of it at all.

The hospital room looked exactly the same, but like it would have changed in the night? And he did feel better, as if his body were a car that had been sent in for a fender-to-fender service.

Who knew a handjob you didn't want could lead to such a turn-around . . .

And it was strange. As he glanced around, he had a thought that it was a miracle he was still on the "outside." But the outside of what—prison? A mental hospital? Something even worse?

Forcing his sloppy brain to come to attention, he tried to remember where he'd been the night before, what had happened before he'd woken up here. . . .

I hit you with my car. I'm so sorry.

He closed his eyes and remembered that woman, that Mels Carmichael. Something about her had pierced through the fog that surrounded him, reaching him where it counted. Why? He had no clue—but under different circumstances, he could have spent a hell of a lot more time with her.

So much more.

But come on, he was not the romance type—his gut was loud and clear on that.

Shoving himself off the pillows, he was surprised he didn't feel worse, and he gave his body a chance to file a different kind of report, one more consistent with someone who had been a hood ornament less than twelve hours ago.

Nope. Still felt better—

Get out of here. Get moving now.

Okay, it would help if he knew who was after him, or why he was running, but he wasn't going to waste time trying to fight with those questions—not when his adrenal gland was consistently pointing at the door and yelling at him to get the fuck—

"I guess you're not a John Doe after all."

Matthias reached for a gun he didn't have and looked across the way. The nurse was back, standing just inside the room, her presence like a draft.

Her affect was different in the daylight. No more seducer.

Maybe she was a vampire. Ha. Ha.

"They found your wallet," she said, holding up a black billfold. "Everything's in here, ID, Visa—oh, and your health insurance card. Your copay's going to be up there, but most of the charges will be covered."

She walked over and put the thing on the rolling table, right beside the card that the reporter had left behind. Then she stepped back like she knew he wanted space.

Long pause.

"Thanks," he said into the conversational void.

She was dressed in street clothes: blue jeans, black clogs, puffy white Patagonia jacket that was pristine. Her hair was down around her shoulders, and she smoothed it even though it was glossy-magazine perfect.

"I also got you some clothes." She nodded over her shoulder. "They're in the half closet behind there. I hope they fit."

"So they're going to let me go?"

"As long as you check out all right this morning. Do you have anyone to go home to?"

He didn't reply—and not because he didn't know the answer for himself. No questions answered, not to anybody. That was the way he was.

Long pause number two.

She cleared her throat and didn't meet his eyes. "Listen, about last night . . ."

Oh, so that's what this was about. "I'm going to forget about it, and you should do the same," he said dryly.

Shit knew he had bigger fish to fry than a rubout forced on him by a beautiful woman.

Yeah, what a sob story that was. Especially compared to the crap he'd done to others—

Memories Loch Ness'ed below the surface of his consciousness, something shocking and monstrous threatening to make an appearance.

Who was he? he wondered.

Abruptly, the nurse's dark eyes, those windows of the soul, locked onto his own. "I'm so sorry. That was really wrong of me. I should never have . . ."

Snapping back to the present, Matthias thought it was funny that in the daylight, all that power she'd had over him was nowhere to be seen. She didn't even appear to be the type of woman who could be so aggressive. She was just a pretty young nurse with a hot body and great hair, who was looking vulnerable.

Had it even happened? They'd probably given him painkillers, and God knew that could fuck your head up.

Then again, if nothing had gone down, she wouldn't be apologizing, would she.

"It was a total breach of protocol, and I've never done anything like that before. It's just . . . you were in so much pain, and you wanted it . . . and . . ."

Had he? He remembered it had been very much the opposite. Except what did he know—he thought he'd actually orgasmed. Maybe that hadn't happened, either.

Which would make sense.

"Anyway, I just thought I'd tell you that before I go—and you'll be out by the time I come back from my days off."

She seemed so honestly ashamed and distraught. And for some reason, he had a feeling it was entirely within his character to take advantage of her, for no other reason than that it would make her uncomfortable.

"It was my fault," he heard himself say—and the instant the words were out, he believed the confession. "I'm the one who should be sorry."

After all, pity fucks operated on the same principle whether the damn things went all the way or not: woe is me; can you take care of my cock; thanks, honey.

The nurse trailed a pale hand on the fake-wood footboard of the bed. "I just . . . yeah, well, I don't want you to think I go around doing that." She laughed awkwardly. "I'm not sure why it matters, but it does."

"You don't have to explain."

As she glanced over, her cautious expression relaxed into an honest smile. To the point where he found himself checking her ring finger for evidence of a marriage certificate.

Nope. Bare.

"Thanks for being cool about it all." She looked over her shoulder at the door. "I guess I should go. Take care of yourself—and please remember to follow up with your own doctor. Head injuries are nothing to fool around with, and memory loss is serious."

"Yeah. I'll do that."

The lie was so easy, he knew he'd told a lot of them in his lifetime. And as he returned her wave, he was processing her like she was a memo or a piece of mail.

Not something human—and that wasn't her fault.

He had a feeling it was his hard wiring.

Great. Nothing like waking up and learning piece by piece that you were a real asshole . . .

He glanced over at the bedside table. The business card and the wallet were right next to each other, one black and thicker, one white and thin.

As he reached his hand forward, he didn't know which one he was going for—

Ultimately, the wallet held the greater allure. Opening the folded leather, he stared at the driver's license that had been slid into the clear slot. The picture was . . . well, he didn't recognize the guy, but the nurse with the magic touch certainly seemed to think it was him. Was this what he looked like? A guy with black hair and a face that was handsome, but cold.

The printed info told him that his eyes were blue—and it looked like they were both working as they focused on the camera. Date of birth was this month. License expired then.

The first name, Matthias, was the one he went by, and the address was in Caldwell, New York, which solved the geographic question—oh, yeah, which he hadn't been aware he'd had.

Caldwell, New York.

Back again. Or at least that's what his instincts told him—

Get out of here. Get moving now.

Urgency aside, he took getting off the bed slowly, and when shit didn't buckle, he pulled out the IVs from his vein and the pads from his chest. Leaning into the monitoring equipment, he muted the alarms before shuffling over to the bathroom.

The light was off, and as he stepped inside, he flipped the switch . . . and it was showtime.

As he met his own reflection in the mirror over the sink, he dragged in a raw breath. His eye on the one side was milky white, and his face was carved with the indelible lines of a lot of past pain—as well as some faded scaring at the temple where his ocular injury had occured.

That photograph on the ID was definitely him, if you added a little gray at the temples, but it had been taken before he'd—

"Sir, I'm going to ask you to get back in bed—you're a slip-and-fall risk. And you should not have taken out the—"

He ignored the new nurse. "I'm leaving. Right now—AMA, yeah, I know."

He shut the door in her face and started the shower. For some reason, as he refocused on the mirror, he thought of Mels Carmichael. No wonder her first reaction had been in the OMG category.

Not exactly a looker—

Christ, why was he thinking like that? What did it matter how anyone viewed him?

In a quick surge of coordination, he reopened the door to the room and stuck his head out. The nurse was gone, but no doubt she was coming back with someone who had Dr. in front of his or her name—time to move fast. He snagged the card that Mels had left and put it in the wallet. Then he grabbed the clothes from the closet and shut himself in the bathroom.

Ten minutes later he had clean hair and a clean body and was dressed in a plain black T-shirt, a black windbreaker, and a pair of loose jeans.

On his way out the door, he snagged a cane that he inferred had been brought for him.

The thing felt normal against his palm, and his gait was much faster with it. Like he was used to using one.

Heading for the elevators, he didn't check in with anyone, no good-byes, no signing on the dotted line. Their billing department would find the man at the address listed on the driver's license.

And maybe so would he.

Adrian's scream woke Jim up and torpedoed him out of bed, his body landing in the attack position. With a crystal dagger in one hand and an autoloader in the other, he was ready for business of the human or Devina variety. Dog, being no dummy, just headed under the box spring, taking cover.

"I'm okay," Ad said. With all the conviction of someone bleeding from an artery.

As Jim shot around the corner, he thought, Yeah. Right.

In the sunlight that streamed through the flimsy drapes, the angel looked absolutely wasted as he sat there sprawled on the floor, dark circles under his eyes, his black hair messed up, his hands shaking as he pulled at the loose collar of his Hanes T-shirt. His piercings, those pieces of metal that circled his lower lip and went up his earlobes and marked his brow, were the only things that sparkled. Everything else was all about the dead-but-breathing.

His pilot light had gone out.

Jim went over and held his hand down to the guy. "Time to get up."

The other angel clasped his palm, and for a moment Jim stiffened, an unpleasant sting tunneling up his own forearm and making his instincts tingle in a bad way. But then he heaved Ad off the floor, and whatever it was disappeared.

"You been to see Nigel and the boys yet?" Adrian asked as he walked around like he was trying to shake whatever had gotten to him.

"What the hell for."

"Good point."

On that note, the other angel went into the bathroom and shut the door. After the toilet flushed, the shower came on, and then the sink.

Going over, Jim settled at the jamb and talked to the flimsy wood. "What was the dream about."

When there was no answer, he curled up a fist and pounded. "Adrian. Tell me."

God knew that Devina used all kinds of tricks to get what she wanted. The idea that she might have B&E'd Ad's mental back door while he was sleeping was a well, duh.

He pounded some more.

When there was no answer, he fucked off modesty and barged in.

Through the clear plastic shower curtain, he got an eyeful of Adrian down on the ground again, this time with tile under his ass: He was crammed in the stall, his knees up, his elbows in against his chest, his head buried into his palms. But he wasn't crying, or cursing, or falling apart, and maybe that was the scariest part. The angel was just sitting under the warm spray, his huge body folded up on itself.

Jim put the toilet cover down and sat on the thing. "Talk to me."

After a moment, the angel said roughly, "She was Eddie. In my dream, she was Eddie."

Shit. "That'll make you scream."

"He was there, too. He woke me up, actually. Goddamn it, Jim . . . seeing him was . . ."

As the sentence trailed off, Jim took particular care inspecting his dagger's blade. "Yeah, I know."

"I'm going to kill her."

"Only if you get there before I do."

Adrian let his arms fall to the sides, so that his fists rested in the choppy pool of water forming around his ass. He looked defeated, but that was just for this moment. That icy rage would be back as soon as that demon came anywhere near them, and frankly, the predictable response was going to be a problem: You didn't want your backup to go rogue on you, and that kind of mental state was hard to reason with.

"I think you need to ask Nigel for someone else," Ad said softly. Like he could read minds.

"I don't want anybody else."

Except that was a lie. He was still coming to terms with his own abilities and weapons—sure, the learning curve wasn't as steep as it had been in the first couple rounds, but he was hardly up to speed. And Devina wasn't the kind of enemy where a marginal performance was even remotely acceptable.

So he needed some rock solid to back him up.

In all honesty, Eddie was the missing piece here. And that was precisely why he'd been taken out by the enemy.

Fucking bitch.

"Do you know anyone else?" Jim asked.

"There was another guy—above me and Eddie, actually. Almost on Nigel and Colin's level. But he ran into some problems—last I heard he was in the In Between. Then again, he was a real wild card. You might as well stick with me in that case."

"We've got to get Eddie back somehow—"

"He's the only one who would know how to do that." Adrian let out a groan and got to his feet, his massive frame rising like a tree. "Maybe Colin."

Jim nodded and refocused on his crystal dagger. The weapon was clear as an ice cube, strong as steel, light as a breath. Eddie had given it to him—

A squeak and a thump brought his head back to his remaining partner. Ad had picked up the soap, but then dropped it, his hands lifting in front of his face, his mouth working like he was trying to curse.

"What's wrong?"

"Oh . . . fuck . . ." Ad flipped them around and looked at the backs. "Shit, no . . ."

"What?"

"They're black." The guy shoved out his arms. "Can't you see? She's in me—Devina's in me—and she's taking over—"

Jim had a moment of what-the-fuck, but he knew he had to step in and reel this situation back to reality, PDQ. Putting his dagger down on the sink, he shoved the plastic curtain out of the way, and grabbed the angel's thick wrists—

That bad-news sensation hit him again, lighting up the nerve endings in his fingers and palms sure as if he'd put them in acid. Focusing on the guy's skin, he wondered just what the hell had happened in that dream.

Except the flesh was completely normal. And people who had lost their best friends were allowed to crack up.

They couldn't stay that way, though.

"Adrian, buddy"—he gave the guy a good shake—"hey, *look* at me."

When the poor bastard finally did, Jim stared into those eyes like he was reaching in and taking hold of a part of the guy's brain. "You are *fine*. There is nothing going on here. She is not in you, she is not here, and—"

"You're wrong."

The bleak words stopped Jim short. But then he shook his head. "You're an angel, Adrian."

"Am I?"

In a grim voice, Jim countered, "Well, put it like this . . . you better fucking be."

After a tense silence, Jim's mouth started moving, words coming out of it, sensible, chill-out syllables crossing the distance that separated them. But in the recesses of his mind, he sent up a prayer to whoever might be listening.

Devina was a parasite, the kind of thing that wheedled into people and infected them.

Made sense that someone emotionally compromised was more vulnerable.

The tragedy, however, was that he couldn't have the enemy in his back pocket.

No matter how much he loved the guy.

Chapter Eight

"What happened to your eye?"

As Mels entered her mother's kitchen, she didn't answer the question, but went straight for the coffeepot. The fact that the thing was in the far corner, and she could drink her mug with her back to her mom, was just an added bonus to the caffeine.

Damn CoverGirl foundation. It was supposed to *cover* up things you wanted to hide. Like blemishes, blotches . . . bruises from car accidents you'd prefer concerned family members didn't know about.

"Mels?"

She didn't need to turn around to see what was behind her: Her mom, trim and small, younger looking than her age, would be sitting at the table across the way, the *Caldwell Courier Journal* open-faced next to a bowl of high-fiber bird food and a cup of coffee. Dark hair, streaked with gray, would be combed down into a neat, freshly trimmed cap, and the clothes would be casual, yet seem perfectly ironed.

Her mother was one of those tiny little women who always looked made up even without makeup. Like she had been born with a can of spray starch and a hairbrush under each arm.

But she was fragile. Like a kind, compassionate figurine.

The china shop to the bull Mels's father had been.

Very aware that the question was still out there, Mels poured. Sipped. Made busy work snagging a paper towel and wiping a counter that was clean and dry. "Oh, nothing—I slipped and fell. Knocked into the shower dial. It was so stupid."

There was a moment of quiet. "You got in late last night."

"I ended up at a friend's house."

"I thought you said it was a bar."

"I went over there after the bar."

"Oh. All right."

Mels stared out the window over the sink. With luck, her aunt would call at any moment, as the woman usually did, and there wouldn't be a need to lie about why she had to take a taxi into work.

The sounds of sipping and quiet crunching filled the kitchen, and Mels tried to think of something halfway regular to say. Weather. Sports—no, her mother wasn't into organized activities that centered around fields, balls or pucks of any kind. Books would do it—although, Mels didn't read anything other than crime statistics, and her mother was still on the Oprah's Book Club train even though the locomotive didn't have an engine or any tracks anymore.

God . . . times like this made her miss her father to the point where it hurt. The two of them had never had any awkwardness. Ever. They'd talked about the city, or his work as a cop, or school . . . or they'd not said a word—and it was cool either way. Her mother, on the other hand?

"So." Mels took another draw on her mug. "Any big plans for the day?"

Some kind of answer came back, but she didn't hear it because the urge to leave was too loud.

Finishing off the last of her black coffee—her mother took hers with cream and sugar—Mels put the mug in the dishwasher and braced herself.

"So I'll see you tonight," she said. "I won't be late. Promise."

Her mother's eyes rose to meet her own. That bowl full of wholesome goodness had little pink flowers on it, and the table-cloth had tiny yellow ones, and the wallpaper had larger blue ones.

Flowers everywhere.

"Are you all right?" her mom asked. "Do you need to go to the doctor?"

"It's just a bruise. Nothing special." She glanced out through the dining room. On the far side of the doily-laden table, past the milky white privacy curtain, a bright yellow Chevrolet pulled up. "Taxi's here. I left my car at the bar because I'd had two and a half glasses of wine."

"Oh, you could have taken mine into work."

"You'll need it." She looked to the horticultural calendar hanging on the wall, praying there was something there. "Today you have bridge at four."

"I could have gotten a ride. I still can, if you want to—"

"No, it's better this way. I can pick up my car and drive it home."

Crap. She'd just boxed herself in. The only way Fi-Fi was going anywhere was if she were on the back of a flatbed—the poor thing had been auto-evac'd to a local service station.

"Oh. All right."

As her mother fell silent, Mels wanted to apologize, but it was too hard to put the complicated *sorry* into words. Hell, maybe she just needed to move out. Constant exposure to all that self-sacrifice and kindness was a burden to bear, instead of a joy to be relished—

because it never ended. There was always a suggestion, an offering, a how-about-this-way, a—

"I have to go. Thanks, though."

"All right."

"See you tonight."

Mels kissed the soft cheek that was presented, and left through the front door in a hurry. Outside, the air was fresh and lovely, the sun bright enough to promise a warm lunch hour.

Getting in the back of the cab, she said, "*CCJ* offices on Trade."

"You got it."

Heading into town, the taxi had shock absorbers to rival cement blocks, and all the seat padding of a hardwood floor, but she didn't care about the rough ride. Too much chaos in her brain to worry about her butt or her molars.

That man from the night before remained with her, sure as if he were sitting beside her.

It had been like that all night long.

Letting her head fall back, she closed her eyes and replayed the accident, double-checking, triple-checking that there was nothing she could have done to avoid hitting him. And then she got tied up in other things, like the way he had lain so still and watchful in that hospital bed.

Even injured, gravely so in some places, he'd still come across like . . . a predator.

A powerful male animal, wounded—

Okay, now she was really losing it. And maybe she needed to look closer at her dating life—which was nonexistent. . . .

Too bad she couldn't shake the conviction that he'd been strangely hypnotic, and wasn't that tacky. What she should be concerned with was his health and well-being, and how likely he was to try to sue her for what little she had.

Instead, she lingered on the raspy sound of his voice, and the way he'd stared at her, as if every small thing about her had been a source of fascination and importance . . .

He'd been hurt a while ago, she thought. The scars at the side of his eye had healed up over time.

What had happened to him? What was his name . . . ?

As she got mired in the land of Questions With No Answers, the taxi driver did his job with no muss, no fuss. Sixteen dollars, eighteen minutes, and a sore tailbone later, she was walking into the newsroom.

The place was already noisy, with people talking and rushing around, and the chaos calmed her nerves—in the same way that taking a yoga class made her jumpy.

Sitting down at her desk, she checked her voicemail, signed into her e-mail, and grabbed the mug she had been using since she'd inherited the desk a little over a year and half ago. Heading over to the communal kitchen, she had one of six coffeepots to choose from: None of them were decaf; three of them were just plain old Maxwell House; and the others were that stinky hazelnut crap or that femme-y macchiato-whatever-the-hell it was called.

Big whatever on the latter. If she wanted a damn caramel sundae, she'd get one for lunch. That stuff did *not* belong in a coffee mug.

As she poured her basic black, she thought about the mug's true owner, Beth Randall, the reporter who'd sat in that cubicle for . . . well, it must have been just over two years. One afternoon, the woman had left and never come back. Mels had been sorry about the disappearance—not that she'd known her colleague all that well—and felt badly to finally get a dedicated spot to sit in under those circumstances.

She'd kept the mug for no particular reason. But now, as she took a sip from it, she realized it was in the hopes that the woman returned. Or at the very least, was okay.

Looked like she was surrounded by missing people.

Or at least it felt that way this morning. Especially when she thought of the man from the night before—the one who she was never going to see again, and couldn't seem to forget.

This was not his house.

As the taxi pulled over in front of a ranch in a modest neighborhood, Matthias knew he didn't live under its roof. Hadn't. Wouldn't.

"You gettin' out or not?"

Matthias met the driver's eyes in the rearview. "Gimme a minute."

"Meter's running."

Nodding, he got out and relied on his cane as he went up the front walk, swinging his bad leg in a wide circle so he didn't have to bend his knee. Things were hardly Home Sweet Home: There was a branch down in the scrubby hedge that ran under the bay window. The lawn was scruffy. Weeds had sprouted in the gutters, reaching for the sun so high above.

The front door was locked, so he cupped his hands and looked into the windows on either side. Dust bunnies. Mismatched furniture. Sagging drapes.

There was a cheapo tin mailbox screwed into the bricks, and he opened the top. Circulars. A coupon book addressed to "Occupant." No bills, credit card applications, letters. The only other piece of mail was an AARP magazine that had the same name as that of the driver's license he'd been given.

Matthias rolled the mag up, shoved it into his windbreaker, and headed back to the cab. Not only was this not his residence, nobody lived here. Best guess was that the person had died within, say, four to six weeks—long enough so that the family had cleaned up the accounts payable issues, but before they emptied the place out to put it on the market.

Getting into the cab, he stared straight ahead.

"Where to now?"

With a groan, Matthias shifted over and got out his wallet. Sliding Mels Carmichael's business card free, he was struck by an overriding conviction that he shouldn't involve the woman.

Too dangerous.

"What'll it be, pal?"

But shit, he had to start somewhere. And his brain was like an Internet connection gone bad.

"Trade Street," he gritted out.

As they headed for the downtown area and got caught in a net of traffic, he stared into the other cars and saw people drinking coffee, talking to passengers, stopping at red lights, going on green. Totally foreign to him, he thought. The kind of life where you nine-to-five'd your way into a grave at the age of seventy-two was not how he'd lived.

So what was, he asked his dumb-ass gray matter. What the fuck was?

All he got back was a headache while he strained for an answer.

As the *Caldwell Courier Journal* facility came into view, he took out one of the ten twenties in the wallet. "Keep the change."

The cabdriver seemed more than happy to get rid of him.

Taking up res on the periphery of the front doors, Matthias loitered in the sunshine, being careful not to meet any stares—and there were a lot of them: For some reason, he tended to attract attention, usually from women—then again, the Florence Nightingale stuff was something the fairer sex was known for, and he did have scars on his face.

Ooooooh, romantic.

Eventually, he took cover across the street at the bus stop, parking it on the hard plastic bench and breathing in the secondhand smoke from people impatient for their public trans to arrive. The waiting didn't bother him. It was as if he were used to lurking, and to pass the time he played a game, memorizing the faces of the people who came and went out of the CCJ offices.

He was extremely good at it. One look was all it took, and he had the person in his database.

At least his short-term memory was working—

The double doors pushed wide, and there she was.

Matthias sat up straighter as the sunlight hit her hair and all kinds of copper showed. Mels Carmichael, associate reporter, was with a heavyset guy who had to hitch his khakis up higher around his hips before they hit the steps. The two appeared to be arguing back and forth about something in the way friends did, and when Mels smiled, it appeared as if she had won whatever debate—

Like she knew he was watching, she glanced across the street, and stopped dead. Touching her buddy on the sleeve, she said something, and then parted ways with the man, cutting through the traffic, coming over.

Matthias plugged his cane into the pavement, and tugged his rags into place as he stood. He had no idea why he wanted to look better for her, but he did—then again, hard to look worse. His clothes weren't his, his cologne was Eau d'Hospital Soap, and he'd washed his hair with the antibacterial stuff, because that was all he'd had.

Naturally, his bad eye, that ugly, ruined thing, was what she looked at first. How could she not?

"Hi," she said.

Man, she looked great in her normal everyday clothes, those slacks and that wool jacket and the cream scarf she wore loose around her neck looking runway fine, as far as he was concerned.

Still no wedding ring.

Good, he thought for no apparent reason.

Shifting his gaze to the right, so maybe his defect wouldn't be so obvious, he returned the "Hi."

Well, shit, now what. "I'm not stalking you, I swear." Liar. "And I would have called, but I've got no phone."

"It's okay. Do you need something? The police called me this morning with a follow-up, and I think they were still planning on speaking with you?"

"Yeah." He let that one stand where it was. "Listen, I . . ."

The fact that he was leaving a sentence hanging seemed very unnatural, but his brain just wasn't producing.

"Let's sit down," she said, gesturing to the seat. "I can't believe they let you out."

At that moment, a bus showed up, rumbling to a halt and blocking the sun, its hot diesel breath making him cough. As the pair of them settled on the bench, they kept quiet while the kibitzers filed on their ride.

When the bus kept going, the sunlight reappeared, bathing her in a yellow light.

For some stupid reason, his eyes started blinking hard.

"What can I do for you?" she asked softly. "Are you in pain?"

Yes. But it wasn't physical. And it got worse whenever he looked at her. "How do you know I need help?"

"I'm guessing your memory didn't magically come back."

"No, it hasn't. But that's not your fault."

"Well, I hit you. So I owe you."

He made a motion to his lower body. "I was like this before."

"Can you remember anything? Prior to the accident, I mean." As he shook his head, she murmured, "A lot of servicemen have come back in your condition."

Ah . . . as in Army, Navy, Air Force, Marines, he thought. And part of that fit. The government . . . yes, he'd had something to do with the Department of Defense, or national security . . . or . . .

But he wasn't a Wounded Warrior. Because he hadn't been a hero.

"They found my wallet," he blurted.

"Oh, that's great."

For some reason he gave it to her.

As she opened the thing and looked at the driver's license, she nodded. "That's you."

Focusing on the *Caldwell Courier Journal* emblem that hung over the door she'd walked out of, he said, "Look, all this is off the record, okay?"

"Absolutely."

"And I wish I had another option. I wish . . . I don't want to get you in trouble."

"You haven't asked me to do anything yet." She stared at him. "What do you have in mind?"

"Can you find out who that is?" He pointed to the driver's license. "Because it's not me."

Chapter Nine

In the silence that followed, all Mels could think about was the fact that she'd been so sure she'd never see the man again.

Guess fate had other plans.

Sitting beside her, he was dressed in black, a big, super-lean male who gave off a tough-to-the-core vibe with his narrowed eyes and his strong jaw . . . and yet nonetheless appeared ashamed of his scars and his handicap.

Looking back down at the driver's license, she frowned. The picture seemed legit, the holograms where they should be, height, weight, and DOB okay, the address right here in Caldwell—not far from her mother's house, as a matter of fact.

He'd probably been on his way home when she'd hit him. Just like her.

Refocusing on the man, as opposed to the image, she had the sense that he was swallowing his pride big-time by coming to her. This was not someone who liked to rely on others, but clearly his life had put him in a place where he had no other choice.

No memory. Few resources.

And with his haunted stare and patched-up body, he had to be a serviceman, back from the war only physically, not in spirit or mind or emotion.

Naturally, the reporter in her liked nothing better than a good mystery—and the fact that she had some culpability in this amnesia he had going on was another reason to jump in feetfirst. But she wasn't stupid. She didn't want to get sucked up into some kind of drama, especially if he was delusional or paranoid.

The picture was him, no doubt.

"I hate putting you in this position." His long, sure hands stroked the cane that he balanced on his thigh. "But I don't have anyone else, and the house at that address? It's not mine. I can't tell you where I do live, but I'm damn certain it's not there. And I checked the mail when I went over." He leaned to the side, grimacing while he took out a rolled-up magazine. "I found this. Name's right, except I'm not over fifty-five. Why would this be in my mailbox, addressed to me?"

She unfolded the thing, the AARP logo looming over a picture of a gracefully aging model in athletic gear. The name on the address was Matthias Hault, and the number and street were the same as what was on the license . . . except he could have lived with his father and shared the same name.

Although wouldn't dads have been glad to see his son show up on the front doorstep?

"I could go to a private investigator," he said, "but that costs money, and right now, I've got two hundred dollars to my name— well, one eighty after I paid the cabdriver."

"Are you sure there isn't someone looking for you?" When he remained quiet, she assumed he was searching that void of memory she'd saddled him with. "What did the doctors say? Again, to be honest, I'm shocked you're up and around."

"So will you help me?" he countered.

That firm line in the sand was something to respect. But she walked over it. "If I do, you're going to have to talk to me. What do the doctors think?"

His good eye traveled around, as if he were looking for an out. "I left AMA."

"What? Why?"

"It didn't feel safe. And I can't give you any more than that. It's all I have."

PTSD, she thought. Had to be.

Maybe if she confirmed his identity, it would set his mind to rest, and help with the recovery.

"Okay, I'll do what I can," she said.

He hung his head, like turning to someone else was a kind of defeat. "Thank you. And all I need is a search on this name. A starting place."

"I can go back inside and do this at my desk right now." She nodded off to the right. "There's a diner down by the river, about two blocks away. You can get yourself something to eat and I'll meet you there ASAP. Ah . . . assuming you can—"

"I can make it," he gritted out.

Or he'd die trying, she thought, measuring the straight angle of his jaw.

Which happened to be very Jon Hamm, as a matter of fact.

The man shoved himself off the bench with the help of his cane. "I'll see you when you get there—and don't worry about rushing."

As he looked down the street, the light got in his eyes, both the one that he could obviously see out of and the one he couldn't.

"Would you like my sunglasses?" she asked. "They're Ray-Bans, about as unisex as you can get. No prescription, either."

She didn't wait for him to tough-guy it and tell her no. She took the case out of her purse and put it forward.

Matthias Hault stared at what she offered for the longest time, as if the simple gesture was a foreign language to him.

"Take them," she said softly.

His hand shook a little as he accepted the case, and he didn't look her in the eye again. "I won't scratch them. And I'll give them back at the diner."

"No hurry."

When he put the shades on, they transformed his face into something . . . undeniably dangerous.

And unrelentingly sexual.

A shaft went through the center of Mels's body, hitting her in a place that hadn't been alive for the longest time.

"Better?" he said roughly.

"I think so."

He was still refusing to look at her, his shoulders and spine set straight, the lines of his mouth tight. Such a proud man, trapped in a position of weakness . . .

She was always going to remember this moment, she thought for no apparent reason. Yes, this moment now, as the sunshine fell upon his harsh, handsome face.

This was a rabbit hole, she realized. This seemingly random intersection between the two of them was going to change things forever.

"There's something I've wanted to ask you," he said.

"What," she whispered, caught up in a moment she did not understand.

"Where did the accident happen?"

Shaking herself, she pulled her brain back to reality. "It was, ah, just outside of the Pine Grove Cemetery. Close to where I live—not far from the neighborhood your house is in."

"A cemetery."

"That's right."

As he nodded and started walking in the direction of the restaurant, she could have sworn he said, "Now, why is that not a surprise."

As dives went, the Riverside Diner was right out of central casting. Naugahyde booths, gingham curtains, waitresses with aprons and attitudes. Food was greasy but in a glorious way, and as Matthias cut into his yellow scrambled eggs with a stainless fork, his stomach grumbled like it had been years since he'd had solid food.

It was late for breakfast, but nothing went better with coffee than eggs and bacon.

As he consumed his meal, the sunglasses his reporter had given him were a godsend, allowing him to keep track of the people coming and going, and the waitresses moving around, and who went into the bathrooms and how long they stayed.

Except surveillance hadn't been why Mels had given them to him.

Damn it. What was it about that woman that made him want to be whole again?

"More coffee?" the waitress asked at his elbow.

"Yeah, please." He pushed his cup over and she poured from the pot, steam curling up. "And another round of everything else, too."

She smiled like she was calculating a bigger tip. "You're a good eater."

When you don't know the when/where of your next meal, you better be, he answered in his head.

His reporter came in just after he'd finished breakfast number two. She looked left and then right; when she saw him sitting all the way down by the emergency exit, she started the long trek past a number of empty booths.

As she sat across from him, her cheeks were red, like she'd rushed. "It must have been crowded when you came in."

"It was." Bullshit—he'd wanted to be near the back in case he needed to get out in a hurry.

The waitress came over with the pot again. "Good to see ya—coffee?"

"Yes, please." Mels shrugged off her coat. "And my usual."

"Lunch or breakfast?"

"Lunch."

"Comin' up."

"You eat here a lot?" he said, wondering why he cared.

"Two, three times a week since I started at the paper."

"And how long ago was that?"

"A million years."

"Funny, you don't look like a dinosaur."

Smiling a little, she took a pull off her coffee cup and got ready for business, her mouth thinning, her lids lowering.

Man . . . she looked hot like that. The intensity. The focus. In this moment, she reminded him of himself—

And wasn't that a miracle, given that he had about as much information on the both of them—and she was a stranger.

"Tell me," he demanded.

"You're dead."

"And here I just thought I felt that way."

During the pause that followed, he could sense her trying to read him. "You're not surprised," she said.

He looked into his half-empty cup and shook his head. "I knew there was something wrong at that house."

"The man who had that name for real was eighty-seven and died of congestive heart failure five weeks ago."

"As false identities go, it's not a very good one, is it."

"You talk like you know about them firsthand." When he didn't comment, she leaned in. "Is there any chance you're in the federal witness protection program?"

No, he was on the other side of the law . . . whatever that meant.

"If that's the case," he said, "they're not taking very good care of me."

"I have an idea. Let's go back to the cemetery—right where the accident occurred. See if it brings anything to your mind."

"I can't ask you to do that."

"You didn't. I offered—" She stopped. Frowned. Rubbed at her eyebrow. "God, I hope I'm not turning into my mother."

"Does she like cemeteries?"

"No, long story. Anyway, I borrowed my friend's car—I can drive you over there after we're done eating."

"No. Thanks, though."

"Why'd you bother to ask about your name if you're not going to keep digging?"

"I can take a cab, is what I mean."

"Oh."

The waitress showed up with "the usual," which turned out to be a chicken salad on wheat with what appeared to be extra tomatoes, and fries instead of chips.

"I think I should take you," she said, reaching for the ketchup.

Matthias watched as two cops came in through the front door and sat at the counter. "Can I be honest with you?"

"Please."

He dipped his chin and stared at her over the tops of the Ray-Bans. "I don't want you to be alone with me. It's too dangerous."

She paused with a French fry halfway to her mouth. "No offense. But considering your physical condition, I could break both your legs and have you unconscious in a New York minute." As his brows shot sky-high, she nodded. "I'm a black belt, licensed to carry a concealed hand gun, and I never go anywhere without a good knife or my heat."

She gave a quick smile, picked up her chicken salad, and bit into her usual. "So, what do you say?"

Chapter Ten

Fortunately, this wasn't a date, Mels thought as things went quiet. Because telling a man you could wipe the floor with him was not a good beginning, middle, or end to a meal.

This was business—yeah, sure, this man's story, whatever it was, wasn't likely to end up in the pages of a newspaper, but it was something to solve, and God knew she never passed that kind of opportunity up.

"Quite a résumé," he said after a long moment.

"My father made sure I could defend myself. He was a cop, one of the real old-school types."

"What's that mean?"

She wiped her mouth with a paper napkin, took another hit of her coffee, and wished she'd ordered a Coke. "Put it this way . . . Now, in the days of video cameras in squad cars, and internal affairs boards, and binders full of procedurals, he wouldn't have lasted a month before he got suspended. But back in the day, he got the job done, and people were safer in this town because of him. He took care of things."

"Rough guy?"

"Fair guy."

"And you approve of his methods?"

She shrugged. "I approved of him. His way of operating, on the other hand . . . let's just say it was for a different era. Before DNA and the Internet."

"Sounds like my kind of man."

Mels had to smile at that. Except then sadness at her father's loss made her look out at the river, and the seagulls which coasted over the sluggish current. "He was never out of control or mean. But sometimes, the criminal element only responds when things are explained in their language."

"You have any brothers or sisters?"

"Just me. And Dad didn't care that I was a girl. He treated me as he would have a son, trained me, taught me self-defense, insisted I learn about firearms." She laughed. "My mother nearly had a heart attack. Still does."

"He retired now?"

"Dead." She went back to the sandwich. "Killed in the line of duty."

There was a pause. And then Matthias said softly, "I'm sorry."

She didn't dare look up, because she'd said too much, and with those sunglasses on, she didn't know where his eyes were—though it didn't take a genius to know they were on her.

"Thanks. Enough about me, though—and enough with that I'm-too-dangerous-for-you crap. I've been taking care of myself for a long time now, and I'm good at it. I wouldn't have made the offer if I didn't think I could handle you."

He laughed in a short burst. "You're awfully sure of yourself."

"I know what my limits are."

"But you don't know me. Neither of us does."

"Which is what we want to fix, right?"

The man sat back. "Yeah."

When she was finished with the sandwich—she skipped the rest of her fries—she paid the bill and got to her feet. "So let's do this."

As he looked up at her, that shaft went through her again, that sizzle of attraction which made no sense heating her up.

"Promise me something," he said quietly.

"Depends on what it is."

"You won't take any chances with yourself."

"Done."

With a nod, he gathered his cane, slid his legs around and then waited for a moment, like he was bracing his body for an onslaught. Her first instinct was to hitch an arm under his to help, but she knew he wouldn't have appreciated that. And staring at him in his frailty wasn't respectful, either, so she did a half turn and pretended to be checking out the backlit menu mounted on the wall over the counter.

A groan told her he was up on his feet, and she led the way to the door. As they passed the few other diners, she felt their eyes go to the man behind her, lingering.

God, what it must be to go through life like that, constantly being stared at. Although . . . chances were good the women saw what she did. Which was nothing limited in the slightest.

Quite the contrary.

Out in the parking lot, Tony's car was a beater, but not in the kept-neat sense that Fi-Fi was. His ride was more like a roaming trash bin.

"Don't mind the clutter," she said as she unlocked the Toyota.

Getting in, she reached over and batted the *The New Republics* and the *Newsweeks* off the passenger seat. Not surprisingly, it took Matthias some time to lower himself, and when he swung his knees in, his boots crunched into the litter in the footwell, mashing Taco Bell into the golden arches, and BK Lounge into Wendy's.

"Your friend's into fast food," he remarked.

"And he eats quick, too."

Hitting the gas, she barged into traffic, shoe-horning the sedan into a hatchback-size space between a cab and a NiMo truck.

"Seat belt," he said.

She glanced over. "Yup. You're wearing one."

"Do you have a death wish?"

"Seat belts don't always save lives."

"So all these people around us are wrong?"

"They can do what they want, and so can I."

"What about tickets?"

"I haven't been pulled over yet. If I do, I'll pay up."

"When. That would be 'when.'"

Pine Grove Cemetery was a good ten minutes away—except for the way she drove. Mels was never reckless; she was just efficient, picking routes that avoided traffic lights and the construction that was going on around the park.

"It's up here on the right." She leaned into the wheel and looked out the windshield. "The place is beautiful, actually. There's something so peaceful about cemeteries."

Matthias made a "meh" sound. "All that eternal rest is just an illusion."

"Don't you believe in Heaven?"

"I believe in Hell, I'll tell you that much."

There was no time to follow up as they came to the front entrance. "The accident happened around here . . . past the main gates. Right about . . . little farther—here."

As she pulled Tony's car over and went to turn off the engine, Matthias was already getting out. Walking quickly with his cane, he stopped in the middle of the road, at the stains where he'd landed.

He looked left and right; then doubled back, going over to Fi-Fi's tire tracks, and the busted tree . . . and finally up to the ten-foot-tall fence that surrounded the cemetery.

Talk about Gothic. Made of iron slats and topped with fleur-de-lis cappers, Pine Grove's boundary was imposing . . . and danger-ous if you tried to scale it.

And what do you know, as she approached, she saw blood on the top of one of the sharp points—as well as a piece of cloth. Like someone had pulled an up-and-over.

"I'll get it," she said, jumping up and snagging what had gotten torn. "Here."

Matthias took the remnant. "Oil cloth, and I'll bet that dried blood is mine. I have a fresh wound on my leg."

Why hadn't he used the front gate? Then again, it would have been locked as it had been after dark.

"Can we go inside?" he asked.

"Right now."

Back in the car, she took them through the entrance and went left, heading in the direction of where they assumed he'd jumped the fence. When she got to the point where they'd found the cloth, she stopped again, got out, and waited for his memory to speak up. If it did.

As he looked around and she gave him some space, the breeze coming through the fluffy green pineboughs whistled in low notes, and sunshine warmed her shoulders . . . and she tried not to think about where her father was—

Further back by some two acres, over in the middle, between the Thomas family's plot and three brothers by the name of Kren-sky.

Guess she remembered.

The last time she'd been here had been the day her father was buried. She'd been in New York City working for about half a decade at that point. He'd been so proud of his daughter in the big city, doing what she'd gone to school for. Journalism—

"This way," Matthias said absently.

As he strode off across the patchy spring lawn, she let go of her past and focused on his present, and together, they made good time even though his stride was uneven and he leaned on his cane for support. Every once in a while, he paused, as if recalibrating his direction, and she didn't interrupt him with questions.

The outbuilding they eventually came up to fit in with all the headstones and tombs, its stone construction echoing the architecture of the entryway gatehouse and the stanchions that regularly marked sections of the wrought fencing.

"I was naked," he said. "I came here and I broke in, and I got—"

He pulled on the door and it creaked as it opened. Inside, he went to the rear wall and matched the torn fabric to some oilskin overalls in the back.

Naked? she wondered. "Where were your clothes?"

He shrugged. "I only know I was here last night."

Outside once again, he started off in the direction they'd been going in, and now things went zigzag—whether it was from keeping the trail or trying to find it, she didn't know and didn't ask. Going along, they passed endless headstones, as well as groundsmen mowing and weeding, and other visitors to the dead.

Finally, after they were nearly a half mile from where they'd left the car, he stopped. "Here. This is . . . Yeah, it started here. I'm sure of it."

The headstone he focused on stood over one of the fresher graves—and on top of the semiloose soil that had been recently put over the coffin, sure enough, there was the imprint of a body, as if someone his size had lain there in the fetal position.

"This is where it started." He leaned on his cane and got down on his haunches. Fingering the dirt, he whispered, "Here."

"James Heron," she said, reading the simple inscription on the grave marker. "Do you know him?"

Matthias looked around the cemetery. "Yeah."

"In what context."

"I have to go." He got to his feet and stepped away from her. "Thanks."

She frowned. "What are you talking about?"

"You have to leave, now—"

"You're in no condition to walk back to town. And good luck finding a cab."

"Please, you need to go."

"Tell me why and I'll think about it."

With a sudden surge, the man stalked up on her, getting close . . . oh, so close. Catching her breath, Mels had to force her feet to stay put . . . and it was a shock to realize it was because they wanted her body to finish what he'd started.

All it would take would be one step forward, and they'd be chest to chest, hip to hip.

Not the brightest idea considering that the predator in him seemed to have come out. But she didn't want to be sensible.

She wanted him.

But that was *not* going to be part of the plan.

Tilting her chin up, she said, "If you think this simmering aggression thing is persuasive, you're wrong. And I'm waiting for an explanation."

He leaned in, the shift at his hips making her keenly aware of how much taller than her he was. How much stronger, even with the injuries. How much his eyes burned even through her sunglasses.

In a low, dangerous voice, he said, "Because you're going to die if you don't get away from me."

Chapter Eleven

Undisclosed location,
Washington, D.C.

"This is your target."

The photo that landed faceup on the glossy table found its way over to the operative by virtue of momentum.

The face was instantly familiar. But who in XOps didn't know the man.

The operative looked up at his superior. "What's the location?"

"Caldwell, New York."

The address was given over verbally, as would any other instructions. And he would not keep the photograph. And this room, in an absolutely unremarkable building in the nation's capital, recorded none of this. No trail. Ever.

"Obviously, he is considered armed and extremely dangerous."

Damn straight the guy was. Always had been—but laurels were nothing that lasted, and there was no "former" in XOps. There was "active duty" and "dead."

And he was going to be responsible for the "dead," in this case.

"The usual rules apply," he was told.

Of course they did: He was going in alone, was solely responsible for the mission, and if he was compromised, he should pray for death—or make it happen himself. All of this was well-known to the small cadre of operatives who had been handpicked by the devil himself. . . .

Matthias. The one who had led them for the last ten years. The cunning chess player, the manipulative mastermind, the violent sociopath who set the tone for them all.

For a moment, it was strange to be taking orders from someone else—but given who the target was. . . .

XOps needed to keep going, however, and his current superior had come up fast through the ranks, clearly positioning himself as the heir to the throne. Which explained what he was doing now. Loose strings were unacceptable.

"Anything else I need to be aware of?"

"Just don't fuck it up. You have twenty-four hours."

The operative reached out a gloved hand and brought the photograph closer. Staring at the face, he thought that if someone had told him the changes that were going to happen in the last two years, he'd have been convinced they'd lost their damn mind.

Yet here he was, looking at the supremely powerful man in the photograph who now had a death warrant hanging over his head: If the operative failed to kill him, the organization would send someone else. And another. And another. Until the job was done.

And, knowing the target, it might take a couple of tries.

His superior picked up the photograph and went for a door that only looked normal. In reality, it was bullet-, fire-, bomb-, and soundproof. As were the walls, ceiling, and floor.

After a retinal scan, the panel opened and then closed, leaving the operative alone to consider his options, which was SOP: Once an assignment had been given over, the methods of execution were up to the delegatee. The brass cared only about the ends.

Caldwell, New York, was merely an hour away by plane, but better to drive. There was no telling the resources his target had, and aircraft could be tracked easier than unmarkeds.

As he left, the fact that he might well be going to his own death was irrelevant—and that was part of the reason he had been chosen from all the other soldiers and civilians who "applied" to get into XOps. Careful psychological and physical screening was conducted over years, not months or weeks, before you were tapped on the shoulder. Then again, the job required an unusual combination of urgency and disassociation, logic and freethinking, mental and physical discipline.

As well as the simple enjoyment of killing other human beings.

At the end of the day, playing Grim Reaper was fun to him, and this was the only legally sanctioned way to do it. Even the canniest serial killers got caught after a while. Working in this capacity for the U.S. government?

His only rate limiter was his ability to stay alive.

Chapter Twelve

Matthias had had to let Mels go.

There hadn't been any other choice. Standing in that cemetery with her, staring across Jim Heron's grave, it had been very clear to him that they were separated by life and death—and she was on the vital side.

He wanted to keep her there.

After they'd argued for a while, she'd left him, walking off with a quick efficiency he approved of. In the wake of her departure, he'd stayed by Heron's final resting place for as long as he estimated it would take her to return to her friend's car—and sure enough, when he eventually returned to the cemetery's front gates, the Toyota trash bin was gone.

Turned out she'd been right about the lack of taxis, but there'd been a bus stop not too far away, and though he'd had to wait a while, he had managed to get himself back downtown.

Better this way. Clean break—at least physically. Mentally, he had a feeling it wasn't going to be quite so cut and dry.

Although there was still a part of her with him in the concrete sense: the sunglasses. She hadn't demanded their return, and he'd forgotten they were on his face.

And covering up his bad eye was going to help in situations like this. . . .

Matthias entered the Starbucks on Fifteenth Street, and cased the place behind the Ray-Bans. The lunch crush had come and gone, and the three o'clock snoozers had yet to crowd in to solve their late-afternoon sags. Only a couple of customers nursing lattes, and a pair of baristas on the far side of the counter.

He picked the one who had the piercings all over her puss, and spiky navy-and-pink hair that looked like it hadn't gotten over the shock of those needle assaults.

Either that or the shit was pissed off at the not-from-nature dye job.

As he approached, she looked up with a counting-down-the-clock expression, but that changed into something else. Something he was used to.

Speculation of the female variety.

He had chosen wisely.

"Hi," she said as she searched his face . . . and then what she could see of his cane and his black windbreaker.

Matthias smiled at her, as if he were momentarily taken with her, too. "Ah, yeah, listen, I was supposed to meet a friend here, and he hasn't shown. I went to call him on my cell phone and realized I've left the damn thing at home. Can I use your landline?"

She glanced over at her comrade-in-lattes. The guy was lounging against the back where the coffee machines were, arms crossed over his thin chest, chin down, as if he were taking a breather standing up.

"Yeah. Okay. Come over here."

Matthias tracked her on the customer side of the counter, exaggerating his limp. "I'll have to call information first, because he was in my contacts. But don't worry, it's just local. I can't believe I forgot my phone."

"Happens to everyone." She was all flustered, those eyes of hers flipping up to him and shifting away like he was too bright to look at for long. "I've got to dial for you, though. You can't come back here."

"No problem." When she passed the receiver over the partition, he gripped it and smiled slowly. "Thanks."

Even more fluster. To the point where she had to take two tries to get through to information.

Matthias casually turned away and made like he was checking the entrance for his "friend" as a recorded voice hit him with, "City and state, please."

"In Caldwell, New York." Pause. Wait for the human to come on. "Yeah, the number of James Heron."

As he held on for the number, the girl picked up a dishcloth and ran it over the counter, all casual. She was listening, though, those brows with the hoops down low.

"H-E-R-O-N," Matthias spelled out. "Like the bird. First name James."

For fuck's sake, how many ways could you spell the damn—

411 came back on the line: "I'm sorry, but I don't have anyone by that last name in Caldwell. Is there another name you'd like to search?"

Well, shit. But somehow it didn't surprise him. Too easy. Not safe enough.

"No, thanks." Matthias pivoted back to the waitress, returning the receiver. "Out of luck. Unlisted."

"Did you say 'Heron'?" the girl asked as she went to hang up. "You mean that guy who died?"

Matthias narrowed his eyes—not that she could tell, thanks to the Ray-Bans. "Kinda. My friend's his brother, actually. They lived together. Phone was under Jim's name. Like I said, my buddy and I were going to meet up here and, you know, talk about it all. It's so hard losing someone like that, and I've been worried about what it's doing to his head."

"Oh, my God, it was *too* sad." The girl shifted the dishrag back and forth in her hands. "My uncle worked with him— happened to be there when he was electrocuted at the site. And then to think he got shot, like, days later. I mean, how does that happen? I'm *so* sorry."

"Your uncle knew Jim?"

"He's the head of human resources for the construction company he worked for."

Matthias took a deep breath, like he was choking up. "Jim was an awesome guy—we were in the war together." He knocked the head of his cane into the partition. "You know how it is."

Four . . . three . . . two . . . one . . .

"Look, why don't I call my uncle for you. Maybe he has the number. Hold on."

The girl slipped out of the partition, paused, and then nodded, like she was on a mission for good, and determined to Do the Right Thing.

As Matthias waited for her to come back, he listened for his conscience to speak up at the manipulation.

When nothing came, he was disturbed by how easy it was. Like the act of lying was so familiar and insignificant, it didn't register any more than the blink of the eyes did.

The barista returned about five minutes later with a number

written in a girlie script that belied all the I'm-a-hard-ass piercing stuff. "I'll dial it for you."

Back behind the counter, she handed him the receiver again, and he listened to the beeping as she pushed the buttons.

Ring. Ring. Ring. Ring. Ring. Ring—

No voicemail. No answer.

He gave her back the receiver. "No one's home."

Then again, what other response was there: Wake up on the guy's grave, and he expected Heron to be answering a call? Long reach from six feet under to AT&T.

"Maybe he's on his way?"

"Maybe." Matthias stared at the girl for a moment. "Thank you so much. I really mean that."

"You want some coffee as you wait?"

"I'd better go do a drive-by on the house. People react to tragedy in . . . funny ways."

She nodded gravely. "I'm really sorry."

And she was. A perfect stranger was honestly sorry for whatever he was going through.

He immediately thought of Mels, who'd also been so willing to help him.

Nice people. Good people. And his faulty memory said he didn't belong in their company.

"Thank you," he said gruffly before limping out.

The forty-caliber handgun in Jim's right palm weighed thirty-two ounces, with ten bullets in the mag and one in the pipe.

He kept the weapon down at his side, by his thigh, as he walked out of the garage. After the mess in the shower, Adrian had left to go get some air and some food, taking his Harley and not his hel-

met. Dog was safely upstairs, resting on the bed in a patch of sunlight. Jim was on guard duty.

Can't you see? She's in me—and she's taking over.

Fuck.

At least he had an outlet: The good thing about the garage was
that it was all the way at the back of a farmhouse property—and the
white main house with its porch and its redbrick chimney had been
empty since he'd started renting here.

No one was going to see. But that wasn't good enough.

Shoving his free hand into his combats, he took out a suppressor. The silencer added ten ounces in weight to the autoloader and
changed the balance, but he was used to the weapon like that.

Now, no one would hear, either.

Standing on the loose pea gravel of the drive, he took a drag of
his cigarette and then held the thing in his left hand. Focusing on
a branch that was thirty feet from the ground, he lifted his weapon
and locked in on the one-inch-thick stretch of oak.

Breathing calmly, he closed his eyes and pictured Devina's face.

Crack!

Thanks to the suppressor, there was no noise from the gun, no
pop, just the kick against his palm, and the impact on the wood.

Crack!

The trigger, like the grip and the barrel, was not only an extension of his arm, but his body, and he didn't need his eyes to re-
adjust the trajectory. He knew exactly where the lead was going.

Crack!

Calm. Centered. Breathing in the belly, not the chest. Unmov-
ing, except for his forefinger and then his forearm muscles as they
absorbed the subtle recoil of the gun.

The impact of the final bullet was softer, but then again, there
wasn't much wood left.

He opened his eyes just as the branch went into free fall, bouncing down through the arms of its brethren, delayed, but not stopped from the hard ground.

Putting his Marlboro back between his teeth, he crushed the fallen pine needles and the scratchy grass under his combat boots as he went over and picked the thing up. Clean cut, relatively speaking. Nothing like what a saw would have done, but considering the distance and the means, it was good enough—

"You are an excellent shot."

The haughty English accent coming from behind him made Jim want to keep squeezing off bullets. "Nigel."

"Have I caught you at an inopportune moment?"

"I still have seven bullets left. You decide."

"Devina has been reprimanded." As Jim spun around and narrowed his eyes on the aristocratic archangel, Nigel nodded. "I wanted you to know that. I thought it was rather important for you to know that."

"Worried that I'm going off the rails?"

"But of course."

Jim had to smile. "You can be a straight shooter when it suits you. So what's your Maker done to my enemy?"

"She's your opponent—"

"Enemy."

Nigel clasped his hands behind his back and went on a quaint little walkabout, his lean figure dressed in the kind of hand-tailored suit Jim was totally unfamiliar with, and fully prepared to stay that way.

"What's the matter, boss," Jim muttered. "Cat got your tongue?"

The archangel shot over a look that might have dropped him dead if he'd been alive in the conventional sense. "You are not the only one with a temper, and I should remind you to watch your tone and words with me."

Jim tucked the weapon into the small of his back. "Fine. Let's drop the small talk. What can I do for you?"

"Nothing. I simply thought it would ease you to know that the Maker has taken action. I told you to let the demon overstep the boundaries. I told you to wait for the response, and it has come."

"What did He do to her?"

"The wins and losses that you both have sustained are permanent. There is naught that He nor any of us can do about where the flags have gone—they are immutable. But He hath decreed that her actions cannot lay unaddressed—"

"Wait, I don't get it. If what Devina did affected the outcome of a round, then her win should be yanked."

"That is not how this contest is set up. The wins are . . ." The archangel looked to the heavens. "The parallel would be personal property, I suppose."

"Mine?"

"In a manner of speaking, I would say yes."

"So if she fucked off the rules, and it changed the result, the Maker should give me back what's rightfully mine. And while we're at it, I'd like to point out that if I'd known who the damn soul had been when it came to Matthias, I wouldn't have been focused on the wrong man."

"And that has been redressed."

"How?"

In the far distance, on the other side of the meadow, a car turned in from the main road and started on the lane that went past the farmhouse.

Shit. Visitors were so not welcome—and the yellow color suggested it was a cab.

The thing didn't stop at the main residence.

Nigel cocked a brow. "I believe it shall be self-evident."

On that oh-so-clear note, his boss disappeared.

"Thanks, buddy," Jim muttered. "Big help. As fucking usual."

Ducking around the corner, Jim nailed his shoulder blades to the aluminum siding. The gun didn't stay in his waistband. Once again in his hand, he was prepared to shoot.

The taxi rolled to a halt in front of the garage.

A moment later, a man he never expected to see again got out of the backseat . . . a nightmare who lived and breathed . . . a blast from the past that he'd just frickin' dealt with.

This was the solution for Devina's cheating on the rules?

"Mother . . . fucker . . ." Jim hissed.

Chapter Thirteen

As Matthias got out of the cab, he told the driver to wait. The garage ahead of him was two stories of utility, with a set of stairs that ran up to its second story on the left. The double doors on the ground level were closed; same with the one at the top landing. Curtains were drawn—

Upstairs in the picture window, thin drapes parted and a scruffy dog appeared, as if it were standing up with its paws on the sill.

Someone clearly lived here.

"Tell the cab to go."

Matthias's head ripped around to the right—and the man who stepped out from behind the lee of the building made him reach out for balance, his memory popping up an instant, vivid recognition.

Jim Heron. Back from the dead.

And from what Matthias's gut told him, the guy looked as he always had, that big, muscled body, the dark blond hair, the hard, cold face. There was no context, however, no running internal commentary on how he knew the man, or what they had done or seen together. One thing was clear, however . . . gun aside, it was obvious this was not the kind of guy you wanted to be around if you were unarmed and without an escape vehicle.

Matthias knocked on the window, gave a twenty to the cabbie, and sent the taxi packing.

As the thing K-turned and went off down the driveway, the sound of its tires crackling across the gravel seemed as loud as rounds of ammunition.

"Is that a gun by your leg or are you just glad to see me?" Matthias said dryly.

"It's a gun. And you want to tell me what you're doing here?"

"I would if I could. Maybe you can help me with that one?"

"What?" When Matthias didn't answer, Heron's cynical baby blues narrowed further. "You're serious. That's an honest question."

Matthias shrugged. "Interpret it as you will. And while you're stewing, I'd like to point out that you're supposed to be dead."

"How did you find me?"

"Information. In a manner of speaking."

As Heron came forward, Matthias noted that the position of that gun with its silencer changed so the barrel was pointing right at his own chest. And he was willing to bet what was left of his nuts that the trigger could be pulled in an instant. Which meant either this soldierlike man was paranoid . . . or for some reason, he thought Matthias was dangerous.

"I'm unarmed," Matthias announced.

"Not like you."

That forty didn't lower; that body didn't ease; those eyes didn't lose their warning look.

"You don't believe me," Matthias said.

"After everything we've been through? Not in the slightest, old friend."

"Were we friends?"

"No, you're right. We were a lot of things, but never that." Heron shook his head. "Goddamn, every time I don't expect to see you again, here you are."

Heron knew the answers, Matthias thought. The man right in front of him was the path to finding out who he was.

"Well," Matthias murmured, "considering you're still breathing, but I was at your grave about an hour ago, I'm not the only one pulling rabbits out of hats. You mind telling me the last time we saw each other?"

"Are you fucking serious?" When he nodded, Heron shook his head again. "You're saying you don't remember."

Matthias put out his hands, palms up. "I got nada."

Calculation was replaced by a brief surprise. "Jesus."

"I wouldn't know. My driver's license says 'Matthias.'"

The laughter that came back at him was chilly. "Mind if I pat you down?"

Matthias balanced his cane against his leg and lifted his arms. "Have at it."

Jim did the deed one-handed, and when he stepped back, there was curse. "Clearly you have lost your mind."

"No, only my memory. And I need you to tell me who I am."

There was a long silence, like Heron was trying to poke holes in the story in his head. Finally, the guy said, "We'll see about any information dump on your past. But I will help you. That, you can take to the bank."

"Not good enough. I need the intel. Now."

"Do you really feel like you're in a position to make demands?"

As Jim led his former boss, Matthias the Fucker, upstairs to the apartment, he was suffering from a serious case of the can't-believes. And yet no matter how much his brain cramped, it looked like pigs could fly, there was a snowball in Hell, and somewhere across town, a twelve-year-old dog was learning how to drive a goddamn car.

Was this what Nigel had been talking about? The redo for round two in the game?

You will recognize him as an old friend and an old foe who you have seen of late. The path could not be more obvious if it were spotlit.

Seemed like focusing on the wrong soul wasn't going to be a problem in this round—assuming Nigel's doublespeak was right and Matthias was, once again, the one on deck.

Which was *not* such a great way of penalizing Devina. Damn it.

Although the good news, if there was any in this particular back-from-beyond scenario, was the memory loss. The old Matthias would never have copped to a weakness like amnesia, so it was probably legit—and God knew that informational black hole was a leg up.

This way Jim only had to work against nature.

The nurture, on top of all that, had been . . . horrific.

Jim opened the door and stood aside. "Humble abode and all that."

As Matthias limped into the studio, Dog rushed over and wagged a greeting, paws skidding on the floorboards.

Given the happy/happy, it was obvious Devina wasn't inside the other man's suit of flesh. Nice tip.

Jim shut the door, and watched his former boss. Same limp. Same voice. Same face. Sunglasses weren't a big surprise given the condition the guy's eye was in. "I'd offer you some food, but I have to wait for my roommate to get back. You're welcome to my couch in the meantime."

Matthias groaned as he sat down. "Still a smoker," he said, nodding to the carton on the table.

"Thought you didn't remember shit."

"Some things . . . they come back."

Jim went over to the galley kitchen and parked it against the sink. For some reason, he wanted to be closer to Eddie. "So let's start with exactly what you do remember."

"I know I woke up on your grave."

"Dead is relative."

"So we're both miracles."

Jim lifted a brow. "At least one of us is. We'll have to see about the other. How'd you find me?"

"Information."

"This phone isn't under my name."

"You gave it to your last employer. I went to the library, reversed the number on the Internet and here you are. Not very good camouflage."

"I'm not hiding from anyone."

"Then why are you dead but living."

"Let's stay focused on you, shall we."

"Okay, so why are you afraid of me." As Jim gritted his molars, Matthias smiled in the way he always had, showing all his sharp white teeth. "That's not memory, by the way. It's the gun in your hand. We're in your humble, out of sight—if I weren't a threat, you'd put it down."

Fucker.

Motherfucker.

Even with amnesia, the guy was a bastard.

On that note, Jim walked over, keeping eye contact with the dark Ray-Bans the man had on. With the suppressed muzzle pointing at Matthias, he put the weapon on the coffee table and pushed it across the pitted wood.

"Help yourself."

"You're giving me a gun."

"Sure, why not. Think of it as a homecoming gift."

"Am I home?"

"Not in this particular place—you can't stay here, and haven't. Ever."

Matthias smiled a little. "Well, I don't want to stay at my house."

"Where's that exactly."

The guy reached into his pocket, took out a wallet, and flipped a driver's license onto the table by the forty.

Jim looked at the ID. It was well-done, with the proper holograms. Last name wasn't right, of course, but the first one and the picture were.

"What do you know about me?" the man demanded.

"Nice mug shot," Jim said as he eased back.

"Not asking you about my future as a model. And why are you avoiding my questions."

"I'm trying to decide how to play this."

"Are we in a game?"

"Yes, we are. And it's got stakes you can't begin to guess at." Jim decided to sit down beside his guest. "Like I said, why don't we start with what you remember."

Those sunglasses lowered as if the man were staring at the floor. Maybe his boots. The cane?

"I was hit by a car outside of Pine Grove Cemetery last night and woke up in the hospital with no clue who or where I was. Today, I backtracked as much as I could and found your grave." The Ray-Bans swung back up and around. "I knew your name the instant I saw it. Knew you as well, the second you stepped into sight."

Jim poker-faced it. "Not a surprise—the pair of us go way back. And that's why I'm going to help you."

"So tell me how I got . . ." Matthias's hand made an awkward sweep of himself. "All this."

"The injuries?"

"No, my tutu and ballet slippers. What the fuck do you think."

"Take off the glasses."

"Why."

"I want to look you in the eye when I answer."

The hand that lifted shook, but he was willing to bet it was a physical weakness, not a mental one. And what was revealed was exactly the way it had been.

"How did the injuries happen," his former boss repeated in a deep voice.

"You tried to kill yourself in front of me. You planted a bomb in the sand and stepped on the fucker right in front of me."

Matthias looked down at his legs, his brows going tight, like he was playing hunt-and-peck with his mental keyboard. "Why did I do that?"

How to answer that one without giving too much away. "You hated the man you were. You couldn't keep going anymore, and you set it up so you didn't have to."

"I didn't die, though."

"Not then, no." Jim got to his feet. "Roommate's back."

A split second later, the sound of a Harley percolated through the windows, getting louder until it rumbled to a halt below.

"You have a good sense of hearing," Matthias remarked.

Jim faced off at the man, wondering exactly how to make the situation work to his advantage. With a sly smile, he murmured, "It's the least of my tricks."

Chapter Fourteen

"You want me to do *what?*"

In reply, a L'Oréal box was thrown out of the shadows, and as the woman caught it, she thought . . . Yeah, wow, great start to the night. She was already tired, cranked off, and ready for it to be one a.m. with her shift over—and this "client" was some freak into hair color?

She was so done with this whore thing; she really was. She was sick of seedy, dark motel rooms, and ugly men with bright ideas— and don't get her started on her "manager."

"You want me to color my hair blond. For real."

A fan of five hundred dollars appeared from out of the corner, the light falling from the ceiling fixture making the bills glow in the dim room. It sure seemed like Benjis from heaven, baby—especially considering the dumb-ass had already paid that to be allowed to come here to this downtown rent-by-the-hour with her.

"Okay, fine." She walked over and snatched the bills. "Anything else?"

The deep voice was quiet. "I want you to blow it dry straight."

"That's it?"

"That's it."

"No sex."

"I don't want you for that, no."

A shiver started at her tramp stamp and chillied up her spine to the nape of her neck. But there was nothing to worry about. There were girls in the rooms on either side of them, and her boss man was out in the parking lot no more than twelve feet away. Plus she carried Mace.

What was he going to do to her.

Muttering under her breath, she went into the bathroom and flicked on the light. In the mirror, she looked like she was forty, with bags under her eyes and hair the consistency of corn husks. The good news was that she did need to touch up her roots—there was a road map straight down her side part, mucky brunette showing at the scalp. But not because she was pulling a Marilyn Monroe.

She'd liked being a redhead. And damn, if her hair was already brittle as hell, this wasn't going to help—

Oh, look, it came with a conditioner. Sweet.

She laid out the squeeze bottle full of creamy shit, the tin tube of color, and the squat thing of postblond goo. Reading the directions took a little time, because she'd always sucked at the whole letter/word stuff, but this wasn't rocket science.

Through the open doorway, she saw that the client had sat down in that far corner, his boots planted widely apart, his hands resting on his knees instead of at his groin. Not much showed of him, the light from above reaching up only so far on his legs. Better that way— made him more anonymous.

Funny, she hadn't remembered these rooms being this dark.

Getting back to business, she punctured the top of the tube with the plastic cap, squeezed the stinky crap into the bottle with the pointy top, and then shook the mixture like she was giving someone a hand job. The plastic gloves were on the back of the directions, and she pushed her hands into them. Thank God they were big, because there was room at the top for her fake nails.

She hit the side part without a glitch, but tangles in the ends made it impossible to get the shit down the length. Getting a brush from her bag, she ripped through from root to split end until she could do the whole job; then made quick work of covering everything that came out of her skull.

The stuff smelled like air freshener and chemical glue, and had the consistency of cum.

Was that what turned this guy on?

Men were such pigs.

During processing time, as her scalp heated up and her nose itched, she texted people about the freak job she was on. No reason to talk to the client—he was still just sitting there, making like a statue.

Thirty-five minutes later she stepped into the shower with a bottle of shampoo that had been left on the counter. The stuff had been half-used by someone else, but there was enough to get things rinsing clean. The warm water felt good, and the conditioner smelled so much better than the bleach.

When she got out, her hair was the color of movie popcorn, all that golden yellow making her white-ass skin glow green. Putting her slut clothes back on didn't help her image much.

Unhitching the hair dryer, she pivoted on her bare feet. "You ready for this?"

The man rose from the chair and came over, stepping into the light. He was good-looking enough, but for some reason, she wanted to give him the money back and leave. Fast.

"I'm going to take things from here," he told her, snagging the dryer and brush from her.

The noise from the hot air roared in her ears as he began to slowly stroke the bristles through her hair. Steady. Sure. As if he'd done this before.

Freak.

When everything was dry and smooth, he clicked the Conair off and put it on the counter beside her.

Meeting her eyes in the mirror, the man just stared at her.

She cleared her throat. "I have to go—"

His face wasn't right all of a sudden, the features seeming to change into. . . .

She opened her mouth and dragged in her last breath to scream just as a blade lifted behind her head.

With a quick slash across her throat, the monster opened a different exhalation route for the air in her lungs, the release not making it high enough to become a cry for help.

Her final image was of a dead, animated corpse that was smiling in the midst of its rotting flesh.

"Party time," a female voice said.

Chapter Fifteen

Suicide.

As Matthias stewed on the word, a man the size of a bus came into the garage's studio apartment, his black jacket, gloves, and leathers making him look like a Hell's Angel. That harsh expression fit the job description, too—and all those piercings didn't mark him as a pussy, either.

Jim made the introductions, classifying Matthias as "a friend," and the leather-wearing roomie as "Adrian."

Suicide.

Trying on the concept for size, Matthias found it fit, and waited for more to come to him: a context, a place, a triggering reason. Nothing bubbled up, even as he strained against the constipation in his head—

With sudden clarity, he looked over at Heron. "The desert."

The man with the answers stopped talking to his roommate and nodded. "Yeah. That's where it happened."

"And you were right there." As Heron nodded again, Matthias's frustration roared. "How the fuck do we know each other—"

Any answer was cut off by the sound of a car pulling up in front of the garage. Instantly, guns were outted, and Matthias joined the party, snagging the one off the table.

God . . . it felt so good against his palm. So natural.

Matthias shoved himself around and played dog, looking through the drapes. As soon as he saw what was in the driveway, he eased back with a groan. "Son of a bitch."

"You know her?" Jim asked from over at the window in the door.

Turning around again, he watched as Mels got out of the Toyota and focused on the Harley. It wasn't a shocker that she'd found the goddamn address; if he'd done it, she could. But he couldn't believe she'd followed through. He'd hit her with the hard reality before they'd split, and most people would have dropped out of the drama right then and there.

I'm a black belt, licensed to carry a concealed hand weapon, and I never go anywhere without a good knife.

"Let me handle this," he said, going over to the door and pushing Jim out of the way—even though the other man outweighed him by as much as a hatchback. "And let me make this perfectly clear—no one touches her. Do you both understand that. No one."

He was physically compromised in some ways, but it didn't take a lot of strength to pull a fucking trigger. And if anybody got too close to that lovely woman down there, he would hunt them down and kill them if it was the last thing he did on earth.

In the heavy silence, two pairs of brows went sky-high, but neither of the men argued with him.

Good thinking, boys.

The instant Matthias stepped out onto the top landing, Mels's head shot up.

Putting her hands on her hips, she somehow confronted him eye-to-eye, even though she was at ground level. "Surprise, surprise."

Keeping the gun way out of sight, he said, "You need to go."

She nodded at the motorcycle. "A dead man's ride?"

"Of course not."

Frowning, she abruptly crossed over the gravel and picked up what looked like one of the cobblestones. Except it caught the sunlight and sent out a flash, suggesting it was metal.

Straightening, she brought the bullet casing to her nose and took a whiff. "Been doing a little target practice?"

As she held the empty round up, he wanted to curse. Especially as she smiled coldly. "This is freshly discharged—no more than twenty minutes, maybe thirty since it was shot out of a gun."

Tucking the borrowed weapon into the small of his back, he came down as fast as he could, and when they were actually face-to-face, he'd never felt so powerless in his life. He'd tried to scare her away; that clearly hadn't worked. Maybe honesty would do the trick.

He traced her face with his eyes, that stubborn, beautiful face. "Please," he said quietly. "I'm begging you. Let this whole thing go."

"You keep talking about danger—but all I'm seeing is a man without a memory on a wild-goose chase. Look, just talk to me—"

"Jim Heron's dead. And I don't know who owns that Harley, or who was shooting—"

"So who are you talking to up there? And if you say no one, you're lying. There's no way you took that bike here. No way—and its engine is still ticking. I bet if I went over and put my hand on the block, it would be warm."

"You really need to let this all go—"

"I'm not putting any of this in the paper—we've already established that. Everything's off the record—"

"So why do you care?"

"I'm more than my job."

He threw up his hands. "Why the hell am I arguing with you. You won't even wear a goddamn seat belt in the car. Why would I expect you to—"

At that moment, the door opened and Jim Heron came out into the sunlight.

Mels looked up at the guy and shook her head. "Well, as I live and breathe . . . you know, you look a helluva lot like a construction worker who was shot and killed about two weeks ago. Matter of fact, I worked on the article in the *CCJ* about you."

Matthias squeezed his eyes together. "Son of a bitch . . ."

The first piece of good news, Jim thought, was that the woman threw a shadow. No chance she was a Devina-ogram.

The second was Matthias's little all-mine performance. That cruel bastard had never called dibs on anyone other than in a target situation—hadn't acted protective toward a living soul. But something in this fire-eyed reporter with the attitude had gotten through to him—and that did not suck.

The female in question glanced at Matthias. Glared at him was more like it. "Not going to introduce us?"

"I'll do it myself," Jim announced as he started down the stairs.

"How refreshing to think manners aren't dead," she muttered. "Then again, with the way you boys go, dead's not really a binary term, is it."

Matthias was not happy behind those Ray-Bans of his, but he was going to have to get over that. Along with a few other things.

"I'm Jim." He stuck out his hand. "Pleased to meet you."

Her expression was all about the oh-please, but she extended her palm. "Do *you* want to tell me what's going on here—"

The instant contact was made, he put her into a trance: She just stared up at him, relaxed, ready to be informed, her short-term memory wiped clean.

Cool. He wasn't sure he could pull it off.

Matthias locked a vicious hold on Jim's arm. "What the fuck did you do to her?"

"Nothing. Just a little hypnosis." He glanced at his old boss. "Here's what's going to happen. She won't remember me—neater and cleaner that way. And you're going to take her to the hotel that I'm reserving a room for you in—"

Matthias was focused only on his reporter. "Mels? Mels—are you okay—"

Jim put his face right up into the guy's eye. "She's fine—haven't you ever heard of Heron the Magnificent?"

Annnnnnnnd out came the gun. Matthias shoved the barrel right into Jim's neck, and suddenly the other man's jaw was right where it had always been, tight, hard, all about the get-'er-done.

"What the *fuck* did you do to her." Not a question. More like the countdown to a trigger pulling.

"Well," Jim said reasonably, "if you pop me in the carotid, you'll never get her out of it, will you."

Actually, if the guy shot him, nothing was going to happen. But they had enough drama going on here, and he wasn't sure he could do this mind trick with two people at the same time. More to the point, given Matthias's tricky mental landscape, Jim didn't want to run the risk of blowing the bastard's brain up with the truth about the whole angel-demon thing. Not yet, at any rate.

That gun didn't waver. "Bring her back. Now."

"You're taking her to your hotel room."

"I'm the one with the gun. I make the plans."

"Think about it. If you're with her, then you can make sure I leave her alone, right?"

Matthias's voice dropped an octave. "You don't know who you're dealing with."

"And neither do you." Jim leaned into the guy. "You need me. I'm the only one who can tell you what you want to know—trust me on this. I'm more aware than you about exactly how buried your past is, and nobody's going to break that barrier but me. So get in that fucking beater, have her drive you to the Marriott downtown, and I'll get there when I'm good and goddamn ready."

Matthias just stayed where he was, squaring off for the longest time. "I could shoot you right now."

"So do it."

Matthias frowned and brought his free hand to his temple like his head hurt. "I . . . shot you, didn't I. . . ."

"We've got a long history. And if you want to find out about it, you will stick with her—no arguments. I've got you by the short hairs, and I'm calling the shots. Nice fucking change of pace, if I do say so myself."

Jim went back to the stairs and ascended, leaving Matthias stuck between a rock and his reporter. At the top of the landing, he snapped his fingers for show and then disappeared into the studio. From behind the drapes, he watched the woman come back on line and the pair of them talk it out.

"So Matthias is the soul," Ad said from between bites of his Reuben.

"Looks like it."

"You sure you want to drag that woman into all this?"

"Did you see the way he looks at her?"

"Maybe he just wants to get laid."

"Good luck with that," Jim muttered. "And yeah, she's going to be an asset for us."

The question now was, Where were the crossroads. Sooner or later, Devina was going to set up a choice, and Jim had until then to get a completely conscienceless, power-hungry despot to do a one-eighty.

Great. Juuuust great.

He was so completely surrounded by job satisfaction at the moment that he was positively choking on the shit.

"Let's get down to that hotel," he said.

"What hotel?"

"The Marriott." He went for his wallet. There was a credit card in it under the Jim Heron name that was up-to-date—and Master-Card wasn't going to know he was technically dead because he hadn't told them.

Adrian wiped his mouth with a Goldstein's Deli napkin. "Are you sure you want this to be so public? Lot of people downtown, and Devina loves to be the center of attention."

"Yeah, but the lack of privacy will tie her hands—first of all, she'll have to clean up any messes. And second, she's going to have to be very careful about how she proceeds in this round—and I can't believe that killing innocent civilians of the human variety is going to put the Maker in His happy place."

Jim went over to the dresser, such as it was, and got his holsters out. Slipping them on, he put his dagger in on one side and another of his guns in the other. Checking his pockets, he went to see how many cigarettes he had—

The folded piece of paper in the ass of his jeans stopped the hunt, and he closed his eyes briefly.

There was no reason to take the newspaper article out; he knew it by heart. Every word, every paragraph—and especially the picture.

His Sissy.

Who wasn't really his.

Always with him. Never forgotten.

Making sure Adrian couldn't see, he outted the piece of eight-and-a-half-by-eleven, unfolded the page, and sneaked a peek at her face. Nineteen when she was taken by the demon, eternal down below in that wall of souls—

Jim frowned and looked to the door. Matthias had been in that vicious hell. What had he seen inside of it. . . .

Or, fuck, what had he done there?

The idea that that girl was in there suffering was enough to make Jim see white with rage.

"Hurry up, Ad," he muttered. "We got to go."

Chapter Sixteen

Riding in the passenger seat of the Toyota, Matthias felt like things were going at a dead run. In fact, not only was Mels obeying all the traffic laws, but they were creeping along at five miles an hour through a construction zone full of jackhammers and paving trucks.

He glanced over at her. Behind the wheel, she was fine, calm, normal, even with the not-a-clue about Jim Heron.

What the hell had the guy done to her?

Man, ordinarily Matthias would have called bullshit on the whole thing. Hypnosis his ass. Except . . . well, he was kind of in the same situation, although instead of losing a couple of minutes, he'd pulled a blank on his whole fucking life.

And what did he know from "ordinary" anymore anyway?

As they stopped at a red light on the far side of the assault on asphalt, he stared through his window. "I don't do well with being out of control."

"Not many people enjoy it." Mels took a deep breath. "I'm glad you're letting me take you back to your hotel."

If you're with her, then you can make sure I leave her alone, right?

He pushed his fingers underneath the rims of the Ray-Bans and rubbed his eyes.

"Almost there," she said. Like she thought he was going to pass out or something.

He wasn't sporting a case of the vapors, though. "You make me feel . . . powerless."

"I don't think that's me. I think that's your situation."

"No, it's you." He had the sense if she were not around, things would be clearer, even if he never remembered another event from his life: In that hypothetical, all he'd have to worry about was himself, and one problem was definitely better than two.

"I've tried to do the right thing," he muttered, and then wondered who he was talking to.

"And you are—by going somewhere you can rest. Things have been chaotic as hell for you in the last twenty-four hours. You need to sleep."

Letting his head fall against the headrest, he closed his eyes and thought of facing off against Jim, fully prepared to pull the trigger and kill the guy.

Sleep did not appear to be what he needed. More like handcuffs and a psych eval: In that moment when his finger had been on the trigger, there had been no hesitation on his part: not with the speed that he'd put the muzzle to the guy's jugular, not because there had been witnesses, and not from any sort of moral hmmm-this-is-a-human-life.

Had he been a soldier? Because that shit was nothing civilian, everything military.

Yeah, he thought, that was it. And he'd been one of the most dangerous kinds of fighters . . . those who had a dead space in the center of their chest. Which meant they were capable of anything.

You hated the man you were.

As the light turned green, Mels took them past a section of minimalls, the stores like LEGOs linked together on the far sides of narrow parking lots. It was everything he never noticed, the cutesy coffee shops, the places that peddled folklore gifts, the low-end jewelers and dollar stores. So banal. So day-by-day. So normal—

"I tried to commit suicide."

Mels hit the brake for a hairbreadth, even though traffic was flowing evenly down the four-lane stretch of byway.

"Did you . . ." She cleared her throat. "Is your memory coming back?"

"Bits and pieces."

"What happened? I mean, if it's not too personal."

Thinking back to Jim Heron, he answered with the other man's words. "I didn't like who I was."

"And who were you?"

Dark as night, cold as winter, cruel as a blade. But he kept that to himself. "You're tenacious, you know that."

She touched her sternum. "Reporter. It's part of the job description."

"I'm learning."

Matthias closed his eyes again and listened to the rise and fall of the engine. When something warm and soft covered his wrist, he jumped. It was her hand, her elegant hand.

On some level, he couldn't believe she wanted to touch him.

Swallowing hard, he gave her a squeeze and then retracted from the contact.

They came up to the Marriott about ten minutes later. The hotel was your typical big-city shindig, looming high over trimmed hedges and a shallow lawn, smack in the center of the business district. Entering the porte cochere, they got tangled in a mess of porters and cars and people with luggage. Then again, it was after three o'clock, which was rush hour for travelers.

"Will you come up?" he heard himself ask, as he wondered who might have followed them—and exactly what kind of relationship he had with Jim Heron.

The word *help* had been tossed around by the guy, except you had to wonder what the motivations were, and it wasn't smart to take anything for granted.

"I'll see you get settled—how about that."

"That's . . . good." He would still have preferred a clean break, but that was no longer possible.

Thanks to Heron.

Although . . . it was no hardship to have an opportunity to be with her a little longer.

Mels idled past all the rolling brass trolleys and the uniformed guys who were humping suitcases out of trunks, and headed down into the parking garage. Through the Toyota's vents, the smell of exhaust bubbled into the car interior, and he cracked a window— but how stupid was that. The air they had entered was the source of the bad smell.

They gave her buddy's car over to a valet, who didn't look too excited to park the POS, and shuffled through a revolving door into a lower-level lobby that was decorated with bloodred carpeting and gold walls. Unfortunately, and in spite of all the flocking—or maybe because of it—the decorations were more bordello than business-class, a grasp for the luxury of a Four Seasons that didn't quite make it.

"I've always thought this place tried to be like the Waldorf," Mels said as she punched the button for the elevator. "But this is Caldwell, not Manhattan."

"Funny, I was just thinking that."

" 'Scuse any bitterness, by the way," she said. "I'm a transplant."

"From New York?"

"Well, I was born here, but I belong there. I'm just waiting to go back."

"What's keeping you in Caldwell?"

"Everything. Nothing." She glanced over. "In a weird way, I envy you your amnesia."

"I wouldn't, if I were you."

Yeah, he really didn't want that for her, and not because he was being a gentleman. Standing beside her, he would have killed to know about her, her family, where she grew up, everything that had brought her to this quiet, fragile moment in time.

"Mels . . ."

Before he could start asking, a family joined them in the wait for the elevator, the daughters running around, the parents looking like they were stuck in a version of hell that smelled like bubble gum, and was populated by short demons in matching fairy princess outfits that asked for ice cream every three minutes.

Ding!

As the doors opened, he put his hand on the small of Mels's back and led her into the elevator. He didn't want to stop touching her, but he dropped his arm, and endured the stares of the children.

Up at the main level's lobby, the hustle and bustle of the porte cochere had invaded the reception area, a line of people snaking out from a bell captain who stood guard at a set of velvet ropes.

"This is a nightmare," Matthias muttered dryly.

"It could be worse. You ever heard of Motel 6?"

"Good point."

When they finally got up to the front desk, he gave his name, and wasn't sure how it was going to work. Typically, you had to present the credit card you made the reservation with to get a room—

"Oh, yes, Mr. Hault, you're already checked in." The woman typed fast on the computer. "I just need your driver's license, please."

Matthias glanced around the lobby. How the hell had Heron managed to get here with his credit card and do the deed? Traffic had been bad, but not that bad on the route he and Mels had come in on—unless of course the guy had pulled a helicopter out of his ass.

And about the credit card, had it been Heron's own? The SOB was supposed to be dead, so you had to wonder how the company was going to send the bill to Pine Grove. Then again, CC numbers were as easy to get as library cards if you knew the right people—and given the look of Heron's roommate, black market access was no doubt a no-brainer.

"Sir? Your license?"

"Yeah, sorry."

As he handed the thing over, the receptionist smiled at him professionally, her expression the equivalent of a facial welcome mat. "Okay, here are your room cards. Just take the elevators over there to the sixth floor. You're in room—"

Not six sixty-six, he thought for no apparent reason.

"—six forty-two. Would you like someone to help you with your bags?"

"No, I'm good. Thanks."

"Enjoy your stay, sir."

As he and Mels headed to the other elevators, he scanned the lobby without moving his head. The people striding around were nothing special . . . just normals dragging their suitcases behind them, or talking on their cell phones, or arguing with their wives/husbands/boyfriends. No one was paying him any attention, and that was why public venues were sometimes the safest places you could be if you were in hiding.

Still, he was glad he had that gun he'd taken from Jim's.

The wait for their second round with an elevator was longer than the first, and when it arrived, Mels stepped forward as did another couple.

He touched her arm and eased her back. "We'll take the next one."

The doors closed as she glanced over at him. "Claustrophobic?"

"Yeah. That's it."

This time he let his hand linger a little. Standing behind her, he was much taller than she was, even though she wasn't short by any stretch—and he wondered what she would feel like against him.

Odd thought to have for so many reasons.

But it led to an undeniable picture in his head—

"Here's another one," she said, stepping out of his hold. "And we'll be alone this time."

Man, when it came to Mels Carmichael, alone had a nice ring to it, it really did.

The trip up to his room was uneventful—assuming he left out the direction his thoughts had turned. And the other positive newsflash was that six forty-two was not far from an emergency exit. Perfect. Inside, the twenty by twenty stretch of bed-bureau-desk-chair was standard issue, although as the door shut itself behind them, he focused on the king-sized mattress.

Except she wasn't looking for an affair with a stranger, and he couldn't perform anyway.

As he walked over and closed the drapes, Mels turned on the bathroom light and leaned inside. "You've got a nice tub."

Without meaning to, his eyes did an up-and-down on her, and yeah, he really liked the way she filled out those slacks of hers.

Shit. He wanted her—bad. Wanted her naked and underneath him, her legs spread wide, her sex taking him inside as he pounded, hard.

Clearing his throat, he said roughly, "Can I buy you dinner? I know it's a little early, but I'm hungry."

For her. Screw the food.

Straightening, she glanced at him, and he was glad he had those glasses of hers on. Nothing good could come out of what was no doubt in his eyes. Lust wasn't appropriate, not in this circumstance—

Hey, check him out. He might be a casual killer, but at least he had some sense of decency.

"Yeah." She smiled a little. "Sure. I could eat something."

As Matthias went over to the built-in desk and rooted around for the room service menu, he told himself he was just doing what Jim Heron had suggested: As long as he was with her, he knew she was okay.

Because he might not know his past, but he was sure about one thing.

He would die to protect this smart, kind woman . . . and her perfect ass.

Chapter Seventeen

Mels finally got to finish an order of French fries.

They came with a hamburger that was done to a perfect medium, a sliver of a pickle with enough bite in it to make her sinuses hum, and an ice-cold Coke that was right out of a commercial, frosted glass and everything.

Over in the mahogany console, the television was on WCLD, the local NBC affiliate, the five o'clock news anchor just starting his reports.

"I have to say," she murmured, picking up the last fry and dragging it through a smudge of ketchup, "these are much better than the ones at the Riverside."

Over on the bed, Matthias was working on his club sandwich, but she could tell he was looking at her. Even through the sunglasses.

He did that a lot, his eyes staying on her as if he liked the way she moved, even when she was sitting down—and for some reason, that made him even sexier . . . to the point where she found herself wondering what it would be like to have that without any barriers.

The looking, that was.

Without the Ray-Bans, she meant—

Shoot, she was making herself flustered.

"You know, you can take those off," she said softly. "The sunglasses."

He froze. And then resumed chewing. After he swallowed, he said, "I'm more comfortable with them on."

"Okay, suit yourself."

He hadn't said a thing about his search for Jim Heron, or how he'd found the address they'd met at. He'd just gotten in Tony's car and let her drive him here.

She wasn't about to argue with the change of heart.

"Don't you have someone waiting at home for you," he said casually.

"Ah, not really. Not much of a personal life, I'm afraid."

"I know how that is—" He stopped himself. "Shit, I actually do . . . know that part."

She waited for him to finish. Instead, he just sat there staring at his plate of half-eaten food like the thing was a TV set.

"Tell me," she said.

He shrugged. "No wife. No kids. No one permanent. Which is why nobody's looking for me—well, at least not in a family sense."

"I'm sorry. What about your parents?"

Matthias winced and then seemed to catch himself.

"No?" she prompted.

"I have nothing on them."

In the silence that followed, she made work out of picking up her tray and putting it out in the hall. Back inside, she knew that it was time to go.

Probably time to let go, too.

Jim Heron was dead—at least according to the not-so-distant archives of the *CCJ*, if not that damn headstone-on-a-grave routine. She'd found his home address through one of the sources that had commented on the story—but of course, he hadn't been there—

A headache cramped her temples, but the pain didn't last as she switched her thinking to Matthias Hault. He was safe here, and recovering well, and when it came to his memory, he was the only one who could get to the bottom of that. She'd done what she was able to in terms of getting him the basics; other than that . . . she could pay up if he sued her, although it didn't look like that was in the cards.

Sure, there was something strange about that house that was supposedly "his," and some things that didn't add up, like who exactly had been at that garage, but if she wasn't going to put it in the paper, those particulars really weren't her business.

Mels approached the bed and sat on the foot of it. As he put his tray aside and looked at her, that shaft went through her again.

She was definitely attracted.

Especially here in this room, where they were alone. Except she really wasn't looking for that kind of complication.

"I'd better go," she said, searching his face.

"So go," he whispered, meeting her eye-to-eye through her sunglasses.

Neither of them moved, his long, lean body as still as hers was.

God . . . she wanted him to kiss her. Which was insane—

"You make me . . ." Matthias took a deep breath.

"What?"

Easing forward, he reached up and brushed her face. "You make me wish I were different."

The touch stopped her heart; then sped it up. "I think you're a better man than you know."

"And that's what terrifies me."

"The idea that you're okay?"

"No, that you think I am."

Mels looked away briefly and wondered what the hell she was doing in this hotel room with him . . . feeling like she wanted them both to lose their clothes along with their inhibitions. But damn it, they were both adults, and she was really frickin' tired of living a halfway life, of wanting things she didn't have, of skimping on her dreams and getting little, if anything, in return.

She wanted to be loud, again. The way she'd been before things had changed and she'd come to Caldwell and cut short . . . herself.

With a frown, she wondered just how long she'd felt this way. And then . . .

She wasn't sure what made her act—his voice? His eyes, which she couldn't see but could feel? His ingrained pride mixing with that churning self-doubt?

Her inner cavegirl?

Whatever the motivation, Mels put her lips against his. Briefly, chastely. Powerfully.

When she pulled back, he appeared stunned. "More out of control, huh," she said quietly.

"You have a knack for . . . yeah."

Well, she had shocked herself, too. But she simply couldn't think of a reason to fight the pull she had toward him. Life was finite . . . and after the last couple of years, she was more afraid of not taking chances in this moment than of flying for a while and crashing in a fireball to earth—

"Mind if I finish what you started?" he said on a growl.

"Hell . . . no."

On that ladylike note, Matthias's hand slid around the back of her neck and pulled her forward, taking over, taking control. And in the second before he had her mouth on his, she thought it was amazing how they were relative strangers, and yet his essence was better than context or time: she felt safe with this mystery man of hers, in spite of all his rhetoric to the contrary.

And holy crap, she wanted him.

Seemed like that was mutual.

Matthias kissed her hard and let her go; then came back at her, like that hadn't been nearly enough. As his tongue entered her, he kept the liplock going, holding her against his mouth, tilting his head, tilting hers. With heat pooling where it hadn't been for so long, she was soaring, crazy and wild—and thought, this was exactly what she needed. This was it, right here, with him.

Sex here in this room, on this bed. With him.

Abruptly, Matthias pulled back, like he needed to catch his breath.

"You in a habit of kissing your stories?" he asked in a husky voice.

"You're not a story. We're off the record, remember."

"Good point." His eyes raked down her body. "I want you naked."

Mels smiled slowly. "Not exactly a newsflash considering the way you just kissed me."

With a groan, he came back at her again, maneuvering her down on the mattress, rolling over on top of her. Man, before his "accident," he must have been really physically dominant with women—not in a violating manner; there was no coercion or sense of being trapped for her. Animalistic was the best way to describe it.

Especially as his leg parted hers, and his thigh pushed into her sex.

Mels surged up against the weight of his chest, and put her arms around him—

With a subtle shift, he held her off, and then stopped altogether. As he pulled away, moved away, there was tension in his face and his body—and not the I'm-about-to-jump-you variety.

"What," she said hoarsely. "What's wrong?"

As Matthias shuffled over to the edge of the bed, his lungs were burning and he wanted to put his head through a wall. Goddamn him, but here he was, with this beautiful, vital woman who had all the signs of serious sexual arousal going for her, and he was . . . willing, but not able.

He wanted her. But there wasn't much he could do about it.

Thinking back to that nurse, to that hand job he hadn't been into, it seemed like some cruel fucking joke that his problem had returned in this circumstance: The distance between him and his reporter was one that no amount of kissing was going to solve. Same with touching or grinding or full-back naked. They were on opposite sides of a grave again; she in the land of the living, he in a cemetery.

For some reason, it made him even more desperate to have her. And with sudden clarity, he knew that in the past, he'd taken whoever he wanted—and had not suffered from a lack of volunteers. But that hadn't meant he had cared about the females.

Mels, on the other hand? This was different. *She* was different.

Except he could never have her properly, not with the way his body was.

"What's wrong?" she said again.

He didn't want her to know. Even if she found out later, he wanted to preserve the illusion he was a real man for a little longer. Assuming he saw her again.

"I can't believe we're doing this," he hedged. Which was the truth. So much of this whole thing—from waking up at the foot of

Heron's headstone to the accident with her—didn't feel right. It was almost as if things were being lined up for him, as if his memory had been taken from him for a purpose.

"Neither can I," she replied, focusing on his mouth like she wanted some more.

She didn't strike him as the kind of woman who was into random hookups. She didn't dress like a whore, move like one, act like one. And she was giving off a hesitant but open vibe, like it might have been a while for her, but she really wanted things to happen.

Tell her to go, he thought. Impotence aside, there were so many other reasons they shouldn't be together tonight. Or ever.

Stretching out next to her again, he tucked his hand around her waist and pulled her to him—but not too close. Not against his hips.

God, she smelled good.

And the feelings were all there in his body, the heat coiling at his pelvis, his heartbeat going urgent, his arms and legs seeming even stronger than they had been. His cock was not with the program, however.

But maybe that was better because he needed to tell her—

"Can I make you feel good?" he blurted.

Okay, that was supposed to have come out as "good night."

"You already have."

"I'm damn sure I can do better."

"Well, far be it from me to stand in the way of excellence."

As he went in and kissed her again, he wondered what she would look like with her shirt open and her bra off, her breasts ready for his mouth, the smooth skin of her stomach leading him down to other territory.

This was incredibly good, all of it, and it seemed so new to him—and not just because he'd never been with Mels before. It felt like he'd never been with anyone. Then again, as far as his memory was concerned . . . there hadn't been anybody before her—

From out of nowhere, an image sliced through his senses. Him and a woman with smooth, dark skin, up against a wall. He had his hand around her throat and her legs around his hips, and he was banging the ever-loving shit out of her—

Matthias jerked back. All at once images flooded his mind, a chronological lineup of every woman he'd been with—young ones, when he'd been young; older, racier ones as he had grown up; then a series of extremely edgy, highly aggressive females.

He saw himself with them all, his body strong and whole, his emotions clear and uncluttered, his heart cold as stone. He saw the women, naked, or half-clothed, armed and unarmed, coming in great bursts of contortion.

"What are you remembering?" Mels asked remotely.

He opened his mouth to speak, but the rush of namesfacesplaces was a deluge he couldn't get out from under, the onslaught clogging his neurons, rendering him nearly unconscious. And as he sagged, he felt himself get eased back against the pillows, no longer the dominant one.

Bringing his hands up to his head, he cursed.

"I'm calling the doctor—"

Matthias snapped out a hold, catching her wrist. "No. I'm okay—"

"The hell you are."

"Just give me a minute."

He breathed shallowly and decided to try giving up the fight. This was the right answer; instead of slamming into him, the memories passed through, the process of the revelations easing. At least . . . until the end. The final recollection was of him with a . . . monster of some sort? Must be a nightmare he'd had . . . but, oh, God, she was hideous, and she was taking him as a way to own him in a dungeon at the base of a long, black well—

Panic acted like jumper cables, hitting Matthias so hard he

jerked from the chest, his torso contracting tight. But he kept a hold on Mels's wrist, making sure she stayed with him instead of hitting the phone.

"Please," he heard her say.

"No . . . doctor . . . it's fading now . . ."

Eventually, he released her, ditched the sunglasses, and rubbed his eyes. "You'd think when things came back, it would be slow and easy."

"Can I *please* get you some medical attention?" She brought up a binder and put it in front of his face. "See? Hotel services has a Doc-in-a-box on call."

"No, honest, I'm all right. It was just overwhelming. I think we take for granted how much we store up in here." He tapped his skull. "Lot of information."

"What kind are we talking about."

He glanced away. "Well, I'm definitely not a virgin. And let's leave it there."

"Oh."

There was an awkward stretch of quiet. And then Mels cleared her throat.

"You know what, I think I should go."

"Yeah."

She got off the bed. Picked up her coat. Put it on. "Before I leave . . ." She came over and wrote something on the little pad on the bedside table. "Here's my cell again—"

A ringing sound came out of her pocket.

"Speak of the devil," he murmured, watching her finish the seven digits before she answered the call.

"Hello?" Her voice was brisk and professional, and he liked that shift of gears, that she could pull it together so fast.

Then again, he liked a lot about the woman.

Mels frowned. "Where? Do we have a 'who' on her? How did

she die . . . Really. Yeah, I'm coming right now. I have Tony's car still—yup." She ended the call and grabbed her bag. "I have to go."

"Something's on the record?"

"And my boss must be having a change of heart. He's actually sending me to a crime scene."

"He doesn't recognize your skills?"

"Not the kind I want him to notice, no." She paused at the door. "Are you sure you're all right?"

"Have you always been a saint," he murmured.

"Not until I met you."

Just as she ducked out, he said, "Mels."

She turned her head over her shoulder, the light from above the door falling on her face. As their eyes met, he would have traded every one of those hookups he'd just seen for a single night with her.

I'm not coming out of this alive, he thought.

So if he ever got a chance to kiss her again, he wasn't going to stop. And who knew, maybe the second try would be the charm.

Assuming there wasn't another volume on his greatest-hits-that DVD.

"Wear your seat belt," he ordered in a low tone.

"Call a damn doctor," she tossed back with a little smile.

As the door shut behind her, he cursed at it. And then thought about how it had felt to kiss her.

Glancing down at his hips, he found himself wishing he was a whole man once again.

Chapter Eighteen

The bar in the lobby of the Marriott was named after the original hotel owner, Something-something Sasseman. At least, that's what the waitress told Adrian in a husky, come-hither voice while she took his and Jim's beer orders. She also found an excuse to drop her pen and bend over, and then walked off like her pelvis had recently been to Jiffy Lube and gotten over-oiled.

Then again, the rest of the clientele in here were leering businessmen likely on the varsity Viagra team, and she was a POA in her midtwenties.

Back in the Eddie days, he would have gone for her in a heartbeat.

Now? File the whole thing under "Meh."

The booth he and Jim were in was covered in red pleather and made sounds that were juuuuust this side of a whoopee cushion anytime one of them shifted positions. The thing was perfect for their purpose, however: It faced out through the fat aperture of the bar at the lobby. No one came or went without their seeing.

Although, given Jim's radar, they could have kept track of Matthias and that woman even if they'd been parked in the back lot: The angel had been sure to touch both of them, and even Ad could feel the tracer spells through the levels of the hotel. The pair were six floors up, close together.

Made you wonder exactly what they were doing.

Probably Parcheesi.

Yeah. Right.

As minutes ticked by and turned into a full hour, the background talk from the drinkers around them was the only thing that filled the silence. The beers they had turned into dinner. The time was . . . endless.

Man, immortality could be a real fucking drag when you didn't give a shit about anything. All you had was time. Great, yawning maws of hours that perpetually chewed on you with dull teeth, eating you alive even as you remained unconsumed.

Well, wasn't he a fucking party tonight.

And his mood didn't get any better as he looked down at his hands. The black stain he'd seen in the shower hadn't reappeared, but he couldn't help checking every second and a half to see if it had come back. So far, so good, except for the whole feeling-like-death thing.

It was literally as if his body had been hollowed out, nothing but the space inside his skeletal ribs remaining—

"She's coming down," Jim said, finishing up the warm inch of beer he'd been nursing. "The woman's left his room."

Ad didn't bother with the dregs of his draft. He hadn't liked it to begin with.

Better than Coors Light, though.

"You stick with her," Jim said as they walked into the lobby. "I don't want her on her own."

"Isn't he the soul?"

"I think so. And assuming he is, she's the key to this."

"You sure?"

"I've seen the way he looks at her. That's all I need to know." Jim nodded in the direction of the reporter who was stepping out of the lobby elevators. "Get on her. I'm going to wait for Devina to show up here."

Ad was not interested in getting foisted off on the GF. He wanted to wait for the demon. He wanted to stand nose-to-nose with her and pray for her to make another crack about Eddie—just so he could show her how much she wasn't getting to him anymore. And then he wanted to stare in her eyes as her frustration flared and she was forced to attack him physically.

At which time he could game-over it. Fight to the death. Go out like a warrior.

The bitch would no doubt beat him, but oh, the joy to take pounds of flesh off her. And the relief to have everything over.

"Adrian? You with me, my man?"

"I want to stay here."

"And I need you on that female. She's got to stay alive long enough to influence him. If Devina gets a goddamn whiff of that connection they're pulling? That woman's going to end up a floater in the Hudson—or worse."

As Jim stared at him, the subtext was based on logic—the strongest person had to face the demon, and right now that was not Ad. And not just because he didn't have Jim's extra flashy moves.

"Do you want to win," Jim said in a low voice. "Or do you want to fuck us."

Ad cursed and turned away, locking onto the trail of the woman and jogging off in the conventional way—because it was too messy to disappear in front of even casual observers.

As she headed for the elevators to the parking garage, Matthias's chippie walked like she was on a mission, and he envied the purpose. Didn't envy her her ride as it turned out. The POS had an engine and a roof—other than that, there wasn't much to recommend the thing.

For shits and giggles, he disappeared himself into the backseat—and onto what turned out to be a Library of Congress's worth of old papers and magazines. The good news was that she picked just that moment to start the engine—but she still heard the noise of his invisible ass compressing countless pages of newsprint. Whipping her head around, she stared into the space he was taking up, and to be nice, he gave her a little wave, even though as far as she was concerned, she was alone in the damn car.

"I'm losing my mind," she muttered as she threw them into drive and took off.

Good driver. Quick on the gas pedal, efficient in her routing.

They ended up in the western part of downtown, at a motel that was only a step up from a dog kennel. After they got out—him remaining invisi, her clearly on the hunt—they joined a convention of cops and reporters who were focused on a room over on the left—

Adrian frowned and abruptly plugged into the scene for real. As the woman he was responsible for approached the badges holding the line at the yellow crime scene tape, he breezed past the flimsy barricade and penetrated the crowd of busy-busy at the door.

What the hell, he thought to himself.

Devina was all over the place, her residual stink hanging in the breeze as if a garbage truck had backed in and left a dump of loose-and-juicy all over the place.

Adrian pressed inside and had to cover his nose to keep from gagging from the stench that didn't reach the sinuses of the humans.

Hello, dead girl.

On the far side of four or five cops, a body was visible through the open door of the bathroom: pale legs, tattoos on the thighs, clothes that were twisted around her body as if she had struggled. Her throat had been slashed, the blood soaking the sparkly thing she'd obviously considered a shirt as well as the chipped tile she was sprawled on.

She was a blonde—thanks to L'Oréal: The remnants of a hair-color kit were all over the counter, and plastic purple-stained gloves lay in the trash. And her hair was straightened—thanks to the Conair dryer and a short brush that had dark strands at its core, lighter ones at the tips of the bristles.

"Damn you, Devina," Ad muttered.

"Is the photographer here yet?" a tired looking man barked out.

The CPDs glanced at one another, like they didn't want to give him bad news.

"Not yet, Detective de la Cruz," someone said.

"That woman drives me nuts," the guy muttered, cocking his cell phone and starting to pace.

As the uniforms clustered around the detective as if they wanted to watch the photog get her ass chewed, Adrian took advantage of the clear shot into the loo, going inside and getting down on his haunches.

Hoping he didn't find anything, Ad lifted the hem of the blood-soaked blouse. "Oh, come *on* . . ."

Underneath the sparkles, the pale skin of the stomach had been scored with symbols, runes not meant for the human she had been, or the men and women who found her, or the family who would mourn her.

They were a message from Devina.

That Ad was going to make sure Jim never, ever saw.

Casting an eye back at the knot of uniforms around that detective, Ad double-checked that the cell phone call preoccupation was still giving him some privacy. Then he passed his palm back and forth over the flesh that had been marked.

Fortunately, the skin still had some remaining vitality left in its cells. But the removal was sluggish.

"—get here, *now*," that detective bit out, "or I'll take the pictures myself. You have fifteen minutes to come on scene—"

Ad frowned in concentration, throwing everything he had into the effort. The runes were carved nearly a quarter inch deep in places, and they were rough, as if made by a jagged knife . . . or more likely, a claw.

"Come on . . . come on—" He looked over his shoulder. The kaffeeklatsching was over, and the detective was heading back.

Retracting his hand, he jumped to his feet—and then remembered that he was still invisi.

"Who touched the body?" the detective blurted. "Who touched this fucking body?"

Shit. The shirt was still up just below her breasts. Not where the thing had started out. And the skin was flushed in an unnatural way, given not just the victim's ethnicity, but also where she was in her dying process. Still, the objective had been met and that was more important than any confusion the humans were going to have sorting what was doing out.

What the fuck was Devina playing at now?

"That bitch," Adrian hissed as he walked out, "is going to pay."

Jim was so done with the people watching in the lobby, but he stayed where he was even as the night dragged on: Matthias was still hanging out in that room of his, and that meant Jim was all about the hurry-up-and-wait.

It was the life of an operative: stretches of total inactivity separated by bursts of life-and-death tap dancing.

Goddamn, this was just like the good ol' times—that hadn't

been good, and didn't feel all that old at the moment because Matthias's backstory wasn't the only one he was thinking about. Ever since his new job as an angel had barged in and taken over his life, it was as if everything that had come before had been wiped clean—except that wasn't the case. Vital distraction was a kind of amnesia; didn't mean you had no history, though—

Looking up at the vaulted ceiling, he frowned. Matthias was on the move.

A minute and a half later, the elevator doors opened and the man stepped out into the lobby, relying on that cane of his, his sunglasses in place even though it was nighttime. All around, people noticed him—then again, it had always been like that, as if Matthias's power created a lighthouse effect even among the mercifully clueless.

Making himself visible, Jim stepped out into the guy's path. "Late-night appointment?"

Those Ray-Bans whipped around, but that was the extent of the reaction. "Babysitting me?"

"Yeah, and I'm not getting paid enough." Jim nodded at the revolving glass doors of the main entrance. "You off to somewhere?"

"Nah, just need fresh air. I feel . . ." Matthias dragged a hand through his hair. "Cooped up. I can't stare at those walls anymore—What? Why are you looking at me like that."

Before Jim could think of a lie, he said, "You're so much more human now."

"What the hell's that supposed to mean?"

Jim shrugged. "Doesn't really matter. Mind if I tag along?"

"Do I have a choice?"

"You could always try to outrun me."

"It's not nice to make fun of cripples."

"Show me one."

Matthias laughed in a short burst. "Fine. Help yourself."

Outside, the night was unseasonably warm with a thick mist choking the air, the moisture hanging between the clouds above and the asphalt below like it couldn't make up its mind whether to be a downpour or not.

Taking out his cigs, Jim lit up and exhaled a stream of smoke. Between the mist, the Marlboros, and the resonant sounds of their footfalls on the sidewalk, the whole damn thing was film noir in real life . . . and that was especially true as they came up to a group of men who were striding along—or marching, as was the case.

What. The. Hell?

The six bastards were all dressed in black leather, which might have marked them as Goths—except the way they walked in formation behind their leader had a professional soldier vibe.

As they passed by, Matthias and Jim moved to the side, and the one in front glanced over.

An ugly son of a bitch for sure, with eyes that were pits of aggression.

Huh . . . in his old life, Jim might have considered them candidates for recruiting. They looked like they could kill anything or anyone in their path, especially the guy in the lead.

But he was different now. And hopefully, so was Matthias.

"I remembered something," his old boss said, after the stretch of concrete was their own again.

"Yeah?"

"Just personal shit. Nothing I was interested in."

As the silence became as prevalent as the fog, Jim took another drag and talked out the exhale. "Waiting for me to fill the void?"

"You were the one who wanted to come along. You could at least make yourself useful."

"And here I thought I was decorative."

"Not for me, buddy." When Jim didn't comment further, Matthias glanced over. "So, I've been thinking about you."

"Not romantically, I hope."

"No, I used to like women. A lot."

"Used to?"

Matthias stopped and faced off. "What I want to know is—"

At the far end of the block, a figure stepped out into the sidewalk with the ease of someone trained to ambush, and the gun that was discharged in their direction didn't make a sound. All Jim saw was the brief flash as the bullet left the tip of the silencer.

With a cursing lunge, he tackled Matthias into an alley, the force of his two hundred and twenty pounds sweeping the other man off his feet, the pair of them going parallel to the ground in slow motion. In midflight, and with perfect synchronization, they took out their guns, trained their muzzles at the shooter, and pulled their triggers—and as their rounds left their silencers, Jim pivoted so that they landed on the damp pavement with him on the bottom, and Matthias using him as a mattress.

There was no time to fuck around, and he didn't need to tell his old boss that—clearly Matthias's preference in nooky wasn't the only thing the guy remembered: he was on his feet and ready to bolt for cover behind a van that was about three yards away—

More shots were fired at them, pinging off the pavement, the GMC's quarter panel, the wheel well. The shooter had followed them and was keeping to the shadows as he closed in.

That kind of stealth was another identifier. Their attacker came at them without sound, and not just because he was using the same kind of autoloader with a suppressor on it that Jim had against his own palm: No footfalls, not even heavy breathing; this was a trained killer, operating in his element.

XOps, Jim thought. Had to be.

With another curse, he looked around for options. The van wasn't good for shelter, because it had a gas tank: he knew where the lines were in terms of what he could survive, but he wasn't exactly sure where Matthias fell on the spectrum of untouchable, and a mushroom cloud over their cover was not a good way to test that shit out.

Grabbing one of Matthias's arms, he helped run the guy down the back of the GMC—and by dumb luck, the thing was parked at an industrial rear entrance to the hotel, the set of ugly steel doors inset into the brick. Jim went right for the handles, latching on, giving a twist.

Locked. Duh.

Annnnnnnnd fuck that for a laugh.

Throwing a blast of energy down into the metal, he blew the locking mechanism apart and threw his shoulder into the reinforced panels. As the pair gave way with a squeal, Matthias froze, the response so quick it was as if he had been trained into the fear.

Jim dragged the man in with him and slammed the way shut. Propping Matthias up, he hit the steel with another blast of heat, this one longer and stronger, putting a quick solder in place to buy them some escape time.

The good news was that it worked—and his old boss was too busy checking his clip to notice the sleight of hand.

Cane in one palm, autoloader in the other, Matthias regained control of himself. "Down that way," he barked like he was in charge. "There has to be an out."

Rather than get into a dick-toss, Jim took off, hitching another hold under that armpit and falling back into the half drag. As they shuffled along, he kept an eye over his shoulder.

It didn't take a genius to figure out who was the target. Matthias had been the former head of XOps, and had "died." SOP was to visually confirm the body, and given that Isaac Rothe had gotten rid of the remains, no one had been able to do that.

Somehow, they'd figured out that Matthias was up and around in Caldwell.

Maybe Devina had an "in" in the organization?

"Did you lock the door behind us?" Matthias grunted.

"Yeah." But chances were good that the assassin was going to have—

The explosion was the short and sweet kind, little more than a flash of light. And then that squeal came again as the operative busted into the corridor.

Up ahead, no doorways. No cover. Just a straight shot as far as he could see.

As if he and Matthias had a single brain, they swung around and both pulled their triggers, emptying everything they had. Bullets ricocheted around as the operative shot back—and it went without saying that Jim shoved Matthias behind him, and used his own body as a shield.

A couple of slugs hit home, the sting unpleasant, but nothing that would kill him or particularly get his attention. And then he and Matthias ran out of shots.

So did the operative.

There was a brief lull, which was a loud and clear "RELOADING NOW," and Jim had no choice but to get running again. Protection spells were great against Devina's minions; not really all that effective against Remington-onset lead poisoning: Keeping his body as a block, he chose one side of the hall and hustled like hell. And as they passed stacks of banquet chairs, Matthias helped as much as he could—but with the damage to his lower body, it would have been better for him to stay still and be muscled off the ground.

Not like they had time to debate deadweight etiquette.

They'd gone about ten feet when Jim realized they weren't being shot at.

No professional would take that long to put another clip in. What the hell—

At that moment, he felt Devina's presence, sure as a shadow passing over his own grave.

Fan-fucking-tastic.

Chapter Nineteen

"Come on, Monty, you gotta give me something."

Unlike the other reporters on scene at the motel, Mels wasn't choking against the police line in front of the open room. She was over on the far end, standing in the fog that had rolled in with her good old friend Monty the Mouth. Monty was a decent cop, but what made him really useful was his ego. He loved to share just to prove he could, and didn't that make him handy.

The difference tonight was that this was her own story. She wasn't background gathering for someone else.

Mels leaned in over the tape. "I know you know what's going on."

Monty jacked his belt up higher on his bay window, and ran a hand over his moussed-back hair. Talk about from another era. A shave job on his dome and a Tootsie Pop and you had Kojak in the twenty-first century.

"Yeah, I was one of the first here. So, you know, on the ground floor."

The problem with Monty was that he made you work for it. "When did you get called in?"

"Two hours ago. Manager dialed nine-one-one and I was the first responder. The guy who rented the room only wanted it for an hour around five, but the front office didn't realize no one had checked out until nine. I knocked on the door. No answer. The manager used his key, and hello."

"What do you think happened?" It was important to use the pronoun *you*.

"She was a known prostitute, so there're three likelies."

After a pause, she filled in, as she was supposed to. "Pimp, john, jealous boyfriend."

"Not bad. Not bad." He rejacked that belt. "No forced entry. Clearly a struggle, as her clothes were messed up. But not everything was blue alley."

"Blue alley" was a reference to the hallway where generations of CPDers had led perps down to intake at headquarters. Over time, the term had codified itself to mean nothing unusual or unexpected when criminals were involved.

"And the surprise was . . ."

Monty leaned in, all state secret. "She'd colored her hair. For some reason, that had been part of the date. Long and blond was how she went. And then he killed her."

"How do you know it was a 'he'?"

Monty shot her a yeah-right look. "And no, I can't give you her name—not released yet because we're tracking down the family. But I know who she is, and she's lucky to have lived through the last two years. Her record's long and there's violence in it—with her as the aggressor."

"Okay, well, you'll call me if you can share something? I don't name sources—you know this."

"Yeah, you're good like that, but no offense, you don't get by-lines very often. Hey, can you set me up with your boy Tony? He's usually on these kinds of gigs."

At that moment, she didn't respect Monty at all, and not because he was unimpressed with her lack of credentials at the CCJ. Damn it, he was not a rock star, and this was not a gig, and for the love of God, could he please stop jacking up that gun belt of his. This was a crime scene and there was someone's daughter or sister and maybe girlfriend or wife dead on the tile in that bathroom.

He could at least feel awkward and slightly dirty about the exchange of information. As she did.

"Dick assigned this to me," she said.

"Really? Hey, maybe you're moving up. And yeah, I'll call you, as long as you keep my name out of it."

"I promise."

"Talk to you later." He nodded to the side, dismissing her. "And make sure you answer your phone when I hit you—I have a feeling about this one."

She lifted the device. "I always do."

As Mels turned away, she reached up to the back of her neck, the hairs pricking at her nape. Looking around, she saw only people who had a purpose: Cops. Detectives. A photographer striding toward the yellow tape like she was pissed off. There were also two news crews across the parking lot, one of which was doing a broadcast, the superbright light putting a dark-haired reporter onstage as they taped.

Mels turned all the way around. Rubbed her neck some more.

Man, this mist was creepy.

Checking her watch, she cocked her phone and hit *send*. When the call was answered, she cupped a hand around her mouth. "Mom? Hi, it's me. Listen, I know I said I'd be home early, but I'm still at work. What? I'm sorry I can't hear— Okay, you're back. Yeah, I'm— Oh, no, don't worry. I'm with about half the CPD—" Probably not the best thing to say. "No, I'm fine, Mom. Yes, it's a homicide, but it's a big case, and I'm glad Dick gave it to me. Yes, I promise. Okay—yup, okay, listen, I have to go—and I'll knock on your door as soon as I get home."

As she hung up, she didn't think that was going to be anytime soon—and she was prepared to wait things out no matter how long it took. The body would need to be photographed, and CSI would also come in and do their thing, and then the victim could finally be removed.

Mels was going to stay until the CPD packed it in, and the newscasters went home, and any other reporter gave up.

Going over to Tony's car, she texted him to let him know that, in fact, she hadn't totaled his vehicle—and that she was going to treat him to lunch tomorrow as well as pick him up at eight thirty on her way in to the newsroom.

And then she crossed her coat around herself and settled back against her colleague's front bumper.

Immediately, she stiffened again and glanced behind her. Nothing but streetlamps on the far edges of the motel's fat parking lot. No masher sneaking up on her, no one at all, as a matter of fact.

So why the hell did she think she was being watched?

Massaging her temples, she wondered if Matthias's paranoia wasn't rubbing off on her. Or maybe it was more like what had happened on that bed had scrambled her brain.

Say what you would about his not remembering much, that man sure as hell knew what to do with his mouth . . .

On some level, she couldn't believe that it had happened. She'd never been into casual hookups, even in college—but if Matthias hadn't stopped them, she just might have let things go to their natural, naked conclusion.

Shocker. Especially as she knew she'd go there again.

If she ever got the chance.

Frozen in the Marriott's basement corridor, with Jim Heron going blanket all over him, Matthias felt like a boxer. And not as in Muhammad Ali or George Foreman. As in their schlub sparring partners, the guys who the real fighters worked over at the gym before they punched the crap out of people worthy of their skills: Gun empty and by his thigh, rib cage panting, head swimming, he was beat to shit with all that running, and running into things. He didn't think he'd been hit, however.

Someone had. The smell of fresh blood wafted down to them, and there was a dripping sound that suggested a pipe had a leak in it—and it probably wasn't something tied to the hotel's water system.

"Stay here," Jim ordered.

Like he was a girl? "Fuck you."

Together, they marched down toward the incapacitated shooter, with Jim in front because he could go a little faster.

Just inside the doors they'd busted through, a man in black, tight-fitting clothes lay flat on his back, eyes fixed and dilated on the afterlife. His throat had been sliced right under the jawline, the arteries and veins not nicked, but split clean apart.

"Messy," Matthias muttered, glancing around and wondering about cleanup—and who in the hell their savior had been.

As he considered the pros and cons of various corporeal disposal techniques, he was dimly aware that he was totally unfazed by the death, the body, the violence of having nearly been gunned down: this was just business as usual, nothing but the practicalities of not wanting the police involved weighing on his mind.

This was how he'd lived, he thought. This was his zone.

Leaning into his cane, he lowered himself to his haunches, one knee cracking like a tree branch. "Do you have a car?"

"Not with me, but I can handle this. Do me a favor and—"

Matthias started working the body over, patting it down, peeling off extra ammo, a knife, another gun.

"Okaaaaay," Jim said dryly. "I'm going to step outside and see if we're clear."

"So you don't know who our Good Samaritan was, either."

"Nope."

The steel door squeaked again when Jim opened it, and for a split second, Matthias was paralyzed with fear, the terror freezing his body from his heart to his heels. Eyes bouncing around, he sought the shadows in the dark corridor, expecting them to jump out and glom onto him.

Nothing moved.

Muttering under his breath, he refocused and yanked up the man's shirt. Kevlar vest had at least one slug in it—so he and Jim hadn't wasted all their lead. No cell phone. And assuming Jim didn't walk out into a bullet shower, it would appear that there was no one waiting in the wings to back this soldier up.

Sitting back, Matthias assessed the steel doors. In the center, around the locking mechanism, there was a scorched blast mark from where the now-dead attacker had blown the shit apart with some kind of a pocket bomb—

In a sudden burst, Matthias remembered his own hands on a detonator, saw himself fingering an IED with a vertical focus. He had prepared the thing for himself, the combination of electronics and blast potential a carefully constructed exit strategy. . . .

Jim was wrong. He hadn't hated himself or what he'd become. He'd just gotten exhausted with being who he was.

And that had been—

The headache came on strong, like his brain had the equivalent of a muscle cramp, the pain wiping his cognitive slate clean, his memories blocked by the agony.

Shit, he wanted access to what was hidden, but he couldn't afford to get stuck defenseless, and crouching over a stiff.

Glancing down into the face of the dead, he forced himself to pull out of the amnesia and note the color change in the guy's skin, the ruddy complexion from exertion draining out and being replaced with an opaque gray. Tracking the death process, focusing on it and it alone, he dragged himself back to reality.

"Do I know you?" he asked the remains.

Part of him was convinced he did. The face was a young white guy's, lean from lack of body fat, pale from lack of sun, as if he were used to working at night. Then again, how many millions of mid-twenty Caucasians were out there?

No, he thought, he knew this kid from somewhere.

In fact, he had the sense he had chosen the son of a bitch.

Had he been in recruiting? For the military?

Jim came back into the corridor, shut the door, and leaned against it, crossing his arms over his chest and looking like he wanted to punch a wall.

"Are we clear?" Matthias demanded.

"Pretty much."

Abruptly, he noticed the holes in Heron's shirt. "Good thing you're wearing a vest, too."

"What?"

Matthias frowned. "You've been hit—"

All at once, his brain coughed up another piece of the past: he saw the pair of them in a stainless-steel room, a cold body on a slab between them, a gun up, a trigger getting pulled . . . at fucking Heron. By himself.

"I've shot you in a morgue," Matthias breathed. "I've shot you . . . right in the chest."

Chapter Twenty

Perfect frickin' timing, Jim thought as Matthias stared at him like he'd sprouted a horn in the middle of his forehead.

This was *so* not a good situation for that memory of his to come back online: Clearly, someone from XOps was on Matthias's trail. It was the only logical explanation—although that wasn't what was blendering his brain.

Devina had evidently saved their asses.

She had come, gone Ginsu, and left. And as the demon never did anything that didn't benefit her, he had to wonder just how much a part of the game this assassination attempt had been. Maybe none—after all, if she wanted to influence Matthias at his crossroads, she needed him to be alive whenever that came.

And Jim had obviously not been doing a bang-up job of protecting the fucker.

"I shot you . . ." Matthias repeated.

Jim leveled a get-over-yourself stare. "You want a medal for it? I'll buy you one off the Internet. But before you go all existential, that's what they make bulletproof vests for, right?"

"You weren't wearing one." Matthias took off the sunglasses and narrowed his eyes. "And you aren't now."

"Okay, right, we're in a public place with a dead body full of slugs that came from our guns. Do you honestly think it's a good call to hang around and to chat?"

"I know him." Matthias pointed to their attacker. "I just can't place where."

"Look, I'm going to take this trash out. If you'd be so kind as to take your motherfucking ass back to your hotel room—"

"Tell me. Or I'm not going anywhere."

For a split second, Jim remembered oh, so clearly, why he'd always referred to the guy as Matthias the Fucker.

"Fine. You were his boss."

"Just what kind of a boss was I?"

They did not have time for this. "Not one I liked, I'll tell you that."

"I was yours, too . . . wasn't I." When Jim didn't say anything further, the guy bared his teeth. "Why the hell are you stringing me along. One way or the other, I'm going to put it together, and all you're doing is pissing me off."

Shit. There was a very real possibility the guy wouldn't move, and Devina would come back—or nearly as bad, the cops or hotel security would turn up.

"Fine," Jim said gruffly. "I'm afraid if you know, you're going to end up in Hell. How's that."

Matthias recoiled. "You don't look like a Jesus freak."

"I'm not one. So can we cut the bullshitting and get moving?"

Matthias shuffled to his feet, hooked his cane over his shoulder, and went to the dead guy's ankles. "You're not dodging the question forever."

"What the hell are you doing?"

"We're going to deal with this together—"

"No, we're not—"

The sound of sirens cut the argument off, and they both looked at the door. With any luck, the cops would pass by, the volume finding a bell curve as the badges closed in and kept the fuck going—

Nope. Someone had seen something, heard something, and done the 911.

As a car screeched to a halt in the alley, Jim wanted to take the easy way out—just whammy Matthias into a trance, poof the stiff, and bend the mentals of the blue unis who were, at this very moment, getting out of their vehicles with flashlights. But the mind-meld shit was tough to do to more than one person at a time. And lighting the corpse on fire would tell the CPD exactly where they were.

Hopefully, those boys in blue would waste some time looking around the alley.

"Shut. It," he barked as he grabbed Matthias around the middle, swung the guy up over his shoulder, and started to book it down the hall.

"Arrrrrreee y-y-you f-f-f-fucking k-kidding mmmmm-m-m-eee—"

The bitch session was cut short, either because Matthias swallowed his own tongue from the rough ride, or because a brain hemorrhage took over thanks to the paint mixing. But goddamn it, they made it to the end of the fifty-mile corridor, and this time, Jim didn't have to hide his blasting the lock. Bursting through, he—

Oh, *shit*.

—ran right into the back of one of the hotel's restaurants.

The good news was it appeared to be the facility used to serve breakfast and lunch out of; the place was a ghost town, the cook tops and stainless steel counters all cleaned up and battened for the off shift. Unfortunately, the B and E had set off the security alarm, and red lights were flashing in all the corners.

"This way," Matthias said, pointing to a set of double doors with round window cutouts in them. "And put my ass down."

Jim unloaded the guy and they took off again, passing by a stove as long as a football field and then a sink big enough to wash an elephant in. As they pounded across the red-tiled floor, Jim looked around for a control panel for the alarm system, some kind of motherboard, but of course they wouldn't put it in the middle of all this Emeril Lagasse. Besides, even if he could disarm the thing, the signal had already been sent.

Busting through the pair of swingers, they went into an open layout of square tables set for hungry people who wouldn't show up for toast and eggs for another seven hours—

On the far side, the tinted-glass walls that separated the eatery from the lobby were showing a trio of running people who had to be hotel security.

He and Matthias both looked to the left, where floor-to-ceiling drapes were drawn back to frame old-fashioned, double-hung windows.

No discussion. They gunned for the only exit they had a chance at. And to Matthias's credit, he didn't try to play hero when they got there; he pulled up short and let Jim unlock the switch and grab the brass handle on the base of the sill.

He put more than just his back into the lift. Tacking on a little mental juice as well, the window slid up with a *crack!* as if it were breaking free of having been painted in.

Twelve-foot drop onto pavement.

"Fuck," Matthias said. "You're going to have to catch me."

"Roger that."

With a coordinated surge, Jim was up and over and into the

loose hands of gravity. He landed solid on his combat boots and held out his arms. Matthias's exit was rougher, his legs hard to bend by the look of it, but the guy wasn't stupid. He gripped the window and dragged it back into place behind him, even though his ass barely fit on the ledge.

As he let himself go and went into a free fall, his black wind-breaker flapped out behind him uselessly, like a parachute with a bullet hole in it.

Jim caught his old boss with a grunt, keeping him from hitting the pavement.

"They found our friend," Matthias said as he shoved free.

Sure enough, far down the side of the building, the cops had opened those double doors and entered the corridor, their flash-lights shining out into the alley from time to time as if they were doing sweeps around the leaking assassin.

Time to get ghost.

Moving quietly and as quickly as they could, the two of them headed in the opposite direction. Unlike in XOps, backup was the name of the game when it came to the Caldwell Police Department, and sure enough, more sirens started to echo throughout the night.

A good fifty yards later, he and Matthias stopped at the other corner of the hotel, did a look-around, and then stepped out of the alley, calm as frozen water.

"Lose the sunglasses," Jim said as he focused on the sidewalk ahead.

"Already did."

Jim glanced over at his old boss. The man had his chin up and his eyes straight ahead. His lips were slightly parted and he was breathing like a freight train, but you wouldn't know it if you weren't looking for signs of hypoxia.

As far as anyone could tell, they were just two Joes out for a stroll, unconnected to any weirdness.

Jim had an absurd urge to tell his old boss that the bastard had done a good job. But that was ridiculous. They'd both been trained by the same drill sergeant, had spent years running exercises on evasive techniques side by side, had been through variations of this precise scenario.

By the time they entered the lobby, Matthias was breathing easy.

It went without saying that the guy would continue to stay at the Marriott. Now that an attempt had been made, and not just dead-ended, but with the involvement of gold badges, it made second tries trickier and riskier, at least for the next couple of days.

Besides, they'd been on a tour of the kitchen. Very professional.

Be a shame not to try the grub.

Mels's tenacity paid off . . . in a sad way.

The news crews left after midnight, and then the cops started paring down. Even Monty left before she did. Finally, it was just the crime scene investigators, two detectives, and her good self.

The yellow line of police tape had gotten smaller and smaller as the staffing had been reduced and she had gotten closer and closer to the open door of the hotel room. So when it came time to remove the victim, she had a clear visual shot at the process. Two men went in with a black body bag, and because of the cramped nature of the bathroom the woman had been killed in, they had to put the thing flat on the carpet and carry her out to lay her in it.

That poor girl.

"Yeah, it's terrible."

Mels wheeled around, unaware she'd spoken out loud. A tall, scary-looking guy was behind her, your typical hard-ass with piercings in his face and a leather biker jacket. Except his expression carried a heartbreak on it that immediately changed her prejudicial opinion of him. He wasn't focused on her; he was staring at the dead girl whose lifeless limbs were being arranged by her sides before a zipper disappeared her into black folds of thick plastic.

Mels turned back to the scene. "I feel so sorry for her father."

"You know him?"

"No. I can just imagine, though." Then again, maybe the guy hadn't given a crap about her and that was part of the reason she got hooked in the life? "It's just . . . she was a baby once. There had to have been some innocence at some point."

"You'd hope."

Curiosity had her sizing him up again. "Are you a guest at the motel?"

"Just a bystander." The man exhaled with a curious kind of defeat. "Man, I hate death."

In that moment, Mels thought of her father for some reason. He'd been removed from the scene of that car crash in a bag, too—after he'd been cut out of the driver's seat by the Jaws of Life.

Was he in Heaven? Looking down on them? Or was dying really just a lights-out kind of thing, like a car being turned off or a vacuum getting unplugged?

There was no afterlife for inanimate objects. So why did humans think that their fate was any different?

"Because it is different."

She glanced over her shoulder and smiled awkwardly. "I didn't mean to think out loud."

"It's okay." The guy smiled a little. "And there's nothing wrong with hoping that your dead are at peace or with having faith. It's a good thing, actually."

Mels refocused on the motel room, thinking it was weird to be having this candid conversation with a total stranger. "I just wish I knew for sure."

"Ah, but you're a reporter. You'd spill the secret."

She laughed. "Like Heaven and Hell are privileged information?"

"You got it. Humans require two things to properly bond: scarcity and the unknown. If loved ones were around forever, you'd take them for granted, and if you knew for sure that you'd be reunited, you'd never miss them. It's all part of the divine plan."

So he was a religious nut. "Well, there you go."

They moved back as the officers grasped the nylon handles of the bag and started walking the victim out. As the grim processional went by, Mels had a feeling why Dick had given her this assignment. Dead girl, grisly scene, mean streets of Caldwell, yada, yada, yada. He was just the kind of asshole to pay her back for shutting him down again.

And the truth was, she *was* rattled, as anyone with a conscience would be. But she was still going to do her job.

Leaning into the doorway, she addressed the man in charge. "Detective de la Cruz? Would you care to make a statement?"

The detective glanced up from his old-fashioned Columbo pad. "You still here, Carmichael?"

"Of course."

"You'd make your pops proud, you know that."

"Thanks, Detective."

As de la Cruz came over, he didn't spare a glance for the big man standing next to her, but he was like that. Unfazed by almost anything. "I got nothing to say yet. I'm sorry."

"No suspects?"

"No comment." He gave her shoulder a squeeze. "Say 'hi' to your mom, okay?"

"What about the hair color?"

He just waved over his shoulder and kept going, getting into a dark gray Crown Vic and pulling out of the parking lot.

As the last officer closed the room door, locked it, and put the CPD seal in place, she turned to the man behind her—

He was gone, as if he'd never been there.

Weird.

Heading over to Tony's car, she could have sworn she was still being followed, but there was no one anywhere near her. The feeling persisted as she drove off, though, to the point where she wondered if paranoia wasn't a virus you could catch.

Matthias was certainly worked up, but he might well have reason to be.

She certainly didn't.

Mels took the shortest way home, which was on the surface roads, and as she went by the cemetery again, she decided to take a little detour.

The house she eventually stopped in front of was on a street where every other garage, except its own, had cheery twin lanterns glowing on either side of its door.

This particular ranch was lights-out inside and on the exterior, a black hole amid all the other occupied-by-owners.

Reaching for the car door, she wanted to poke around a little, look in some windows, maybe find an unlocked way into the garage. But as soon as she made contact with the handle, a wave of dread came over her, sure as if all the ambient someone's-watching had coalesced into an actual bogeyman who was coming up from behind her with a knife.

Mels gave the eerieness a second to pass, in case it was heartburn from that burger and fries at the Marriott, but when it just sat on her chest, she put the car back in drive and turned around in the middle of the street.

Probably the mist that was still hanging in the air.

Yeah, it was the serial killer—movie fog that made the night seem darker and more dangerous than it really was.

Driving off, she hit the door lock and held on to the wheel hard.

She didn't loosen up until she pulled into the familiar driveway of her parents' house, the headlights of Tony's car washing up and over the front of the Cape Cod she'd grown up in.

For some reason, she focused on the shutters on the second floor. The ones outside of the dormer of her bedroom.

Her father had fixed them when she'd been ten years old: After a Nor'easter had come in and blown both of them off, he'd gotten a shiny aluminum ladder and lugged the heavy old wooden things up, balancing them on the eaves, rescrewing the pinnings, making it all right.

She'd held the base of the ladder, just because she'd wanted to be a part of it. She hadn't been worried that he'd fall. He'd been Superman that day.

Every day, actually.

She thought of that stranger by the motel, the one with the pros-elytizations and the piercings. Maybe he did have a point about that scarcity and surety stuff when it came to some people. But for her, if she knew for certain her father was okay, she would actually find a measure of peace herself.

Funny, she hadn't realized until tonight that she might need that.

Then again, since his passing . . . she'd made a point not to look closely into things.

It was just too painful.

Chapter Twenty-one

At just before five a.m., Jim was in Matthias's room at the Marriott, staring at the muted television from a chair in the corner. About two hours previously, he'd gotten a text from Ad saying that the reporter was home safe at her mother's and the angel was going to check on Eddie and let Dog out. The next report had been forty-five minutes later—Ad was going to try to catch a few.

Over on the king-sized bed, Matthias was sleeping like a corpse: on top of the covers on his back, head on the pillow, hands linked across his sternum. All he needed was a white rose between his fingers and a canned organ and Jim could have been paying his respects.

Why the hell had Devina helped them?

Christ, the only thing worse than her going against him was her rescuing him. And he hadn't needed her lifesaver. He had tricks up his sleeve, damn it. He had been just about to bust out a light show.

Maybe she was trying to suck up to the Maker.

How fucking galling was that—

The five a.m. *Wake Up, Caldwell!* newscast led with a reporter covering a murder scene downtown, the woman standing in front of a motel, turning back and nodding to an open room where police were going in and out. Then there was a cut to a box of hair color and the mug shot of a hard-used woman with stringy red hair.

So much sin in the world, Jim thought.

And on that note, he needed more ammo.

When a commercial for Jimmy Dean sausage came on, his stomach would have ordered room service if it could have picked up the phone and dialed.

"Can you at least tell me my own name?"

Jim glanced over to the bed. Matthias's eyes were open, but he hadn't moved, like a snake coiled in the sun.

"I've only ever known you as Matthias."

"We were trained together, weren't we. Last night we had the exact same moves at the same time."

"Yeah."

Sensing where this line of questioning was going to take them, Jim outted his cigarettes, put one between his teeth, and then remembered they were in a public place. And wouldn't it be ironic to get booted out of the hotel for lighting up when they'd broken in the back entrance, traded open fire, left a body, and broken out again?

Har-har-hardy-har-har.

Jim refocused on the TV, which was playing a deodorant commercial. For a split second, he envied the dudes portrayed in the scene: all they had to worry about were their armpits, and as long as they used Speed Stick products, they were good to go.

If only the solution for Devina came in both aerosol and stick.

"Tell me how I killed myself." When Jim didn't answer, the

other man said, "Why are you so afraid to talk about it? You don't strike me as a pussy."

Jim scrubbed his face. "You know what? You should sleep less. You're a pain in the ass well rested."

"I guess you're just a pussy, then."

As Jim exhaled hard, he wished it were smoke. "Fine, you know what I'm worried about? That when you find out who you were, you're going to become that man again and I'll lose you. No offense, but this clean slate you've got going on is a blessing."

"You make it sound like I was evil—"

"You were." Jim locked eyes with his old boss. "You were infected to the core, to the point where I'd come to the conclusion that you were born that way. But seeing you like this . . ." He motioned with his hand. "It's a surprise to find out that you weren't."

"What the hell happened to me?" Matthias whispered.

"I don't know anything about your past before you came to XOps."

"Is that what the organization was called?"

" 'Is' called. Not 'was.' And yeah, you and I did train together. Prior to that, I don't know shit. There were rumors about you, but they were probably the result of hyperbole based on your reputation."

"Which was . . ."

"You were a sociopath." The man cursed softly and Jim shrugged. "Listen, I wasn't a saint, either. Not before I joined, certainly not when I was in. But you—you set a new standard. You were . . . something else."

There was a period of silence. Then, "You're still not telling me anything specific."

Jim rubbed his hair and thought, Well, hell, there were so many *anythings* to choose from. "Okay, how about this one. There was a man, Colonel Alistair Childe—name ring any bells?" When Matthias shook his head, Jim really wished they were outside so he could light up. "He was a good guy, had a daughter who was a lawyer. A son who had some problems. Wife died of cancer. He lived up in Boston, but had a lot of dealings in D.C. He got too close."

"To what."

"The firm, so to speak. You had him kidnapped and taken to his son's crack house, where your operatives pumped the kid full of an overdose of heroin and filmed Alistair screaming as the son foamed at the mouth and died. And you thought you'd done the guy a solid, because, in your own words, you took the kid who was broken. The threat, of course, was that if Childe didn't clam it, you'd off the daughter, too."

Matthias didn't move, barely breathed, just blinked. But his voice was the tell. Rough and full of gravel, it barely got the words out: "I don't remember that."

"You will. At some point. You're going to remember a whole lot of shit like that—and some stuff that I probably can't even guess at."

"And how do you know so much?"

"About the Childe thing? I was there when you went after the daughter."

Matthias's eyes closed, and his chest went up and down slowly, as if there were a horrible weight on it.

Kind of gave Jim some hope. Maybe the reveal would yank him further out of the sin.

"If that's true, I can see why you're concerned about my moral compass."

"It's the God's honest. And like I said, there's so much more."

Matthias cleared his throat. "So how exactly did this happen?"

As he gestured around his eye, Jim found himself sucked back into their shared past. "I wanted out, but XOps don't have no retirement option, and you were the only one who could grant me a discharge. We argued about it, and then you showed up where I was on assignment in the desert. You told me to meet you alone at night far the hell away from camp, and I figured this was it, game over. Instead, you were by yourself. You looked me in the eye as you lifted your foot and put it down in the sand. The explosion . . . it went upward, not out. You never meant it for me, and it wasn't a mistake." Memories of that hut, of the gritty sand in his eyes and the blast smoke in his nose, came back hard and fast. "Afterward, I carried you out of there, took you where you could get help."

"Why didn't you leave me to die?"

"I was done playing by your rules. It was time that the all-powerful Oz didn't get what he was after."

"But if you wanted out, and you'd killed me—who would have fucked with you? Assuming you're telling the truth about all this, you would have been free."

Jim shrugged, "I had you over a barrel. You didn't want that little suicide secret getting out, so I had the best of both worlds. I was free and you were going to spend the rest of your life looking like shit and being in pain."

Matthias laughed in a harsh burst. "Strangely, I can respect that. But I don't get why in the hell you're helping me now."

"Job change." Jim reached for the remote. "Look, we made the news."

As he unmuted the TV, a different newscaster filed a report on the body that had been found, gee whiz, right where they'd left it in that service corridor. No suspects. No identity on the victim— and good luck with that. Even if they found something, the aliases set up by XOps were impenetrable. Further, time was ticking for the coroner: The body was going to disappear from the morgue any minute—if it hadn't been removed already.

Just another cold case that was going to get stuck in a file cabinet down at the CPD.

"What kind of work do you do now?" Matthias asked.

"Independent contractor."

"Still doesn't explain why you're helping a man you hate."

Jim stared at the guy and thought of everything Matthias represented in the war with Devina. "Now . . . I need you."

As Mels got ready for work, she broke a nail getting dressed, and then spilled coffee on her blouse in the kitchen. Under the bad-luck-comes-in-threes rule, she had a feeling she was on someone's hit list, but at least her mother was at an early morning yoga class—and that meant she could get out the door without a lot of chatter.

Sometimes, talking to her mother about her job was tough. Like the woman needed to hear the details of that poor girl at the motel?

Hardly good breakfast conversation.

Besides, Mels wasn't feeling talkative. It had been a long night, what with writing up her piece on the murder and sending it into editorial so it could be copyedited and put up online first thing. And today, she was going to focus on further reporting so she could submit a more thorough article for tomorrow's paper edition.

With any luck, Monty was going to let his fingers do the walking to her cell phone, so that mouth of his could do what it did best.

On the way to pick up Tony, she got stuck in a line at the McDonald's drive-thru, but there was no way she was turning up at her buddy's apartment without breakfast. Finally, with two sausage biscuits in a bag and a pair of coffees in the console, she was back in business in the borrowed Toyota.

As she pulled over at the curb in front of his building, the guy hefted himself off the front steps and waddled his way over, his bulk making him seem much taller than he really was.

"Have I told you lately how much I love you?" she asked as he got in.

Tony grinned. "If that's breakfast, then yes, you have."

"I got you a matched set." She handed the bag over. "One of the coffees is mine."

"Better than a pair of earrings." He unwrapped one white package. "Mmm, edible."

"I really appreciate your letting me borrow your baby."

"Come on, where do I have to go? Long as I can get to work and back, I'm good." As he chewed, he frowned and picked a receipt out of the ashtray. "You were at the Marriott yesterday?"

Mels put the directional signal on, and pulled out into traffic, wishing that her friend wasn't so damned observant. "Ah, yeah, I was."

"What time?"

Mels kept her eyes on the road ahead, recognizing the Reporter Voice she was getting hit with. "It was last night. I was just visiting a friend."

"So did you see all the commotion?"

"Commotion?"

"You don't know what happened?"

"I was called out to that murder scene in the west end. What are you talking about?"

"Wait, you got put on that prostitute with the hair color?"

"I did. So what went down at the Marriott?"

As Tony took his own damn time finishing the first Mc-whatever-it-was-called, Mels's stomach churned. Man, if he tried to start the second one, she was going to jump out of her skin—

"There was a shooting in the basement of the hotel. Eric's assigned to it. There were bullets exchanged in the alley, and someone broke in through one of the rear delivery entrances to the restaurants. Nine-one-one was called and they found a man with no identification and no weapons on him dead from a knife wound."

"I thought you said there were bullets involved?"

"Oh, he'd been shot at all right. But that wasn't what killed him." Tony made a slicing motion across the front of his neck. "Slit wide."

A shiver went through her.

Because you're going to die if you don't get away from me.

Mels told herself to calm down. That was a big hotel in a not-good-after-dark part of town. Murders happened, particularly among drug dealers and their clientele—

Tony rifled around in the bag to get out biscuit number two. "Apparently, the guy would have died from the gunshots, except he had one hell of a bulletproof vest on. Eric said the guys at the CPD were drooling over the thing. They'd never seen one so sweet." The gentle sound of another white wrapper being turned back was followed by a fresh whiff of unhealthy-and-awesome.

"So what did you find out last night?" he asked around his mouthful.

Mels pulled a rolling stop and hung a left onto Trade, her head tangling up: Matthias had been going to bed when she'd left him—although that didn't mean he couldn't have gone out after she'd—

"Hello? Mels?"

"Sorry, what?"

"When you were at the motel. What'd you find out?"

"Ah . . . right, sorry, not much. The woman was killed after she colored her hair—her throat was slashed."

"Two in one night. It's an epidemic."

Well, there was that, she thought. No one could be in two places at once, right?

Okay, now she was being crazy. "Yeah. Weird."

Five blocks later, they came up to the CCJ building, and she parked around back, giving the keys to Tony as they walked over to the rear entrance.

"Thanks again," she said.

"Like I told you, whenever you want. Especially if you buy me breakfast. And will you stop putting dollar bills in my drawer when you take a Twinkie? You know you're welcome to my stash."

It was true. Tony had a boatload of food grade petroleum in his desk and she had been known to partake from time to time. But she wasn't a mooch.

Mels opened the door and held it for him. "I'm not going to rob you."

"If I give you permission, it's not robbing. And besides, you don't take, like, what, more than a Ho-Ho or two a month."

"Pilfering is pilfering."

They hit the shallow stairs that led up to the glass doors of the newsroom, and he got the door this time. "I wish everyone felt like that."

"See? It's not your job to feed us all."

The instant they stepped through, the ringing phones and fast voices and scurrying feet was a familiar theme song, sweeping into her body, carrying her to her desk. As she sat down, the dull roar smoothed over the anxiety about Matthias, and she signed into her computer without conscious thought—

The manila envelope landed on her desk with a slap, startling her.

"Got something pretty for you to look at," Dick said with a sly smile.

She reached for the packet and slid out . . .

Well, wasn't she glad she'd given both those sausage biscuits to Tony: They were photographs of the prostitute's body, eight-and-a-half-by-elevens in color, all up close and personal.

As Dick hovered over her like he was waiting for her to chick out, she refused to give him any satisfaction, even though the center of her chest ached at the images . . . particularly the one that showed the neck wound in detail, the deep slash cutting through the skin and into the pink-and-red muscle and pale gristle of the throat.

When Mels put the photos down, she made sure that was the one on top, and noticed that Dick, for all his Big Man attitude, refused to look at the image.

"Thanks." She kept her eyes steady on his. "This is going to help a lot."

Dick cleared his throat like maybe he'd pushed the asshole act a little far, even by his own low standards. "Let me see your follow-up ASAP."

"You got it."

As he sauntered off, she shook her head. He should know better than to give her father's daughter a challenge like that.

And P.S., the fact that he would at all was just gross.

Kind of made her think about the way Monty used tragedy for his own purposes.

Frowning, she went through the photographs again, and then focused on the one that was taken on the morgue slab. There was a strange rash on the lower abdomen, a reddening of the skin, as if the victim had been sunburned—

As her cell went off, she answered it without looking at the number. "Carmichael."

"Hello."

The deep voice sent a burst of heat right through her core. *Matthias.*

For a split second she wondered how he'd gotten her number. But then she remembered that she'd given him her business card—and written the thing down.

"Well, good morning," she said.

"How you doing?"

In her head, a Ping-Pong match started up between what Tony

had told her in the car and what that kiss had felt like. Back and forth, back and forth—

"You there, Mels?"

"Yes." She rubbed her eyes, and then had to stop because the bruised one didn't appreciate the attention. "Sorry. I'm okay, how are you? Any more memories coming back?"

"As a matter of fact, yes."

Mels straightened in her chair, her interest shifting, locking on. "Like what?"

"I don't suppose your Nancy Drew would mind checking something out for me?"

"Absolutely. Tell me what you want to know." As he spoke she took notes, writing down names, murmuring *uh-huhs* at the pauses. "Okay. This is no problem. Do you want me to call you back?"

"Yeah, that'd be great."

There was a strange pause. "All right," she said awkwardly. "So I'll call you—"

"Mels . . ."

Closing her eyes, she felt him against her, his body pressing in, his mouth taking over, that dominance that was intrinsic to his personality coming out.

"Do you know what happened at your hotel last night?" she said abruptly.

"Yeah. I spent hours thinking about you."

She closed her eyes briefly, fighting the seduction. "The police found a dead body. That had a very fancy bulletproof vest on it."

Another pause. Then an even response: "Huh. Any suspects?"

"Not yet."

"I didn't kill him, Mels, if that's what you're asking."

"I didn't say you did."

"That's what you're thinking."

"Who are these people to you?" she cut in, making little boxes around the names he'd given her to research.

"Just things that have bubbled up." His voice became distant. "Look, I'm sorry I called you about them. I'll get the info somewhere else—"

"No," she said firmly. "I'll do it and I'll phone you back."

After she hung up, she stared into space. Then she rose from her desk chair and went down a couple of cubicles. Leaning over the top of yet another gray partition, she smiled in a fake way that her colleague didn't know her well enough to spot. "Hey, Eric, what's up?"

The guy's eyes shifted away from his computer monitor. "Hey, Carmichael. What can I do you for?"

"I want to know about that murder at the Marriott."

The reporter smiled, all cat-and-canary. "Anything in specific?"

"The vest."

"Ah, the vest." He rifled around the paperwork on his desk. "The vest, the vest . . ." He pulled a sheet free and spun it to her. "I found this on the Internet."

Mels frowned as she read the specs. "Five thousand dollars?"

"That's what they cost before they're customized. And his was."

"Who the hell can afford that?"

"Exactly what I'm asking myself." More rifling. "Big-time security firms are one. U.S. government is another—but not for your Joe Schmo FBI agent, mind you. You'd have to be very high-level."

"Any VIPs in the hotel?"

"Annnnnd that's what I looked into last night. Officially, the staff can't give out names, but I overheard the night manager talking to one of the cops. There's nobody special under their roof."

"What about that area downtown?"

"Yeah, I mean, there're some big businesses around the neighborhood, but they were all closed as it was way after normal business hours. And it defies logic that some dignitary was walking around Caldwell and one of his security team happened to go rogue and get his throat in the way of someone's knife."

"When did it happen?"

"'Round eleven o'clock."

After she'd left and gone to the crime scene. "And no clue on the identity?"

"Not a one. Which brings us to the next hi-how're-ya." Eric chewed on the end of a blue Bic. "No fingerprints."

"At the scene?"

"On the body. He didn't have any fingerprints—they'd been etched off."

Mels's ears started to ring. "Any other identifiers?"

"A tattoo, apparently. I'm trying to get some pics of it as well as the body, but my sources are slow." His eyes narrowed. "Why all the interest?"

Fancy bulletproof vest. No prints. "What about weapons?"

"None. He must have been stripped." Eric leaned forward in his chair. "Saaaaay, you're not trying to sweet-talk Dick into getting you a byline on this, are you?"

"God, no. Just curious." She turned away. "Thanks for the info. I appreciate it."

Chapter
Twenty-two

When the phone rang about a half hour later, Matthias just stared at the thing. Had to be Mels getting back to him.

Damn it, this was a mess. . . .

After Jim had taken off to go do breakfast or errands or some shit, naturally, the first thing he'd done when he was alone was call Mels and try to find out if that story was true about the father and the son up in Boston. It hadn't dawned on him that she'd have heard about what went down in the basement, but come on, sloppy thinking much? It was all over the cocksucking news. Even nonreporters who didn't keep up with that kind of shit knew.

The phone stopped its electronic ringing. But she was going to redial.

God, her voice when they'd spoken. She'd sounded suspicious, and in so many ways that was the best thing for her. Yet it killed him.

When the phone started going off again, he couldn't stand it.

Grabbing his cane, he walked out the door of his room and headed blindly for the elevator. As he took it down, he had no clue where he was going. Maybe breakfast.

Yeah, breakfast.

It was what people did at nine a.m. all over the country.

Annnnnd, of course, the only restaurant that was open for business was the one he'd gotten to know intimately the night before—and as he walked past the colored glass wall, he decided to go off Marriott property to—

"Matthias?"

At the female voice, he pivoted around. It was the nurse from the hospital, the one who'd given him a helping hand, so to speak. Outside of work, she was fresh as a daisy, with her dark hair loose around her shoulders and a pale dress hanging below her knees.

She kind of looked like a bride.

"What are you doing here?" she said as she came over. "I thought you'd be home recovering."

As people walked by her, they all stared, men with hot speculation in their eyes, women with varying degrees of envy and dislike. Then again, she was stupidly beautiful.

"I'm okay." He tried not to stare at her. It was like looking into the sun, painful on the eyes. "How about yourself?"

"My mom's come into town. Or rather, she was supposed to be here by now. Her flight was due in a half hour ago, but it got delayed in Cincinnati because of storms. I've been debating whether to wait or go home—we were going to have breakfast. Is that where you're headed now?"

"Ah, yeah."

"Well, then, how about we go dutch. I'm starved."

Her black eyes positively sparkled, to the point where they made him think about the night sky. But it wasn't enough to make him want to cop a squat in the—

"Okay," he heard himself say, like some third party had taken over his mouth.

Together, they walked over to the maître d's stand.

"Two," Matthias said as the man did a double take at the nurse, and then froze like a deer in the headlights, apparently struck stupid by all the lovely.

"I'd like a window seat," she said, smiling slowly at the guy. "Perhaps over . . ."

Not the window he jumped out of, Matthias thought.

". . . there."

Bing-fucking-o.

"Oh, yes, sorry, right away." The maître d' got with the program, snagging a couple of leather-bound books and leading the way. "But there are some better views across the room, overlooking the gardens?"

"We don't want the sun to be too bright." She put her hand on Matthias's arm and gave him a little squeeze, as if she wanted him to know she was watching out for his bad eyesight.

Man, he really didn't like her touching him.

As they walked across the room, the nurse created a total stir, men peering over the tops of their *Wall Street Journals* and their coffee cups and sometimes their wives' heads. She took it all in stride, like it was just the normal course of things.

After they sat down in front of the window he'd violated with Jim, coffee materialized, and they mulled over the menus. The civilized bullshitting that came with picking and choosing among the fifty different plates of good-morning got on his nerves. And he didn't want to eat with her, although to be fair, he didn't want to eat with anybody.

The stuff with Mels was the problem. Yeah, he'd called her with that info search, but the bigger truth was, he'd just wanted to hear her voice.

He'd missed her through the night—

"Penny for your thoughts?" the nurse said softly.

Matthias looked out the window at the building across the alley. "I just realized—I don't know your name."

"Oh, sorry. I thought it was on the whiteboard in your room."

"Probably was, but it could have been in neon lights and I don't know if I'd have noticed."

This was a lie, of course. In fact, there hadn't been a nurse listed, just a doctor, and there hadn't been a name tag on her scrubs.

Which seemed a little strange, come to think about it. . . .

She took an elegant hand and laid it on her breastbone—which seemed like an invitation to check out her cleavage. "You can call me Dee."

He stuck with her eyes. "As in Deidre?"

"As in Devina." She glanced away, as if she didn't want to go into it. "My mother has always been a godly woman."

"Which explains your dress."

Dee shook her head ruefully and smoothed the skirt. "How did you know this getup isn't me?"

"Well, for one thing, it looks like it belongs on a forty-year-old. The jeans and parka are more your age."

"How old do you think I am?"

"Twenty-five-ish." And maybe that was why he didn't like her touching him. She was so young, too young for someone like him.

"Twenty-four, as a matter of fact. It's why my mom's in town, actually." She touched her sternum again. "Birthday girl."

"Happy birthday."

"Thanks."

"Your father coming in, too?"

"Oh . . . yeah. No." Now, she closed up completely. "No, he's not coming."

Damn it, the last thing he needed was to get all into her personal shit. "Why not."

She fiddled with her coffee cup in its saucer, turning it back and forth. "You are so odd."

"Why."

"I don't like to talk about myself, but here I am babbling away."

"You haven't told me much, if that makes you feel better."

"But . . . I want to." For a split second her eyes dipped to his lips, like she was wondering things about him she really, really didn't need to. "I want to."

Nope. Not going there, he thought.

Especially not after Mels.

Dee leaned in, those breasts threatening to break out of that dress. "I haven't been able to stop thinking about you."

Great. Wonderful. Fucking perfect.

In the tense quiet, Matthias briefly eyed the big window next to them. He'd already been out the thing once.

If things got awkward, he could do it again.

Mels hung up her office phone and leaned back in her chair. As the squeak sounded, she made a new tune out of it, rocking back and forth.

For some reason, her eyes locked on that coffee mug that had been left behind by the other reporter.

When her cell phone went off, she jumped and fumbled with the thing. Quick check of the screen and she wanted to curse—not because of who it was, but because of who it wasn't.

Maybe Matthias was in the shower.

People took showers in the mornings.

Yeah, for, like, a half hour, though? She'd been calling every five minutes.

"Hello?" she demanded.

"Hey, Carmichael." It was Monty the Mouth; she could tell by the cracking of his gum. "It's me."

Well, at least she did want to hear from the guy. "Good morning."

"I got something." His voice dropped, all secret-agent style. "It's explosive."

Mels sat up, but didn't get too excited. With her luck, "explosive" was more hyperbole than H-bomb. "Oh, really?"

"Someone tampered with the body."

"Excuse me?"

"Like I told you, I was first on scene, and I snapped some photographs—you know, in an official capacity." There was a rustling over the connection, and then a muffled conversation, like he was talking to someone and had covered up the receiver. "Sorry. I'm at the station house. Let me get out of here and call you back."

He hung up before she could say anything, and she had images of him dodging fellow officers on his way to the parking lot like he was one of Eli Manning's receivers.

Sure enough, when he called back, he was out of breath. "Can you hear me?"

"Yeah, I got you."

"So my photographs of the body have something on them the official ones don't."

That was her cue to OMG, and in this case, she didn't have to fake it. "What's the difference?"

"Meet me and I'll show you."

"Where and when."

After she hung up, she checked her watch and dialed Matthias's room phone again. No answer.

"Hey, Tony," she said, leaning into the aisle between their cubicles. "Can I borrow your—"

The guy tossed the keys without missing a beat with whoever he was talking to on the phone. As she blew him a kiss, he covered his heart and gave her a little swoon.

Striding out of the newsroom, she got in Tony's Toy and headed across town, using a route that just happened to . . . well, what do you know, it was the Marriott hotel.

And she was a good half an hour early for her meeting with the Mouth.

By crazy luck, she found an open, metered parking spot just across from the lobby entrance—except it took her two tries to get the car in place, her parallel-parking skills rusty from her using too many garages since she'd moved back to Caldwell.

Plus, feeling like a stalker didn't help her at the wheel.

As she walked into the lobby, she felt like someone from security should stop her and turn her away, but no one paid her any attention—which left her wondering exactly how many other people were to'ing or fro'ing over things they felt icky about.

At the elevators, she hopped a ride to the sixth floor along with a businessman whose wilted attire and red eyes suggested he'd flown in the night before from somewhere far away.

Maybe even flapping his own arms.

Stepping free, she hung a right and went down the carpeted hall. Room service trays were set out next to doors, treacherous welcome mats with their smudged plates, half-empty coffee cups, and stained napkins. At the far end, a maid's cart was parked in front of an open room, the light from inside spilling into the corridor and highlighting fresh toilet paper rolls, folded towels, and a lineup of spray bottles.

Matthias's door still had the Do Not Disturb sign on it, and she took that to mean he hadn't checked out. Putting her ear to the panels, she sent up a quick prayer that he wouldn't pick this moment to open up.

No running water. No muttering from the TV. No deep voice on the phone.

She knocked. Knocked a little louder.

"Matthias," she said to the door. "It's me. Open up."

As she waited for a response that didn't come, she glanced over at the maid who had come out with a plastic bag full of trash. For a split second, she considered playing the whole I-forgot-my-key-card thing, but in post-9/11 Caldwell, she had a feeling that wasn't going to work—and might end up with her getting tossed out on her hey-nanny-nanny.

Well, wasn't this a credit to her character: The invasion of his privacy wasn't even on her no-go radar; it was the fear of getting caught that stopped her.

Disgusted with herself, and pissed off at him, Mels hit the elevator again, and when she got to the first floor, she intended to march out to Tony's car, get in the damn thing, and be wicked early for her meeting with Monty and his flapping gums.

Instead, she casualed her way around the lobby, peeking into the gift shop, wandering down to the spa . . .

Yeah, 'cuz of course he'd be buying bathrobes and getting a cucumber wrap on his face. Right.

When she came up to the main restaurant that was open, she nearly abandoned the wild-goose chase, but it only took a moment to peer in—

On the other side of the tables of diners, sitting at a window, Matthias was eating with a brunette woman in a limoncello-colored dress.

Who was she—

Was that the nurse? From the hospital?

"Would you like a table for one?" the maître d' asked.

Ah, yeah, that would be a negative—unless the thing came equipped with an airsick bag. "No, thanks."

Across the way, the brunette started to laugh, throwing her head back so that her hair flowed all around. She was so perfectly beautiful, it was as if she were a moving photograph that had been touched up in all the right places.

As Matthias sat accross from her, he was hard to read, and in an absurd moment of possessiveness, Mels was glad he was wearing her sunglasses. Like that was the equivalent of her pissing on his fence post.

"Are you meeting someone, then?" the maître d' asked.

"No," she replied. "I do believe he's busy."

Chapter Twenty-three

Dee's laughter was . . . well, kind of divine, as a matter of fact. To the point where it fritzed out part of Matthias's brain, and he couldn't think of what he'd said that was so funny.

"So how's your memory?" she asked.

"Spotty."

"It'll come back. It's only been, what, a day and a half?" She leaned to the side as her plate of eggs, sausage, toast, and hash browns arrived. "Give it time."

His bagel looked anemic in comparison.

"Are you sure that's all you want?" She gesticulated with her fork. "You need to put on weight. Myself, I'm a strong believer that a big breakfast is the only way to start the day."

"It's nice to be around a woman who doesn't pick at her food."

"Yup, that's not me." She motioned for the waitress to come back over. "He wants what I have. Thanks."

It seemed rude to point out that if he ate that much he was go-

ing to explode, so he just pushed the bagel aside. She was probably right. He felt out of it, sluggish and empty, the club sandwich
he'd had for dinner with Mels having been long burned off thanks
to that ninja motherfucker with the happy trigger finger.

"Don't wait for me," he said.

"I wasn't going to."

Matthias smiled coldly and passed some time glancing around
the room. Most people were exactly what he'd expect in a hotel like
this . . . except for one guy over in the corner who looked seriously
out of place: He was wearing a suit that was cut better than everybody else's, and seemed dated even to the fashionless eye.

Hell, the getup might have been worn to a flapper party—or
maybe back in the Roaring Twenties themselves—

As if sensing he was being looked at, the man lifted his eyes with
an aristocratic air.

Matthias refocused on his dining companion. Dee was going at
her food with precise cuts of her fork, the thin edge pushing easily
through the scrambled and the hash.

"Sometimes not remembering is a good thing," she said.

Yeah, he thought, he had a feeling that was especially true in his
case. God, if that story Jim had fed him was—

"And I didn't mean to be evasive about my father," she said.
"It's just . . . he's nothing I like to think about." Her fork drifted
down to settle on the plate as she stared out the window. "I'd do
anything to forget him. He was . . . a violent man—an evil, violent
man."

With a quick shift, her stare came back to his and locked on.
"Do you know what I'm talking about. Matthias—"

Abruptly, another one of those headaches came from out of nowhere, barging through his thought processes and zeroing in on his
temples, twin shots of pain heating up on either side of his skull.

Dimly, he saw that Dee's perfect red mouth was moving, but the words weren't reaching him; it was as if he had pulled out of his body, even as his flesh stayed where it was . . . and then the very interior of the restaurant began to recede, sure as if the walls had hinged loose and fallen outward, morphing all *Inception*-like until suddenly he wasn't sitting in a Marriott's pseudo-fancy eatery anymore, but somewhere else—

He was on the second floor of a farmhouse, rough wood planking marking the floors, walls, and ceiling. The stairwell in front of him was steep, the banister made from pine that had darkened to the color of tar from the oils of countless hands having gripped it.

The air was stale, and stuffy, although it wasn't hot.

Matthias looked behind himself, into a room that he recognized as his own. The twin bed had mismatched blankets and no pillows . . . the bureau had scratches on it and pulls that were halfway attached . . . there was no rug. But on the little table next to where he slept, a brand-new radio with fake wood trim and a silver dial sat pristine and out of place.

Glancing down, he saw he was wearing a ragged pair of pants, and that his feet stuck way out from the rolled-up hems; his hands were the same, oversized compared to his thin forearms, his extremities too big for the rest of his body.

He remembered this stage of his life, knew that he was young. Fourteen or fifteen—

A sound brought his head around.

A man was coming up the stairs. Overalls were dirty; hair was slicked with sweat, as if a hat or a baseball cap had been locked on it for hours; boots were loud.

Big man. Tall man.

Mean man.

His father.

All at once, everything shifted, his consciousness de-coupling from his flesh such that he was no longer able to control the body he was in, the steering wheel having been taken over by someone else.

All he could do was stare out of his eye sockets as his father turned the corner at the head of the stairs and stopped.

The skin on that lean face had been weathered to the point of cowhide, and there was a tooth missing on one side as he smiled like a serial killer.

His father was going to die, Matthias thought. Right here, right now.

However improbable that was, given the difference in their sizes, the man was going to hit the ground and be dead in a matter of moments—

Abruptly, Matthias could feel himself start talking, his lips forming sounds that didn't register on him. They had an impact on his father, however.

That expression shifted, the smile dissipating, that dental gap disappearing as the thin mouth flattened. Rage narrowed those electric blue eyes, but it didn't last. Shock was next. As if something that he had been confident about now seemed less than certain.

And all the while, Matthias kept talking, slow and consistently.

This was where it had all started, he thought to himself: this man, this evil man who he'd lived alone with for too long, this sick bastard who had "raised" him. Now was the time for reckoning, however, and his younger self felt nothing as he spoke the words he did, knowing full well that he was finally caging the monster.

His father's hand grabbed onto the front of the overalls, right over his heart, crushing the material, the dirty, chipped nails digging in.

And still Matthias kept talking.

Down to the floor. His father went down on his knees, his free palm thrown out to the banister, his mouth cranking open so wide that the other missing teeth, the ones in the back, showed.

He had never expected to get caught. That was his killer.

Well . . . technically, the myocardial infarction was what did him in. But the proximal cause was the fact that their ugly secret was out.

Death took its own sweet time.

As his father flopped over on his back, his hand now shifting to his left armpit as if it hurt like a bitch, Matthias stood where he was and watched the dying process roll in and take over. Apparently, breathing was difficult, that chest chugging up and down without much effect: Beneath the tan, his father's color was receding.

When the view switched back to the bedroom, Matthias realized that he had turned away and was walking, going over to the radio, sitting down, turning it on. He could still see his father struggling like a fly on a windowsill, limbs contracting this way and that, head arching back as if he thought maybe a different angle would help increase the oxygen flow.

But it wasn't going to help. Even a fifteen-year-old farm boy knew that if your heart wasn't pumping, your brain and vital organs were going to starve no matter how many deep breaths you took.

Out on the prairie, they got only five stations and three were religious. The other two played country and pop, and he twisted the dial, going back and forth between the pair. From time to time, just because he knew his father was going to meet his Maker sometime soon, he let a sermon ring out.

Matthias felt nothing other than frustration that he couldn't get hard rock to play. Seemed like Van Halen was a better match to his father's kicking it than Conway fucking Twitty or Phil fucking Collins.

Other than that, he was calm as a pond, level as concrete, set as a table leg.

Hell, he didn't even care that the abuse was over. He'd just wanted to see if he could get rid of the old man, like the effort was a science project: he'd made the plan, gotten the pieces into place, and then woken up that morning and decided to set the first domino falling at school.

Thanks to his particularly malleable, softhearted, very religious homeroom teacher.

Standing out in the hall, he'd cried in front of her as he'd told her the hell he'd been living in, but that show of tears had just been to give her some extra motivation. In truth, the grand reveal was no more internalized than a change of clothes: As he'd manipulated her with the truth, he'd been cold as ice on the inside, taking neither satisfaction that the first part was done, nor excitement that it was finally happening.

Everything had gone down fast after that, and that had been the only thing that he hadn't banked on: He'd been immediately sent to the school nurse, and then the police had come, and paperwork had been filled out, and off he went into the system.

They'd sent only women to work with him, as if that would make it easier on him. Especially during the "physical exam" part—which they'd expected him to get really upset by.

And who was he not to give them what they wanted?

He had not expected to go into foster care within two hours, however.

The thing was, the only goal he'd really wanted was this part here, this endgame with his father on the floor—and he'd had to run away and hot-wire a car to make sure he got home before the police took his father to jail when the man came in from the cornfields. Everything was a waste if he blew the final act.

But it had worked out just fine.

In the last few moments of his father's miserable life, Matthias twisted the radio knob over to one of the religious stations—and paused for a moment. The sermon was about Hell.

Seemed appropriate.

He watched as the final breath was taken and then the stillness came. So strange, a human being suddenly stepping over to the other side, that which had been animated becoming indistinguishable from a toaster oven or a throw rug or, shit, even a clock radio.

Matthias waited a little longer as the pallor in that face went completely gray. Then he got up, unplugged his radio, and tucked the thing under his arm.

His father's eyes were open and staring up at the ceiling, much as Matthias's had done at night over the years.

He didn't flip the guy off, or spit on him, or give him a kick. He just walked past the body and went down the stairs. His final thought, as he left the house, was that it had been an interesting mental exercise . . .

And he wanted to see if he could do it again—

"Matthias?"

Letting out a shout, he jumped in his chair, the restaurant rushing back at him, those walls popping into place again, the ambient sounds of people eating and talking filtering into his brain once more.

As other diners looked over at him, Dee leaned in. "Are you okay?"

Her beautiful face was cast in perfect lines of compassion, her lips parted as if his distress was making it hard for her to breathe.

The removal he'd felt in his younger self slipped back into place over the center of his chest, as if the memory had recalibrated his internal hard wiring, tightening him up like a car that had had alignment problems: As he regarded the woman across from him, it was from a vital distance, a chilly objectivity putting space between them even though their chairs were no farther apart.

Emotions could be so easily faked, as he himself knew.

The smile he gave her felt different on his face—but also very familiar. "I'm perfectly fine."

The waitress came over at that moment with his huge breakfast, and as she put it down, he could have sworn Dee sat back and smiled to herself in satisfaction.

Standing with the maître d', Mels was through being StalkerGurl. Bad enough that she had come to the Marriott on the hunt, but to have found Matthias with that nurse? Now she had two reasons to feel like crap: She didn't respect herself, and only a fool would compare anything but Sofia Vergara to that other woman.

As a plate the size of a countertop was put down in front of Matthias, he looked across at his eating companion with a sly smile, and—

His head turned for no good reason just as she pivoted away.

Their eyes met, and instantly, that cynical expression of his changed into something she couldn't read—and told herself she didn't care about.

Whatever. This was none of her business.

And she was certainly not going to bother with anything theatrical. Instead, she calmly headed for the lobby's revolving doors—

"Mels!" came a hiss behind her.

There was no pretending he hadn't come out after her, and no reason to ignore him.

"I didn't mean to interrupt your breakfast," she said as she halted and he came up to her. "And I'm on my way to a meeting. When you didn't answer your phone, I figured I'd swing by."

"Mels—"

"That story you asked me to check out was true. Except they spell the last name with an E. Child'e'. The son died of an overdose, and the father was at the scene when it happened. The daughter is still alive—a defense attorney up in Boston. Father works for the government in various capacities. At least that's what's been in the papers. I can't speak to things that aren't in the public domain." As he just stared at her, she kicked up her chin. "Well, what did you expect me to come back with?"

He rubbed his face like his head hurt. "I don't know. I . . . When did the son die?"

"Not long ago. Two and a half years, maybe—"

"Your breakfast is getting cold."

Mels glanced over at the nurse. The woman was focused solely on Matthias as she approached, like he wasn't talking to anybody.

Okay, the female looked incredible in that dress, her body turning what was quintessentially demure into hot-dayum—

Abruptly, a flashback from the Seinfeld epi with Teri Hatcher shot through her head . . . yeah, those double-Ds were probably real and spectacular, too. Meanwhile, she herself relied on Wonderbra technology to push her into a C-cup range.

"I was just leaving anyway," Mels said. "I'll be late for my meeting otherwise."

This got her a dismissive look from the nurse, those dark brown eyes not just hands-off, but fuck-off. "Come on, let's go back to the table."

Matthias just kept staring at Mels, to the point where she felt as if he were trying to tell her something. But he had cold eggs and hot legs to worry about, so his proverbial plate was full enough without her.

She threw them both a wave and fell into the foot traffic funneling out through those revolving doors.

On the far side, the sunshine was bright and cheerful as she headed for Tony's car, and the sedan was warm inside. Settling into the driver's seat, she gave herself a stiff lecture before starting the engine—except it didn't do any good.

Not even the part about how a man who was mysterious and unavailable was likely to, given her reporter's instinct, seem oh, so much more appealing than your average schlub—but that didn't make him a good bet.

Maybe this was why she was still single. It hadn't been for lack of dating invites. It was more likely the fact that the men who had asked her out had had steady jobs, and nice enough looks . . . and their memories.

No shadows, no excitement.

Nah, she was into someone with a possibly shady past and a breakfast companion who had Barbie's body and TV-commercial hair.

Healthy, realllllly healthy.

Starting the car, she nudged into traffic, her rendezvous with Monty the Mouth set for a park about seven blocks from the hotel.

At least the timing of it all was in her favor: If she had to go back to the newsroom and pretend to be working while she stared at her computer screen, she was liable to lose it.

Goddamn men, she thought as she found another free meter, pulled a better parallel and got out.

Following the instructions she'd been given, the whole thing with Monty had shades of spy movies, with her going over to a bench under a specific maple tree. All she needed was a newspaper to hide behind and a secret word and they'd be in total shaken-not-stirred land.

Monty showed up ten minutes later, in plain clothes that marked him as a swinger type. He was in a good mood, the subterfuge clearly giving him the kind of drama injection he needed.

"Walk behind me," he said in a low voice as he passed by.

Oh, for crissakes.

Mels shifted to the vertical when he got ten feet ahead of her, and she kept his meandering pace, wondering why the hell she was putting herself through this.

After a little stroll, they ended up down at the river's edge, at the big Victorian boathouse where people launched their canoes and sailboats when the weather got warmer.

Stepping inside, her eyes took a moment to adjust to the dim interior, the diamond-paned windows not letting much of the sunlight in, the racks of rowboats and stacks of buoys and lineups of paddles and rolled-up sails making the place seem crowded. And it was loud in a sense, too—all around, the water clapped in and out of the docking cribs, the slapping noises echoing through the empty slips—

With a sudden explosion, barn swallows shot out of their early nests, dive-bombing them both before escaping into the open air.

As her heart settled back into a normal rhythm, she said, "So what have you got?"

Monty took out a large, flat envelope and handed it over. "I printed these out at home this morning."

Mels slipped a finger under the metal butterfly clip and freed its hold. "Who else knows about this?"

"At the moment, just you and me."

One by one, she slid out three color photographs, all of which were of the victim: the first was a full-body with the shirt down, the second closer with the shirt up, the third tight on what appeared to be a series of runes.

Cecilia Barten.

That was the name that went through Mels's head as she examined the images: Sissy had been another girl, younger, and far, far outside the kind of life where getting murdered was a job hazard.

Her body had been found in a quarry just recently with the same kind of characters carved into her abdomen. She'd had her throat slit, too. And she'd been blond.

"You saw the pictures from the crime scene, right?" Monty asked.

"Yeah." Mels refocused on the close-up. "The skin was red, but there was nothing like this on it. Wait, so tell me, off the record if you have to—how did this go down? You said you were a first responder—"

"*The* first responder. I went into the room with the manager, and promptly followed procedure. I cordoned off the door and called for backup."

"Where was your partner?"

"She'd called in sick, so I was out alone—budget cuts, you know how it is. No replacements. Anywho, while I was waiting, I took the pictures."

She hated people who used the word *anywho*. "You moved the shirt."

"I was examining the body and the scene in my official capacity."

Creep. "Why take the pictures at all though, if the official photographer was coming?"

"The real question is, Where did that lettering go."

Man, this just wasn't right, Mels thought.

Looking over at him, she asked, "So what can I do with this?"

"Right now, nothing. I don't want to be accused of tampering with the body."

But you did, didn't you. "So why give these to me?"

"Someone has to know. Maybe I'll go to de la Cruz—or maybe you can put this out in the *CCJ* and just say it's from an anonymous source. The thing is, the time of death was clocked at around five or six, so the killing happened fairly soon after whoever took the room occupied it. I got there at, like, nine fifteen. That leaves four and a half hours for someone to get in there and get out."

What he was missing, though, perhaps deliberately, was the fact that those runes had disappeared between when he'd arrived on scene and when the CPD photographer had taken pictures. The body couldn't have been alone for very long and scarification didn't just up and disappear.

This was *really* not right.

"Okay, just let me know what you feel comfortable with on my end," she said. "Whenever you decide."

He nodded at her like they had sealed some kind of a deal, and then started to walk off.

"Hold up, Monty—quick question on something else."

Her source paused in the doorway. "Yeah?"

"You know that man they found dead at the Marriott?"

"Oh, you mean the stiff in the delivery entrance? The one who disappeared from the morgue?"

Mels stopped breathing. "Excuse me?"

"You didn't hear about it?" He came in close to share the report. "The body's gone. As of this morning."

Impossible. "Someone stole it. Out of the St. Francis morgue."

"Apparently."

"How does that happen?" As Monty shrugged, she shook her head—and knew that whatever was going on with the missing corpse, it wasn't good. "Well, I hope they find the damn thing. Hey, you don't happen to know what kind of bullets were in that vest the victim was wearing?"

"Forties."

"And I heard there was a tattoo on the body?"

"I don't know. But I can find out."

"I'd appreciate it."

He gave her a wink, and a sly smile. "No problem, Carmichael."

When she was alone, Mels went through the pictures again, one by one . . . and decided Caldwell probably had another serial killer on its hands.

Not exactly the kind of job security she or the CPD were looking for.

And she had to wonder if he wasn't a man in blue.

Chapter Twenty-four

As Devina folded her napkin beside her empty breakfast plate, she smiled across the table at her prey. All in all, things were going well. Matthias was starting to remember, and that little door she'd opened about his father had brought back just the kind of light she liked to see in his eye.

That old man of his had been key, of course, the beginning of the evil, proof positive that infection could happen even human to human, not just demon to human.

But she had to be careful to walk that line.

"I'll get the check," Matthias said, lifting his hand to signal to the waitress.

"You're such a gentleman." She reached into her bag and started shifting her lipsticks from left to right, counting. "I'm glad we ran into each other."

. . . three, four, five . . .

"Stroke of luck." He glanced over at the window, like he was making plans. "What were the chances."

. . . six, seven, eight . . .

"What are you going to do today?" she asked, her heart starting to beat as she closed in on the end of the count.

. . . nine, ten, eleven . . .

He answered her with something she didn't follow, but then, she was nearly finished.

Twelve.

Thirteen.

As she exhaled, she took the last tube out and popped the lid. Focusing on Matthias, she willed him to watch her mouth as she exposed the soft, blunt tip of the lipstick and began to run it over her flesh.

He did precisely as she wanted, but the response was not what she was after, the regard clinical, not sexual. As if she were an instrument he was briefly considering using.

Devina frowned. When he'd stepped out to go chasing after that fucking reporter, there hadn't been any of this remoteness. He'd been naked while fully clothed, trained on that woman like she was something inside of him, rather than separate and apart.

The demon tucked her lips in and released them, feeling her mouth plump back up—and to make sure he got the point, she inserted a thought in his head of her mouth around his cock, sucking, pulling, swallowing.

It didn't work.

He just glanced over at the waitress, took the check she gave him, and wrote his room number down.

The sound of a hard wind rattling all the windows in the place had people looking around, including Matthias: Sitting across from the guy, Devina seethed, her temper flaring and touching the elements outside the hotel, kicking up a gale that came from the south.

All she could think of was how Jim had toyed with her—and now this lame-ass cripple, who was going back to Hell as soon as this round was over, was blowing her off.

Bastards. Both of them.

She stood up and slung her bag over her shoulder. "How long are you staying?" she bit out.

"Little while longer."

True enough. Things were moving fast with him, even if he didn't know it, and this round was going to be over very quickly.

Maybe she should take him up to his room and remind him that he was a man, not a robot—and that those "injuries" weren't going to be a problem as long as he was with her.

Good luck with your reporter on that one, she thought.

"I'm heading out right now," he said. Like he was dismissing her.

Devina narrowed her eyes, and then remembered that she had a role to play. "Well, I'm sure I'll see you around."

"Seems like it. Good luck with your mother."

As he turned away, she kind of wanted to fuck him for reasons other than the round. He had the same kind of strength Jim did—as well as that essential elusiveness.

She should have paid more attention to this man when she'd had him. Fortunately, he was going to come home soon.

In the meantime, she needed to take care of that reporter. That was not the kind of influence she needed in this game.

And accidents happened all the time. The Maker couldn't find fault with her for that.

Matthias took a cab to the offices of the *CCJ* and waited in the parking lot behind the building. He figured Mels had borrowed that Toyota to come over to the hotel, and sure enough, her friend's ride wasn't parked along with all the other beaters with trash in them.

As if having a wastepaper basket for a whip was part of the journalist job description.

Hanging out by the back door, he stood to the side, bracing his ass against the building, and leaning on his cane. Overhead, clouds came in and covered the sun, the shadows on the ground taking over as the sunlight faded away.

He was being watched.

Not by the stragglers who came and went out of the exit . . . or the smokers who lit up, exhaled like chimneys for a brief time, and went back inside . . . or the people driving around the crowded parking lot looking for a spot.

It was a steady, constant watching from a fixed position over on the right.

Could be someone in one of the cars parallel-parked along the outside perimeter of the newspaper's lot. The only other option was the roof of the building across the way, as its walls had no windows.

He needed to get some ammo. Without bullets, the forty with the silencer that he'd "borrowed" from Jim was nothing but a delivery system for blunt-force trauma—which wasn't exactly useless. Just not quite as deadly or long range—

The Toyota he'd been waiting for eased around the corner and pulled in. When the car stopped abruptly, he knew she'd seen him.

Mels parked in the first available, got out, and walked over with her chin up and her hair blowing in the breeze.

"Working off your breakfast with a good walk?" she asked.

A subtle sting inside his chest lit off as he met her eyes, and it gradually intensified, the sensation becoming hard to breathe through.

"I'm sorry," he said roughly.

"What for?"

All he could do was shake his head, his voice gone. The cold, calculating clarity he'd felt after the visions of the past had come to him was gone. In its place, he was a destination undefended, stripped of fortifications.

"Matthias? Are you all right?"

Somehow it happened: He stepped forward and put his hands on her waist . . . and then he was holding her close, putting his face in that hair she'd left loose.

"What happened?" she said softly as she started to rub his back.

"I don't . . ." Ah, shit, he was out of his damn mind. "I can't . . ."

"All right, it's okay . . ."

They stood there together as thunder rumbled like the skies disapproved, and lightning flickered across the underside of the cloud cover.

Goddamn him, but he wanted to stay where they were forever: When he was against this relative stranger's warm body, there was no past and no future, only the present, and that lack of landscape or horizon was a kind of shelter—

Rain started to fall in big drops, to the point where it was as if they were pelted with marbles.

"Come inside," she said, taking his hand and using a pass card to enter the building.

A strange chemical perfume in the air tingled in his nose. But it wasn't floor polish or window cleaner; it was ink from the presses.

"Here," she said, going over to a maroon door, turning a handle, and pushing the way open with her hip.

The conference room beyond had mismatched chairs and a long table that was a cobbled-together mishmash of components, the Frankenstein of office furniture. There was a Poland Spring watercooler in the corner, though, and she went over and got him a paper cup full.

"Drink this."

He did as he was told, and as he swallowed, he tried to pull it together.

Mels hopped her butt up on the table, her legs swinging back and forth slowly. "Talk to me."

Ah, shit, how could he tell her what he remembered? For fuck's sake, why had he even come here. . . .

Well, at least he knew the answer to that one. He wanted to be honest with one person. Finally. He just had to make the connection with her, like he was in a free fall, she was a rope to catch, and the words he needed to speak were the grip he'd have on his lifeline.

"I killed my father."

Her feet froze in midswing, her shoulders tensing.

"It was after years of him . . ." Say it. Say it. Fucking say it. "He was a violent man, and he drank. There were . . . things that happened that shouldn't have and I . . ."

The light in her eyes gradually shifted back, compassion coming to the front once again.

But when it looked like she might hit her feet and try to hug him, he put both hands up. "No, I can't—I'm not going to get through this if you touch me."

"Okay," she said slowly.

"I don't even know why I'm telling you this."

"There doesn't have to be a reason."

"It feels like there should be."

"You know you can trust me, right? I may be a reporter, but I meant what I said—that's my job, not who I am."

"Yeah." He rubbed at his hair and then took off the sunglasses. "I'm sorry, but I need to see you clearly."

She frowned. "There's no need to apologize."

He turned her Ray-Bans over in his hand. "I thought you preferred these on me. You know, back at the diner—so you didn't have to see my face."

"That wasn't why I told you to keep them. You're not ugly to me, Matthias—not by any stretch. And you don't have to hide yourself."

Somehow, he knew that wasn't going to last. He had a feeling the more that came to him, the worse the picture of who he was was going to get—like a paint-by-numbers where you thought you were making a pretty portrait, but it turned out the subject was Michael Myers.

"I boxed him in," Matthias heard himself say. "I went to my homeroom teacher, and then the school nurse, and I told them everything, explained the absences, and the bruises, and the . . . other stuff. I was fifteen. I'd kept it all in up until that point—"

"Oh, God, Matthias—"

"—but then I let the cat out of the bag, and the system took over. He had a heart attack in front of me when I told him the secret was everywhere."

"And that's why you think you killed him? Matthias, you didn't do anything wrong."

"Yeah, I did. I watched him die. I didn't call nine-one-one, I didn't run for help, I stood there and watched him as he went down to the floor in front of me."

"You were a victim of abuse and in shock. It's not your fault—"

"I did it on purpose."

Now she frowned again. "I don't understand."

"I didn't care what he did to me. That shit was more of an annoyance than anything." He shrugged. "The whole thing about coming forward was just a mental exercise to me. See, I knew him." He tapped his temple. "I knew the way he thought, the things that made him tick. He liked being mean and having power over me. He was a not-so-bright guy who worked with dumb animals and corn stalks all day long—it wasn't until he had to deal with adults who were on his level that his inferiority complex came out. He used to threaten to kill me if I told anyone, and that was his tell. The secrecy was so important to him, and not just because it's illegal to fuck with your kid. I *knew* it was going to get him, and more than stop the abuse . . . I just wanted to see what would happen."

"Wait, let me ask you something. How long had you been with him?"

"My mother died in childbirth."

"So your whole life."

"I was somewhere else for a while, but then I came back to him."

"When you were little."

"Yeah."

"And it doesn't occur to you that you were just a young kid saving yourself?"

"That was the end result, but not my motivation. And that's what's rattled me so badly."

Mels shook her head. "I think you need to be a little more forgiving of yourself."

Ah, hell, she wasn't going to get it. He could see it in her eyes—she had made up her mind about him, and nothing was going to change her opinion.

"Matthias isn't my real name."

"What is?"

It had come back to him. Over breakfast.

He stared at her for the longest time, lingering on her face and her neck and on her lean body . . . and then going back to her smart eyes.

He wasn't going to give her that information. He couldn't.

In the silence that followed, he felt an overriding need to be alone with her again, and not in public. In his room. In that hotel bed with the sheets that smelled like lemon. He wanted a little of her before he left, as if she were some kind of medicine that might keep him alive just awhile longer.

Because he was going to die soon, he realized.

It wasn't paranoia. It was . . . as inevitable as his past was written in stone.

"I'm running out of time," he said softly. "And I want to be with you before I leave."

"Where are you going?"

"Away," he answered after a moment.

Chapter Twenty-five

Mels stopped breathing as the conviction that Matthias was a missing person hit her hard, without regard to the fact that he had a driver's license and, supposedly, a house: Standing in front of her, looking her in the eye, it was as if he weren't even in the room.

Here for a split second, gone forever.

"Why are you leaving?" When he just shook his head, she asked, "Is that why you won't tell me your name?"

"No, it's because it doesn't matter. It's just syllables. I haven't been that person for so many years, it simply isn't relevant."

"I'm not so sure about that." As he shrugged, she had to push. "And you don't need to go anywhere."

For one thing, she didn't believe people could see into the future, and that meant if he took off, it was of his own free will—and that decision could be unmade at any time. By him.

Except . . . the problem with that argument was that she felt it, too, the sense that they didn't have an ever-after waiting for them. They'd met because of an accident, their lives colliding, and just as that impact hadn't lasted long, neither would they.

The injury was what was going to be forever.

She had this awful feeling she was never going to get over meeting this man.

"How much longer?" she demanded.

"I don't know."

Getting off the table, she went over and wrapped her arms around him, laying her cheek against the beating heart behind his ribs. As he held her back, she wondered why he was the one she felt such a connection with. Those others, the conventional ones, hadn't gotten through to her.

This man, though . . .

Matthias eased back and touched her face. "Can I kiss you here?"

"You mean on my cheek or in this conference room?"

"Well, you do work here, and—"

She pressed her lips to his, silencing him. Who gave a shit where they were. There were plenty of interoffice relationships, and people who had brought husbands and wives and partners into the building.

Besides, if her boss could sexually harass her, she should be able to kiss the man she actually wanted under this roof.

Closing her eyes, she tilted her head and brushed his mouth again, letting her lips cling to his. And as he kissed her back, she wished she could capture the moment and make it physical somehow, turn it into something that she could hold in her hands, or put somewhere safe like she would a book or a vase.

But life wasn't like that. You didn't get to hold on to the moments that defined you or touch the things that touched you—not in the palm of your hand or with the tips of your fingers, at least.

Destiny's machinations were as elusive as a sculptor's tool, swooping in, changing your contours, and then moving on to the next piece of clay.

With a steady shift, Matthias's palm slid up to the nape of her neck, taking control. And as his tongue licked between her lips, she opened for him, wishing that this was somewhere private as heat magnified inside of her, the walls of her body sending it endlessly ricocheting around, faster, hotter, faster, hotter—

Mels frowned as she realized her hand was touching something hard at the small of his back.

Not a brace.

There was nothing medical about it.

Ducking under the flap of his windbreaker, she found . . . the grip of a gun.

She pulled the weapon out of his waistband as she stepped back.

It was a forty, and she quickly checked the chamber. Empty. Same with the clip.

"You're not the only one with a permit," he said remotely.

She gave the autoloader back to him. "Guess not. Can I ask you where you got it?"

"I bought it."

"And forgot the ammunition?"

"It wasn't a package deal."

"You know what? The victim who died at your hotel just last night was shot at by this caliber of gun."

"And you think I did it because I'm out of ammo."

Mels shrugged. "You told me not to get involved with you because it could kill me. You show up with a gun after someone is shot at the Marriott. Call me Einstein."

"I didn't kill that man."

"How do you know it was a male?"

"It's all over the news."

Mels crossed her arms over her chest and stared at the floor, thinking nothing good was going to come out of where this conversation was going.

"I think I'd better take off."

"Yeah," she said.

Talk about whiplash. From kissing to this in less than five seconds.

"I'm sorry," he murmured at the door.

"Why are you apologizing?"

"I don't like leaving you like this."

Well, that made two of them.

As the door clicked shut behind him, she wondered if she would ever see Matthias again—and gave herself a steady lecture about keeping her head tight and not letting her libido get her into dangerous situations.

Not something her father would have approved of. Not something smart women did.

Damn it. . . .

After fifteen minutes of kicking her own butt, she went up to the newsroom, got herself a mug of strong-and-black, and returned to her desk.

"Tell me you haven't wrecked my car, too."

She jumped and glanced over at Tony. "Wha— Oh, no. Here are the keys."

"Guess you just look like you've been in another accident."

Go. Fig.

Easing back in her chair, she stared at her computer screen.

"You okay?" Tony asked. "You need a Twinkie?"

Mels laughed. "I think I'll try Maxwell House first, but thanks."

"What's up with the puss?"

"I'm just wondering how it's physiologically possible for scars to remove themselves from a dead body."

Okay, not the question she'd actually been thinking about, but a fine, socially acceptable substitute. She'd also have asked it eventually. Tony was a walking encyclopedia.

Now it was his turn to ease back and stare at nothing. "Not possible. Scars are scars."

"So how could you explain two sets of photographs, one that showed a pattern on the skin and one that didn't?"

"Easy. Someone got busy with Photoshop."

"That's what I'm thinking."

What she didn't get was the "why." Although she had her suspicions as to the "who."

Mels let her head fall to the side. Any tampering wouldn't have been done by the official photographer—while the woman had been snapping away, there'd been half a dozen men in that room with her, and if she'd changed anything in the images later, they would have hollered about the discrepancy the second they saw the pictures.

So that left Monty, a man who masturbated his ego by talking to the press when he shouldn't and trying to create drama where there was none. What were the chances that he'd tinkered just for kicks and giggles?

Mels snapped into action, going into the CCJ's database.

"Either that," Tony tacked on, "or it was a case of divine intervention."

"I got the tattoo."

At five o'clock, Mels looked up from the final version of her story on the prostitute. Eric was standing in front of her, a folder in his hand, a shit-eater on his face.

"From the Marriott victim who disappeared from the morgue?"

"The very one."

"Lemme see?" she said, holding out her hand.

"It's, ah . . . yeah." He passed the pictures over. "Not my style. I'm more of a tribal guy."

As she popped the top fold, Mels's brows lifted. The photograph was in color, but that wasn't necessary—at least not where the ink was concerned. The tattoo's depiction of the Grim Reaper was done in black and white, and with eerie detail . . . to the point where even in the photograph, the glowing eyes under the ragged hood and the bony hand pointing out to the viewer seemed to call upon her specifically.

"Pretty gruesome, huh," Eric remarked. "And nice cemetery, too, don't you think."

True enough on the background: The horrible figure was standing in a field of graves, the headstones stretching far into the landscape beyond, the decaying robes sweeping out and obscuring that which seemed to go on forever.

"What are these hash marks at the bottom?" she wondered.

"It's got to be a count of something—and not loaves of bread, I'm willing to bet."

"Could be gang related."

"That's what I was thinking, especially given that there was a body recently in the morgue with something similar on it—according to my source."

"What does the CPD think?"

"I'm looking for the answer to that right now."

Mels glanced up. "So you've done an Internet search on the image?"

"There are a thousand representations of the Grim Reaper on the Web—and some of them are in people's skin. From what I could find, none look exactly like that, but all of them sort of look like that, if it makes any sense."

"How did your source get these? I heard that everything was wiped cleaned from the intake file."

St. Francis was in an uproar over the incident; it was as if the man had never been through their system at all.

Clean. Very clean.

"My buddy happens to be a tattoo buff. He took the pics on his own phone as the body came in."

"Handy dandy," she murmured as she returned the folder. "So, if we assume the ink is gang related—what the hell was the guy doing wearing a state-of-the-art bulletproof vest? And what about the disappear? Gangs aren't that sophisticated, financed or dogged about their dead—breaking into a hospital to get a body back? And then pulling an IT scrub? Not going to happen. Mob's the same."

Eric chewed on that mangled Bic of his. "It's got to be government of some sort. I mean, who else could pull it off?"

She thought of Matthias's empty autoloader. "I hear the bullets were from a forty?"

"The gun that was used against the guy? Yeah—and the good news is that the police took the vest along with the clothes and boots into evidence so they're still around." Her colleague's eyes narrowed. "So, are you going to tell me why you're so interested now?"

"My dead girl got slit in the throat as well." Although, really, what were the chances the two killings were related?

"Ah, so you're collecting neck injuries."

"Just being thorough."

"And how's your story coming on that prostitute? Anything new?"

"I'm working on some things."

"Let me know if you need any help."

"Back at you."

As Eric walked off, she realized that the newsroom was largely vacant. And she was nearly out of time when it came to her deadline.

Rereading her article, she was dissatisfied. No new information other than the victim's identity, and when she'd called the family, she'd gotten a rather shockingly uninterested no comment.

How could you not be upset at your daughter's death?

Mels didn't like sending her piece in as it was. The writing was fine, and spell-check had done its job, but the real story was with Monty and his photographs and she couldn't put any of that in yet.

With a curse, she hit *send*, and vowed that she was going to get to the bottom of it all. Even if it didn't go into print.

Switching her screens, she reassessed the side-by-side of two images that she'd put together an hour before: they were both of similar markings carved into abdominal skin. One was from that Cecilia Barten girl who'd been found at the quarry on the outskirts of town just days before . . . and the other was what Monty contended had been on the prostitute's belly.

The pattern of scratches looked like some kind of language: There were identical characters in both photographs, although they were not in the same sequence—which in her mind didn't rule out in the slightest the Monty-as-Photoshopper theory. If anything, it was perfect, tying the death at the motel to that of the Barten girl without making the manipulation a one-for-one obvious.

In fact, the more she thought about it, the more she decided the tampering fit with Monty's routine. If he was the "source" for a new serial killer, how much fun would that be for him. . . .

Except she had to wonder. When no one else was killed like those girls, what was he going to do? And his job was at risk. He was already walking a line by giving info like he did. Raising the stakes by lying about it was just too foolish.

Maybe he was simply getting sloppy.

Then again, what about the hair color? The prostitute had colored hers right before she'd died, to a shade of blond that matched the Barten girl's. That wasn't something that had changed between photographs; that had actually occurred.

What if Monty was a copycat killer?

"How's your car situation?" As Mels jumped, Tony halted in the process of packing up his stuff. "You okay over there?"

"Yeah, sorry. Just thinking."

Her buddy slung his bag over his shoulder. "You need to borrow my vintage wheels again?"

Mels hesitated. "Oh, I couldn't bother you with—"

"Not to worry. Just drive me home and she's all yours as long as you bring me breakfast again tomorrow morning." Holding up the keys, he swung them back and forth from their KISS logo tag. "I really don't need the damn thing."

"One more night," she hedged.

"Two more sausage biscuits with coffee, you mean."

The pair of them laughed as she shut down her computer. Getting up, she took the photographs Monty had given her, stuffed them into her bag, and linked an arm through Tony's.

"You're a prince among men, you know that?"

He smiled. "Yeah, I do. But it's nice to hear it once in a while."

"Listen, do we know anyone who's good with photographs?"

"You looking for a portrait of yourself?"

"I'm talking about analyzing."

"Ah." He held the back door open for her. "As a matter of fact, I know just who you can talk to . . . and we probably can meet him on the way home."

Chapter Twenty-six

Jim had not expected to pay another visit to the St. Francis Hospital morgue anytime soon. Once through the park with the slabs and the stiffs had been more than enough for him.

Of course, the good news was, he didn't have to die this time. And the *rigor mortis* wasn't his own.

What a great standard to measure shit against.

The trouble was, things were way too quiet on the home front. And that meant he had to go looking for Devina—and he figured a good place to start was with the operative's body down at the morgue.

He still didn't believe for a second that the demon had just been lending a helping hand the night before when she'd arrived with her sharp and shiny to "save" them. And after a day spent tailing Matthias, and waiting for her to do something more than breakfast, he'd told Ad to hold the farm—and come here to the land of Lysol, piss-green tile, and scales that were used to weigh brains and livers.

He wanted to take a good look at that "operative's" body.

In the quick draw of last night, he hadn't been able to pay a lot of attention to the remains—and although he wasn't sure what they could tell him, it was the only leftover around . . .

Assuming he got to them before the XOps recon folks did.

His first clue that all wasn't well in the land where coroners were kings was the police presence out in the hall in front of the morgue: Blue unis were everywhere, milling around the basement facility, chatting one another up. And then as Jim ghosted through the morgue's double doors, there was another bottleneck of badges in the reception area, this one mixing with members of the medical staff.

Somehow, the place had become a crime scene.

Gee. What a surprise.

"—time did you come in?"

The scrubs being questioned over at the desk crossed his arms over his chest and shoved out his patchy goatee. "I told you. My shift started at nine a.m."

"And was that when you arrived?"

"That's when I clocked in. I already told you—"

Jim left that interview where it was devolving, and headed out of the paper-pushing part of the afterlife enterprise and into the chilly clinical section. Stepping through the Staff Only doors, the fluorescent-lit area beyond was kitted out with more stainless steel than a smelting factory, what between the five workstations, the half dozen deep-bellied sinks, and all those godforsaken scales.

Over on the far wall, the rows of cold-storage compartments were latched closed, as if the folks at St. Francis weren't entirely sure zombies were a work of fiction—except for a single one in the corner. That was open wide, with various guys in navy blue polo shirts dusting and peeling for fingerprints in a radius around the gaping mouth.

Whaddaya want to bet the operative's body had disappeared.

Shocker.

Jim cursed as he went over, and found no sign of Devina any-where in sight—typically, in her wake, a nasty smell lingered like a Glade PlugIn gone bad. Here? There was the slightest whiff inside the refrigerator unit, but nothing that was recent.

Looked like XOps had come to Merry Maid the aftermath, not the demon.

"Damn it."

As he spoke out loud, a couple of cops looked over to where he was standing, like they were expecting to see a buddy of theirs.

When they frowned and went back to work, Jim considered go-ing upstairs for a visit—and he wasn't talking about the ER or the inpatient rooms of the hospital. But what would Nigel the archan-gel do for him? Trips to Heaven hadn't really helped in the past, and shit knew he was pissed off and frustrated enough already.

He was just about to leave when something dawned on him.

Going down the wall units, he looked at the names that had been printed on index cards and slipped into brackets on those shoulder-wide doors.

Sure enough, at the other end, there was one that read, BARTEN, CECILIA.

On some level he was surprised her remains were still here, but then he reminded himself that it only felt like forever since he'd found her in that quarry. In reality, it had been a mere matter of days, and she was, after all, part of a criminal investigation.

Not that any member of the CPD was going to be able to find Devina and hold that demon accountable for the death.

That was his job.

Lifting his hand, he touched the stainless steel. Sooner or later, Sissy's mother was going to have the chance to bury her child, and that kind of cold closure was rather like the cooling space the bod-ies were kept in, wasn't it.

A lock-in where the grief was stored for the rest of someone's days—

Jim frowned and cranked his neck around, his senses going off on a lot of levels.

With a curse, he pushed his way out of the examination facility, through the receiving office, and into the hall beyond.

Seek, he thought . . . and ye shall find.

Too bad everyone showed up at the same time.

"You know what I like most about hospitals?" Tony asked.

As Mels walked with him up to one of St. Francis's huge buildings, she waited for the automatic revolving door to give them an opening. "Not the food."

"Au contraire—the vending machines." As they shuffled through the entrance together, he shoved his hands into the front pockets of his khakis and came out with all kinds of change. "They've got such a good selection here."

"Well, you can put your quarters away—it's my treat."

"Tell me something . . . why aren't we dating?"

Forcing a laugh, she thought . . . man, he didn't want her to answer that. And neither did she.

As they came up to a knot of medical staff and visitors playing elevator bingo, they hedged their bets on the first set of doors because it was the least congested. Seconds later, there was a *bing*, that particular car arrived—and it was headed down.

"We have chosen wisely," Tony said in an affected voice.

Mels laughed as they waited for some uniformed security guards to step out; then they got in along with a construction guy and his tool belt.

Miracle the man could still walk with all that hammer and screwdriver stuff hanging off him.

When they arrived at the basement floor, Tony hung a louie,

and so did she. Hammer guy followed suit, making it three for three, although he stepped out in front of them, heading for the distant sounds of nails being struck and band saws whining their way through two-by-fours.

"We may have to wait," Tony said as they followed the signs to the morgue. "Suraj said he'd sneak out when we got here, but—"

Both of them stopped as they turned the corner.

CPD blue unis were everywhere, choking the entrance to the morgue.

"Guess the investigation is still in full swing," she muttered. "You sure your buddy can get out of there at all?"

"Yeah, let's see how he's doing," Tony said as he texted on his phone.

As her mind locked onto something other than Matthias, it was just the distraction she wanted—and she hoped this took a while. God knew the last thing she needed was free time and a car. She was liable to end up back at the Marriott, where Matthias might well be having dinner with Hot Stuff—or worse.

But come on, the fact that he had a forty-caliber gun did not mean he'd shot anybody. She had a nine-millimeter in her purse and that didn't make her a suspect in every shooting downtown—

"Damn it."

Tony looked over. "Huh?"

"Nothing. Just frustrated."

"Maybe this will still work—" As his cell let out a Tweety Bird sound, he checked the text. "Oh, good, Suraj's not going to leave us hanging. Let's wait over in . . . Oh, look. Vending machines. What a surprise."

Sure enough, across from the morgue there was a break room with all kinds of caloried slot machines. "You planned this."

"Not the cops part."

As they went in and Tony sized up the offerings, Mels paced

around the tables that were bolted to the floor and the orange plas-tic chairs that were not—likely because the latter were so ugly and uncomfortable no one would want to steal them.

Remembering her promise, Mels took out her wallet and counted her dollar bills. "Don't hold back. I got plenty."

"This is just a snack before dinner, really. And I don't like to eat alone." He looked over his shoulder. "Hello? Wingman?"

It was sad that she found it relaxing to think of nothing but what kind of overprocessed, mass-produced, worse-than-nonorganic she wanted.

Sure sign she needed a vacation. And a life.

"Have you made your choices?" she said as that band saw down the hall got to screaming again.

"You'd better believe it."

Seven singles into the machines later and Tony had a collection of nacho bags and candy bars in his hands.

"Now it's your turn," he said.

"I don't have your metabolism."

Tony rubbed his belly. "Neither do I."

She picked M&M's, the plain old-fashioned kind that she'd loved as a kid, but she'd run out of bills. Putting her hands into ev-ery kind of pocket she had, she brought out a palmful of loose coins and fished her way around for quarters—

Mels froze.

"What?" Tony asked from where he'd sat down.

A bullet casing. That was what.

In her frickin' pocket?

Except then it came back to her as she picked the thing out of the mismatched coins . . . that garage out in the farm country. Where she'd found a Harley with a warm engine, Matthias with a lie on his face, and . . . something else. . . .

Some*one* else—

A sudden sharp shooter went through her head, the pain clogging her thought processes, and shutting everything down . . . but for the conviction that she'd seen something important out there. What had it been, though?

Pushing hard, her mind just couldn't seem to put a name to the proverbial song, and the more she tried, the more it hurt.

"Mels?"

"I'm okay. No, really, just—I probably need the sugar."

Tony nodded as he popped open a bag of Cool Ranch Doritos. "A pick-me-up is never a bad thing."

A compact guy in a white coat came in. "Hey, sorry to keep you waiting."

Tony got up to shake hands. "Suraj, hey, man."

Shaking herself back into focus, Mels put the bullet in her purse and struggled to get through the hellos.

"We don't mean to take you away from your work," she said as they all clustered around one of the tables.

"Yeah, well, there's hasn't been much of that going on today." Suraj smiled, his teeth white against his beautiful skin. "The police have been here grilling us about that body that disappeared since this morning."

"What can you tell us?" Tony asked around a mouthful of crunching.

"Off the record, it's the one that was found in the Marriott basement last night." Suraj shrugged and settled back into his orange seat like his butt was well familiar with the ugly chairs. "I don't know much. I came in at noon for my usual shift, and the CPD was all over the place. Rick's been the guy on the front lines of the questions—he was the one who discovered the body was gone. Went to pull it out to do an autopsy, and . . . nothing. Not there. It's too weird—I mean, it's not like the dead guy walked out or something. But no alarms went off, and bodies are not easily hidden—not as if you're going to smuggle one out under your armpit. Plus, this place? Eyes everywhere. Security cameras, people—"

"Has this ever happened before?" Mels asked.

"If it did, it was before my time. Then again, I've only been here a couple of years. It's a mystery."

"Will you let us know when you can give a statement?" Tony interjected.

"That'll have to come from my boss, but I'll keep you posted under the table as much as I can. Now, what can I do for you?"

Tony glanced over at Mels as he picked up a little Cheetos bag and motioned to the guy with it. "So, Suraj isn't just good at what he does here. He's also got a knack for photo analysis, which is why I think he can help you."

Suraj smiled again. "I'm a jack of three trades, actually—I also make a mean chicken tikka masala."

"With the garlic naan," Tony added. "Pure awesomeness."

"So what kind of image are we talking?" his friend asked.

Mels took out the folder Monty had given her. "Before you look at all this . . . I can't tell you who gave these to me or in what context they came into his or her possession."

"What you're saying is, I should forget I ever saw them."

"Exactly."

As the man palmed the folder and opened it up, Mels frowned and looked around. That sense of being watched ratcheted up again, tingling her nape and making her clench her hands. Except there was no one in the entryway. No one in the hall beyond. Nobody lurking behind Tony's vending machines or under the godforsaken chairs or the bolted-down tables—

"I know this case," Suraj said as he flipped through the pictures, and Tony leaned in for a look-see. "Yeah, this is the prostitute who was found at that motel—I recognize the clothes. These markings were not on her abdomen when she came in here, though."

"And that's the issue." Mels reeled her paranoia in. "The official photographs of the body don't show anything, but these, which are claimed to have been taken before the CPD ones, do. So I want to know if these images are touched up in some way."

Suraj looked across the table. "Do you have the files for these images? JPEGs? GIFs?"

"No, the printouts were given to me, and they're all I'm going to get."

"Will you let me take these into my workspace for a minute? I've got a microscope back there."

Mels eased in closer. In a low voice, she said, "The police do not know about these photographs, and I'm not sure what their owner is going to do with them."

"So keep it quiet."

"But know that I will not obstruct justice if that's what this comes down to. I haven't had them long, and I will move fast with the authorities as appropriate."

"But you probably don't want me scanning these into my computer and doing an analysis that way, do you?"

"I'd rather not make any copies—especially not in e-form."

"Okay, I can tell a lot under the microscope." The guy got up. "Give me ten and I'll see what I can do."

As Suraj left and Tony played point-and-shoot with one of the rubbish bins, Mels rubbed the back of her neck and thought of what she'd found in her damn pocket.

"I don't suppose you know anyone who's into ballistics?" she said.

"As a matter of fact, I do. What you got?"

Mels massaged her temples. "A headache, actually."

"You haven't bought your food yet. Much less consumed it."

"Good point, my friend." She got up and headed for vending heaven. "Very good point."

Chapter
Twenty-seven

As Jim stood just inside the break room across from the morgue, he got up close and personal with the fact that invisibility had its benes—and sometimes could put your balls on the rack.

He'd known the moment Mels Carmichael had entered the St. Francis medical center complex, and given the number of cops in the basement, it hadn't been a total surprise that she'd beelined for right where he was. Unfortunately, he'd also sensed a reflection of Devina somewhere around—but he couldn't quite pinpoint it.

And then he'd seen those photographs.

Unlike the reporter, her buddy with the munchies, and the doctor-type in scrubs, he knew *exactly* what those markings were—as well as who put them there.

And who had taken them off the body.

Those runes in the skin of that dead woman were exactly what had been on Sissy's abdomen. A language, a marking, maybe even a message. And what Devina could carve in could probably be lifted—after all, she routinely created a three-dimensional image of perfection over her true, walking/talking corpse self.

An eraser job was not outside the realm of possibility. . . .

As the guy with the hospital pass hanging from his lapel got up and left, Jim followed him and those pictures into the morgue, even though there was nothing he could do—and leaving the reporter was probably not the brightest idea.

Except why would Devina be fucking around with killing some random human woman? You'd think she'd be too busy worrying about the game—and that prostitute had clearly not been a virgin, so it wasn't like she could be used to protect the demon's mirror—

Hair color. Blond hair color.

Straightened hair.

Just like Sissy.

What were the chances. "Motherfu—"

The hospital guy stopped dead in the middle of the CPD clog and looked behind himself—and Jim sent a reminder to his mouth that invisible was one thing; silent was another.

As the man led the way down a hall and into a cramped, tech-heavy office, Jim stayed out of the way, settling back against a whiteboard marked with a grid of names, dates, and procedures. When the phone rang minutes later and the guy got distracted, Jim wanted to yank the cord out of the wall and refocus the bastard.

But come on. He already knew the deal; the question was who to be more pissed off at. Himself. Devina—

Jim frowned, as something dawned on him. During the check-ins with Adrian this morning, the angel had mentioned he'd been hanging out at a murder scene with the reporter.

What a frickin' coincidence.

It was a good half hour before the man got up from his crouch over the scope to head back out to the reporter and her carbo-loading friend.

"So what's the verdict," she asked as he sat down.

"Okay, first the caveats. Without the digital file itself, or the ability to pixelate it and run a scan, I really can't give you a one hundred percent—"

The sound of clanging above their heads had all three of them looking up and then shielding their eyes as a shower of fine particles sifted loose from the ceiling squares.

"How long's this construction been going on?" Tony asked while a shrill grind of a saw played chaser.

"For. Ever." The man lined up the photographs on the table. "Anyway, disclaimers aside, here's what I think. From what I can see under the scope, it appears as if there was no retouching done—but that's not really saying much, given that I only have the print-outs, and people can do some pretty subtle, sophisticated stuff with images if they have good enough equipment."

Mels inhaled deeply. "Well, thank you—"

Suraj put up his palm. "Wait, I'm not finished. I saw that body. There was a rash in the abdominal area, but obviously that's not what's in these photographs. And I remember that pattern—it's also on the girl who was found in the quarry—"

Another sound, louder, like thunder, reverberated through the ceiling . . . as if something had been dropped on the tiles directly overhead.

The last thing Jim saw before all hell broke loose was Mels sending a glare heavenward. One second later, a six-by-eight-foot section of the suspended ceiling broke free of its maze of girders and swung down in one piece, hinging on where it was still attached.

Firing right at Mels.

Jim flipped into action, surging forward, shoving her off that orange chair and out of the way. His back and shoulders took the brunt of the impact, the sharp-edged weight cutting into him, drawing blood as everyone in the room shouted and ducked for cover.

The pain caused him to reveal himself, but that wasn't the biggest problem. Looking up through the dark hole in the ceiling, he locked eyes with . . . a construction worker who was illuminated by the light flooding upward from the break room.

Standing with his boots planted on the rafters and his hands on his hips in the vast space above, the man was not right.

His eyes were black as the depths of Hell.

"Devina," Jim hissed.

All at once, the worker grabbed his chest and started falling forward, his body slumping with a curious grace, the ends of all those tools on his belt flaring out like a model's hair in front of a fan.

Jim played buck-stops-here for the second time, catching the guy in a sloppy grab because loose, limp bodies, though they weighed less, were messier than hunks of ceiling.

There was an abrupt explosion of talk, but Jim didn't pay any attention to it. He was too busy easing the unconscious worker onto the floor—and sensing Devina's abrupt departure.

Damn it . . .

"Oh, dear God," Mels said, crouching down.

A sharp elbow pushed Jim aside, the man with the hospital badge getting on his knees and putting fingertips to the side of the construction guy's throat. As Jim stepped out of the way—

"Jim Heron."

Jim looked at the reporter, who was staring up at him as she rose from the floor. Fucking hell, he thought as she squared off at him.

"Well?" she demanded, seemingly undaunted by the fact that she'd nearly been killed. "And don't deny it. I've seen your picture in a lot of places."

"I'm his twin brother."

"Really."

The medical guy looked up. "Someone call extension nine-zero-zero-zero on that phone. Tell them we're outside the morgue."

Matthias's girl snapped into gear, discharging the directive calmly and quickly. When she came back, she went over to her newspaper colleague, who, in spite of the drama, had managed to peel back the wrapper of a Snickers bar and get munching.

"You okay?" she asked him.

"Close call," he muttered, staring at the medical drama on the floor at his feet.

Mels relocked her eyes on Jim, and then she grimaced and rubbed her temple like it was aching.

Things turned into a convention at that point, with other construction people arriving, along with hospital staff, security, and a couple of cops who'd heard the crash.

When the worker who'd fallen through the ceiling was finally put on the stretcher, he opened his eyes. Blue as the sky now. Not black.

Not a surprise.

Man, that demon had some kind of balls: If the conventional theory of a higher power held true, then the Big Guy Upstairs knew everything that happened, at every moment, all over the planet—from each blossom that bloomed to the feathers on a sparrow, to . . . big hulking construction workers who free-fell into break rooms at major metropolitan hospitals because they'd been temporarily possessed.

No doubt Devina had intended that chunk of the building to fall down on Mels. And wouldn't that have been a destabilizer in the game: Matthias finally bonds with a chick, and then she dies on him?

Great setup for decision making.

And to think Jim had assumed the demon was being too quiet?

Keeping free of the congestion, he disappeared himself, figuring that Mels would assume he'd walked off. Instead, he stayed put, and stuck close to that reporter—and had to admit he was impressed. She was a tough bird, answering the questions that hospital security gave her, keeping tight for her friend as well as the guy who'd done the microscoping, working with crowd control as the injured SOB on the stretcher was removed from the scene.

She looked around from time to time, as if she were searching for someone, but in the end, all she could do was describe her "savior" to the St. Francis security set. She didn't name names, however. Then again, she didn't really know who he was, did she.

As far as Matthias's reporter was concerned, he just bore a striking resemblance to a dead man. That was it.

Funny, much as Jim didn't approve of so much his old boss had done over the years, he found himself not faulting the guy's taste in the opposite sex.

And he was going to have to get her and Matthias together ASAP. Not just because it would make defending them easier, but who knew when the crossroads would come . . . and Matthias would have to choose his way.

The more time his former boss spent with that female . . . the better off they were all going to be.

Where the hell was "Jim Heron," Mels wondered when she and Tony were finally free to go.

"Good thing I had that food," her buddy said as they got back on the elevator they'd taken down to the basement a lifetime ago. "It's frickin' eight o'clock."

"Yeah." She pushed the *up* button. "Yeah . . ."

Tony's palm landed on her shoulder. "You okay?"

She took a deep breath as they began to rise. "Don't ask me that until we get upstairs. Between my car accident and what just happened, I'm worried there's another big crash coming my way. Things happen in threes, you know."

"That's just superstition."

"I hope you're right." To think she'd been worried about the morning coffee stain/fingernail three-pletion. This current streak of catastrophe she had going on was way over and above anything that could be handled with a Tide-to-Go and an emery board. . . . after a moment, she said, "Ah, Tony, I have another favor to ask you." God, was she really going to do this?

"Name it."

"Remember when I asked if you knew someone in ballastics? I need a bullet casing analyzed."

"Oh yeah, sure—I got a couple of guys I can call. What's your timeline?"

"As soon as possible."

"Let me make some calls and see who'd be willing to do it for you."

"You're a lifesaver."

"Nah. That guy down in the basement? He's the hero."

"Don't shortchange yourself."

As they arrived at the lobby, she stepped out and . . . well, what do you know. Jim Heron, or his twin brother—or whatever—was waiting across the way, lounging against the wall, looking as inconspicuous as any six-foot-plus guy who was built like a brick shithouse could be.

Putting her hand on Tony's arm, she stopped him and gave him back his keys. "Hey, I'm going to cab it home, okay?"

Her friend frowned. "I can take you back—it's not that far out of the way."

"I'm going to head over to the newsroom—"

"It's late and we've had a hell of a night already."

True enough—and chances were good she was going to be reliving the near miss for a while. But she wasn't losing her chance to talk to the superhero who'd stepped in at just the right time . . . and who now appeared to be waiting for her.

Mels leaned in and gave her buddy a kiss on the cheek. "I'll see you tomorrow."

Tony said good night and ambled off toward the revolving doors. As he took out his phone, she was willing to bet he was calling for takeout, and for some reason that made her like him even more.

Pivoting around, she clashed eyes with Heron—or whoever he was—and found his casual stance was nothing to be fooled by. His size alone was vaguely threatening, and that grim expression didn't make her think of daisies and daffodils, either.

And yet she wasn't afraid as she went over to him.

Bullshit this man was a twin . . .

Then again, why hang around a public place where someone might recognize him as she had?

"I thought you'd left," she said.

"Nah, I've been here all along."

"Business at the hospital?"

"You could say that."

"Security wants to talk to you."

"I'm sure they do."

As he fell silent, she waited for something, anything, to come back at her. There was nothing. He just stood there, meeting her stare as if he were prepared to do that for the next hundred years.

"I suppose I should thank you for saving my life," she muttered.

"No reason to. I'm not sentimental."

"Well, you look like you've got something to say to me—"

"Matthias needs you."

Her brows popped; then she glanced away fast. And even though she'd heard him just fine, she muttered, "I'm sorry?"

"Can you come with me? He's back at the hotel."

Mels looked at the man again. "No offense, but I'm not going anywhere with anybody. And if you don't mind my asking"—not that she cared if he was offended down to the tips of his combat boots—"what is he to you?"

"An old friend who I'm trying to help. He hasn't been right for a long time, and the way he talks about you gives me hope."

Now she just blinked. "He doesn't know me any better than I know him."

"Does that really matter?"

She laughed in a hard burst. "Ah . . . yeah. It does."

Jim Heron's "twin" shook his head. "Look, I've been worried about him for years, okay? He's heading for a brick wall right now, flailing around, searching for purpose, and I'm exactly that kind of asshole to drag anything and anyone into this who will help him find his way."

"And you think that's me?"

"No. I know it's you."

She let loose another laugh. "Well, you should have seen who he was having breakfast with earlier today."

The man cursed. "Let me guess. Brunette with legs down to there?"

"As a matter of fact . . . yes. Who is she?"

"Bad news." The guy shoved a hand through his dark blond hair. "Please—look, I just . . . I really need your help. I can't go into specifics, but Matthias and I were in the service together for twenty years, and I don't need to tell you what war does to people. You're a reporter. You're a human being. You can extrapolate from there. He needs . . . a reason for living."

She thought of the gun at the small of Matthias's back. Then remembered him curling his body into her as they stood in the parking lot behind the *CCJ*'s offices.

I'm leaving soon.

"If you think he's a danger to himself," she said roughly, "you should be calling the proper authorities. Other than that . . . I'm really sorry. But I can't do this—"

"Please." The man's eyes seemed to shimmer, not with tears, but with a light that reminded her of sunrise on the ocean. "He's come too far to lose everything now."

Boy, those pupils of his were hypnotic. And she had the sense that she had stared into them before . . . stared into them and . . .

As that headache came back, she closed her eyes and wondered if she had any Advil in her purse. "Why the hell do you think I'm any kind of answer for the guy?" Except even as she tossed that out, she thought of the connection between them and knew exactly what Heron-whoever-he-was was talking about. "I shouldn't matter this much to him."

Make that, he shouldn't matter this much to *her*.

He was armed for godsakes. And staying in a hotel where someone had been shot—

"But you do."

Mels popped her lids and frowned at the guy. "Be honest with me. Did you follow me here tonight?"

"Yeah, I did. I wanted a chance to talk to you, but wasn't sure how to approach you without freaking you out."

"Well, you nailed that one," she said dryly. "Just save my life."

"So in that sense, you owe me, right?"

She had to laugh. "I cannot believe you're laying that on me."

"Like I said, I will do anything in my power to save him."

"Save him? Interesting choice of words, Mr. Heron."

When the guy said nothing further, she stared into his face for the longest time. "Goddamn it."

"Is that a yes?"

Turning away and heading for the exit, she expected him to follow her out to the cabs lined up at the curb. And he did.

"Tell me something, Mr. Heron—and that is your name, right? Jim Heron." He didn't answer; then again, he didn't have to. "Do you believe that bad luck comes in threes?"

As a taxi rolled into position in front of them, Heron got the door for her. "I don't know about numbers. But lately, the shit's been coming in brunette."

With another curse, Mels squeezed past him . . . and got in for the ride.

Chapter
Twenty-eight

Matthias was in the dark. And it wasn't the kind of dark that came with a room that didn't have any lights on or when you were walking around at night in the country. This was not even the kind you got when you shut your eyes and wrapped your head in a blanket.

This was the one that seeped in through your skin and filled the spaces between your molecules, the one that polluted your flesh into a permanent state of rotting, the one that wiped clean your past and your future, suspending you in a choking, adhesive solution of sorrow and despair.

He was not alone in this horrible prison.

As he writhed in the weightless void, others did the same, their voices mixing with his own as pleas escaped from cracked lips and the endless begging for mercy rose and fell like the breathing of a great beast. From time to time, he was chosen for special attention, clawed monsters with fanged maws latching on, yanking and pulling. The wounds they imparted always healed as quickly as they were wrought, providing an ever-fresh canvas for their masticating artwork.

Time had no meaning; nor did age. And he knew he was never getting out.

This was his due.

This was his eternal payment for the way he had lived his life: He had earned this place in Hell through his sins upon the earth, and yet still, he argued the unfairness to the others he was trapped with. Tough debate, though. There was little on the good side to support his bid for freedom; more to the point, nobody was listening.

He had had his mortal shot. He had chosen his path.

But oh, God, if he'd known, he would have fought the tide in himself, derailed his actions, shifted the consequences away from where they had taken so many lives—including his own.

Trapped in the darkness, tortured with his fellow sinners, desolate and despairing to a degree that even the worst nightmare couldn't approach, a great uncorking occurred, his emotions bubbling up and over—

"Matthias?"

He woke up with a shout, his head flipping off the pillow, his arms punching forward as if he had something to fight.

But there was nothing in front of him. No one tangled with him.

And there was light.

In the dim glow from the bathroom, Mels . . . his beautiful Mels . . . was standing at the foot of the bed in his hotel room. She had her coat on and her purse hanging off her shoulder, as if she had just arrived from work . . . and her expression was nothing remote, everything involved.

Bad dream, he told himself. It had been a bad . . .

The fuck it had been a dream—

"Matthias," she said gently, "are you all right?"

At first he couldn't fathom why she was asking him that. Yeah, he'd had a nightmare, but—

Ah, shit, was he *crying*?

Wiping his cheeks with flat palms, he scrambled off the bed and excused himself for the bathroom. Crying in front of her? Yeah, fuck that for a laugh.

"Just gimme a minute."

Shutting himself in, he braced his hands on the counter and hung his head over the sink. As he cranked the faucet to make it seem like he was doing something other than trying not to be a pussy, he sagged into the modest strength of his arms, attempting to shed the conviction that where he'd been in that dream was in fact not a place he'd actually been to.

Wasn't working.

The Hell he'd just seen was a memory, not a nightmare. And wasn't that enough to get his hands shaking.

Splashing water on his face didn't do shit, and neither did a hard scrub with a white towel. After he used the loo, he went back out—had to. Any longer in the bathroom and Mels was liable to think he'd hanged himself by the belt or something.

As he emerged, he found her sitting in the chair by the windows, her hands in her lap, her head tilted down like she was assessing whether or not she needed to trim her nails.

Aware that he was just in the T-shirt and boxers that he'd bought in the lobby gift shop—and that his ruined legs were on display from midthigh down—he got back under the covers.

"I'm surprised you're here," he said softly as he put the Ray-Bans on.

"Jim Heron's so-called brother brought me over in a cab and let me in."

Damn that man, Matthias thought.

Mels shrugged, like she knew he was pissed. "And you know what?"

"What."

"I don't buy the twin crap for a second. I think that *is* Jim Heron, and that he faked his death for some reason—and I think you know why."

In the pause that followed, it was obvious she expected him to fill in the details, but his brain had pretty much shut down. He didn't want her around the guy, much less alone with him—because he couldn't trust anyone. Especially not with her.

"You were meeting with him when I came out and found you at that garage. Weren't you."

"It's complicated. And as for his name, that's not my story to tell."

"He told me you two had served in the military together." She waited again for him to fill in some information. "It's clear he feels responsible for you."

As the past churned behind the shroud of his amnesia, at least he didn't have to lie to her. "So much of it is . . . a haze. Nothing more." He traced her with his eyes. "I'm glad you came."

There was a long pause. "You want to tell me what you were so upset about just now."

"I don't think you'd believe me."

She laughed a little. "After the last day and a half, I'm more likely to, trust me."

"Why?"

"Everything feels . . . wrong. I mean, it's just been a weird ride, you know." She stared at him as if she were taking his temperature, his blood pressure, and his heart rate from across the room. "Talk to me, Matthias. You gotta open up—and if you can't give me your memories, just tell me where you are."

Closing his eyes, he felt as though he were boxed in, unable to answer, but incapable of ignoring her.

Finally, he murmured, "What would you say if I told you I believe in Hell. And not from a religious standpoint, but because I'd been there—and I think I was sent back here to do something." Man, she was quiet. "I don't know what it is, but I'm going to find it out. Maybe it's a second chance—maybe it's . . . something else."

Cue even more of the silence.

Lifting his lids, he measured her. "I know it sounds crazy, but . . . I woke up naked on Jim's grave, and I think I was put there. Everything before that is a blank, and yet I have this sense that I'm suppose to do something, that there is purpose in my being here . . . and that I don't have forever."

Mels pushed her hair back and cleared her throat. "The blank part is because you've got amnesia."

"Or maybe it's because I'm not supposed to remember. I swear . . . I've been to Hell. I was trapped there with these countless other people in a prison where all there was . . . was suffering. Forever." He rubbed his sternum, and then left his hand where it was, over his heart. "I know it here, in my chest. Just like I know that you and I were supposed to meet the night we did, and we're supposed to be together right now. And yeah, that's nuts, but if the afterlife doesn't exist, why do so many people believe it does?"

Mels shook her head. "I don't know the answer to that."

"I'm glad you're here," he said.

The longer she didn't reply, the more he knew he'd pushed her too far . . . except then she smiled in a sad way.

"My father believed in Heaven and Hell. And not just in theory. Kind of ironic, given how he ran his life. Then again, perhaps he felt like he was personally in charge of the 'wrath of God' side of things on earth."

"He was a churchgoer?"

"Every Sunday. Like clockwork. Maybe he thought it would get

him off the hook for some of his more . . . shall we say, physical cor-
rections of behavior."

"Nothing does that."

As her eyes shot to his, he wanted to curse. Way to go—making
it sound like her pops was in the basement. "What I mean is—"

"He did a lot of good things, too. Saved women and children
from horrible situations, protected the innocent, made sure people
got what they deserved."

"That should work in his favor, then." Lame. So lame. "Look, I
don't mean to suggest—"

"It's okay—"

"No, it's not. I don't know what I'm saying." He put his palms
up. "Don't listen to me. It was just . . . a shitty nightmare—yeah,
nothing but that, and I don't know . . . a goddamn thing."

Liar. Such a liar. But the subtle signs of relief in her, from the
easing of her shoulders to the way she released her breath low and
slow, told him it was worth it. One hundred percent.

"His name was Thomas," she said abruptly. "Everyone called
him 'Carmichael,' though. He meant the world to me—he was
everything I looked up to. Everything I want to be—God, I don't
know why I'm talking about this."

"It's okay," he said softly—because he was hoping that if he
didn't make a lot of noise, she would keep talking.

No such luck. She stopped, and he was surprised by how much
he wanted her to go on. Hell, he'd take any kind of conversation:
her grocery list, her thoughts on air pollution, whether she was a
Democrat or a Republican . . . the theory of relativity.

But man, details of her past? Her parents? That was true gold.

"What about your mom?"

"I'm living with her, actually—since he passed. It's . . . kind of
strained. I had so much more in common with him. With her? I
feel like a bull in a china shop. She's nothing like he was."

"Maybe that's why they worked. Opposites attract and all that."

"I don't know."

"How'd he . . ."

"Die? In a car wreck. He was in a squad car on a chase, and the perpetrator's vehicle blew a tire. Dad swerved to avoid hitting them, lost traction himself, and ended up slamming into a parked utility trailer. They had to cut his body out of the driver's seat."

"I'm . . . so sorry."

"Me, too. I miss him every day, and even though he's gone, I'm still trying to impress him. It's nuts."

"I think he would be proud of you."

"Yeah, I'm not so sure of that. Caldwell is a small pond."

"It's the one he played in."

"Not as a low-level reporter, though."

"Well, considering the way you've treated me, how could anyone not feel right about the way you turned out? You have been . . . really good to a stranger."

Mels stared across the bed at him. "Can I be honest with you?"

"Always."

There was a long pause. "You don't feel like a stranger to me."

"It's the same for me," he said softly. "I feel like I've known you my whole life."

"You don't have any memory."

"I don't need specifics on this one."

She looked down at her hands again, at those blunt nails. "Listen, I need you to tell me about that gun—"

"Like I said, I got it from Jim, when I was at the garage to see him. I took it because I didn't feel safe being unarmed."

"So Heron is alive, and I'm right that the twin thing's a lie." Her eyes met his. "I need to know."

He rubbed his face. "Yeah, it is—but let me be clear. His reasons for playing dead are his problem, not mine. I'm not involved in that shit, and it's going to stay that way."

After a moment, she nodded. "Okay, thanks for telling me. And I guess I can forgive the guy considering he saved my life tonight."

Matthias did a double take, his palm tingling like it wanted to find that gun. "Saved you? How?"

As Matthias sat up in the bed, he was suddenly looking like a very dangerous guy, his body tense, his expression filled with a protective anger that made him seem capable of nearly anything—in her defense.

Mels shifted around, that attraction she'd felt before surging.

"How did he save you," came the growl.

"Well . . ." As she searched for words, she loosened her coat, letting it slide from her shoulders and pool in the chair. "I was at St. Francis following up on some work, and there was a construction zone. Some guy was working overhead, and the ceiling wasn't strong enough to support his weight or something. A bunch of girders and tiles fell down—and like, from out of nowhere, this Heron guy jumps into the room and puts his body in the way. He caught it all, even though God only knew how much it weighed. And then the construction man fell through the opening. He'd had a heart attack, I guess? We were meeting with one of the guys who works in the morgue and he started CPR right away. It was bizarre."

Matthias took a deep breath. Like he was profoundly relieved.

And reactions like that were the reason she trusted him. In spite of all the other stuff.

Mels shook her head. "It was just a freak-accident/close-call kind of thing. But man, I was lucky he was there."

"Can I ask you a favor?"

"Sure."

"Come over here." He held out his hand. "And not because I'm going to make a move on you. I just . . ."

Mels got to her feet right away and crossed the distance between them, sitting down on the edge of the bed beside him, her body leaning toward his. As he took her hand, he rubbed the inside of her wrist with his thumb.

The stroking, more than any words he could have spoken, made her feel precious.

"I'm really glad you came here," he said, again.

"So am I."

Reaching forward, she took the sunglasses from his face, and his eyes dipped down like it was hard for him to let her see him properly.

"I told you, you don't have to be ashamed," she said quietly.

He laughed with an edge. "About what?"

"The way you look."

His eyes swung back. "What if I told you that wasn't the problem."

"Then what is?"

"I'm not sure you want me to answer that."

Leaning in, she traced the scars at his temple, and brushed over the brow above the eye that no longer worked. "I like the truth."

He cursed low in his throat. "Goddamn it, woman . . . you're killing me."

"No, I'm not."

Matthias's lids closed for a second, like he was digging deep for self-control. "Do you know what I'm regretting most at this moment?"

"What?"

"That I didn't know you before. That way I could . . ."

"Could what?"

As he focused on her mouth, she had a quick urge to lick her lips—and as she gave in to it, he shifted under the covers like his body needed something from her.

Man, it was hot in the room all of a sudden.

"I want to make love to you, Mels. Right here, right now. Matter of fact, I've wanted you all along. The instant I saw you in the hospital—that's when it happened for me."

Okay . . . wow. And maybe another woman could have played things coy—but she wasn't interested in games.

"Me, too." God, had that come out of her mouth? "I mean, look, it's been a while for me, so this is all a huge surprise . . . but there was something different about you from the moment I—" She had to laugh a little. "The moment I hit you with my car."

That hand of his captured hers again, the stroking resuming.

"Thank you," he said.

"For what?"

"I don't know."

She wasn't sure she believed that. "Do you really think you're not attractive?"

"You just saw me in boxers."

Mels shook her head. "I'm not one of those shallow chicks who needs a guy all jacked up with muscles. There's so much more to it than that."

"Maybe, but I'm pretty certain you'd like your man to be able to have sex with you."

Mels opened her mouth. Shut it. Opened it again.

"Exactly."

Shit. That probably should have occurred to her, given the other scars on his lower body. . . .

"Straight up, Mels, the only reason I haven't completely jumped you is because I can't. I . . . can't." He threw up his free hand and let it fall back down to the bedspread. "And you know what sucks? I've been with a lot of women."

Annnnnnnd that made her chest hurt. "Before you were injured . . ."

He nodded. "Of all the things for my memory to come back on, right?"

Cue another kick in the solar plexus. "You remember them?"

"I hate it—because I would trade every single random fuck for just one night with you." He brushed her face with his fingertips and then brought his thumb to her mouth. With the same gentle pressure he'd put against her wrist, he caressed her lower lip. "I'd give up every one of them. Matter of fact, it feels like . . . a curse to have finally found someone like you, only to have it be too late. And that's where it's at. It's too late for me, Mels, and that's how you're killing me. When I look at you, when I see you move, when you smile or take a deep breath, I just . . . I die a little. Every time."

Mels felt tears prick the corners of her eyes, an emotion she couldn't define striking her heart and making it ring.

"You liked kissing me," she said roughly.

"No. I loved it. I want to be doing it right now. I want . . . to do other things to you, just to make you feel good. But that's as far as it would go—and whereas that's more than enough for me, I know at some point, tonight, tomorrow, next week . . . it's not going to be enough for you."

She pressed a kiss to his hand. "I thought you were leaving."

"I am. That was just a rhetorical example."

Maybe. But it gave her a little hope, and she suddenly needed that like she had to have air.

"Mels, I—"

Swooping in, she stopped whatever it was he was going to say with her own mouth. At first, as the contact was made, his lips were stiff against her own, but that didn't last. Soon enough, he was moving against her, wanting, taking. Licking. Nipping.

When she finally eased back, she was out of breath. "Don't make up my mind for me, okay?"

It was clear she wasn't the only one affected, because his chest was rising and falling with an urgency that turned her on.

"I don't need sex to be happy with you," she told him. "It's honestly not that important—"

With a sudden surge, he all but pounced on her, pushing her back against the mattress and kissing her hard and deep. As his body covered hers, his tongue entered her, owning her in a way that was so complete, she hadn't realized until that moment exactly how anemic any other man had been.

That heat that had sprung up exploded, the blood in her veins going into a roar in the space between heartbeats.

And that was before his hands started to undo her clothes.

Chapter Twenty-nine

As things went all Barry White and shit in the hotel room, Adrian backed out of there quietly, passing through the closed door and emerging into the hallway.

Jim had turfed the babysitting to him and taken off as soon as the reporter was at the Marriott, and that was all fine and dandy—but he wasn't into live porn unless he was personally involved, thank you very much. He was, however, completely into giving that pair plenty of Devina-free time. Shutting his eyes, he placed his palm on the wood of the exit he'd used and put a seal on the room, not just at its entrance, but all around the inside and into the bathroom.

Then he settled against the tone-on-tone wallpaper and shoved his hands in his pockets.

Now he knew why Jim smoked. Helped pass time when the dead zones came.

Man, that poor bastard Matthias, he thought. Then again, there were worse things than having a limp dick. Plus, that was what happened when you stepped on land mines or bombs or whatever the hell it had been: You blow your shit up, you can't expect to be able to bone your female—

Down at the other end of the hall, the elevator doors opened and a woman stepped out, along with a daughter who was probably five or six. The former looked like she'd been through a war—or at least a lineup of bouncers: her hair was a mess, her sloping shoulders were strung with bags, and a lone suitcase was trailing after her on wheels like a sulking dog. The kid, on the other hand, was all firecracker, bouncing up and down, running up and back, her voice shrill enough to shatter glass.

Or, in the alternative, make you want to break it with your own head.

Adrian sat back while the parade went by him, keeping himself invisi. But that didn't last—the little girl picked up on his presence, slowing to a stop and staring at where he was standing.

"Come on, Liza," the mom said. "We're down this way."

"Mommy, there's a angel here—"

"No, there isn't."

"But mommy, there so is! There's a angel right here!"

"There is *no* one there. Will you come on?"

As the child just looked at him with big hazel eyes the size of car tires, Exhausto-mom came over and did a drag-away.

But mommy dearest had nailed it, he thought.

He didn't feel like an angel. Never had, really—and Eddie's death had taken away any small sense of responsibility to live up to the name. That dead SOB had been the standard to measure himself against. The one who was good and true. The compass . . .

Unable to stay still, Ad pushed himself out of his lean and headed for the elevator. Jabbing a finger into the *down* button, the doors opened immediately, the car that the mother/daughter pair had used still in place. On the ride down, he made himself visi, fixed his hair in the bronze mirrored panels, and straightened his leather jacket.

The prep work did nothing to improve his image. Then again, the problem was his expression. He looked like he was ready to bite someone's head off.

Ding!

As the doors opened, he stepped out and long-legged it to the bar. Unfortunately, the place wasn't seedy enough to attract the kind of woman he was after: no half-dressed Goths in the mix, with Prozac smiles and knees that liked to fall open—but that didn't mean he couldn't find a volunteer.

Taking a seat in a darkened corner, he let his need for sex waft out from his body.

And whaddaya know, every woman who came in, walked by, or even registered for a room all the way across the lobby looked in his direction.

The waitress who'd served him and Jim the night before came right over. "Hi."

Her smile was half-lidded and really not professional. Especially as her eyes drifted down everything he had to display.

Which happened to include an unapologetic hard-on.

"What can I get you?" she drawled.

She was good-looking in a way that was tied primarily to her youth. Skin was glowing, hair was lush and healthy, body was banging. A closer gander at her features suggested that if you added twenty years and twenty pounds she'd be anonymous in middle age, but he was all about the here and now anyway.

"They give you any breaks at this place?" he said in a low voice.

"Yeah." Smile got even bigger. "They do."

"When."

"Ten minutes."

"Where can I have you."

Her lips parted like she needed more oxygen. "Where do you want me . . . ?"

"Here. Now." He glanced around the bar. "But that would give people a helluva show."

As his eyes swung back, he looked her up and down, and pictured fucking her from the front, her legs wide around his hips, his cock going in and out as he watched the sex. . . .

Okay, the theory didn't really excite him as much—but that was the difference between porn and true penetration. The actual? That was what he was after.

The conversation with his waitress around The Plan was hushed and quick, but it wasn't a business transaction. She was not a whore being bought; she was a red-blooded woman who wanted a good fuck just like he did.

With things set, Adrian left the bar, his body humming, his heart cold as a meat locker. As they'd discussed, he hung a louie and took the ornate stairwell down to the spa. On the descent, the sound of his heavy boots echoed up into the marble ceiling, and the scent of sea salts and minerals and perfumed oils made him want to breathe through his mouth, not his nose.

He sneezed when he got to the bottom, but at least he didn't have to go through the glass doors of the spa. If the shit smelled this strong on the outside, the interior would probably melt his sinuses.

Taking another left, he went down a whitewashed hall that was marked with black-and-white photographs of half-naked chicks in geometric poses. The door at the end was marked with a discreet Staff Only sign, and he waited at it with no patience whatsoever, breathing that thick air that clogged his lungs.

Shit. He couldn't breathe—

His waitress opened up and grabbed his hand. "This way."

It was a different world on the far side. No pictures, no smooth walls, just old, exposed brick and flooring that had a worn groove down the center. But it wasn't like he'd come here to enjoy the scenery—at least, not the hotel's.

Looking over her shoulder, the female smiled in a manic way, like this was more fun than she'd had on her shift for, like, ever. "If anyone sees us, you're my cousin from out of town, okay?"

"Sure, whatever." Provided no one caught them in the act. Kissing wasn't going to be the half of it.

He followed her into a staff room that was in shambles, all kinds of bags and clothes strewn around mismatched furniture, the combustion of multiple perfumes creating a stale smell that made the place seem hotter. On the other side, there was yet another door, and this one opened up into an even dingier hallway that was clearly the colon of the original hotel structure.

And currently used, at least partially, as a storage area: Lined up against the rough walls, banquet chairs were stacked six to eight feet tall, the brass of all those legs and the bloodred velvet seats providing some kind of cover.

"We have fifteen minutes," she said, putting her arms around his neck.

Adrian took the woman's mouth like he was going to take the rest of her, hard and deep, his tongue extending and finding hers. In response, she clawed at his back, her nails digging into the leather of his jacket as one of her legs lifted from the floor and curled around his thigh. With rough hands, he popped her skirt up. She was wearing stockings that had looked professional enough in the bar; in reality, she had them pinned to a garter belt, and was sporting a thong.

The cheeks he grabbed onto were firm and high, and he spun her around in front of him, her hair swinging in a circle as she faced the sweaty brick wall. Getting down on his knees, he bit one side of her ass, sinking his teeth into her flesh as he took that thong south.

The sexual urge he rode had nothing to do with her. She was just the living, breathing equivalent of a StairMaster, something to work his edge off with, a vessel to pour the overspill of his anger and frustration and grief into.

And given the ease with which she met him here, and kissed him here, and was letting him do her here . . . he had the feeling this was not the first time she'd let herself get used like this.

Maybe she was using him for the same reason.

With the thong around her ankles and her skirt up over his head, he went down on her from behind, taking her with his mouth, penetrating her with his tongue. She tasted good, her electrolyzed sex supersmooth and ultrawet against his lips, everything fragrant and clean, as if she had standards for herself.

After she'd come a couple of times—he had no idea of the count, because the truth was, he didn't really care—he got up and initiated a trade of places so he had his back to the wall. As the woman made like she was going to try to suck him off, her knees bending as her painted nails did the deed on his zipper, he stopped that bright idea by picking her up by the thighs and splitting her legs around his hips.

He didn't want her mouth on him.

Too personal, as weird as that sounded.

Just as Ad was about to push inside her, he froze.

Jim Heron was standing opposite them, the angel's arms crossed over his chest, his eyes narrowed and pissed off.

Nice timing. Fucking great.

But he wasn't stopping now. His balls were tight as fists, and the top of his cock was about to blow off.

Ad shrugged at the guy and entered the woman. If Jim wanted to watch, that was fine. Hell, if he wanted to join in, that was okay, too.

Although the latter seemed unlikely, given that I'm-going-to-kick-your-ass expression.

Whatever.

Closing his eyes, Ad gave himself over to the slick compression he'd taken solace in so many times in the past.

God, he missed Eddie so much it hurt.

Six floors up, in his room, Matthias was unleashed. Unhinged. Unraveled.

As he kissed Mels, he went to the buttons on her silk blouse and freed them one by one, the fine fabric parting to reveal even softer skin . . . and a pair of cotton-covered breasts that knocked him the hell out. God, it was all too much already, the noises of their lips together, their panting breath, their clothes shifting around—the sight of her. And then there was the way she moved against him, her body undulating in waves that brought those breasts up to his chest and then her hips into his.

He wanted his mouth all over her, and that was going to happen *now*—starting with her throat. Nipping his way down the smooth column to her collarbone, he brought his hand to just beneath her breast, brushing his thumb against the cup of her bra.

He meant to tease a little—didn't last.

"Oh, God, yes . . ." she said as he felt her up.

At the sound of her groaning voice, he had to pause and collect himself, his head ducking into her hair as he struggled for control: The need to consume her was so great, he was a little shaken by it, because he didn't know himself enough to trust that he wouldn't hurt her.

There was no going back, though.

That bra was gone a heartbeat later: Springing the front clasp, he stared down at her pink nipples and her pale curves.

He growled at that point. At least, he assumed that noise came from him.

Either that or a puma had somehow slipped into the room.

Matthias dipped his head and sucked one tip into his mouth, his tongue swirling around, flicking, licking. He didn't leave the other side alone, couldn't—his fingers pinched, then tweaked her tight little nipple, telling it to hang on; he'd be there in a second—

A sudden sting at the nape of his neck told him she had dug in, and abruptly, her thighs went wide as if her sex were dictating her movements, not her mind—and that vital core that defined her as a woman wanted what he could give her.

Or rather . . . wanted what he might have given her, if he could have.

Shit.

Even with her bumping and grinding against his pelvis, and in spite of the heat that was raging in his blood, his body couldn't respond as a male's should. There was no hard arousal to sink into her, no erection she could grab onto, no thick cock she might wrap her lips around in payback for what was going to be done to her in another minute or two.

As a crushing sadness came over him, threatening to derail the session, a single moan from her was enough to get him back online: None of that mattered. All he wanted was to make her feel good, so when push came to shove—or rather, when she was going to want something to be pushable or shovable—he was just going to have to get creative.

Lifting his head, he stared into her flushed face and her wild eyes. That hair of hers was loose around the pillow, all wavy and spread out, and her cheeks were the color of Christmas.

Man, she was incredible.

Keeping their eyes locked, he rose up off her so that he was kneeling between her split legs. And in that pause, before things got really serious, he imagined himself as he had been, strong, powerful, his body as dominant as his will was.

As it stood now, he was glad he had the undershirt on. And he felt . . . really lucky.

She had everything to offer; he had nothing. And yet she wanted him anyway.

It was at that moment that he fell in love with her.

The shift in his heart and soul made no sense, and yet the emotional logic was so persuasive, the center of his chest resonated with a warmth that had never been there before: He knew without the specifics that he had spent a lifetime engaged in complicated cruelty, and yet here he was, naked before her though he was clothed, accepted for who he was on the inside, not for what he didn't look like and couldn't do.

The revelation changed him internally, putting him into a gear that was slower than the mad rush that he'd all but tackled her with.

Now he moved deliberately, his hands going to the button and zipper of her slacks, and undoing things at an unhurried pace. Opening the fly wide, he curled down and pressed a kiss to her lower abdomen, halfway between her belly button and the top of her sensible, mind-blowingly erotic bikini panties.

Who needed that fussy lace and satin crap? Simple cotton did it for him, as long as she was the one wearing it.

Man, he wanted to suck on her through the damn things.

"I'm gonna get you naked," he said in a voice warped with sex.

With another one of those holy-shit moans of hers, Mels cranked her head to the side and watched him pull off what covered her lower body, one hand drifting to her mouth and touching it.

Matthias reached up and edged her fingers between her lips. "Suck on them for me—oh, fuck, yeah . . ."

She did exactly what she was told, her cheeks drawing in as she complied, then her tongue parting through her fore- and middle fingers before the knuckles disappeared from sight again.

"Like this?" she said after pulling them free.

He had to close his eyes. It was either that or pass the fuck out . . . because all he could imagine was his cock in that wet, warm hold, her down at his hips, her head going forward and back as that suction was all around him.

"You're beautiful," he growled as he tossed her pants over his shoulder.

Time to get to work.

His lips lingered along the top edge of the panties, tracing the way to one hip while his fingers trailed his mouth, touching lightly, caressing. When he got to the side, he took the cotton off her body, slipping it down her long legs.

He made love to her with his mouth.

It was the best sexual experience of his life. Everything was about her: how she felt, what she liked, how far he could push her before he had to let her climax . . . and it was amazing. He also had no intention of stopping anytime soon. Cupping her with his palms, he lifted up her hips and tilted them as he stretched out, ready to stay forever.

And it wasn't like he couldn't get inside her.

Straightening his tongue, he penetrated her core rhythmically, alternating the surges with great laps that tickled the top of her sex. Quicker. Deeper. Harder. He wanted her to fall apart on him over and over again, to keep coming against his lips, to burst free and twinkle back down to earth for the rest of their natural lives.

"Give me what I want," he said. "Give me what I need. . . ."

Putting his fingers in his mouth, he slicked them up and sank them in, and oh, man, it was good. Especially as she orgasmed, the pulsing clenches something that seemed to flood through him as if he were releasing along with her.

When it was over, he paused to catch his breath, and she lay there in glorious abandon, her breasts heaving, her body loose all over, her skin flushed.

It took her a while to recover. She even tried to speak a couple of times, but couldn't follow through.

Kinda made a guy feel like a man.

"That was . . . unbelievable."

Her words were more purr than voice, and wasn't that just fucking great.

As Matthias smiled, he felt just a little evil—not in a bad way, but in the masculine way—like when you had the woman you wanted naked, on her back, on your bed, and you had every intention of showing her some more attention.

"Would you like me to keep going?" he said on a dark drawl.

Chapter Thirty

As Jim stood in that underground hallway, he was ready to rip his wingman a new one.

Of course, to do that, he'd have to peel that waitress off the bastard—and as much as he was a hands-on kind of guy, he wasn't prepared to get that close to the Saran Wrap situation.

Fucker.

Literally.

And, yup, this happy little bump and grind put him in an even worse frame of mind: He'd come down to the Marriott ready to rip Adrian a new one over those photographs of that prostitute—and instead of finding the angel on the job, outside Matthias's room? The SOB was nailing this chick in the same hallway where that operative had been killed by Devina the night before.

Like Jim didn't already have a hair across his ass.

Those photographs, those goddamn photographs . . .

Adrian had said he'd been to a murder scene with Mels—and

now the woman was showing up with pictures of a female victim whose hair had been dyed blond, and whose throat had been slit wide, talking about a pattern of runes that had been in the skin of the abdomen, but was now—gasp!—not there anymore?

That angel had to be the "why" behind the disappearance.

So it was time to have a come to Jesus with Mr. Eraser.

Meeting Adrian's stare, he dared the guy to keep up with the fucking, and—shocker—the son of a bitch did.

The waitress was having a great time—at least, going from what Jim could see from the rear, her head thrashing, that hair flying, those arms contracting around Ad's neck. For a moment, Jim thought back to some of his own sexual exploits—but then he settled on memories that weren't relevant in the slightest:

Him with Devina. Used and abused by her and her minions in her Well of Souls.

He had no idea why he'd dwell on the shit. That hadn't been about sex; it had been torture, plain and simple, and God knew he'd been trained for that.

Still, the images stayed with him, lingering in the background like a stink.

Made no sense. He'd had bones broken before—on purpose, by an enemy. He'd been cut in the past, too—strung up by his feet and beaten like a punching bag . . . oh, yeah, and that time in Budapest when he'd been packed into that car, driven out to the country, and left for dead after getting worked over with a claw hammer—

Abruptly, the waitress moaned the way women did when they weren't faking it: this was not a contrived, pretty little sound engineered to make a guy think he was a sex god. This was the real kind, when the female was coming so hard she wasn't even aware of the animal grunts she was throwing out.

As she thrashed, Adrian supported her up off the floor with barely any effort—then again, the chick was synched up hard, locked on him tighter than a coat of paint. And, shit, their movements were so universal, him pumping in an ever-increasing rhythm, her getting tossed around as those penetrations were received, absorbed, enjoyed. Watching it all, Jim probably should have been aroused. Should have wanted in.

At the very least, he should have stayed pissed off.

Instead, panic tingled on the fringes of his mind, memories of his arms pinned down and his own legs spread putting a fine sheen of sweat above his upper lip.

He turned away, not because he was so angry he was going to kill Adrian, and not because he was disgusted or too modest for the show.

His stomach churned.

The hands that took out his cigarettes shook ever so slightly, and the sounds as Adrian orgasmed made him shut his eyes for a second.

Naturally, the horny bastard went for a twofer with no recovery time.

And Jim couldn't actually start smoking until the woman was gone.

Great.

When the pneumatics were finally over, Jim glanced across his shoulder. Adrian had slid the girl down to the ground and was letting her rest her head against his pecs. As he stroked her hair, he seemed utterly detached from her, to the point where he might as well have been in another zip code. Matter of fact, except for the instants when he'd shot his load, he appeared to have been on some kind of erotic autopilot the entire time.

Why the hell did he bother?

The waitress checked her watch, pulled herself together, and kissed Ad on the lips. Just before she left, she took a pen out and grabbed for Ad's hand. With big strokes, she inked a number into his palm, and then curled his fingers up like she'd given him some sort of gift. Then on a twirl of her hair, she was off, all but skipping down the corridor in the direction that would take her to the restaurant's kitchen.

Adrian did up the front of his pants with efficiency. "Before you get on your high horse, I put a protection spell all over the room. They're fine."

Jim lit up and exhaled hard, the smoke shooting out of his mouth. "What the fuck would Eddie think about this?"

Those already icy eyes narrowed into slits. "Excuse me?"

"You heard what I said."

Adrian jabbed a finger. "You do not play that card. Ever—"

"What would he think about you down here, fucking some chick on the job." Jim turned his coffin nail around and looked at the bright, glowing tip. "And you didn't even seem to enjoy it—so it's not like you're off post for a good reason."

Waves of rage distorted the air between them, the other angel's anger so palpable it was practically a light source.

"I'm going to tell you this once," the guy said. "And only once—"

"Eddie wouldn't have been impressed by this—"

The attack was so fast, so vicious, Jim didn't have time to ditch his cigarette. As Ad locked on Jim's throat with both hands, that lit tip went up . . . and came down right in the collar of his shirt.

But the burn was the least of his problems.

Jacking his hands between them, he split that hold wide-open and snapped a head butt out, catching the other angel right in the soft cartilage of the schnoz. Except, apparently, Adrian didn't have any feeling there either—he just threw out a curving right-hander that slammed into the side of Jim's ear like an SUV.

Listing off to the side, he caught himself on a stand of chairs and one-eightied his momentum, pitching himself back at the guy—

who happened to have found his fighting stance and was clearly ready to turn this into a UFC free-for-all.

There was a huge part of Jim that also wanted a good, bloody hand-to-hand fight with the guy. But it was hard to pull the soapbox, superior thing about Eddie when he was prepared to go a hundred and fifty rounds with the dumb man-whore down in this corridor.

One gut shot put a stop to the whole thing.

Jim faked out like he was coming in high, and Ad was so pissed off and juiced, the guy fell for it. As he left his navel undefended, Jim went in low and fast—so fast there was no chance to block, and so low that the cock and balls were involved.

Motherfucker was going to sing the high notes like Justin-cocksucking-Timberlake for a while.

Adrian caved in around his groin, his hands formed a protective cup that was about three seconds too late to protect his nads.

Jim shook the now-crushed cig out of his shirt. His skin had been burned on his shoulder, but compared to the ringing in his ears, it was nothing.

Wonder if he had a concussion.

More dementia was *not* what they needed in this round.

Standing over the bastard, Jim said in a guttural voice, "I know what you did."

Adrian let one knee go down to the concrete floor. Then the other. "Duh. You frickin' watched."

"The prostitute. The runes on her stomach. You burned 'em off her, didn't you."

Ad started flapping his lips, but the curses didn't carry far.

"Let me make myself perfectly clear." Jim leaned over and put his face right in the guy's grille. "You ever keep information from me again, and you're off the team—if Nigel won't arrange for it, I'll fucking take care of the job. Do you understand me."

Not a question.

As Adrian's eyes lifted, they were like two blowtorches mounted through the back of his skull, but Jim didn't give a shit. The angel could go volcano if he wanted; they were *not* going to operate on any other terms.

When Ad finally spoke, the words were hoarse, the other angel's lungs still more focused on reoxygenation from the shot to the nuts than allowing him to bitch. "Do you think Devina . . . did that because it was going to *help* you?"

"Not the point." Jim shook his head. "You do *not* get to edit this game—"

"Oh, so I'm an asshat because I was trying to help you—"

"I need to know what she's doing."

Ad fell back on his ass and scrubbed his face. "Come on, Jim, she's trying to fuck your head because you won't let her fuck your body. That and a physics equation and you can solve the mysteries of the goddamn universe. You know this. So why are the particulars of the message important."

"If I can't trust you, I don't know where I really stand."

"And if she gets under your skin, we've lost both you and Eddie."

Their competing logic drained the final vestiges of emotion out of the air, leaving a pervasive exhaustion that was clearly communal.

"Goddamn it," Jim breathed, as he sat next to the guy.

"That about covers things."

Jim took out his Marlboros. The pack was mangled, a couple of the cigs cracked in half and therefore unusable. But he found at least one that was still intact enough to light.

As he lit up, he glanced over at where the fucking had gone down. The weakness he'd felt in those moments was just one more reason to hate the enemy.

Adrian glanced across. "Eddie would have done the same thing about those runes."

"No, he wouldn't have."

Those eyes turned hard again. "You didn't know him longer than a matter of weeks. Trust me—he did what was necessary in all circumstances, and anything that has to do with Sissy Barten is your Achilles' heel."

"Obstructing information—"

"Can we just drop this—"

"—is as close to a crime as men like you and I have."

"—and get back to work."

As tempers simmered again, like their respective pots had been returned to the godforsaken stove, Jim cursed. See, this was the problem with Eddie being gone. No ref to call the shot or the foul and get the pair of them back on track.

No voice of reason.

And Ad kind of had a point. Jim was a little obsessed about Sissy, and Devina was smart enough to know that. But after years of being in the field, the one thing Jim knew to value as much as his own competence was intel—information was always the best weapon and the strongest shield you had against your enemy. If you knew their thinking and their actions, their locations and their movements, you could formulate your strategy.

"There isn't a lot of solid ground in this game," Jim said after a while. "I'm fighting on sand, against an opponent who's got her stilettos on concrete. Shit's already stacked against us, and if you're filtering, that's one more thing I gotta frickin' worry about."

Adrian looked over, all dead fucking serious. "I wasn't trying to fuck you. Honest."

Jim cursed out an exhale. "I believe you."

"I won't do it again."

"Good."

In the aftermath, although they didn't hug it up or some shit, he figured they could give themselves gold stars: This argument had gone so much better than that first one at the side of the road. Back then, Eddie had had to pry them apart. Guess they were making progress.

"One last question."

Adrian glanced over. "G'head."

"What did it say?"

As silence stretched out, Jim figured it wasn't a good sign. Yup . . . if someone like Ad was actually choosing his words, it was a really bad goddamn sign.

"Do you want to win this?" the other angel demanded. "And I'm not talking about just this round. I'm talking about the whole goddamn war."

Jim narrowed his eyes. "Yeah. I do."

Jesus, he realized, that actually was the truth.

"Then don't ask me to translate. Nothing good's going to come out of it."

There was a tense silence while Jim measured his partner: man, Adrian was meeting him right in the eye, without any kind of pre-varication, everything in that big body still as if he were praying for the right answer to come back at him.

Shit, the burn to know to the particulars was like the worst kind of indigestion . . . but it was hard to argue with the other angel's dead-and-serious.

"Okay," Jim said roughly. "Fair enough."

Up in Matthias's room on the sixth floor, Mels lay lax on the bed, her arms loose, her legs twitching involuntarily, her mind blown and then some.

She felt like she'd had the best workout she'd ever gotten at the gym, followed it by the most incredible yoga session, and topped things off with a visit to a spa that specialized in deep-tissue massage and reflex-frigging-ology.

Oh, and also sat down at a DIY sundae bar that had hot fudge made out of Lindt truffles.

Bliss. Pure bliss. The best sex she'd ever had, even though they hadn't actually had sex . . .

Next to her, Matthias was curled on his side, his head on the only pillow left on the bed, one arm tucked in, a little self-satisfied smile on his harsh face. Looking over at him, unexpected tears pricked the corners of her eyes. He'd been so generous, not asking for anything in return, seemingly satiated just by the act of making her feel good.

"What's wrong," he said quietly as he brushed away a tear with his forefinger. "Did I hurt you?"

"No, God no . . . I just . . ." It was hard to explain without running the risk of his feeling inadequate—and that was the last thing she wanted, after all he had done for her. "Just emotional, I guess."

"Bullshit. You know what it is." His voice was level, his hand steady as he stroked back her hair. "And you can tell me."

"I don't want to ruin this." She sniffed a little. "It was so perfect."

"So what are these for?" Matthias turned that forefinger around so she could see the glistening on the tip. "Talk to me, Mels."

"I really wish I could give you the same . . . you know, I want to do those things to you."

His expression didn't change, but she knew she'd hit him where it hurt: She could tell by the way his breath stopped, and then abruptly resumed—like he'd reminded himself to draw air.

"I'd like that, too," he said roughly. "But even if my plumbing worked, what I've got to offer you isn't worth seeing, much less touching."

"I told you, you're—"

"And besides, what we did is more than enough for me." Now he smiled, though his eyes remained grave. "I'll always remember it—and you."

A cold wave of dread rippled through her, replacing the warmth.

"Do you have to go?" she asked after a moment.

"Yeah, I do."

Mels reached over and pulled the blankets around her body. "When?"

"Soon."

"Do me a favor?"

"Anything."

"Tell me before you do. Don't let me find out because I can't get ahold of you. Promise me that."

"If I can, I will—"

"Not good enough. Swear to me that you'll tell me—because I can't . . . I don't want to live with the uncertainty. That'll be hell for me."

He closed his eyes briefly. "Okay. I'll let you know. But I need something in return."

"What?"

"Stay with me tonight. I want to wake up with you."

Her body eased, her heart unclenching. "Me, too."

When he held his arms out, she nestled in against him, putting her head against his chest, hearing the beat of his heart as his hands circled her back, and rubbed slow and even. Talking about sex and departures made her anxious; the contact, however, calmed her down to the point where she began to drift off.

Unfortunately, she had a feeling he wasn't doing the same, and wished there was some way to have him relax. But it appeared this was yet another thing about them that was a one-way street.

"Matthias?"

"Yeah?"

I love you, she finished in her head. I love you even though it doesn't make sense.

"After you go, can you ever come back?"

"I don't want to lie to you," he said hoarsely.

"Then I guess you'd better not answer that."

Matthias turned his face into her hair and kissed her. "I won't leave you hanging."

Oh, but he would. After this was all over, she had a feeling she was going to be looking for him in any crowd, on every sidewalk, around each corner.

For the rest of her life.

Loss just plain sucked, she thought. And one would assume that as you got older, along with the other skills that you developed whether you wanted to or not, you'd get better at it.

Instead, it just seemed to kick up all the full list of things that you'd been forced by fate to leave behind: The fact that he was going to peel out of her life like a car pulling away from a curb made her feel as though her father had died yesterday.

Mels shifted her arms so she could hug him as well. And of course, the instant her hands made contact with his body, he stiffened—but screw that. He was going to have to let her touch him in some way.

Battered though he was . . . scarred though his skin remained . . . he was beautiful to her.

"You've ruined me for other men, you know," she said.

He laughed harshly. "Not unless you like the Frankenstein types—"

Mels jacked her head up. "Stop it. Just—stop it. You can't keep me from giving a crap about you, and you're just going to have to suck it up if I want to put my hands on you. We clear?"

In the dim light that came from the bathroom, he started to

smile, but then lost the expression, a strange emotion filtering through his features.

In a low voice, he said, "You're an angel, you know that?"

Mels rolled her eyes and put her head back on his pec. "Hardly. You haven't heard me curse yet?"

"Who says angels can't have potty mouths."

"No way."

"Oh, and when have you met one lately?"

For some stupid reason, an image of Jim Heron jumping forward and putting his own body in the way of that ceiling panel shot into her head.

Unless he'd shown up at that very moment, she might have been killed.

"Actually, maybe you have a point," she said on a shiver. "I could see how they're out there . . . I really could."

Chapter
Thirty-one

"Pablo, are you kidding me?" The woman jacked forward in the chair. "This is . . . *blond.*"

The inflection in that high-pitched voice made it sound as if someone had taken a dump on the crown her head.

As opposed to turning her tacky-ass bright red hair into a yellow that perfectly complemented her chemically peeled complexion.

Frankly, Devina was a little offended. The shit was hot.

Staring out of Pablo's eyes, the demon put the man's hands on his hips and decided that being in a service industry didn't suit her. What a pain. In. The. Ass. Bitch had been thirty minutes late for the appointment, had wanted a soda while she processed—like this place was a fucking restaurant?—and then had whined about the temperature of the rinse at the sink.

And now this attitude.

"I tink you vill like eet when eet's blown dry."

The voice Devina spoke with was smooth and slightly accented with a no-way-to-place South American-ish variant. Then again, Pablo was a self-invention, apparently, a human who, much like she did, chose to clothe himself in ways that made him better than he really looked, sounded, and came from.

He was actually from Jersey.

She'd Googled him at his desk when things had been cooking on that head, because there had been nothing else to do—and God knew talking to the client was enough to make her want to have Pablo shoot himself in the head.

Maybe she should have let a couple of the assistants stay? Nah, then she'd have had to deal with them as well.

"Let mee vork viz eet," she said though Pablo's mouth as she ran the man's hands through the long, wet tangles. "I vork wiz eet. You see."

The client went on a tirade, reminding Devina of some of those nutjobs from the *Bridezillas* marathon she'd caught on WE TV the other night—and also of why she could never be a lesbian. Jim Heron's flavor of swinging-dick, macho-bullshit double cross was easier to put up with than this inexorable, soul-sucking, passive-aggressive melodrama:

". . . blahblahblah! Blah-blah! Blah blah blahblahblahblah *blah blah* . . ."

The blabbering kept up for a while, but like all deluges, eventually the shit stopped. "Fine," the bitch said. "But I'd better like it."

Devina smiled with the stylist's mouth and picked up a brush and hair dryer. Using the kind of long, even strokes she did her own hair with, she set about straightening the semi-curly lengths. As she worked, she thought back to a month ago, when she had come in for her own appointment on time—Pablo was the best in town, after all—only to find this nasty-ass woman had barged in, all on fire about the cut she had been given. Pablo had deferred to the loud noise because there had been no other choice, plopping her into the chair, hitting the hair with a spray bottle of water, getting out the scissors.

Devina had been delayed nearly an hour, and all for less than a sixteenth of an inch taken off the ends.

Like the bitch did her hair in the morning with the help of a tape measure?

Sometimes karma really did come back and bite you on the ass.

It took forever to dry the combination of extensions and real stuff, but Devina wasn't worried about an intrusion: she'd locked the front door of the salon, and there was no way to see inside this far back. Also, the quiet location was another thing working in her favor. Pablo's establishment was in the ritzy part of town, on a street jam-packed with stores that sold French bedding, English stationery, and Italian shoes.

This was the land of the country-club wifey, and that meant everything else but this salon closed at six o'clock.

Generally speaking, fembots had to earn their keep when their husbands came home.

And on that note, Devina had a feeling that the chick in the chair was someone's second wife. Between the fake boobs, the Botox, and the too-thin thing, she was a brittle, jumpy version of a woman—which was what came when you liked things you couldn't afford, and had sold yourself to an old goat to get them.

Then again, maybe she was banging her "Pilates teacher" on the side.

When Devina finally had Pablo's hands put the dryer and the brush down, the bitch was leaning forward in the chair, fluffing everything out and turning this way and that.

She liked it.

"Well, I'm not paying you. This wasn't what I asked for, and I hate it." Except she was making these pursey puckers with her injected lips, like she was posing for a camera. "I am *not* paying."

Actually, this was good. Less of a chance that she'd be tied to Pablo. Devina wasn't about to lose her stylist, and he was just a medium in all this, a pass-through point that wouldn't remember a thing.

The client picked up her ridiculous Takashi Murakami LV bag—like someone hadn't told her you needed to be fifteen to carry that shit off? "I don't know how much longer I can keep coming here."

Hah. Devina knew the answer to that one.

Not. Long.

Pablo's mouth started flapping, that falsely accented voice doing all kinds of ego petting as the target marched into the changing room and shut the door.

With a little time on her hands, Devina sent Pablo's legs over to the reception desk. She wanted to check and see when her next appointment was, but everything was computerized, and although she could Google stuff, she was no hacker.

It was at the end of this week, wasn't it?

When the woman came out—clothed in a "fashion-forward" ensemble that appeared to have been put together by a color-blind cubist who hated her—she seemed to already be getting into the habit of swinging the blond around.

This woman deserved to die on too many levels to count.

"Pablo" escorted his client to the door, and that meant it was time for Devina to pare off from her host. As she separated herself from the Jersey-boy-gone-Rio, she left him with no memory of having seen his last client. As far as he knew, the woman who was now a blonde hadn't showed up—and the police, when they found the body, wouldn't be able to trace the hair color to him.

Devina hadn't used the stuff at the color bar. Too complicated. More L'Oréal.

And during processing, she'd slipped out the back and put the box and the used tube and bottle in some random car that was parked two shops down.

No one was going to associate this with Pablo—and if they did, he was going to pass any lie detector with flying colors, because as far as he was concerned, he'd never seen the bitch.

Outside, the air was crisp, and Devina assumed an anonymous male image as she fell in lockstep behind the newly blonded. The woman immediately got her cell phone out, like she was all excited to share her tale of trauma at the hair salon.

Sorry, sweetie, that was a no-go.

With a quick blink of energy, Devina knocked out the iWhatever—which was yet another public service. No doubt she had just saved somebody who didn't care a fifteener of indignant Louboutin-stamping about The Tragedy at Pablo's.

As the woman stopped and tried fixing the problem by smacking the cell phone against her palm, Devina walked by, hands in the pockets of her jeans, head down, affect calm.

She continued along the row of darkened shops, checking the environs. No one else was on the sidewalks; nobody was passing by on the road; nothing was doing.

She knew when her prey resumed walking thanks to the *clip-clip* of those stilettos over the concrete. And there was the cursing, of course.

When the blinkers flared on a lone black-on-black Range Rover half a block down, Devina smiled. There was a cross street that cut through the lineup of shops about ten feet away, and that was just what she needed.

Willing four streetlamps to suddenly extinguish themselves, she slowed her pace and let those loud shoes catch up.

It was a case of perfect execution.

Literally.

Devina sprang herself around at just the right moment and grabbed a handful of that blond hair, securing a grip strong enough to rip the female off her feet. Then, in a quick succession of moves, the demon dominated the situation, taking control of arms and legs that flailed around, shifting a palm so that the mouth was covered, holding hard and fast.

Superior strength was leveraged to drag the victim into the cut-through, into further darkness as more streetlights were willed off.

There wasn't any time to waste. Yes, this part of Caldwell was a snooze-fest at night, but a car could come by at any moment, and it would be nice to enjoy the killing in peace.

As dense shadows swallowed them both, Devina wasn't worried about the Maker getting pissy about this kind of thing. She'd been on the earth since time had begun, her nature expressed through exactly this sort of shit.

And no one could argue that this pain in the ass was part of Jim Heron's great quest to win the game. This was a sideline issue.

Now . . . if this female happened to be killed in a manner similar to the way another girl had been murdered? If there was a pattern carved into some skin that was of a runic nature exactly like said other dead body? If there were some commonalities in ethnic group and hair color?

And if that crap happened to bother Jim Heron, causing distraction, disquiet, and dysfunction?

Well, as her therapist always said, you could only control yourself and your actions.

If Jim couldn't handle the shit, it wasn't Devina's fault . . . or problem.

Chapter Thirty-two

Mels woke up to the feel of hands traveling across her belly and dipping in between her legs. Half-asleep, she eased onto her back and turned into the warmth, finding Matthias's mouth in the darkness. Instantly, they returned to where they had been most of the night, pressed in tight, the heat pooling in her sex, the tension twisting in her gut.

As her lover went downward, pushing the covers out of the way, he found her breast and began to suckle on her as his talented fingers eased in right where she wanted them.

The idea that she was going to lose him soon made everything feel first-time intense, as if her body understood exactly what her mind was stuck on: Enjoy this now, because the memories are going to have to last a very, very long time.

It was hard to imagine she would find this with anybody else.

"Come for me," he demanded against her nipple.

The release squeezed her thighs against his hand, trapping him deep inside of her, the jerking of her hips rubbing the top of her sex on his wrist in just the right place.

As she gasped his name into the darkness and went rigid, the sweet sting of the orgasm continued beyond the first rush of pleasure, and she opened herself up to it, hoping to hold on to the fleeting sensations and turn them into an infinity.

But, of course, it didn't last.

Real life didn't come with forever.

When Matthias nuzzled her throat and tucked her in against his chest, she wished he were naked, too, but anytime she'd tried to pull his shirt off or even put her hands under it, he'd redirected her.

Opening one eye, she groaned when she saw the clock. Six thirty a.m.

The night was over.

Crap, she was on the verge of going teary.

And damn it, she'd forgotten to tell her mother that she wasn't coming home. She also had no car. And she didn't want to go to work.

What a great way to wake up.

"I'd better get going," she said gruffly.

"Yeah." He loosened his hold on her, pressed a kiss to her mouth, and then separated them completely.

Was now the moment, she wondered. Time for him to honor his promise?

"How about dinner?" he said instead.

The smile that hit her face was so big it was a wonder it didn't light up the room like a camera flash. "You got it."

The fact that she was going to see him in twelve hours made the hit-the-bathroom-and-re-dress thing so much easier, and then, like a gentleman, he showed her to the door, still in his Hanes T-shirt and boxer shorts.

As they stood together in between the jambs, he looked like he might say something . . . but then he let his actions speak for him: He kissed her so deep and long, she thought they would never come up for air.

Mels left before she couldn't leave, and the elevator ride seemed to take forever.

Outside at the curb, she was pleased to find that even though it was before seven in the morning, there was a line of taxis waiting.

Getting into the back of one, she met the guy's eyes in the rearview. "Two forty-two Pine Way."

"Out in the 'burbs, huh."

"Yup."

He nodded, put them in gear, and didn't say another word. Thank you, Jesus.

As they took the ramp up onto the Northway, joined commuter traffic that was just starting to heat up, she stared at the city from the elevated highway. There was a beauty to the urban landscape, the tallest buildings reflecting the pink and peach of the sunrise off their mirrored flanks, the roads relatively clear, the day just beginning and therefore making downtown look young.

Then again, after a night of sex, and the security of a dinner date, she probably had so many endorphins in her bloodstream, she was incapable of seeing the world as anything other than a tourist postcard.

It wasn't until they came up to the great iron fencing of Pine Grove Cemetery that her bliss started to take a backseat.

What would you say if I told you I believe in Hell. And not from a religious standpoint, but because I'd been there.

Mels closed her eyes, the stress creeping up her spine and settling in at the base of her skull.

I think I was sent back here to do something. I don't know what it is, but I'm going to find it out. Maybe it's a second chance.

Matthias had sounded anything but crazy when he'd told her that. He'd seemed to believe with absolute clarity in what he was talking about, and when she'd been looking at him, staring into his eyes, she'd come pretty close to believing it, too.

But maybe that was the way of crazy people. They were normal except for the salient, damaging fact that their reality filter was way off from everyone else's. To them? What they thought they saw and what they believed to be true *was* the real thing.

So they could look you in the eye with total sincerity and talk a whole lot of bullcrap.

If she took away the extrapolation, he'd woken up on a grave, naked. Had clothed himself somehow and gotten over a ten-foot-high iron fence. Then jumped out in front of her car.

And this added up to a reject from Hell for him.

Oh, and people were after him. . . .

Plus he was armed.

Panic trembled along her nerve endings as logic started to re-place emotion, and the conclusion that she'd put herself in danger loomed.

Except he'd never hurt her. Never threatened her. They'd been in a public place—a hotel room with thin walls.

And a man who had saved her life at the hospital had vouched for the guy.

Crazy madman or lost soul?

Which was he. . . .

More to the point, where was she in all this?

Mels was rubbing her tired, aching head when they pulled up in front of her mother's house. After paying the driver, she put the front walkway to use, and studiously refused to look at the dormer where her father had done all that work.

He wouldn't have approved of her coming home early in the

morning, wearing the same clothes she'd put on the morning before, her hair a mess even though she'd pulled it back, her lips swollen.

Unlocking the door, she didn't need the scent of coffee or the sound of a spoon against a china bowl to tell her that her mother was up. She'd probably stayed awake, too—

Cutting through the family room, Mels saw a half-done crossword puzzle next to her mother's favorite chair, along with a mug that appeared to have the dregs of hot chocolate congealing in the bottom.

Picking the thing up, she brought it with her into the kitchen. "Hi. Listen, I'm really sorry I didn't call. It was rude of me—I just lost track of time."

Her mother didn't look up from the granola, and when she was silent for quite a while, Mels found it difficult to breathe.

"Do you know what the oddest part is?" her mother said eventually.

"No."

"If you didn't live here, I wouldn't have known that you didn't come home—I wouldn't have worried." Her mother frowned into her coffee. "Don't you think that's strange? You're a grown woman, legally and in practice nothing more than a roommate of mine. You are no longer a minor child that I'm to look after. So you'd think it wouldn't matter."

Mels closed her eyes, that distance between her and her mother so vast she wondered how they were able to hear each other at all.

This was, of course, her fault—and not just the part about not calling the night before.

With a soft curse, Mels went over and poured herself a cup of Folgers. When she turned back around, the way the sunlight fell on her mother's face went through her like a knife: Something about the angle of the illumination seemed to pick out every single line, wrinkle, and imperfection, until the age was so screamingly obvious, Mels had to look away.

In the silence, she thought of her father. Of everything he had missed since he'd died, all the days and weeks and months. The years.

Of how much time her mother had had to miss him. Of the house that the woman had to take care of herself. Of the nights— the long nights made longer thanks to a daughter who had her head up her ass.

Mels went over and sat down. Not across the table, but next to her mother. "I think I'm falling in love with someone."

As her mother's head snapped up, Mels was a little shocked, too. She hadn't shared anything about her life for . . . yeah, since she'd moved in—and before then, it wasn't as if she'd been filing long editorials.

"You have?" her mother whispered, eyes wide.

"Yeah, he's . . . well, he's the man I hit with my car, actually."

Her mother breathed in. "I didn't know you'd been in an accident. Was it . . . when you told me you hurt yourself in the shower?"

Mels looked down at her hands. "I didn't want to worry you."

"I guess that explains the fact that your car's been gone."

"It wasn't anything serious. Honestly, I'm fine." Well, except for the fact that she felt like crap for lying to her mother.

In the silence that followed, she braced herself for some kind of an oh-you-can't-be-serious, either about Matthias or Fi-Fi.

Instead, her mom just said, "What's he like?"

"Ah . . ." Mels covered up the pause by taking another sip of coffee. "He's a lot like Dad."

Her mother smiled in that gentle way of hers. "That doesn't surprise me."

"He's . . . yeah, I don't know how to explain it in specifics—he just reminds me of Dad."

"Is he a Catholic?"

"I don't know." They'd never talked religion—well, except for the whole back-from-Hell thing—but now that her mother brought it up, she thought it might be cool if he was. "I'll ask him."

"What does he do for a living?"

"It's complicated." Christ, did he even have a job?

"Does he treat you nicely?"

"Oh, yes. Very much so. He's . . . a good man." Who might be crazy as a loon. "He takes care of me."

"That's important, you know. Your father . . . he always took care of you and me—"

"I'm really sorry about last night."

Her mother palmed her cup and stared into the distance. "I think it's wonderful that you found someone. And that you came home safe this morning."

Oh, shit . . . she hadn't thought about that part of it—of her mother not just up and waiting, but likely replaying that night when members of the CPD had come to the front door.

"Can I ask you something about Dad?" Mels said abruptly.

"Sure."

Man, she could not believe she was going there. "Did he treat you well? Because he was gone a lot, wasn't he. Working."

Her mother's eyes swung around. "Your father was very committed to this city. His job was everything to him."

"What about you? Where did you fit in?"

"Oh, you know me, I'm not much for being the center of attention. Would you like some more coffee?"

"I'm good."

Her mother got up with her bowl, went to the sink, and rinsed out the uneaten granola. "So, more about your mystery man. Can you tell me his name?"

"Matthias."

"Oh, that's a nice name."

"He has amnesia. He can't tell me much more than that."

Brows lifted, but there was no censure, no concern, no flip-out. Just calm acceptance. "Is he in the care of a good doctor, I hope?"

"He was seen at the ER, yes. And he's okay—it's coming back."

"Does he live here in Caldwell?"

"He does right now." Mels cleared her throat. "You know, I'd like you to meet him."

Her mother froze over by the sink. Then she blinked fast, like composure was hard to keep. "That would be . . . lovely."

Mels nodded, even though she had no idea whether it was even possible. The thing was, though, she'd given so little to her mother, and at the moment, Matthias was—or at least seemed to be—the biggest deal in her life.

So it seemed appropriate to open up about him.

Although, boy, after all this time, the whole sharing thing felt odd and awkward . . . the interpersonal equivalent of a training bra, or a set of braces, or a learner's permit.

More significantly, it hadn't been until this moment, on this morning, in this kitchen, that Mels realized that for all the sum total of her age, she hadn't grown up. Not really. She'd checked out of life on a lot of levels after her father died, her feelings regressing and getting buried under career goals that had soured into a sustained dissatisfaction with everything.

Matthias had shaken her up.

Woken her up.

And she didn't like what she saw in the lines of her mother's face.

"Yeah," Mels said. "I don't know how long he's in town for, but . . . I'd really like you to meet him."

Her mother nodded and seemed to take an inordinate time sponging around the counter. "Whenever you like. I'm always here."

God, that was true, wasn't it.

And why had she felt like that was a burden she had to bear?

Mels glanced at the digital clock on the stove and stood up with her cup. "I guess I'd better go get ready."

"Would you like my car today?"

"You know what . . . yes, please."

Now her mother really smiled, the expression lifting some of the perma-sadness that had been there since . . . well, forever, it seemed.

"That's good. I'd like to help in any way I can."

At the archway into the hall, Mels stopped. "I'm sorry."

Her mother's answering smile struck her not as weak, but as accepting.

Huh. It wasn't until now that she realized the two were very different—and she had to wonder why she'd mistaken the latter for the former.

"It's okay, Mellie."

"No, it really isn't," Mels said as she turned away and headed for the stairs. "Not at all."

Generally speaking, Matthias wasn't in a situation where he should be making dinner plans of any kind.

It was just impossible not to want another hit of Mels naked with him in bed.

Or on the floor. Against the wall. Over the bathroom sink.

Wherever.

The bottom line was that it was time for him to get going. He'd been too long in Caldwell, too exposed in this hotel . . . and too close to Mels.

Time to take off.

And it was in the dour spirit of having to leave Caldwell that he walked out of the Marriott, Jim's gun with its silencer packed at the small of his back, a baseball cap he'd bought at the gift shop pulled down tight to the sunglasses.

The day was warmish, and with the spotty cloud cover that had rolled in overnight, the temperature probably wasn't going to improve much—

"Out for a morning stroll to the candy store?"

Matthias stopped and turned around. Jim Heron had magically appeared behind him, and somehow, that wasn't a surprise.

What was a shock was the emotion that hit as he looked into the other man's eyes.

Jabbing his palm out, he said gruffly, "Thank you."

Dark blond brows popped, and Heron went preternaturally still as pedestrians broke pattern and swung wide to avoid them, the herd of rushing people re-forming on the far side.

"What," Matthias said, keeping his hand where it was. "Too proud to accept a little gratitude?"

"You've never thanked me or anybody else before. For anything."

In the silence, a moment of clear resonance set up shop in the center of Matthias's chest, the kind of thing that told him that the statement was true.

"New leaf," he muttered.

As Jim clasped what was offered, he said, "What's the gratitude for?"

"Taking care of my girl last night. I owe you one."

After a pause, Jim said in an equally rough way, "You're welcome. And I can take a guess about what's gotten you up and moving. Come back to my place—I've got plenty of ammo there."

Considering that would conserve cash, Matthias gave the idea a big fat yes. "Where you parked?"

"Over here."

A quick trip across the street, and then he was sitting side by side with the guy in a black Explorer.

As they hit the main highway, for some reason he kept having the urge to look into the backseat, and he gave in to the paranoia from time to time. There was nothing/no one back there, however.

What the hell—

"So how's your memory doing?" Jim asked.

"Same as." Matthias left things there, because the whole back-from-Hell theory seemed too weird to put out there. It was one thing to share that shit with Mels. Spouting it to Jim seemed . . . like he was dropping his trou in front of the guy.

Not going to happen.

Matthias reached out and put the radio on. "—body of a woman found at dawn on the front steps of the Caldwell Library. Trisha Golding, second wife of Thomas Golding, CEO of CorTech, was discovered with her throat cut and some of her clothes removed early this morning by a street sweeper. CPD units responded immediately, and are still on site. Officially, the homicide department is downplaying the possibility of another serial killer in the city, but a source inside tells WCLD exclusively that the term is being used in connection with this victim and the case of another young blond woman found . . ."

As the report droned on, Matthias noticed that Jim's hands gripped the steering wheel tight enough to turn the knuckles white.

"What's the matter?" he asked the guy.

"Nothing."

Yeah, right. But it wasn't his job to pry, and besides, he had enough shit on his own plate.

Just one more night here, he promised himself. One final night with Mels, and then he was going to take his last hundred dollars, spring for a bus ticket, and . . . go down to Manhattan.

There was something he needed there. He could feel it.

But man, what a tall order. New York City was how big? And he had how little cash left? And yet he had the sense that if he got to the Big Apple, he was going to be directed to . . . whatever the fuck it was.

Which was why he had to ammo up—he wasn't taking any chances on what might be waiting for him.

Hadn't been a lot of nice surprises lately.

Except for Mels Carmichael.

Chapter
Thirty-three

Mel didn't make it into the CCJ.

Her phone rang just as she left the house, and as she got it out of her purse to answer, she groaned. There were three voicemails that she hadn't picked up over the course of the night, and this was Dick the Prick.

Something had happened while she had been . . . otherwise occupied.

"Hello?"

"Don't you check your damn phone."

"I'm sorry." And no, she was not going to explain that she had been "busy" or Dick might jump to the conclusion as to why—and be right for once. "What's up?"

"You know, a reporter's job is twenty-four/seven, Carmichael."

Well, the last two days were the first time he'd really treated her as one. "Has something happened?"

"Didn't your radio wake you up this morning?" When she said

nothing, he cursed. "There's another dead blonde—found on the steps of the Caldwell Public Library. I wanted you there an hour ago—"

"I'm on my way now."

This got her a heartbeat of silence—like he'd been looking forward to shanking her on a get-moving rant. "Don't screw this up."

"I won't." Mels smiled to herself. "By the way, I'm working a special angle on that prostitute with a source at the CPD. I know something no one else does."

Now he actually sounded a little impressed. "Really?"

"More later."

As she hung up on him, she left out the "hopefully" part, because she didn't want to be equivocal with her boss—and besides, there was no way Monty wasn't going to let her come forward. He was going to need the hit that snitching provided him.

Turning the radio on, she—

"—homicide department is downplaying the possibility of another serial killer in the city, but a source inside tells WCLD exclusively that the term is being used in connection with this victim and the case of another young blond woman found . . ."

Gee, wonder who that "source" was?

Monty was not monogamous, that was for sure.

Caldwell's municipal book repository had always reminded her of the one in *Ghostbusters*—a.k.a. the New York Public Library. In fact, you had to wonder if there hadn't been some conscious modeling on the bigger-and-better that was down in Manhattan: Across the facade, there were the requisite Corinthian columns and up above, a pediment with the gods and, yes, even two massive stone lions stood guard on either side of the imposing Neoclassical entrance.

Parking her mother's car at a meter, she put in four quarters and jogged across Washington Avenue. It was obvious where the body had been found, and yeah, score one for visibility: The screening that had been put up was smack-dab in the center of the stone stairway that rose to meet the three main doors.

With police tape running from one lion's perch to the other's, all access was cut off, so she hung back, trying to find Monty.

For some reason, he wasn't around, and like the other reporters, she didn't get much from anyone else: nobody from the CPD was saying anything other than, "News conference at eleven."

Eventually, Mels took a break and hit the Au Bon Pain across the way, scoring a piping-hot no sugar/no cream and a pecan roll the size of her head. Back out by the crime scene, she ate her sugar bomb and found the walkie-talkie was not her friend. Fueled by stimulants, her mind replayed every second of the night before. . . .

Although all of her thoughts weren't of the boom-chika-wow-wow type. Doubts lingered in the spaces between the kisses that she remembered, a strange, ambient fear making her edgy.

Even if they had dinner tonight, he was still leaving.

And other issues remained . . .

With a grim resignation, Mels took out her phone. Hitting up Tony's cell, she waited one ring . . . two . . . three—

"Where's my breakfast?" he said.

Mels laughed. "Still at Mickey D's, I'm afraid."

"You know, I could always *make* you borrow my car again."

"I've got my mom's today. Tomorrow, though? We could be in business again. Listen, did you happen to talk to any of your ballastics guys?"

"Oh, crap. Yeah, I did. I have one who's willing to meet with you."

"I don't suppose he's on the force?"

"Mind reader, are you?"

"Well, I have to go over to H.Q. for a news conference in about an hour, so I'll be down there."

"Okay, here's the thing. He's a little uncomfortable about it. He doesn't want any trouble, and he's only doing this because I set him up with his wife a couple of years ago. His name's Jason Conneaut, and he's in the CSI unit. Let me give him a call and see how he wants to handle things—he may not want to meet you on CPD property."

"Thanks so much, Tony. Just call or text me."

"Roger that."

As she hung up, she thought, man, wasn't it going to be awkward if the casing she'd found in her pocket with her change matched certain others.

And part of her wasn't sure she wanted to know—but that anxiety was precisely why she had to follow through. It was one thing being off-kilter because she was falling in love and she didn't want to get hurt—and the guy in question was not a safe bet emotionally speaking. It was another to let that crap get in the way of her job, her safety, or the public interest.

Staring over at the library steps, she really didn't like where her thoughts went.

And it wasn't just the unknowns about Matthias.

For so long, she had lived a tamped-down, flat life, frustrated but unwilling to make any changes, trapped in neutral in Caldwell—to the point where she hadn't even recognized the hole she'd dug herself.

The question now was, What was she going to do about it all.

"So you're going to see the reporter again, right?"

As Matthias sat on Jim's sofa and loaded the borrowed gun, he really didn't want to talk about Mels. "Thanks for this. And for the early lunch."

The pastrami and ryes that the guy's roommate had shown up with had seemed a little much to tackle at eleven a.m., but his stomach had gotten on board, and now, all that was left of the meal was the crumpled paper the sandwiches had been wrapped in, and a bunch of dead-soldier potato chip bags.

"Aren't you?" Jim said again.

Matthias rubbed an eyebrow with his thumb. "Yeah. But after tonight, I'm leaving."

"Where to?"

"Here and there."

"Caldwell's a good place to be. Big enough to get lost in, small enough to be able to control."

Not the point, Matthias thought. And, as much as he trusted Heron on some levels, he wasn't saying a damn thing about going to Manhattan.

Over in the corner, the decrepit TV flashed the logo of the local NBC affiliate, and then cut to the news desk. The instant the change happened, Jim shifted around and stared at the screen, his focus so intense, his eyes looked like they might blow the thing up.

"—WCLD-Six news team bringing you the latest in news, weather, and sports." The anchorwoman was an Almost There, her hair a little too blond, her voice a little high, her hands a little twitchy, the package not quite on a New York level, but certainly a cut above the Midwest markets. "Our top story today is the discovery early this morning of a victim on the steps of the Caldwell Public Library. Caldwell Police Chief Funuecio held a news conference at eleven this morning and our crew was there. . . ."

Matthias let the report drone on in the background as he focused on the change in Heron. And he wasn't the only one: the roommate came in with the empty trash bin, took a look at Jim, and did a one-eighty with a curse, heading right back out the door.

What the hell was going on?

"—a strange pattern on the lower belly of the victim. The images that we are about to show you are graphic, and viewer discretion is advised."

On the screen, a close-up of what was clearly skin and scratches was flashed, the etches that had been carved into the flesh appearing to be some kind of language—

Matthias blinked once. Twice. And then a part of his brain broke free so violently he let out a holler and threw his hands up to his head—

A black prison . . . bodies writhing . . . one who didn't belong . . .

Oh, God, there was one who hadn't belonged. . . .

Pain racked him, his body remembering things that had been done to him on a visceral level as memories careened into him, the nightmare he'd had the evening before revealing itself as a vital living memory, what had happened in the recent past locking onto him with teeth that tore and claws that ripped through him—

"Matthias? Matthias—what the hell's happening?"

Jim was in front of him, except he couldn't see the man, both his eyes blinded as his lids fluttered up and down.

"Oh . . . God . . ." he heard himself moan as he listed to the side.

Hell . . . he had been in Hell, tortured and claimed, sucked down into the eternal prison after he'd been shot by . . .

"Isaac Rothe," he blurted. "He killed me, didn't he. He shot me because—"

Alistair Childe. The one Jim had told him about, the man whose son had been taken and whose daughter was in danger . . . Matthias had gone after the daughter, but she'd had a protector, a trained, highly effective protector, who, in the end, had prevailed by shooting Matthias in the chest.

He had died on the floor of the elder Childe's house—

More memories came to him, the impacts like physical blows, the agony dragging screams from his joints and limbs.

"Matthias, buddy—"

Abruptly, the vision of a blond girl, a young blond girl with runes on her stomach and a tattered, bloody sheath around her, cut through everything . . . and stayed with him.

"She was down there with me." Abruptly, his voice became strong and clear, untempered by the maelstrom in his skull. "The girl . . . was trapped with me."

There was a pause. Or maybe his hearing had gone, too?

"Who," Jim said in a frozen voice.

"The girl with the blond hair . . ."

Twin grips locked on his forearms, and he knew Jim had grabbed him. "Tell me her name."

"The girl with the blond—"

"What was her name?" Jim's voice cracked at that point. "Tell me—"

"I don't know. . . ." Matthias felt himself get shaken hard, as if Heron were trying to rattle loose the answer. "I don't— I just know she was an innocent . . . who didn't belong. . . ."

Cursing, low and vile, got his attention.

"Who is she?" Matthias heard himself ask.

"Was she okay?" Jim demanded.

"There is no shelter in Hell," he replied. "We were all in there together, and they were merciless."

"Who were?"

"The demons . . ."

Chapter Thirty-four

"Well, I wouldn't be married if it weren't for Tony."

As Mels laughed a little, she couldn't help noticing that the man walking casually beside her was looking over his shoulder. "Tony's a good guy."

"The best."

After the news conference, she'd met Jason Conneaut as arranged at this open-air mall a couple of blocks from the station house. It was clearly a case of the lost-in-a-crowd theory at work, and she had a feeling they were going to be fine on the anonymous front: They were just two more people in a flood of shoppers going in and out of stores like Victoria's Secret and Bath & Body Works and Barnes & Noble.

No big deal.

"So here's the casing," she said, surreptitiously passing him an envelope that had a bulge in it. "I wrapped it in Kleenex so I didn't lose the damn thing."

"Can you tell me where you got it?"

"No, I can't. But I can tell you what I'm looking for." Now she was the one glancing around. "I want to know if it was discharged from the same gun that was used in the shooting at the Marriott the other night."

Tony's friend locked a pair of pale eyes onto hers. "If it is from the same gun, I am going to be required to disclose who gave it to me."

"I'll do you one better than that. I'll tell you who it's from and where to find them."

Oh, man . . . please let it not come to that.

Tony's buddy visibly relaxed. "Good, because I don't want trouble."

Mels stopped and put out her palm. "You have my word."

As they shook on it, he said, "This could take me a day or so."

"No problem. Call me when you're ready—I won't bug you."

After they parted, Mels took a little stroll by the shop windows, pausing from time to time. The city had closed off this five-block stretch of street to form a pedestrian way quite a while ago, but this was the first time she'd done a crawl—and it felt good to blend in with everybody else, to pretend that her life was boring/normal and she wasn't hooking up with a relative stranger who was armed and had friends like that Heron guy.

She was standing in front of yet another store when she frowned and took out her cell. It wasn't to answer a call or a text, though.

She was checking the date. . . .

Well. What do you know.

It was the day her father had died.

At first, she didn't know what had made her think about it, but then she saw that she'd stopped in front of a shoe store that had a Winter Clearance Sale sign hanging over a lineup of snow boots—that still might be useful in the spring in Upstate New York: late April could bring all kinds of different weather from cheery sun to miserable gray rain to snowstorms . . . or even sleet and freezing rain . . . that turned the roads superslick and dangerous, and made stopping impossible . . . and increased the likelihood of vehicular death. Especially during high-speed police chases.

She closed her eyes briefly. Then made a phone call that never would have happened before.

"Hello?"

At the sound of her mother's voice, Mels felt tears prick her eyes. "You didn't say anything about it this morning—and I forgot."

There was a pause. "I know. I didn't want to remind you if there was a chance it wasn't on your mind."

Funny, it was the first time she'd reached out. Then again, three years later, the missing and the mourning were too deep to handle with any kind of composure.

"How're you holding up?' she asked.

The surprise in her mom's voice made her want to kick herself in the ass: "I . . . well, now that you've called, I'm better."

"You must miss him like I do."

"Oh, yes. Every day." There was another pause. "Are you okay, Mels?"

This was said in the tone of who-are-you-and-what-have-you-done-with-my-previously-unreachable-daughter?

"Do you have plans, Mom?"

"The girls from bridge are taking me to dinner."

"Good. I . . . may be home late again."

"It's okay—and thank you for letting me know. Thank you—" A choked sound cut that sweet voice off. "Thank you for calling."

Mels focused on the heavy treads of the snow boots that the store was practically giving away. "I love you, Mom."

Long silence at that point. Reaaaaaaally long. "Mom?"

"I'm here," came the rough reply. Which was followed by a sniffle. "I'm right here."

"I'm glad you are." Mels turned away from the shoes, from the mall, from the people. "I'll let you know if I'm staying the night at his place, okay?"

"Please. And I love you, too."

After she hung up, Mels walked back to the station house in a daze, entered through the front door, and headed straight out the back to the parking lot where she'd left her mother's car.

She didn't go to the CCJ offices.

Heading out of the city, she properly stopped at the lights and hit her directional signal appropriately and didn't tailgate . . . but had no idea where she was going.

Until the gates of the Pine Grove Cemetery loomed.

Part of her groaned. She didn't want this. Not with everything else that was going on in her life at the moment. Then again, under the Drama Loves Company rule, maybe the timing was ideal.

She had no trouble finding her father's grave site, and as she eased over to the shoulder of the lane, she was not surprised to see that his plot had been planted with all kinds of spring flowers, like daffodils, tulips, little crocuses.

Her mother being thoughtful, of course. And she no doubt came for visits not just on special days but on a regular basis.

Getting out, Mels crossed over the pale green lawn, the young grass springing back into place and covering her tracks.

Other headstones had debris on them, little bits and pieces of trees or patches of lichen or moss dotting the tops or the bases. Not her father's. His was clean to a polish, no evidence of the passing of three sets of seasons.

When Mels finally knelt down, it was to trace the cross that had been inscribed deeply into the gray granite.

Matthias's deep voice came back to her as he had talked about Hell with the kind of conviction she might have used to discuss working at the paper, or living in Caldwell, or losing a father.

Personal experience had marked his words.

Mels went over the crucifix again with her fingertips. Funny, she'd never paid much attention to the religious stuff people put on grave markers, whether it was the angels with their wings up-raised, or the Virgin Mary with her head tilted down, or the Stars of David—whatever the religion, she'd seen them as decoration, not serving any kind of divine purpose.

That didn't feel true at the moment.

She was glad her father's patch of earth was marked with the symbol of faith, and she was glad he'd always gone to church on Sundays—even though, growing up, she'd hated that she missed a day of sleeping in.

Abruptly, she prayed with a kind of burning fear that made no sense that he was in Heaven.

To have a loved one in Hell would be . . . unthinkable.

Jim was losing his godforsaken, ever-loving mind.

As Matthias's lax body slumped into the sofa, his mouth moved like he was trying to speak . . . but nothing came out. Like there was a traffic jam on his cognitive byway.

"Talk to me," Jim barked, trying to get through to the guy. "Did you know her? Did you see her? Is she okay?"

That mouth worked up and down, especially when Jim shook the guy again. "Matthias—"

"The girl—she's in there." Matthias pawed the sunglasses off his face and stared straight into Jim's eyes—yet seemed not to focus on what was actually in front of him. "In Hell. The blond girl is there—I was with her."

"Is she okay—" Dumb-ass question. Of course Sissy wasn't. "What . . ."

"I was really there," the man said as he tried to push himself up, like maybe some vertical would help clear his head. "And I was brought back to . . . why was I brought back? What am I supposed to do?"

Even though a big part of his mind was stuck on Sissy, Jim forced himself to get back in the game: this was the moment he'd been waiting for. This was his opening, the way in.

But shit . . . Sissy . . .

Jim cleared his throat. Twice. "Ah, you're back because we need you to make the right choice this time."

"Choice?"

"At the crossroads." Jim prayed he was going to make some sense. "You're, ah, you're going to come to a moment where you need to choose, and if you don't want to go back where you were, you have to pick the righteous path, not . . . what you're used to."

"So it's true? About Heaven and Hell?"

"And you've got a second chance."

"Why?"

"The devil cheats."

Matthias suddenly focused on him. "You were there. Down below . . . oh my God, you were there—and that woman, thing—whatever—shit, the *nurse!*"

"I'm sorry?"

"The nurse who took care of me at the hospital after I was hit—who ran into me at the hotel!"

For a moment, Jim wanted to punch his own head. "Let me guess. A brunette?"

"It was her down below. And you were with her . . . she had you strapped down on—" The guy stopped abruptly. "Um, yeah . . . you were there."

Great. Fucking wonderful.

Matthias had seen the fun and games?

And then it dawned on him. If Matthias had, Sissy must have as well— Christ, and he'd thought her catching him in the aftermath had been bad enough?

The urge to kill curled his hands into fists.

"Just how are you involved in all this?" Matthias demanded, eyes narrowing—

A dull thwack cut off whatever Jim might have replied, the sound something he was way too familiar with to misconstrue. And yet he couldn't have heard it right, could he?

No, he thought as he reached for his forty, that had been a bullet going into wood: The confirmation was Adrian's sudden appearance in the apartment. The angel was outing his gun, and looking like he was frustrated as shit.

"We've got company," he barked.

"Not Devina." Jim would sense her, and as much as he would have loved to see the bitch and give her a piece of his goddamn mind he wasn't picking up on any vibrations.

"No, the other kind of visitor."

Fuck. XOps must have staked out the Marriott and seen them leaving. Not a surprise—just really sucky timing what with Matthias still looking like someone had unplugged him from his power source: The guy was better, but not fully back online.

"Let me go out there," Jim said in a bored voice. "I know how they're trained—"

"What's happening?" Matthias said as he pushed himself upright.

"Nothing—"

"Nothing—"

Matthias grabbed the gun he'd been feeding lead into, the surge of energy a surprise. "Let me—"

"You stay here with Adrian—"

"Fuck that—"

"FYI you're the target."

"And you think that makes my aim bad?" Matthias focused on Ad. "What did you see out there?"

"Not much. I heard a stick crack off to the side and caught a flash of black that wasn't a shadow. Next thing I knew I was hit—annoying, really."

There was a heartbeat of frozen silence as Ad realized what he'd said—and so did Matthias.

"Do you need a doctor?" Matthias asked.

"No, I'm good."

As the angel turned away, there was a hole in his jacket the size of a pea—and it was precisely in the center of his back, execution style. Clearly, XOps was still teaching its recruits how to be good little marksmen: If Adrian had been alive in the conventional sense, he would have been dead within seconds, the integrity of his heart muscle reduced to hamburger in his rib cage.

Bet that operative out there had been surprised when his target merely looked over and glared like someone had been snapping gum in a movie . . . then disappeared into thin air.

"Hell of a vest you must be wearing," Matthias muttered.

"You stay put," Jim commanded. "Ad, you—"

And that was when the wind came up from out of nowhere, the howling signifying so much more than a change in weather, the light draining from the sky not because a storm had arrived in the Jim Cantore sense, but because the demon's minions had showed up.

Shit, one look at Adrian and Jim knew they were in trouble. The angel's face had that nasty cast it took on when his mood meant you couldn't deal with him. And what do you know: Outing his crystal dagger, he dematerialized right in front of Matthias, heading into the fray alone, obviously prepared to die out there.

"Did I see that right?" Matthias said calmly.

Jim glanced over and went for his own dagger. "You stay here. We'll take care of this."

Matthias didn't seem all that bothered about the poof. Then again, he'd just gotten part of his backstory right, so he was clear that demons existed—and reality was pretty fungible when it came down to brass tacks.

He was, however, checking that gun like he was going to use it.

"Don't even think about it," Jim snapped. "I need you safe."

Jogging to the door, he glanced back to see if the guy was paying attention, but the status of Matthias was not what caught his eye. Dog had gone over to the crawl space where Eddie was and had curled into a sit right against the door . . . as if he were guarding the angel's sacred remains.

Which was good.

At this point, he'd take any help he could get.

As Matthias parted the drapes a little and looked out, Jim dematerialized, and prayed he could get things under control before his old boss acted on any bright ides.

Last thing he needed was a pair of wild cards.

Chapter
Thirty-five

As Matthias searched the pebbled drive, he smelled something bad—and not in the conventional, three-week-old-leftover sense. This stench was in more than just his nose; it penetrated the very pores of his skin and twisted his gut . . . and he knew what it was.

This was the Hell that he had been in made manifest. This was the horrid infection that had festered in his flesh.

It was back.

It was coming to get him.

A paralyzing fear took over his limbs, freezing him in place, rendering him incapable of thought or action. The torture and the helplessness, the goddamn eternity of what he'd found in Hell was a misery he couldn't bear again—

Fuck. That.

The fighter in him surged to the fore and cut off the emotions, the cold logic that had for so long defined him taking over and re-establishing control, shutting the door on anything and everything but the fact that they were *not* taking him. No fucking way was he going back there.

He didn't care what he had to sacrifice or who he had to kill—he was *not* going down again.

Gun was loaded. Body was willing. Mind was sharp.

That was what he knew for sure. The rest he was going to have to figure the fuck out.

A quick check for exits other than that side door yielded a big fat zero: Looked like that was the only ingress/egress—unless, of course, he considered windows.

In the bathroom, he found just what he was looking for: a three-foot-across, four-foot-high set of panes that opened out to the rear woods. Quick check and he thought, Shit, the sky had grown dim as the gloaming, the sun not just covered up, but consumed by the thick cloud cover that had blown in from wherever. But a sudden rain-storm was not what he was worried about: down on the ground, in and among the pines, shadows were moving, and not because some-one was working a flashlight around the forest.

Fury threw open the center of his chest. Crossroads? Fuck that—try payback. In this moment, he had a chance to get back at those bastards, and he was damn sure going to take a pound or two out of them on the way to the exit.

As he popped the latch on the window, he was suddenly feeling like Mr. Popular and was so ready to return the love to whoever got in his path—XOps, cops, demons, whatever the fuck.

The window pushed all the way up like a dream, nice and quiet and smooth, but it let in the gale that was blowing outside, the cold wind hitting him in the face. Hefting himself off the floor and through the relatively small opening, he was grateful for two things: one, that he didn't have his old body—because his formerly broad shoulders and big barrel chest would have been a tight squeeze; and two, that it was dark as the inside of a hat even though it was afternoon.

Good for him: Cover was his friend—at the moment, he was a sitting fucking duck.

The window was set about five feet up from a six-inch ledge that ran around the garage, and with a messy series of arm and leg rearrangements, he turned himself around, planted the toes of his Nikes on it, and closed the window. If he went to the right, he had to go around the corner that led to the stairwell. To the left? There was a sloping roof that would cut the distance to the ground and increase the likelihood that he wouldn't shatter his bad leg like a piece of glass when he landed.

Louie it was.

Shuffling along the ledge, he hung on to the sill for as long as he could; then he had to dig into the siding with his fingernails, clawing a hold to keep that center of gravity in his ass from peeling him off the side of the building.

The wind didn't help.

But he made it to the half roof.

Wasting no time, he scrambled to the far edge and dropped off. The second he landed on the packed leaves and soft earth, he ducked into a crouch and put up his gun. All around, there were sounds of movement, suggesting there were a lot of people, things, whatever the hell, in the forest behind the garage.

He didn't move anything but his eyes.

The lack of depth perception made long-distance shooting tricky, so that, coupled with his compromised mobility, made it a sit-and-wait situation.

Spider to the fly, and all that shit—

Someone heavy was coming 'round t' mountain from the left, fast and hard, the ground vibrating from the force.

Matthias trained his forty on whoever/whatever it was.

A three-dimensional shadow shot out from the lee of the garage, the faceless, formless creature ambulating like a sprinter on some version of two legs. But all wasn't well in its seedy little world: The thing appeared to be wounded, a smoking trail left in its wake as it seemed to be running for its unholy life.

What followed in its path blurred the distinction between good and evil.

Jim's roommate was like an avenging angel or some shit as he pursued what was clearly his prey. With a crystal knife up over his shoulder, and a warrior's wrath distorting his face, Adrian was hell-bent on killing that demon.

And that was exactly what he did, right in front of Matthias.

The man leaped up into the air, the lunge closing the distance between the two even as the demon ran his heartless chest out. Shit wasn't going to go well, though—the point of that flimsy glass knife was in the lead, and there was no way that was a good idea: That "weapon" didn't look strong enough to cut paper.

Wrong.

As the tip penetrated the nape of that creature, the shadow let out a screech that was like metal streaking across metal—exactly what Matthias had heard for the centuries he'd been in Hell. And then the demon crumpled under the impact, Adrian's weight trapping it on the ground.

What happened next was kind of like IMAX-3D, with some kind of splatter technology thrown in. Jim's roommate incapacitated the thing by hacking pieces off of it—an arm here, a leg there—and that was when the blood went flying. Acid was more like it. One drop on the back of Matthias's hand, and he cursed at the sting, grinding it off on the dirt—

A second shadowy form jumped out from behind a tree, as if its appearance had been spawned by the trunk. Adrian was ready, however, spinning around, meeting it head-on as the first writhed on the forest floor.

This one he didn't waste time with. Right through the head,

and that seemed to be the knockout drop that was required to kill the fuckers: another earsplitting screech and then that shadow was no more, gone in a blink—

Just as Adrian turned back to the demon on the ground, two more came out from the trunk that had birthed the other one, like the conifer was just coughing the fuckers up.

Matthias didn't hesitate. Pent-up hatred gave him superstrength as he jumped out and opened his clip, alternating between the pair, that acidic blood going flying as the demons faced off at him.

"Come and get it!" he yelled.

Adrian started cursing, but fuck that. Matthias was unleashed as he went for hand-to-hand, still pulling that trigger in a controlled manner as he rushed at his enemy.

"Take a dagger!"

The other man's command registered through his fury, and he spared a half second to glance over his shoulder. The instant he did, one of those glass weapons came end-over-end at him, flying through the air with perfect trajectory.

Matthias snatched it midflight with his free hand, and then he was immediately in business: His instincts took over, his body responding in a coordinated rush that had the forty up and pumping to hold off the one on the left as he buried that dagger into the temple of the shadow on the right.

Good-bye, sucker.

Without losing a beat, he turned on the other and did the same, even though that acid was going everywhere, and he had a lot of skin exposed—and the shit hurt.

More shadows came.

An impossible-to-beat deluge—and he was out of bullets.

Matthias tossed the useless gun over his shoulder and sank down, ready for anything. Crossroads, huh? Guess this was it—and if the right decision Jim Heron had referred to was the urge to fight?

Got it.

As the nearest shadow zeroed in on him and attacked, he had a fleeting sadness that he wouldn't see Mels again, that this was it, that he knew he wasn't walking away from this battle.

But . . . if there was an afterlife in a bad way, maybe there was a Heaven, too. Maybe he was going up this time instead of down.

Maybe he could somehow get back to Mels and let her know angels existed.

Because he knew that for sure now.

She was one of them.

Out in front of the garage, Jim was invisi and waiting for the operative to show himself. The second the bastard did, he was going to swoop in and feed a gun muzzle to the motherfucker—he wasn't taking any chances with Matthias, and shit knew he didn't want Devina appearing from out of nowhere and "saving" his ass again.

There was enough of her in the woods, fuck them all very much.

Man, he hoped Ad was keeping it together back there.

And P.S., the fact that the minions showed up at exactly the same time the operative did didn't bode well—and it made him worry about that reporter. Usually Devina's good timing was bad news for him, and he didn't think this was going to be an exception.

Where are you, he thought as he traced the tree line, watching for the inevitable peekaboo. That bullet hadn't been discharged by a shadow; he knew that much—and no one else had a clue they were here, or had cause to show up with a lead-based welcome wagon.

Back behind the garage, the sound of screeching made him twitchy, his body ready, willing, and panting to join the fray out in the forest. But Matthias was up in that studio, and Jim wasn't going to give this operative a chance to infiltrate and pop the bastard.

In Hell. The blond girl is there—I was with her. . . .

Jim cracked his knuckles. His vengeance was getting harder and harder to suck up, that fault line of fury threatening to break him in ways Devina's physical torture couldn't get close to. The bitch was smart—killing those other women. It kept Sissy right in the forefront, loud as a fire alarm, bright as a goddamn neon sign.

It was the most effective thing the demon had done so far to get under his cool—

Over to the right, a shadow moved—and it wasn't the Devina kind. It was a man dressed in black from head to foot, a mask covering his face.

Jim observed from his superior position of not-fucking-there as the operative slipped from trunk to trunk. You had to admire the focus. In spite of the fucked-up weather, the God-only-knows-what out back, and the relative lack of cover, the guy was a study in cold calculation, every footfall exactly where it needed to be. And he was well equipped, with a good-looking gun and silencer, and no doubt a bulletproof vest under the black fleece—after all, operatives were hard to find, difficult to train, and extremely expensive to support.

Not the kind of resources you squandered.

There was no backup, at least not that Jim could sense or see. Operatives did work in pairs from time to time, but that was rare and usually only when there were multiple targets.

And clearly, they were just coming for Matthias.

Which was not going to happen. Not under Jim's watch.

Crossing the pea gravel, he zeroed in and didn't waste time with any showboating or big reveal from out of thin air just to get a rise out of the fucker.

In honor of the tradition he had been trained in, Jim simply let the other man pass by and then fell in step behind him, unnoticed even as he let himself become visible. Then, with quick coordination, he gripped both sides of the operative's head and snapped the man's neck with one vicious jerk. As the body went loose, Jim let it drop where it did, and stood his ground.

In the unlikely event there was another operative in the woods, that was going to flush him.

Heartbeat.

Heartbeat.

Heartbeat.

Jim stretched it a little longer and then was sure it had been a solo job again. Stepping over the newly dead, he fell into a jog around to the rear—

Talk about your melees.

Minions were swarming the back forty, going up against Adrian and— Shit, was that *Matthias* with a crystal dagger?

Sure as hell looked like it.

And he was holding his own.

The first impulse was to jump in there, but Jim stopped himself. This ambush bullshit was just too obvious. And he didn't believe that the minions were going to kill Matthias—nope, not with Devina stepping in when she had back at the Marriott.

Narrowing his eyes on the fighting, he whistled once, the shrill sound cutting through the grunting and cursing. When Adrian glanced over, Jim popped up his palms—the universal sign for, You got this?

When Adrian nodded and returned to work, Jim gave Matthias another quick measure. The bastard was on fire, that broken body somehow working with enough deadly coordination to score some serious hits—and not because the minions were giving it to him easy once they engaged with him.

They were, however, focusing on Adrian, none of them singling Matthias out until the guy forced them to.

Devina had definitely given a no-kill order to those shadowy sons of bitches: Jim had squared off with them enough to know that they were capable of far greater offensive strategy—and the shit Adrian was dealing with was proof.

Time to go.

Jim hightailed it around to the front, threw some buffering over the corpse so that in the unlikely event someone got lost and made it all the way down the drive, they wouldn't find a dead guy as a welcome mat.

Then he was out of there, going Angel Airlines to downtown Caldwell.

The reporter was the one exposed at the moment, and that was where Jim needed to be.

Chapter Thirty-six

As far as Adrian could tell, the final minion showed up shortly after Jim disappeared.

The second that angel was gone, the seemingly endless supply of Devina's PITAs dried up—proof that keeping the guy on site had been the reason for the attack.

Ten minutes later, the last shadow was dispatched, stabbed through the head by a crystal dagger wielded by Matthias.

As Adrian turned and looked at his wingman, he was breathing hard and steaming from the blood that had splattered on his shoulders.

That crippled SOB had sure as hell pulled it together in the nick of time.

"You okay?" Ad demanded between heaving gasps.

Matthias's knees buckled and he gave himself over to gravity, letting his ass hit the ground—at least until the black blood that had been spilled on it ate its way through to his BVDs.

The man popped up off that grass like he'd been kicked in the can. "Fuck! This shit is—"

"Don't rub your ass with your hand, idiot. Then your palm'll get covered in it."

Annnnnnd that was how Matthias ended up dropping trou in front of Ad.

The guy all but ripped open the front of those black slacks, and then his flat ass and thin legs let the rest happen.

"Better?" Ad said dryly as he looked around.

"Except for the stiff breeze on my 'nads, yeah."

Ad's eyes went back to the man's lower body . . . and for some reason, his mind got stuck on the reporter in that hotel room the night before, the two of them all sexed up, but going nowhere.

That must really suck, he thought.

Clearing his throat, he nodded at the garage. "I got a change in there for you."

"I'm ready for one."

Matthias bent down, used the crystal dagger to slice open the pant legs, and then stepped free of them, leaving the burned-out remains smoldering on the ground like a car that had been bombed and abandoned at the side of the road.

Looking over, he tossed the dagger in a perfect end-over-end sequence at Adrian. "Thanks for the weapon—that was fun."

Then the guy turned away and made like he was heading around the garage.

No questions. No demands of, "What the fuck?" Just, Hey, good party, my man.

Adrian hightailed it to catch up, thinking that Jim had been right about his old boss. Even half-naked, with some of his clothes still smoking, the fucker was tight as a bank vault—and Ad's kind of guy, apparently.

Matthias stopped as he came around the corner. "Looks like we had another kind of company."

Sure enough.

The dead operative was lying like a doormat on the fringes of the forest, half on/half off the pea gravel of the drive. Talk about bad shape: the body was chest-down, but the head was owl-backward, those dead eyes focused on the skies above.

That musta hurt.

Ad went over and crouched. "You go up and I'll get rid of him—"

"Not a chance." As Ad looked up, Matthias planted his feet and got his glare on. "Those things out back? Those are your world. This." He jabbed a forefinger at the stiff. "Is mine. Get me some fucking pants while I strip him."

Well, what do you know. Just because his balls didn't work didn't mean the guy was a pussy.

"And bring me a belt," Matthias muttered as he knelt down onto the ground, and started to pick over the carcass like the best kind of vulture. "I'm not your size anymore."

Adrian wasn't the type to be dismissed, especially by a mere human. But Jim's old boss had earned some respect in that forest, and there was no arguing with the way he was handling the postgame wrap-up on a man who'd been sent to kill him.

After Ad did a quick scan of the property to make sure nothing was doing, he flashed up inside the studio—no reason not to, considering the focus Matthias was showing the dearly departed. After a quick check-in with Dog and Eddie, both of whom were right where they needed to be, he grabbed a set of leathers in case the shit hit the fan again, and looked around for something, anything he could leverage as a belt.

Back down on ground level, he dropped the pants by Matthias's nearly bare ass. "Here."

The guy took a pause in his peel job and started to get to his feet. When he faltered, Adrian extended his palm.

Matthias looked up as if he wanted to throw a fuck-off out into the airwaves, but as he made a second attempt and didn't get far, he slid his hand against Ad's. It took no strength at all to get him off the ground, but the subtle pull made the difference between Matthias's staying where he was and his being on the vertical.

As the man's head dropped to take off his Nikes, Ad felt a pang in his chest. To be disabled was a kind of curse. And yet through heart alone, Matthias had done a man's job out in the back—had even stepped in during a moment when Ad might have gotten hurt.

"Thank you," Adrian said.

Matthias's brows twitched—which was apparently his version of OMG. "What for?"

"Stepping in."

"You could have handled it," he said gruffly as he yanked up those pants.

The leathers were painfully loose on him, and when Adrian handed over an extension cord, the stare he got back was all about the *really?*

"Best I could do."

Matthias did the duty, snaking the stiff black cord through the loops, pulling shit tight, and tying it in a knot. Then he was back to work.

"No cell phone, ID has his picture on it and not much else, ammo, piano wire, good knife—but not as flashy as the ones you have." Matthias glanced around. "We need to find his car and get him the hell out of here. They're going to send more, but let's clean up this mess before things get complicated and the morgue at St. Francis runs the risk of losing another body."

"I'll get the keys to the truck. In the meantime, let's stuff him in the garage."

"Roger that."

Ad went for the F-150 that Jim had driven before he'd fallen into the battle between good and evil. By the time he'd backed the thing out, Matthias had tied the operative's arms and legs together, and was dragging the body toward the bay that had been opened.

The effort was making him limp like someone had hit his bad leg with a Louisville Slugger. And broken the bat in half.

Adrian stepped in and took the torso. No comment. No fuss.

"Worried he's going to wake up?" Adrian drawled, nodding at that thin copper wire that had been used to secure things.

"Lately, I'm not taking anything for granted."

The truck that Adrian had pulled out was not new, but it was in good condition. Unfortunately, as Matthias grunted and dragged his bones up into the passenger seat with the help of his cane, the same couldn't be said for himself.

He was old and in bad condition.

The fight he'd had such a blast with hadn't ended as far as his body was concerned, every sharp jab, quick counter, and bracing blow lingering in his joints and muscles. He felt like he'd been in a car accident.

Again.

But he liked it. Everything . . . from the killing to the cleanup . . . felt like a familiar set of clothes or a destination he'd lived at for a long, long time.

After Adrian drove them out past the white farmhouse that appeared to be unoccupied, the man hit the brakes at the main road.

"Preference?" he said.

As with the fighting, the analysis came to Matthias with perfect clarity and confidence: "The operative would have driven by this lane first, coming from the direction of downtown because he'd have taken a car up from Washington, D.C., on the Northway. Then he'd have doubled back and gone past again."

"So right."

"No, left. He'd have double-checked a third time before identifying the best place to park. And then after finding it, he would have located another, less obvious solution." Matthias nodded in that direction. "Left."

"Do all you guys have the same brain?"

"I had a very specific recruiting strategy and type."

"And what was that?"

Matthias focused on the man beside him. "You. Without the metal in your face."

"I do believe I'm blushing."

As Adrian made the turn, Matthias cracked a smile, and then got to searching the shoulders of the road. They were definitely out in the sticks, overgrown evergreens and early blooming forsythia crowding the asphalt on both sides like fans at a velvet rope.

One mile out. Two miles. Three—

"There," he said, pointing through the front windshield—but like Adrian hadn't seen the unmarked buried to its quarter panels at the side of the road?

Adrian eased by the vehicle at five miles an hour under the turtle-like speed limit so they could check things out. Pulled over like it had broken down, the unremarkable unmarked had a bright pink CPD seal on it—like the cops had already been by, assessed the Taurus, and put the owner on notice to get his shit the hell home or have the ride impounded.

Adrian doubled back and drew up close. "Are you sure this is—"

Matthias got out of the truck and peeled the sticker off easy as pie. "If this was real, you'd need a straightedge."

Tossing the "seal" inside the truck, he stepped back and looked left and right. No one around, and no one down the road in either direction.

Taking the heel of his cane, he—

Shattered the driver's window.

Reaching in, he popped the locks and opened the door. No alarm—but XOps never put alarms in their cars. The primary directive, aside from getting your target dead, was no attention—ever. That just made for shit to clean up.

Naturally, there had been no keys on the operative, but that was also protocol. XOps left nothing behind, no bodies, no weapons—no cars, either. The key would be attached to the undercarriage so that the recon folks could sweep in and reclaim the Taurus—but he didn't have the time to go prostrate and screw around in the tall grasses.

Matthias pivoted around. "Can I have one of your daggers?"

When one was presented to him hilt-first, he lowered himself behind the wheel of the sedan and put the tip into a juncture in the plastic casing that covered the steering column. With the heel of his hand, he slammed the blade home and twisted until the section snapped free, exposing the guts.

As far as the average member of the public was concerned, the automotive industry had progressed past the point of manual manipulation, new cars run by their electrical systems and their inner brains—which meant the days of breaking and entering and hotwiring were over.

Good news for regular drivers. Not so helpful when you were trying to build in flexibility during assassinations. And that was why XOps unmarkeds were all modified for just this kind of infiltration. If you couldn't find the key, if you didn't have time to retrieve it, if a hundred thousand other unknowables were in your way? Get in and get gone.

Cross the wires. Hit the gas. On the road.

When they got back to the garage, Matthias drove into the open slot the truck had vacated and dragged himself out. Using the sedan's hood, sides, and trunk, he steadied himself as he felt around the base of the car—

Aha.

The magnetic box he brought out from down under was four inches long, two inches wide, and thin as a finger.

It was coded, however, with a tiny keypad. He'd forgotten that part—

From a corner of his brain, a four-digit series of numbers trembled on a ledge, just about to fall into his consciousness.

Adrian strode in. "What's—"

Matthias held up his palm. "One sec . . ."

Closing his eyes, he changed tactics. Fighting and forcing his memory hadn't worked; maybe taking a passive approach would.

And hopefully the result wouldn't be another time-out like the one he'd sported right before they'd been attacked.

Breathe. Breathe. Breathe—

The universal code popped into his head, jumping free of the choke hold that had strangled it into inaccessibility—and along with the numeric sequence came friends . . . lots and lots of friends.

All at once he was flooded by passwords, and alphanumeric combinations, and even color sequences.

Something grabbed his arm. Jim's roommate.

Good timing, as his legs started to go out, a dizzy twirl in his skull turning his body into a goddamn ballerina, even as he didn't move.

Overwhelmed, he could only watch what played across the backs of his eyelids, the seemingly endless catalog revealing itself with all the grace of a bull charging through a crowd.

He retained the information, however.

Especially as other things started to come in for a landing. Things like accounts, and Web sites . . . and personnel files.

Chapter Thirty-seven

"Monty, where are you . . . you loose-lipped son of a bitch . . . ?"

Glancing at her watch, Mels ducked back into the boathouse at the river's edge, double-checking that her source hadn't come in from the opposite end. Nope. Just her and the empty slips and the pissed-off barn swallows and the stacks of rowboats and life preservers.

When Monty had called and wanted to see her, she'd refused to play that follow-the-leader-through-the-park game again, and his lateness made her wonder if maybe he was in a sulk at his spy-guy parade getting rained on—

"Shit!"

All around, swallows burst back into the boathouse, forcing her into a duck and cover as they bitched in circles for a minute and then reescaped out into the open air.

"Monty, where are you?" she said to all the no-one-else around her.

Going over to one of the boat slips, she looked down into the water. Man, there was something inherently creepy about not being able to see the bottom. Made you wonder what was really down there—

A creak brought her head up. "Monty?"

Off in the distance, a child squealed in happiness. A car horn went off.

"Is someone there?"

All of a sudden, the sunlight dimmed as if God had decided to conserve energy, or maybe someone had thrown a tarp over Caldwell.

In the darkness, the interior of the boathouse closed in on her. Yeah, okay. Time to go.

Mels shoved her hand into her purse as she headed for the exit, a spike of paranoia making her search out her Mace—

Someone got to the doorway first, blocking the way out.

"Monty?"

"Sorry I'm late."

She relaxed at the sound of the familiar voice. "I was just about to give up on you."

"I would never let you down."

Mels frowned as the man took a step forward. Then another. "What's that cologne you're wearing?"

"Do you like it?"

God, no. It smelled like he needed to take a shower. "So you said you've got something for me?"

"Oh, yes. I really do."

As he approached her, he somehow managed to keep his body between her and the exit, and then he was right in front of her, hands in his pockets, head down like he was looking at his feet.

That child, the one probably playing on the swing set in the park, laughed again, the sound filtering in and making her feel the isolation like a draft.

I gotta get out of here, she thought in a rush.

"Listen, Monty, I've got to—"

And that was when the man looked up, black eyes glittering with threat. It wasn't Monty. She didn't know who the hell it was—

Mels attacked first, cocking her hand back on her wrist and taking the hard heel of her palm and jamming it right up into the guy's jaw. As his head flew back, she threw a vicious blow to the gut, which curled him forward again, bringing his face right in to range. Locking onto both sides of his head, she brought up her thigh and slammed her knee into his nose; then shoved him out of the way.

With a burst of speed, she gunned for the door—

The man was there. Right in front of her.

Ripping her head to the side, she checked to see if it wasn't a second attacker. There was no way he could have moved that fast—

Those eyes. Those black eyes.

What would you say if I told you I believe in Hell . . . because I'd been there. . . .

Mels staggered backward, until one heel hit a wet spot and slipped. Or maybe . . . the man with the obsidian stare had pushed her without touching her—

Free fall.

As she went loose into thin air, she threw her arms out and found nothing that could help her regain her balance. . . .

Splash!

Hitting the water was a shock. Cold and grasping, the river seemed to dig into her, sucking her in and holding her down. Opening her mouth, she was flooded with a nasty taste as she tried to claw her way back to the surface.

She got nowhere, sure as if a Hawaii-style riptide had set up shop in the Hudson.

Closing her lips so she didn't take any more water in, she felt the burn in her chest quickly become a screaming heat, and panic gave her a burst of energy. Thrashing against the black void, she fought with that newfound power—putting everything she had into saving her own life.

She got nowhere.

Arms and legs slowed down.

Heart rate sped up.

The fire in her lungs became volcanic.

After an eternity, the dull roar in her ears receded, and so did the cold of the Hudson, and the pain in her chest. Or maybe it was more that all that was still going on—she was just starting to lose consciousness.

How was this happening?

How the *hell* was this happening?

Dimly, she readied herself for the whole life-before-the-eyes thing, getting good and braced for a list of regrets, for the faces of the people she would miss most—of which Matthias's would definitely be one . . .

Instead, she just felt more suffocation and a sense that, aw, crap, this was how it ended?

As a last thought, it was pretty uninspiring. . . .

Following the tracking spell he'd put on that reporter, Jim showed up at what appeared to be some kind of boat club facility down at the Hudson River's edge. Overhead, the sky was so choked with clouds that it could have been after midnight instead of afternoon, but that wasn't the doom-and-gloom he was worried about.

The instant he got within range, Devina's presence was a scream that ran up the nape of his neck—

And then the reporter's signal disappeared.

Bursting in through the open door, he stopped dead as he saw Devina standing by herself, stilettos planted on the planks of the docking platforms.

"Surprise, surprise," she said, kicking up her chin and moving her hair over her shoulder.

For a split second, he nearly launched himself at the demon. He just wanted his hands around her throat, squeezing as she fought against him, squeezing until he snapped her head clean off her goddamn spine.

But the reporter was the reason he'd come.

Searching the place, he found . . . nothing. No one. Just waves clapping under the cribs, the restless water chatting all around.

"Where is she?" he demanded.

"Where is who?"

In the water, he thought.

Jim jumped forward and shoved the demon out of the way, hoping she landed on her bony ass as he started looking in all the empty slips. Man, the river was murky, the lack of light making it seem opaque.

"What are you looking for," he heard Devina say.

Stalking around, he got nothing but churning current—and wasn't fooled. The demon had come here for a purpose . . . and was staying for one, too. "I want you to leave. Right now."

"It's a free world."

"Only if you lose."

Devina laughed. "Not the way I see it—"

He shot over to his enemy and got nose-to-nose with her. "Leave. Or I'll destroy you right here and now."

A nasty glint came into her eye. "You can't talk to me like that—"

Before he knew it, one of his hands locked on her throat, his little fantasy coming true as he began to channel energy into the hold—

From out of nowhere, a light source entered the boathouse—no, wait, it was him. He was glowing.

Fine, whatever. He was so angry he could have gone disco-ball, for all he cared—especially as his other palm joined the party. And for a moment, Devina just laughed at him again, except then something changed. She started to struggle to breathe, her fingernails coming up to try to peel his grip from her neck at first with anger; then with something close to fear.

As that glow he was giving off spread throughout his body, it grew stronger, until it started to throw shadows—and he kept squeezing, pushing her back until she was trapped against the rowboats that had been stacked up on risers, shoving his body against hers to hold her in place. He was shaking with power from head to foot, and somehow he knew he was turning her on—which was not the case with his arousal. Yeah, he was hard, but what part of him wasn't? Every muscle was clenched, from his jaw to his thighs, his shoulders to his ass.

He was going to fucking do it.

Right here, right now. Fuck Nigel and those English pricks who were in charge of him. Fuck the game, the war, the conflict—whatever you wanted to call it. Fuck it all—

Something exploded behind him, displaced water hitting his legs.

And then there was a great, dragging gasp for air, followed by hacking coughs.

Jim broke his concentration for a split second to see what it was—and that was all Devina needed. The demon ethered out of his hold, coalescing into a black scatter of molecules with a screech, and then firing herself at him.

The impact was like ten thousand bee stings across every inch of skin he had, and he yelled, not out of pain but frustration, as he went down in a heap.

Devina didn't counterattack but moved on, casting herself into the sky she'd darkened, becoming one with the evil clouds above.

Gone, gone, gone . . . for now.

From his vantage point of cheek-on-plank, he watched her go with a curse through his gaping mouth . . . and then focused on the reporter saving herself.

Over at the closest slip, a pair of arms shot up out of the water, pale hands latching onto the decking, nails penetrating the wood. And then with a great heave, the woman drew her wet, cold self out of the river's depth.

She ended up flopped next to him, the pair of them not moving as they recovered.

"We . . . have . . . to . . ." she coughed, "stop meeting . . . like this."

Chapter Thirty-eight

Off in the distance, someone was talking. Jim's roommate.

Matthias couldn't focus on the sounds, however, his neuropathways jammed with all those profiles, Internet addresses and codes—all the way back to his first e-mail addy and the sequence of the bicycle lock he'd used in grade school . . . and Jim Heron's dossier.

"Matthias—talk to me. What's doing." Not a question. A demand—and he wanted to follow it. He and the roommate had developed a kind of working relationship, what with those black things, and now the whole dead-body/car problem, so he felt compelled to comment.

Except he couldn't talk.

Something gripped his ass—no, wait, that was the ground or a seat. He'd been made to sit down. Blinking his eyes, he tried to see through the video game that was playing in front of him, but he got nowhere.

"Matthias, buddy—you gotta talk to me."

With a shaky hand, he rubbed his eyes. That helped. When he

opened up again, he could see Adrian's piercings up close and personal.

"Hey, you back?" the guy asked.

After a while, Matthias muttered, "Why did you do that?"

"I didn't do shit to you—"

He waved his hand around that fierce puss. "With the piercings. I mean, really. Do you think you need to look like more of a hard-ass?"

There was a heartbeat and then the big bastard laughed. "She was hot. The more I got, the more time I got to spend with her."

"The piercer?"

"Yeah."

"So it was a chick thing?"

Adrian shrugged. "The pain made the sex better."

"Ah."

At that, Matthias looked away. Strange. Before PLMD—or Poor Land Mine Decision—sex had been like eating and breathing, something he just did. Now . . . the loss of that part of himself seemed to take on epic proportions.

Then again, if he was honest, that was more about Mels. If he hadn't met her, he wouldn't have cared. Hadn't cared, actually, over these last couple of years of halt-and-lame.

"So did you stroke out on me?" the roommate asked.

"Just things coming back." Not a fun ride, but if he kept this up, he might actually remember why he had this need to get down to Manhattan.

"But you're all right."

The fact that he didn't get grilled about the particulars—which he wouldn't have shared anyway—was a nice touch. "Yeah. Now back to the stiff."

When he went to stand up, his legs wouldn't hold him, sure as if they were made of paper.

"Let me get your cane and your sunglasses," the guy said, heading out of the garage.

Left to his own devices, Matthias was determined not to keep sitting next to the rear tire of the unmarked like something that had dropped off a mud flap. Reaching up, he planted a hand on the bumper, and with a groan, got himself vertical.

Palming his way around, he leaned in through the driver's-side door and popped the trunk.

He was staring into the empty space when the roomate came back. Taking the cane, he put the Ray-Bans in place and shook his head. "There isn't going to be anything on or in the car. We're thorough like that." He went around to stand over the body. "I say we put it all in the Hudson at nightfall."

Shit, he had dinner plans.

"Make that midnight," he amended as he shut the trunk. Then, "No, two a.m."

"You have something on tonight?"

As the roommate hairy-eyeballed him, he clammed up; he wasn't talking about Mels. Trouble was, though, he couldn't assign this disposal to anybody else, mostly because he had to see the sedan sink into a watery grave with his own eyes: Until his memory was back in its entirety and he was on his way—whatever that meant—he couldn't risk any third-party complications.

Nothing like a dead body to get the CPD riled, and XOps? They claimed their men.

Adrian stroked his square jaw. "What if I told you we could do it now."

"How."

"Trust me."

"Who do you think you are, Houdini?"

"Nah. Don't have a straitjacket big enough for this POS. But I do know where to go with it."

As Adrian stood there in neutral, his eyes were steady, his breathing calm, his vibe one of total confidence.

Matthias didn't give a shit about people's words. But he was willing to bet on affect, which was oh so hard to fake.

Unless, of course, the SOB was delusional.

Matthias thought back to that fight in the woods—most guys who handled themselves like this one did were the product of years of training and experience in the business of mortal-stakes risk management.

"So what's your plan?" Matthias said.

"Dump the damn thing now."

"In the river? It's broad daylight."

"Won't matter where I'm thinking of."

Matthias glanced over at the stiff and thought fondly of the way things bottomed out in water. "Let's get him into the trunk."

Adrian went over to the body as Matthias hit the release and popped the rear compartment open again. Rigor mortis was in effect, which was good for carrying, not so hot for cramming something in a relatively tight space: Both of them had to throw muscle into getting those knees bent up and pretzeling the torso, the effort proving that a golf bag was so much easier to deal with—especially given that shit made by Callaway always came with handles.

"I'll drive," Matthias said.

"You like to be in control, don't you."

"You'd better believe it."

The two of them piled in, and he hot-wired the engine again.

K-turn. Out the drive. Past the farmhouse.

"Where we doing this?" he asked.

"Hang a left. We're heading north."

They'd gone about five miles when the roommate looked over. "So you like that reporter, huh."

"I don't remember."

"Liar."

"I have amnesia, you know."

"You like her."

Matthias glanced across the seat. "Please don't tell me that you're trying on a career change as a *yenta*?"

"We're going to be driving for a while. Just making conversation."

"Silence is a virtue." There was a pause. "Besides, I don't know why you're interested."

"I fucked a chick last night."

Matthias's brows went up behind Mels's Ray-Bans. "Well, good for you. You want a cookie? Or a commemorative stamp?"

"It was like . . . you know when you sneeze?"

"Are you kidding me."

"I'm serious. When you sneeze, like, it's a relief of an irritation."

Matthias gave the guy a long, hard one—as in stare. And then decided, yeah, he kinda knew what the bastard was talking about. "But that's because you can afford to be blasé."

"You with that reporter got me thinking is all."

Don't ask. Don't ask— "Why."

"Take a left up here. Time to cut down to the river's edge."

Matthias did as he was told, thinking it was probably a good thing that the conversation dried up.

"Take a right here."

He hit the brakes and eyeballed the break in the tree line—and the sharp rise. "That's a footpath."

"Unless you drive on it with a car. Then it's a road."

Matthias eased the Taurus off the asphalt and onto the twin tire grooves carved out through the rugged undergrowth. Talk about taking your time. Between the puddle holes and the steep ascent and the occasional downed branch that was the size of a body, it was not a road less traveled, but a road no-traveled.

Or should have been.

And yet they made it to the end—which was a modest cliff, as it turned out. And twenty feet down? There was a whole lot of lake.

As Matthias put the engine in park, he glanced over at the roomate. "This is perfect."

"Duh."

The water below looked like an offshoot of the river, a supplier that channeled the rainfall from the mountains to the Hudson when the level got high enough—which it was now, thanks to the spring rains. The site was also perfectly isolated—evergreen everything all over, with no houses, no other roads, no people.

There was only one problem. "We don't have a ride home. And I can't walk that far—"

Adrian pointed across the seats.

In the trees, hidden just out of sight, was the Harley that the guy had used before.

Matthias cranked his head back around. "When the hell did you have time to get your bike out here?"

Jim's roommate leaned in. "Considering what you and I fought this afternoon, are you really asking me to explain shit."

Matthias blinked, the rational part of his brain cramping up briefly—and then releasing. "Good point."

As Adrian got out and started to clear the way to the lip of the cliff, throwing big branches off to the side like they weighed no more than paper clips, Matthias put the sedan in reverse to give them a little bit of a runway; then he got busy finding a heavy rock and dragging it over to the open driver's-side door. All they needed to do was put the weight on the accelerator, flip the engine into gear, and get the hell back.

Adrian was going to have to do that part.

"You humans always take the hard road," the roommate muttered as he came over and got the gist.

Matthias glanced across his shoulder. "Humans?"

"Whatever."

Three minutes later, Adrian jumped out from behind the wheel as that sedan roared forward in a straight line, did a swan dive off the cliff, and plowed into the lake with a massive splash.

Matthias went to the edge and watched the bubbles rise to the surface. "And it's deep enough."

The roar of an engine brought his head back around. Adrian had mounted up and was combat-booting that big-ass bike out from the tree cover.

Not exactly the most discreet way of getting them away from the scene. But with his limp, he was hardly in a position to argue for quiet.

As he mounted up behind the roommate, he knew there was a GPS on the sedan—so XOps was going to come and take that body out of the trunk at some point. But at least he was making them work for it. And as for the proximity to Jim's? It wasn't as if they didn't know where the guy lived.

Besides, Jim wasn't the target.

As Mels lay on her back and stared at the boathouse's rafters, she tried to get her bearings while water dripped off her hair and her clothes.

Cold was the big one. Gratitude was the second. Third was a big WTF. . . .

Held under the water. Choking. On the verge of death. And then just before her strength left her completely, whatever had pulled her under released its hold: Her arms had suddenly found traction against the river, pulled her up to the surface, gotten her to the air.

As she had broken free, coughing out the water in her throat, her vision had cleared, and from over the edge of the dock she'd dimly seen Jim Heron attacking someone in her defense—

The swallows came back, flapping around and finding their nests, suggesting time was passing.

"Are you okay?" Heron asked her on a mumble, as if he'd been hurt.

Any answer she could have given him was drowned out by his starting to retch. Curling over onto his side, he pushed himself up on bowed arms as his stomach staged a full-on revolt.

Okay, she might have just nearly drowned, but he looked like the one who needed medical intervention. Scrambling around, she prayed that her purse hadn't gone for a swim as well—

Thank God. It was over by where she'd felt that great push on her body, hiding among some PFDs.

Mels meant to stand up and walk to it; she really did. But the vertical thing didn't go well, and instead, she had to drag herself across the dock, fits of coughing still grinding her lungs, her head all fuzzy. Except she wasn't about to give in to all that.

They needed help.

When she got to her purse, she cranked the thing open. Her cell was right in the proper pocket. So was her wallet. And so was her collapsible raincoat—which was going to come in handy in another few minutes when she changed out of her soaked clothes.

Clearly she hadn't been the target of a robbery.

Crab-legging it back to Heron, she said, "Is there any way you'll let me nine-one-one this?"

He shook his head until another round of the barfies took over.

Of course he wouldn't. "So who am I calling?"

She had to repeat the demand twice before the digits started rolling out of his mouth, and she immediately punched them into her phone. When she hit *send*, she wondered who was going to pick up.

Ringing. Ringing. Ringing—

Distortion, big-time. Like whoever answered was standing next to a jet airplane. Then there was a rustling as if the phone were changing hands . . . and the roar dissipated somewhat. "Yeah."

Pause. And then for no good reason, she got a little teary. "Matthias?" When nothing came back at her but that noise, she spoke louder. "Matthias? *Matthias!*"

He had to shout in return. "Mels? Mels! Are you—"

"I'm with Jim. Heron, that is. Listen, we've got some trouble here—"

"What happened—"

"I'm okay, but Jim's down for the count—"

"Was he shot?"

"I don't know what—"

"Where are you?"

As she gave their location, she leaned to the side and looked out the boathouse's open door. There was that laughing child and a mother far across the lawn, at the park with the benches. And no one else.

Hard to know whether that was a good or a bad thing.

"Mels, is it safe to stay where you are?"

Reaching into her purse, she took out her holstered nine-millimeter autoloader. Flicking the strap free, she palmed the weapon, and checked the clip. Fully loaded.

"I'll make it safe."

"Listen, Adrian and I need to get a vehicle—we're on his bike. But we're coming right away."

"You just get here as soon as you can. I'll handle things until then."

Hanging up, she kept the cell in her left hand, the gun in her right, and went over to Jim.

There was a scent coming off him, and she recognized it as what she'd smelled when that man had approached her—and unless she was reading things wrong, it seemed as if that was what was making him so sick.

Reaching out, she put her hand on his shoulder. "I'm not going to leave you."

No way. He'd saved her twice—which made him an angel in her book.

No matter how harsh he looked.

Heron glanced up, seeming to pull out of the vortex of his nausea. "I'm supposed to protect you."

She frowned. "Why?"

"Because . . . you are the key to him."

"Him who?" she whispered.

More throwing up cut him off, but she knew the answer. "Did Matthias send you to me—"

As her phone started ringing, she jerked it up. Unknown number.

No way she was going to hit *send* and answer the damn thing.

She had enough to worry about right now, thank you very much.

Chapter Thirty-nine

Three hundred and fifty years. Maybe four hundred. Shit . . . try a thousand.

That was how long it took to get from Caldwell's rural fringes into downtown in that F-150 truck.

Matthias was ready to peel his own face off when Adrian finally pulled over into a parking space next to a green stretch of park. Not even a second later, the pair of them got out and left their ride like it was a piece of junk at a landfill.

No running, though, in spite of the fact that he was in a panic. Long strides with his cane, but no running. Just him and a buddy, out for a go-nowhere stroll—no BFD.

From behind Mels's Ray-Bans, he scanned the park. Clear except for a mother and a daughter on the swings.

Just as Mels had described, there was an old Victorian boathouse on the river's edge, the diamond-paned monolith sitting on the shore like a cedar-shingled hen about to lay an egg. And the closer they got to it, the more Jim's roommate looked like he wanted to kill someone.

Matthias felt the same way.

The open doorway into the thing was broad, but the interior was as dark as the sky had gotten before those shadows had shown up at the garage. As Matthias's good eye adjusted, stacks of faded blue and red and yellow rowboats appeared, and so did a wall of orange PFDs. Birds of some sort flew out from the eaves over the half dozen empty slips.

For some reason, he hated the sound of the water smuckering up around the cribs, the sucking and clapping noise predatory.

"Mels?" he said softly. "Mels—"

Down the way, from in between some shrink-wrapped sailboats and what looked like a convention of rudders, she stepped out.

"Oh, shit, Mels . . ."

Nailing his cane into the dock, Matthias shot forward, and as he came up to her he threw his arms around—

Snapping back, he barked, "You're wet."

"I know. Jim's over—"

"To fuck with him—"

She looked across his shoulder at Adrian and froze, like maybe she recognized him. "Ah, he's behind there. I don't know what's wrong with him—but he really isn't well."

The roommate was on it, heading into the space where she'd hidden herself and the other man.

"Who hurt you," Matthias growled as he ripped off his coat and wrapped her up, trying to get some warmth into her. "It wasn't Jim, was it—"

"God, no." She pushed away, but drew the windbreaker close around her. "I . . . I, ah, slipped and fell into the water, and he came—"

"Were you here alone?"

"I was meeting a source about a story. Some folks don't want to be seen in public talking to a reporter." She crossed her arms over her chest and lifted her chin. "And I'm not really loving this interrogation vibe."

"Tough."

"*Excuse me.*"

"You expect me to believe that you just *oops!* and went into the river? And how in the hell did Jim know where you were?"

Matter of fact, how had the guy gotten out here?

"Accidents happen, you realize." Mels jutted forward on her hips. "And as for Heron, why don't you ask him that question."

As if on cue, Adrian came out with the guy, holding him off the ground by the waist, Jim's combats duffing the docks.

Yeah, okay, no one was asking shit of Heron: He was pale as a ghost and lax as a bolt of wet cloth.

"Got to get him somewhere warm and safe," Adrian muttered, like he was talking to himself.

Matthias nodded over his shoulder. "My hotel room is close by. Let's bring him there."

Mels stepped in. "We can't get him through the lobby without attracting—"

"Good idea." Adrian hitched up Jim's deadweight and addressed him. "You can put a show on, right, boss?"

Boss? Matthias thought.

"And I'm coming, too," Mels said, as she disappeared behind the sailboats. "Give me a minute."

Little more than sixty seconds later, she came out a changed woman. Literally. She'd lost her wet pants and shirt and replaced them with a black dress; pulled her hair back smooth to the base of her neck and tied it with something; and put on a pair of flats.

Who knew an entire wardrobe fit in that bag of hers?

She walked right up to him. "Do yourself a favor and do not *ever* address me in that tone of voice again. I'll let it go once. Next time I'm going to knock the attitude right out of your mouth—are we clear?"

Okay. He could almost be hard right now.

"Let's go," she announced, ducking under Jim's other side and putting his arm over her shoulder. "Man, you're heavy. . . ."

As the pair of them took the patient toward the door, the sight of her touching the other guy made Matthias want to take the bastard and throw him off the docks with an anchor around his neck.

He followed because he wanted answers—and he wanted her.

Man, nothing was sexier than a woman who could take care of herself. But, shit, two close calls in twenty-four hours?

She was definitely going to tell him what had really happened here.

When the F-150 pulled up to the valets in the Marriott's underground parking garage, none of the boys in livery expected a clowncar exodus out of the cab. But that's what they got.

Surprise, Mels thought as she was the first one out.

From a distance, she guessed she looked presentable in her cobbled-together outfit, but up close she smelled like dead fish, and the reality was, she was only wearing a collapsible raincoat and what were essentially socks with hard bottoms as shoes. But like management was going to detain her for being a hot mess?

Or a cold mess, as it were . . . because that chill from the river and the scare was still in her bones.

Next out of the truck was Matthias, and the valet took a step back from him. Smart move: His mood was downright nasty, his face so tight he seemed like he was going to explode—but that was his damage, not hers. If he wanted to talk, he could do it adult-to-adult, at a volume lower than a yell.

Leaning in, he helped Jim out, all casual-like, as if the guy were just suffering from some jet lag, or maybe a little stomach flu. And Heron managed to pull it together. Although he was shaky if you knew where to look for the trembling, he walked by himself to the double doors of the lower lobby, each step measured and deliberately steady.

"Adrian" was on him fast, long-striding over, putting an arm around the guy and helping him to stay standing.

Somehow, she didn't think it was a coincidence that the man at the motel was tied with Heron. But now was hardly the time to press the issue.

And it was eerie. People coming in and out of the double doors didn't spare Jim a glance—and it didn't appear to be because they were being discreet.

How could they have missed someone who looked so drunk and wobbly? Generally speaking, it was the kind of thing that would draw stares.

It was as if the guy weren't there at all.

A strange warning tingled along the nerve receptors across the nape of her neck—

At that very moment, Adrian looked over his shoulder, his eyes gleaming in a way that didn't seem human at all—and yet wasn't threatening. "You coming, Mels?"

Shaking herself back from the silliness, she strode up the stairs and joined the three men by the elevators. "Yeah. I'm here."

Oxygen deprivation had obviously affected her brain—or maybe her adrenal gland was just on high alert after the past couple of days, and who could blame it. On the other hand, there was no reason to get lost in la-la land. Jim Heron was not invisible. People were not acting bizarrely. And there was no reason to turn life into a comic book where people had magical powers.

She was a reporter, after all—which meant she was into nonfiction.

After taking the elevator to the main floor, they then had to trek across the carpet to the other bank of up-you-go's. Fortunately, most of the people standing around and waiting were in travel-exhausted mode, to the point where someone could have roller-skated in wearing a Bozo suit and strumming a ukulele and they probably wouldn't have been noticed.

Yup, that was why no one paid them any attention.

When you were jet-lagged and felt like death, other people were simply not on your radar.

"I need a bathroom," Jim wheezed out.

"Two minutes," Ad answered.

The elevator was quick to open, fast on the ascent, and before they knew it—and before things got messy—they were on the sixth floor, shuffling at nearly a jog to get the impending eruption in range of Matthias's toilet.

The second they got into the room, Jim and Adrian disappeared into the loo. Which left her standing face-to-face with—

"I'm sorry."

As Matthias spoke, her brows popped. Given his scowl, he obviously still had his panties in a wad, so an apology was the last thing she expected.

"You're right, I shouldn't have jumped down your throat like that." He shoved his hand through his hair and left the stuff roughed up. "I'm finding it increasingly difficult not to think of you as mine—and that means that when I show up at an isolated location, and you're soaking wet, and cold, and clearly rattled, I feel like I let you down, because I wasn't there for you."

Okay, now her mouth wanted to fall open.

"You're a strong woman and you can take care of yourself—but that doesn't mean I'm not going to have all the stereotypical guy reactions when my female gets hurt or is endangered. I'm impotent, but I'm not genderless." He cursed. "Not saying it's right, just telling it like it is."

He met her right in the eye.

And in the silence that followed, all she could think of saying was . . . I love you, too.

Because that's what he was telling her in this moment—it was in his steady stare, his calm, grave words, his proud jawline.

God, he reminded her so much of her father: Shoot first, ask questions later, but always call a spade a spade.

"It's all right," she said roughly. "I know things have been anything but normal lately. Everyone's keyed up."

On that note, it was a shock to realize she wanted to I-L-Y the man—but she kept that impulse in check. It was . . . too early. She'd only met him how long ago? Two days? Three?

Abruptly, he paced around, that cane cocked at a steep angle that suggested he was hurting. Halting over by the windows, he parted the drapes and looked out. Not for the view, though, she guessed. It was like he needed an excuse to stop.

"I want you to promise me something," he said harshly.

"What's that?"

"After I'm gone, I want you to start wearing your seat belt."

For a moment, Mels didn't speak, the reminder that he was leaving like a slap in the face. "Ah . . ."

He looked over his shoulder. "I'm serious, Mels. Will you do that for me."

Mels went across and sat on the bed, random things filtering through her brain: She really wanted a shower. . . . God, she hoped someone didn't find her clothes before she got a chance to go back and get them . . . had she really walked into the Marriott like a hooker with no underwear on under a raincoat?

All of that was just cognitive dissonance, however, a strategy to avoid the request.

Deciding to man up, she said, "Do you know why I don't wear one?"

"You have a death wish."

"My father had one on, and that was the reason he was killed in that car accident." As Matthias turned around slowly, she nodded. "The seat belt trapped him in place. Without it, he would have bounced out of his seat and not had half his body crushed. See, his vehicle hit one of those flatbeds that carries lawn equipment? And the metal edge of it penetrated through the door. When the paramedics got to him, he was still alive, because the compression was slowing the blood loss down. Hell, he was even still conscious. He . . ." She had to clear her throat. "He knew he was going to die there in that goddamn car. The instant they cut him loose, he was going to hemorrhage out—and he . . . he *knew* it. He was awake and aware—he must have been in such pain. I don't . . . I don't know how anyone deals with that moment. But you know what he did?"

"Tell me," Matthias said quietly.

For a second, Mels got lost in the confrontation she'd had afterward in his sergeant's office—when his boss had refused to give her details of the death.

But damn it, she was Carmichael's daughter, and she had a right to know.

"First, he wanted to be sure the suspect had been apprehended—and he got on his high horse when it turned out that his colleagues had focused on him instead." She had to laugh a little. "Then he . . . he made them swear that my mother would never find out the way he died. He wanted her to think it had been instantaneous—and that's what she believes. I'm the only one in the family who knows how . . . how much he suffered. Finally, he told them to look after Mom—he was really concerned about her. Not me, though. He wasn't worried about me, he said. I was tough like he was. . . . I was his strong, independent daughter—"

As she choked up, tears pricked.

Then fell silently.

She wiped her cheek. "Finding out he thought of me like that was actually the proudest moment of my life."

There was a heartbeat of quiet. Then another. Then so many more.

Strange, she thought. That moment in the sergeant's office had changed her life, and yet she had compartmentalized it and frozen it as part of a past that was something to be left behind.

And yet now, in this hotel room, with Matthias focused on her, and Jim Heron throwing up his liver on the other side of the wall . . . things began to weave together, the past and the present like a pair of boxcar trains that had finally been pushed close enough together to lock on.

She brought herself back into focus. "Anyway, ever since I found out the specifics, I haven't been able to . . ." She cleared her throat. "It's not a death wish—call it a misappropriation of logic, maybe, but I don't want to die."

God knew, she didn't want to die.

As Matthias came over to her and sat down, she got ready to be hit with all kinds of, *But you know the statistics, chances are you won't be in the same position he was, blah, blah, blah.*

Instead, he just put his arms around her.

It was curiously devastating, the kindness, the protection, the silent understanding.

Leaning into his chest, she said, "I've never told anyone that before."

She felt him kiss the top of her head, and with a shudder, she gave herself over to his strength—and it was phenomenal.

She hadn't had a clue the burden she'd been carrying around all these years by herself.

Funny, as they sat close together, the warmth from their bodies magnifying, she decided that he had told her he loved her with an apology . . . and she had reciprocated with that story.

Proof that profound things could be said using lots of different vocabularies.

"He needs to lie down."

As Adrian spoke up from the bathroom doorway, Matthias held her closer. "He can have this bed."

"Thanks, man."

Mels went to get up, and was surprised when Matthias came with her. And then the two of them ended up on the wing chair and footstool by the window, with her sprawled out along his body.

It was as if he couldn't bear to ever let her go.

And she felt the same.

Chapter Forty

Adrian carried Jim to the bed and tucked his worn-out ass in. The poor bastard was shaking badly, his skeleton rattling against its prison of skin, trying to get free—but at least he wasn't sick to his stomach anymore.

As Ad straightened, he glanced across the room. Matthias and Mels were in a chair together, the woman with her head on the man's shoulder.

It was pretty damn clear that Devina had tried to throw some mojo around with the reporter, and Jim had obviously not stood for that shit. Made you wonder what kind of condition Devina was in.

Talk about walking with a limp. An angel could only hope.

"You guys want food," he said to the lovebirds.

"Doesn't he need a doctor?" Matthias shot back.

"Just time."

"What's wrong with him?"

"Food poisoning."

"Bullshit."

Ad glanced at Mels pointedly and kept his yap shut. It was no disrespect to the reporter—and it wasn't because she was of the fairer sex, either. Matthias was one of them: He'd been to Hell, and he knew Devina even if he didn't totally remember her. He was also inextricably mixed up in all this.

Mels, however, was not, and the less she knew, the tighter in the head she was going to be when all this was over—assuming she survived: It could be a real shocker to discover exactly how much of reality was malleable, and how many nightmares were true. And once you'd had that mental download, it was impossible to return to the halcyon days of only worrying about your dry cleaning and your property taxes and whether you had enough milk for your cereal in the morning.

This truism pretty much explained all of after-midnight radio.

The good news was that at least Matthias got the point, the guy nodding once, and zipping his lip.

Seeing them together, Ad almost felt bad that this pair wasn't going to last. Matthias was a short-termer, at best—at worst, he was part of a slippery slope that landed all of them in Devina's goddamn wall. And Mels? Given what Devina was capable of, the reporter would be lucky if the only place she ended up in was a pine box.

Odd, he thought. He hadn't felt anything except pain and rage since Eddie had been killed. But seeing these two together, he was . . .

Oh, what the fuck did it matter. He had his own problems—and Jim's recovery was one of them.

"I'm all right," the other angel said, as if on cue.

"Shut up and lie down."

"You suck as a nurse." But the guy did what he was told—likely because his body didn't give his brain a choice.

Mels sat up. "A doctor has to take a look at him."

"If it makes you feel any better, he's been in this condition before. Just give him an hour or so." Maybe longer. "He'll be fine. Where's the room service menu?"

"What exactly happened to him," she demanded.

Ad turned around toward the desk. "Ah, here it is. Let's see . . ." Thumbing through the laminated booklet, he eyed the entrees. "Nice selection."

As he debated between a New York strip and the roast beef, there was some conversation in the background—Matthias telling his girlie to chill out and that they'd get the answers when Jim woke up.

Maybe, maybe not, Ad thought.

After passing the thing over to them, Ad hit the phone and ordered the crap out of dinner. Hanging up, he glanced at the couple. "We're ruining your date night, aren't we."

Cue the foot shuffle on both sides—nice touch, as neither of them were standing up.

"I really can go," Jim said, pushing himself off the pillows.

"Will you quit it?" Adrian snapped, abruptly feeling caged. "Fuck it, I'm going out in the hall to wait for the grub."

The truth was, his brain was humming, and everything in that room was in danger of getting on his nerves: that woman, Matthias, Jim with his barfing. He suddenly wanted to scream at all of them, at himself, at fucking Eddie for dying, at Devina—

Always at Devina.

Out in the corridor, he shut the door and leaned against it, closing his eyes.

"Mommy, it's the angel again!"

Oh, for *fuck's* sake.

And he'd forgotten to go invisi.

Lifting his lids, he stared down at that little girl with the big eyes. Tonight, her hair was pulled back in a ribbon that matched her blue dress, and her smile was so open and honest, it made him feel a million years old.

"You're a angel!" The skinny thing seemed capable of speaking only with exclamations—like maybe the height differential required greater volume. "Can I see your wings?"

The mother hightailed it down the hall and arrived with that same cloud of exhaustion, the weight of whatever world she was living in clearly wearing her out. "I'm sorry. Come on—"

"Please? I want to see your wings."

Ad shook his head. "I don't have any. Sorry."

"You do—all angels have wings."

"I'm not an angel."

The mother put an arm around her daughter's shoulder—and was no doubt ready to pull a fireman's hold on the kid if things didn't get moving. "Come on. We've got to go."

Mom refused to make eye contact—then again, the child was doing enough of that for the pair of them.

"Come *on*."

The whining started, but the little girl allowed herself to be pulled away. "I want to see your wings. . . ."

Adrian focused on his combat boots, locking his eyeballs on the steel toes, letting the mother steer that precious cargo over to the elevators and off the floor.

"Rather harsh on the wee one, don't you think?"

Adrian exhaled a curse at the familiar aristocratic inflection.

Fantastic, a visit from upstairs. Just what he needed. "Hello, Nigel."

The archangel stayed quiet until Ad glanced up. Another nice outfit, go fig: The dandy was kitted out in a fitted linen suit with a matching waistcoat in a white so bright it made Ad want to Ray-Ban it up like Matthias. Cravat was candy-striped pink and white. So was the pocket square.

SOB looked like an ad for Orbit gum.

"I thought I'd come and check on you," Nigel said, hauteur turning the kindness into condescension. Or maybe that was just Ad's mood.

"Not Jim?"

"Him as well."

"We're great. Havin' a ball, and you?" As those shimmering eyes of the *Capo di tutti capi* narrowed into slits, Ad cocked his head. "Tell me something—if you're so concerned about your team down here, why don't you bring Eddie back."

"That is the Maker's purview, not mine."

"So talk to Him. Make yourself useful."

"Your tone leaves a lot to be desired."

"So sue me." As Nigel just stared at him, Ad refocused on his goddamn boots. "Now's not a good time to expect anything much from me."

"Which is the tragedy, is it not. Because this is precisely the moment when you are needed the most."

Adrian threw up his hands. "Nigel, buddy, boss, whatever the fuck you want me to call you. Give me a break, will you—"

"Your statement to that child is correct. You are not an angel—not with this attitude."

Ad banged his skull against the door. "Fuck you. Fuck all this."

There was a long silence—to the point where he wondered if the big man hadn't poofed it back up to Heaven.

Except then Nigel said softly, "We are depending on you."

"I thought it was Jim's job to be the golden-boy savior."

"He is ill. And now—now is the turning point."

Adrian looked over at the Englishman. "I thought you weren't supposed to influence things."

"I am allowed to advise."

"So what the hell do you want me to do?"

Nigel just shook his head slowly, as if Adrian had disappointed him so thoroughly, he had lost the ability to speak.

Then the archangel disappeared.

Which, if you considered the takeoff literally, meant he didn't want Adrian to do shit.

Down at the far end of the hall, the employees-only door opened and a room service guy came out with a stainless-steel cart. He was moving fast, like this was something he did a lot.

"That for six forty-two?" Adrian said as the uniform got closer.

"Yup."

"That's me." He jammed a hand into his ass pocket and took out his billfold. Peeling off a twenty, he handed it over. "Where do I sign."

"Hey, thanks, man." The kid took a white slip out. "And right here."

Ad scribbled something, and knocked so that Matthias would open up. When the guy did, the waiter went to roll things into the room, but Ad stepped in between the doorjambs.

"We've got this."

"Okay, just set it out here when you're done. Have a good evening."

Fat chance of that.

Matthias held the way open as Ad pushed dinner into the room, and, man, the whistle of the cart's wheels seemed way too loud. So did the closing of the door. So did the soft voices that sprang up as the reporter and Matthias arranged stuff on the desk and asked Jim if he could stomach any food.

Ad backed away, that hum in his head making him feel as if the barometric pressure in the room had exploded. Pulling at the low collar of his muscle shirt—like that was going to help?—he backed into something.

Ah, yes, the door again.

Perfect timing. He *had* to get out of here.

The sad truth was that he was better at anger than responsibility. More competent at fighting than logic. And that bastard Nigel hadn't given him anything to rail against.

Yet being pissed off wasn't bringing Eddie back, and it wasn't going to change the game or the fact that all of them, even that bitch Devina, were locked on this path, the rules of the conflict defining the landscape and trapping them in the game.

The whole goddamn thing made him want to scream—and left him missing Eddie so bad it hurt. With his buddy around, he'd always had a check and balance . . . had relied on Eddie to make decisions and provide that all-important pull-back-from-the-ledge when it was appropriate.

Except he was a grown-ass man—angel, whatever.

Maybe it was time to do that shit for himself.

Abruptly, he stared at the pair across the room.

As Mels started popping the covers off of plates, Matthias was hanging back, his eyes all but eating her up.

From out of nowhere, Jim's voice banged around Ad's head. *He's the soul, but she's the key to all this.*

Eddie would not have wasted time stamping his boots and getting frustrated, wouldn't have allowed himself diversions into the land of cocktail waitresses and grungy service corridors, would have stayed sharp even when shit didn't seem fair.

Adrian dragged in a deep breath, and on the exhale, the path became clear to him.

Applying Eddie logic, he knew what he could do to help.

Little bit of a game changer, but . . . what are you going to do. Nigel wanted him to get involved? Roger that.

Besides, it was what Eddie would have done.

As Matthias sat back down in the wing chair with his food, the weight blessedly off his tired, aching legs, he watched Mels as she ate at the desk.

French fries again. With a hamburger, done medium. And a Coke.

The subtle glow from the craned lamp was kind to her face, downplaying the circles under her eyes and the lingering bruise next to her temple. But he noted it all—along with the tension that ran down into her shoulders. Two near misses? In twenty-four hours? He was able to write off the construction guy falling from heaven—but down at that boathouse?

He had this awful suspicion that someone had tried to hurt her. Or worse.

And yet here she was, as pulled together as anyone else.

He thought about what she'd said about her father and was pretty sure that if the guy had been alive, he'd be stalking the streets for whoever had pushed her into that cold water.

Guess that was up to Matthias now—and he was prepared to meet the challenge.

As if she knew he was looking at her, her eyes shifted over and she smiled. "Aren't you going to eat?"

He wasn't hungry for food at this moment. Not in the slightest. Something about the almost-tragedy made him want to be with her skin on skin, like that was the only way he could be sure that she had survived for real.

Matter of fact, in his mind, he crossed the distance between them, pulled her up against him, and undressed her as he kissed the ever-loving shit out of her.

Not a bad plan, except the bed was full—and somehow he doubted that nearly drowning was an aphrodisiac to women.

"Matthias?"

He nodded and picked up his fork, putting food into his mouth and chewing like a robot. The silence that followed was all about waiting: Adrian waiting for Jim to feel well enough to get up; Jim waiting to recover; Matthias waiting for a moment alone with Mels, followed by some one-on-one with Jim to find out exactly what had gone down.

"Can I talk to you for a minute," Adrian said abruptly.

Matthias glanced up. The guy was looming by the bed, a huge, dark figure who was grim as a graveyard.

How had this friend of Jim's not been recruited into XOps, Matthias wondered. "Ah, yeah. Sure."

"In private."

Wiping his mouth with his napkin, he dropped the white square onto the arm of the chair and got to his feet. "Where to."

Adrian looked around, and then nodded at the bathroom door.

"I'll be right back," Matthias told Mels.

The little room was cramped enough with the toilet, the counter, and the cut-in for the shower/tub combo. With Adrian in it, the thing assumed matchbox proportions.

"What's up?" Matthias asked.

"Take the sunglasses off, wouldja?"

"Afraid you can't read me?" When there was no answer, he removed the Ray-Bans and stared at the other man with his good eye.

"You're very important in all this," Adrian said in a low, even voice. "So we've got to do everything to help you."

"You and Jim?"

"That's right."

"Who are you, exactly? Because I don't remember you from the good ol' days." He narrowed his eyes. "And not because of the memory-loss bullshit. I don't know you at all."

"No, you don't. But you're never going to forget me."

"What the hell are you talk—"

The man's hands shot out and clamped on both sides of Matthias's head, locking on as the eyes boring into his seemed to change—into a color he'd never seen before.

Matthias tried to jerk back, shove away, dodge out of the hold, but there was no going anywhere. He was stuck where he was, sure as if someone had bolted his feet to the floor—

In a warped voice, the other man started speaking in a language Matthias had never heard. The words were deep and rhythmic, almost a song—except no, they were so much more than sound, the syllables becoming solid in the air, forming strands of rainbow-colored light that encircled his body, one upon another upon another upon an infinite number, as threads would be woven to form a binding.

He fought against it all, thrashing, pushing, the memories of being trapped in that dark Hell giving him strength—

He got nowhere . . . and still the gossamer spooling from that voice, those words, that cadence wound 'round him, covering him from head to foot, forming an interlocking prison that tightened, tightened . . . and somehow removed him from the bathroom he'd walked into.

Matthias started to yell, but he had the sense that sound wasn't traveling, that whatever was going on with him was on a different plane—

The suction came next, the great pull making him feel like his internal organs were being drawn through his skin, his body somehow getting turned inside out. The pain was a stunner, a moan of agony rippling up his throat and breaking through his lips as he continued to fight within the cocoon—

Everything started to move.

The vibration began as a barely noticeable hum, but it soon reverberated within its bandwidth, multiplying until he was rattling within the physical sheath of the words, banging from side to side at a million miles an hour . . . until he was sure he was going to shatter.

And then came the rotating. Slowly at first, and then with gathering momentum, everything turning until the cage of light spun hard and fast around him. As the rotation took on impossible speed, pressure built to a bursting point, his ears popping, his lungs barely able to draw breath, his body taken to the limit of physical endurance.

He was going to get blown apart, every molecule he had straining—

The maelstrom started to lift, the whole construct rising from his feet, lifting . . . lifting . . . up his ankles, his calves, his hips . . . over his shoulders . . . and then finally off the top of his head, sailing free of him.

In its wake, he fell as if boneless, going down to the hard floor in a clatter of body parts.

But it was not over.

From the vantage point of his cheek on the tile, he stared up at an impossible sight. The spinning, shimmering chaos hovered above the other man; then began a descent, overtaking Adrian, covering first his head, and his pecs, followed by his whole torso . . . until he was subsumed by the maelstrom.

Behind the filaments, the man struggled as if being invaded, his body jerking and spasming, the grimace of agony suggesting he was where Matthias had just been.

Snap!

With a sharp sonic note, whatever it was dispersed in the same way it appeared, thread by thread coming loose and dissipating into the air like smoke, the cocoon peeling itself off strand after strand . . . until Adrian fell to the floor.

Matthias lifted his head and looked down his body. Then measured the other's.

Ironically, the pair of them had landed in exactly the same position, one hand up, the opposite down, one leg stretched out, the other curled up.

They were precise mirrors of each other.

Matthias reached out to touch the roommate—

He blinked. Blinked again. Jerked off the floor.

Holding his hand in front of his face, he moved it forward and back, the distance changing.

With a shout, he surged for the counter and yanked himself up toward his reflection over the sink.

What he saw was impossible.

His cloudy eye, the one that had been ruined by his actions two years ago, was the same blue as the other.

Jumping to his feet, he leaned all the way into the glass, going nose-to-nose with himself—as if that would tell him the truth or something . . . and he supposed it did, just not in a way he would ever have thought possible: Proximity simply proved that the scars on his temple had, in fact, faded.

To the point where if he hadn't been looking for them, he wouldn't have noticed them.

Matthias stepped back and stared down at his body. Same height. Same weight. But the aches were gone, and so were the numbness and the random sharp shooters that had been racking his bones with such consistency that he noticed them now only in their absence.

He lifted up his pant leg. Scars lingered in the skin of his calf, but like the ones on his face, they were nothing as they had been. And a deep knee bend that should have left him gasping for breath didn't faze him.

He looked at the man on the floor. "What the fuck have you done to me?"

Adrian grunted as he sat up, and then struggled to haul his way off the tile. When he finally straightened, a wince buried his eyes in low brows. "Nothing."

"Then what the *hell* was that?"

The other guy turned away. "I'm going to check on Jim."

Matthias reached out and snagged the man's arm, a spike of fear hitting home. "What did you do to me?"

Except he knew. Even before Adrian looked over that thick shoulder, he *knew*.

He had been healed. By some miracle, Adrian, the roommate, whoever the hell he was, had done what two years of doctors, surgeries, drugs, and rehab had not.

His body was whole . . . once again.

Because Adrian had taken on all the damage.

Staring into the man's now milky eye, Matthias didn't dwell on the metaphysical stuff, the holy shits, the amens, or even the thank-you's.

All he could think of was, How the hell was he going to explain this to Mels?

Chapter Forty-one

"Hi, Mom, how are you?"

As the reply came over the connection, Mels put another French fry in her mouth. "I'm still at work, yeah. But I wanted to call to let you know I'm okay."

Man, those simple words had connotations above and beyond the hour of the day and the reference to "work."

Closing her eyes, she forced her voice to be level. "Oh, you know how the CCJ is. There's always something going on. . . . Hey, how did bridge go?"

For once, instead of feeling weighed down by the mundane, everyday conversation, she embraced it. Normal was good. Normal was safe. Normal was totally far from cold water and an invisible hold and the specter of death.

She was alive. So was her mother.

This was . . . really good.

And it was interesting how much the response mattered. As well as the follow-up she asked—about how Ruth, their next-door neighbor, had played. And also the laugh about the trump that hadn't gone well. She truly listened, actually cared, and that gave her a sense of how much she had been going through the motions lately.

Guess the shock of that chilly water had further woken her up.

Opening her lids, she focused on Jim Heron, lying so still under the covers.

What had really happened down at that boathouse?

"Mels? You there?"

She gripped her phone a little tighter, even though she was in no danger of dropping the thing. "Yeah, Mom, I am."

How would tonight have been if things had ended differently?

A wave of fear burrowed into her bones, replacing her marrow with Freon, and a sudden shivering made her feet tap under her seat, and her fingers drum on the desk next to her nearly empty plate of food.

She looked to the bathroom and wondered what Matthias was doing in there. For a little bit, there had been some kind of dull noise, like the shower was running, but now there was just silence.

"Mels? You're awful quiet—are you okay?"

I almost died tonight. . . .

Okay, apparently the composure she'd been sporting since she pulled herself out of the Hudson River had been on account of shock: A crying jag was suddenly threatening.

Except she wasn't going to fall to pieces on the phone with her mother. "I'm really sorry—I'm just . . . glad to hear your voice."

"That's sweet of you."

Other things were said, more nice and normal things, and then Mels heard herself explain that she wouldn't be home until late.

"But I'm just downtown at the Marriott—I have my phone on and it's never far."

"I'm really glad you called."

Mels looked up into the mirror that was over the desk. Tears were rolling down her face. "I love you, Mom."

There was a stretch of silence. And then the three words came back at her, in a surprised tone that sped up the waterworks on her end.

Two times in one day. When had that happened last?

As her mother hung up, it was a miracle Mels could find the end button on her cell. Next move was to take the napkin out of her lap, drape it across both palms, and lean down into the soft cloth, pressing it to her face.

The sobs racked her, throwing her shoulders out of whack, making the chair squeak. There was no stopping the explosion, no thought, not even any images.

And the emotional snap was not just about the river or Matthias; it went further than the present, stretching all the way back to her father's death.

She cried because she missed him and because he'd died young. She cried for her mother and herself.

She cried because she'd almost died today . . . and because Matthias's leaving was like knowing that the man she loved was dying sometime very soon—

The warm weight of a hand on her shoulder brought her head up. In the mirror, she saw that Jim Heron was behind her—

"You're glowing," she said with a frown. "You're—"

Wings.

The man had wings over both his shoulders, beautiful gossamer wings that rose up into the air, making him appear to be just like an—

Wrenching around, Mels looked up to confront the man, but he wasn't anywhere near her. He remained in the bed under the covers, a still, silent mountain.

Turning back, she saw only herself in the glass.

At that moment, the bathroom door opened.

Matthias stepped out slowly, one hand gripping the doorjamb to steady himself.

The instant she saw him, she knew something was different. "Matthias?"

He came to her with careful, cautious steps, as if he'd been on a boat and his legs still thought he was on the open seas.

Then the door to the hallway opened and shut, Jim's colleague leaving the room.

"Matthias?"

When he got in front of her, he lowered himself to his knees. As his eyes lifted to hers, she gasped. . . .

Over on the bed, Jim picked that moment to get his act together. Anger, more than time, cleared his mind and gave him the strength to motivate. His body was still polluted as shit, but he was done lying around, waiting to feel normal again.

Throwing off the covers, he groaned as he went upright.

Naked was not good news.

Oh, man, neither was his stomach.

"Can I borrow some clothes?" he asked, knowing Matthias and Mels were over by the desk.

Someone cleared a throat. Matthias. "Ah, yeah—that bag by your feet."

Bending forward, he picked it up. The thing was from the gift shop down in the lobby, and as he opened the neck, he told his gut to hang tight with any bright ideas. Inside, there were a couple of pairs of black sweats and some T-shirts with Caldwell's city logo on them.

"Are you sure you're good to go?" Matthias asked.

"Yeah—where's Ad?"

"He just left."

Jim sent out his instincts—his wingman was right in the hall by the door. Good.

The buck-ass-naked problem was rectified sitting down, so he didn't flash the lady his ass. Shirt was a little tight and the sweats were high-waters, but like he was worried about his wardrobe?

As he got to his feet, he weaved and put a hand on the wall.

"You sure you don't need to lie down some more?" Matthias asked.

"Yeah."

"Your cigarettes, phone, and wallet are by the TV."

"You're a lifesaver." Because man, the instant he saw that red pack and his black lighter, he was able to take a deep breath. Snagging the vitals, he shoved them into the sweats and headed for the door. He didn't look back—couldn't.

He was too pissed off for conversation right now.

"Call me if you need me—Ad knows the number," he muttered as he hit the exit.

Out in the corridor, he looked around. "Adrian," he barked.

The other angel became visi across the way, his powerful body propped up against a little phone/table/bouquet arrangement, his eyes on the floor, his brows down like he had a headache.

"I got a meeting to go to," Jim said. "I'll be back."

The guy gave a little wave and a nod. "Take your time."

"Roger that."

Jim didn't bother with hoofing it out of the hotel—good job, as he'd left his boots and socks in Matthias's room.

Angel Airlines took him where he wanted to go.

Back to the boathouse.

Night had since fallen, and the exterior lights on the place were strong enough to create a glow inside, uneven shadows being thrown everywhere, the birds in the eaves watching him from their nests with suspicious little eyes.

Walking to the empty slip Mels had "fallen" into, he was ready to kill his enemy.

So much for that bitch turning over a new leaf. She might have gotten shanked by the Maker with Matthias's redo, but clearly shit wasn't sticking.

No surprise.

Closing his eyes, he sent out a summons to the demon, demanding that she come to him.

And as he waited, his body regained its full strength, like his fury was a car battery and her imminent arrival a set of jumper cables.

Naturally, Devina took her own sweet damn time to show, and as he walked up and down the dock with his bare feet chilled by the cold planks and his hands cranked into fists, all he could think of was what Matthias had said about Sissy in the Well of Souls . . . and how those two dead women had been made out to be like his girl—

Not that she was his.

God, he could just picture Sissy's mother picking up the newspaper and seeing the coverage on the front page of the CCJ. Like losing her daughter in the most horrific way possible wasn't bad enough? She had to read about a copycat killer?

"You rang," the demon said, her voice nasty and sharp.

Jim pivoted around, and the first thing he noticed was what she was wearing: His enemy had jacked her spectacular fake body into a blue dress he'd seen before.

Well, wasn't this a Hallmark moment. It was the one she'd had on the night they'd first met in that club across town—and he remembered her in it, standing under that overhead light, a stunningly beautiful lie that was pure evil.

In terms of the calendar, that intersection of previously divergent paths had taken place mere weeks ago. In terms of experience, it was many, many lifetimes in the past.

Hatred made him hard down below, the arousal not tied to anything he found attractive, but rather everything he didn't.

He wanted to rip her apart and hear her scream. He want her to know what it was like to be powerless and at the mercy of someone who didn't give a fuck.

He wanted her to beg—

As if she sensed exactly where he was at, the demon smiled like she'd been given a birthday present. "Looking for something in particular, Jim?"

Chapter
Forty-two

Mels heard the door shut behind Jim Heron, but she paid no attention to the man or his departure. Her eyes were locked on Matthias's face. By some . . . miracle, he had been transformed—utterly transformed: His coloring was warm for the first time since she'd met him, the skin no longer gray from pain. His scars had faded. And his eyes . . .

His *eyes*.

The one that had always been cloudy was now clear, sure as if a faulty contact lens had been the problem and he'd just taken the thing out.

Except there hadn't been some kind of Bausch + Lomb malfunction, had there.

"What . . ." That was as far as she got, her voice fading from confusion.

"I don't know." Matthias shook his head. "I . . . have no idea. . . ."

She reached up and touched the barely distinguishable scars. "You're healed."

How was this possible—

With an abrupt shift, Mels's eyes shot to the mirror, the image of Jim Heron standing behind her returning with every detail.

And then she heard Matthias's voice. . . . *I believe in Hell . . . because I've been there. . . .*

Oh, God . . . literally.

"There's more to all of this, isn't there," she said in a stilted voice. "And it's got to do with Heron."

Matthias turned his lips against her palm and planted a kiss. That was all the reply she got.

In the silence that followed, she thought about something she'd said to her father years and years ago. She'd been a typical teenager at the time, disagreeing with everything and everybody: She'd announced, as they'd driven home from church, that she didn't believe in God, or Heaven, or Hell—so why did she have to have every single Sunday morning ruined.

Her father had looked into the rearview mirror and replied, "Just because you don't believe doesn't mean it's not real."

Staring into the face of the man she loved, she didn't believe the transformation—and yet she could run her fingertips down his now-unmarred skin.

And as she thought more, she found that there was little understanding any of this: Not the way things had started outside that graveyard . . . not the two men who surrounded Matthias . . . not what had happened to her under that water . . . and not this, either.

But as her father had said, that didn't mean it wasn't real.

"I want to kiss you." Matthias focused on her mouth. "That's all I know."

She so got that. In this swirling confusion and post-shock emotion, the only thing that made sense to her—the only thing that seemed tangible—was that she wanted to be with him in whatever way she could.

Mels lowered her lips to within half an inch of his, and whispered, "I think the bed's empty now."

Matthias closed the distance, brushing at her mouth. Then he rose to his feet and scooped her up, one arm under her knees, the other beneath her arms.

"Oh, wait, I'm too—"

She didn't get to the *heavy*. He lifted her from out of the chair and held her up strongly from the floor, carrying her over to the bed without a limp.

"What happened in that bathroom?" she said again.

Instead of an answer, he laid her out on the duvet and then straddled her legs, looming large above her. "I don't know—and that's the truth. I went in and . . . Adrian . . . Look, let's not talk right now. Let's . . . do other things—putting words to it is not going to make it any more understandable."

She had the sense that he was right. Nothing made any sense, except for the need to be with him—and that was especially true as he took a fingertip and ran it down the side of her throat to the juncture of what she was wearing.

"Where did you get this dress?"

"It's a raincoat. Collapsible—I always keep it in my bag."

"So no zipper?"

"No." He smiled a little, but then grew serious—like he was remembering why she'd needed a change of clothes. "Don't think about the boathouse," she told him. "Not right now."

After all, two could play at the shut-it game.

"How can I not," he said darkly. And yet he leaned down and kissed her, hovering above her body, his hands going to the tie that kept the two halves of the coat together—

"You're naked under this?" he breathed.

"As a jaybird."

He eased back a little. "I can't decide whether that's the hottest thing I've ever heard . . ."

"Or?"

"Or if I want to kill any other man who saw you in this."

"I'm not showing anything."

"Not the point."

The possessiveness in that deep voice had her smiling—especially as he parted the coat and ran his big hands down her body. His mouth followed next, his lips soft, his teeth sharp as they nipped gently, lingering on each one of her breasts until her nipples were tight and peaked.

She stopped him before he got too far. "I'd love a shower—want to join me?"

From under heavy lids, his eyes glowed. "I think we're doing just fine."

"Come with me."

As she sat up, he rolled to the side. "How about I watch?"

"If that's what you want."

The growl that came at her was a big, fat *yes, ma'am* if she'd ever heard one—and far be it from her not to start the show early: As she got off the bed naked, she deliberately stretched her arms over her head and arched her back, her breasts heavy and taut.

Especially as she cupped them both, and thumbed the tips.

"God . . . damn," he groaned.

Mels took her own sweet time walking around the end of the bed, letting him look at her body as her hands went to her hips and then her butt. There was such freedom in the privacy, and the way the light from the desk hit her from the side, and how his hot stare followed her every move.

"You coming with me?" she asked.

"Yeah . . ." He went to sit up, but then frowned, looking down at himself in confusion. "Ah . . . yeah."

"You can keep your clothes on," she said gently, not wanting him to feel embarrassed. "And there's plenty of room in the bath."

He shook his head like he was clearing it. "Yeah." He laughed awkwardly. "By the way, that appears to be the extent of my vocabulary at the moment."

Flashing him her backside again, she heard the rustling of him getting off the bed, and then his warm palms were on her waist and he pulled her against him. Kissing her shoulder, his hands moved around and palmed her breasts, lifting them, caressing them.

"Mels . . . God, you feel good." He nuzzled her nape and went behind her ear. "You're . . ."

"Wouldn't you like to see how talented I can be with a bar of soap?"

"Oh, *fuck.*"

"I'll take that as a 'yes.' "

Inside the loo, she leaned in and started the shower while Matthias put the toilet seat down and lowered himself onto it, rubbing his jaw like he was hungry and looking forward to a meal.

"You'll be leaving that open, of course," he said.

"The curtain?"

"Yeah."

"And if I don't?"

"I'm going to rip it down off that rod."

She pushed the thing out of the way. "Well, we can't have you wrecking the place."

Mels stepped under the warm spray and went into another arch, putting the front of her body into the water. Then she turned and soaked her hair, letting her head fall back on her spine, the rush from above feeling like hands all over her.

His hands.

The soap was one that the hotel provided, a little bar that had been worn down by his use—and as she wet it, she smelled ginger, the humid air carrying the fragrance upward into her nose.

So slippery.

Across her neck and to her breasts, then farther, to her belly and over her hips . . . she went everywhere with the soap, the suds covering her skin before sliding downward in delicious trails—some of which went between her thighs.

Matthias was frozen where he sat, his eyes all over her, as if there were too much for him to look at—

For a moment, she lost her rhythm, that mystery of the healing returning to her . . . but then he spoke up.

"Do you need some help with your back?"

The rasping sound of his voice refocused her. "Patience."

"Don't have any."

"Learn some." As he cursed, vile and low, she smiled at him and leaned down to her legs, letting her breasts hang slick and full. "It's good for the soul."

"So are you. And for godsakes—don't stop, ever."

Happy to comply, she was slow and careful with her ankle and her calf, her nipples swaying back and forth, brushing the top of her thigh as she worked—

"Let me take over from here." He leaned forward and snagged the soap. "Oh, sweet Jesus . . . I have to touch you."

She was not going to deny him. Anything.

He wet his hands in the waterfall that had formed off the side of her hip; then he was on her flesh, the silky suds magnifying the contact as he swept up the back of her leg and lingered so close to her core . . . before attending to her inner thigh, stroking, plying, getting her hot in a way that had absolutely nothing to do with the temperature of the shower or the air in the room.

Mels closed her eyes.

She was at once in her flesh and flying free of it, grounded on the tile and soaring in the air, stretched between the extremes of wanting this delicious torture to last forever . . . and being desperate to get to the release that was even now threatening to bring her to her knees.

"Give me your other leg."

Opening her lids, Mels put her hand on his shoulder to balance herself and lifted her opposite foot.

All she could think about was his head between her thighs.

"You're getting wet," she said roughly.

His burning eyes lifted to hers. "I hope that makes two of us." As she nodded, he laughed in the back of his throat. "Say it for me."

"Say what."

"How wet you are, right here . . ." His hand swept to her core, his long fingers slipping into the heat, rubbing just enough to have her crying out—before easing free. "Say it."

He picked that moment to open his mouth and slide what had touched her in between his lips, his cheeks hollowing out as he sucked, a sound of approval resonating in his chest.

"*Say it,*" he commanded.

Mels could only moan something relatively close to, "I'm so wet. . . ."

His smile was all bad boy with fantastically dirty intentions. "You going to wash your hair for me?"

He stared at her breasts as he spoke, like he was picturing them moving back and forth as she worked her arms over her head.

Roger. That. And then hopefully they could go back to other things . . .

It was the work of a moment to grab the little bottle. The cap was already off, and as she poured the shampoo into her palm, the stuff was honey-thick and golden yellow in color.

Matthias's eyes stuck to her breasts as she reached up to the crown of her head. Sure enough, the back-and-forth motion was carried to what he was so captivated by, and she knew she was getting to him by the way he stroked her leg from ankle to thigh, going a little higher with every pass.

Until he was where she wanted him to be.

As his slick fingers touched her sex again, she jerked in pleasure—and that was good timing for the rinse part. With the water carrying the shampoo out of her hair, he teased and probed, the friction taking her to the brink.

"I want to see you come," he ordered.

No problem. The sound of his voice coupled with the way he penetrated her was more than enough to pitch her headlong into a massive orgasm, her palm slapping against the wet tile as the tension snapped in her core and the sensation rippled throughout her body.

Something came out of her mouth . . . his name, yes, that was it—and she said it twice.

The water was shut off as she was recovering, and a towel wrapped around her.

"You clean enough for your standards?" he said as he lifted her out.

She was pretty sure her reply was "yes"—it was certainly the word in her mind. God only knew what she spoke—

With a surge of demand, Matthias pressed his mouth to hers and licked his way inside as he rubbed her with the soft terry cloth. And then he was carrying her back to the bed.

As he laid her out, she thought he was going to kiss her again, and closed her eyes while lifting her chin.

He did kiss her. Just not on the mouth.

He went right to the center of her, parting her thighs wide, latching onto her sex, sucking her in. The sensation of wet on wet sent her over the edge again, her body racked with an orgasm that was only part release.

The other half was just another crap load of want.

Down at the boathouse on the river's edge, Devina could feel the heat rolling off the angel who was facing off in front of her—and goodness, gracious sakes a-fuckin'-live, that burn wasn't just anger.

He wanted her.

And even better than that, he hated himself for it: He utterly despised the arousal that was making a circus tent out of the front of those God-awful sweatpants he was wearing.

The combination was better than absinthe and oysters, an aphrodisiac that nearly made a demon forget that he'd double-crossed her in the last round.

Not quite, though. She could still hear him saying those words. *I lied.*

And what do you know, on her side as well, fury slammed head-first into love, the two extremes magnifying each other.

Jim's voice came out in an incredible growl, the tone low and mean, rippling with the power in his body. "I want you to cut the shit, Devina."

"What exactly are you referring to, Jim." She let the purr loose in her voice, because it was there—and it would piss him off.

The fact that she was getting turned on too was going to be another slap in the balls to him.

God, who knew they'd have a date tonight of all nights! She'd have spent more time on her hair.

"I want you to leave that reporter alone."

"Which reporter? Brian Williams? Diane Sawyer? Or someone in print, perhaps?"

Jim's hand flashed out and grabbed a hunk of her hair, yanking it so hard she nearly came then and there.

Leaning in, he looked like he was going to bite her. "Funny, I didn't think your methods were working for you."

"That first win with Matthias is still *mine*," she spat, her head cranked to the side.

"No soul to keep, though, huh."

"A small price to pay to win the war."

"That where you think you're headed?" He closed in, bending her even harder. " 'Cuz it's not how I see things going."

They were both straining, their faces together, their bodies curled in tight. And all around them it was quiet—not just because it was dark outside. He had a spell in place—even in his anger and his preoccupying hatred, he still had enough left over to make sure that pesky humans didn't interrupt them.

It was positively romantic.

And on that note, she ripped herself out of his hold, leaving him with a handful of brunette strands.

Okay, that stung. Which was kind of fun.

"You want me," she said, passing a hand over the bald spot and regrowing more of those perfect waves.

"To die. Yeah, I do."

"Number one, I'm immortal. And number two, let me teach you a little lesson, Jim—"

"I don't need shit from you."

She smiled and stared pointedly at his sex—which had made a tent out of the most dreadful pair of sweatpants she'd ever seen. "I'm not sure about that. And I'd listen closely to this, if I were you—you are a new player in town. Me and the Maker? We go back further than that proverbial twinkle in your father's eye. He *created* me, Jim. I am as beloved to Him as your boss, Nigel. I am the balance—without me, there is no Heaven, no goodness, no peaceable hearts-and-flowers bullshit, because when it comes to free will, contrast is required if the gifts are to be relished. I am *His* idea."

The angel crossed his arms over his chest. "Then why is the game predicated on your destruction?"

"More like it's predicated on Nigel's." She looked him up and down, measuring his body, that big, muscular body that she'd had in so many different ways, both willing . . . and not. "You know, I chose you, too—it wasn't just your 'boss.' In the beginning of all this, I agreed with Nigel that you'd be the one on the field. You were part evil and part good, as equal as we could find." Devina walked back over to him. "So if you have a problem with the way things are being handled with any ancillaries like that reporter, it's your fucking fault."

"*Mine?*"

She put her fingertip on his chest. "You were supposed to be half-and-half, good *and* evil—except I gotta say, you've disappointed me and under-represented my side. Therefore, you've left me no choice but to *act* in precisely the way I was designed to conduct business—"

When his hand shot out again, she locked a deadly grip on his wrist. "You touch my hair once more and I'm going to fuck you up . . . instead of fuck you good."

"I don't want you—you make me *sick*."

Her hand zipped right down to his cock and gave it a squeeze. "Really."

Jim broke it off this time, slapping her away, stepping back. Abruptly his voice became level, but that was a lie. "The blondes aren't working on me, Devina. You're wasting your time with them."

"Am I? Or is that just what you want me to believe." She came forward, bringing them back together, reuniting their bodies. "I think it's the latter."

"It's not getting to me, demon." He lowered his lips back within range. "And it's your funeral if you push the rules too far—or do you think having another go at one of the souls is the worst thing your Maker can do to you? I'm thinking it isn't." Jim leaned himself even closer to her, until their mouths were nearly touching. "I'm thinking He can do so much worse."

Just to piss him off, she bit him on the lip, the blood tasting good.

He didn't even hiss.

No, instead he turned his head and spit. Then he just looked at her—like he wanted to kill her with his bare hands.

How. Delicious. Was. That.

God, she was beyond ready for some good, old-fashioned, no-holds-barred fucking, the kind that was going to leave marks and have her sore for days.

And in the tense, almost-there silence, she considered her options. More lecturing. More needling.

Or . . . she could take a match out and light this bomb.

"If I were you, I'd be nicer to me," she said, extending her tongue and lapping up the freshly welled blood on his lower lip. "Because I have something you want, don't I—and things could get pretty uncomfortable for your little girl if I'm so inclined. What's her name? Sissy, is it—"

Boom.

Chapter
Forty-three

As Matthias went down on his woman, only part of his mind was on the sex. The other half was busy reporting on developments south of his waistband.

It appeared as if he was hard as a two-by-four—and just as long.

Licking at Mels's core, sucking on her, going deep with his tongue, he couldn't believe the erection that was now, at this very moment, enjoying the friction of being trapped between his lower belly and the mattress.

Surprise!

He'd first noticed the change in his body as soon as he'd gotten Mels naked on the bed. One look at her perfect breasts and he'd felt a shock nail the head of his cock.

He'd glanced down at his hips and then figured he'd lost his mind.

Except, when he'd gotten up off the mattress to follow her into the bathroom, he could have sworn the shift of the pants over his pelvis registered a very specific kind of hi-how're-ya.

And now, with her coming against his face, the heart of her open to his mouth, her taste hitting the back of his throat, he knew the impossible had happened.

Reaching down, he shoved his hand between his legs.

The moan that came out of him went right into her sex.

He *was* hard.

Rock-hard.

And desperate, apparently: because a single, quick stroke on the top of those borrowed leathers and he had to collapse into Mels's leg, the shock, the gratitude, the—

Logic pulled all the whoo-hoo'ing up short, reminding him that just because he had an erection, that didn't mean he could finish the job.

"Matthias?"

As he cleared his throat, Mels clearly knew something was doing, his woman rising off the pillows. "What is it?"

Straightening, he got on the mattress and balanced on his knees. Then he took her hand and drew it forward. He didn't trust his voice, but then again, there was no need to talk this out. The instant she felt him, she was going to understand.

Thinking back to that craziness with Adrian in the bathroom, he still had no idea what had happened—but in addition to getting his vision back, he was now hard, and he was more than willing—and, thanks to that guy, he appeared to be, after so long, able as well.

He nearly teared the fuck up.

To be with her, *really* be with her . . .

That man was an angel, capable of miracles.

Matthias placed her palm on himself. The second contact was made, his hips jerked forward, his cock pushing into her touch, his molars locking from the shock of the pleasure.

Mels stiffened—natch.

Speak, you fool, he said to himself. Say something.

Instead, all he could do was rub himself against her, rolling his hips—which kind of counted as begging, he supposed.

And oh, sweet Jesus . . . Mels took over from there, her face rapt, her eyes gleaming as she gripped him through the pants.

Falling to the side, he let her claim him, his body going loose as she knelt between his legs and went for the waistband of the leathers Adrian had lent him.

"Are you okay with this?" she asked him.

He appreciated the fact that she was being sensitive about the whole scar thing. But then . . . somehow they weren't so deep anymore, were they?

"Yeah, if you are—"

She shut the whole issue down by loosening the extension cord tied around his waist. "Interesting belt."

"It's black."

"So it matches," she said with approval.

And then he was naked but for his underwear.

Funny, with the view of her breasts he was currently enjoying, he could have been getting both arms amputated and he wouldn't have cared.

Except he had to look down at himself, and not because he was checking out his legs.

Okay, still not in his imagination: His cock was straining against the thin cotton of his boxers like it was prepared to rip a hole in them to get at her. And it was strange . . . that long, thick length hadn't seemed like a true part of himself when it had been working before— maybe that was a result of his past; who knew; who cared. Yet in this moment, the damn thing seemed more vital than even his mind.

Still, he needed to warn her that this might not end well—

The instant her hand touched him, the second that warm palm

circled him through the material, his body responded with a tremendous rush, his mouth cranking wide to let out an explosive curse.

When he opened his eyes again—he hadn't been aware of shutting them—he saw her face close to his own.

"How's that feel?" she asked huskily. Even though she knew.

And then she got him completely naked.

With a surge, he grabbed her shoulders and brought her to his mouth, kissing her hard as she started to stroke him for real, her grip moving up and down on his shaft, slow at first, then faster, each pass sweeping over his head and squeezing.

Matthias got utterly lost in what she was doing to him, and in that awesome disorientation, he licked into her lips, going deep, burying a hand in the thick hair at the base of her neck. More—he needed more—

In a quick shift, he pulled her over his chest and followed through on the roll, mounting her.

"I want in you," he said against her mouth.

She nodded immediately. "Let me see if I have something."

With a quick kiss, she left the bed and went for her purse. Rummaging around, she muttered a prayer. "Thank God."

When she turned around, she had a pair of condoms. "Just so we're clear, these were a friend of mine's—and I carried them for her when we went out. That's the truth."

And he believed her.

Enough with the talking, though. "Come here," he demanded, holding out his hand.

Things moved at warp speed as the necessities were taken care of; then they were right back where they had been, her thighs split, him poised over her core.

While he kissed her, plying her soft lips, she used that talented hand of hers to guide him right to the heart of her. And he took it from there. With a powerful surge, his hips pushed forward, and the penetration was something he felt to his marrow, the slick heat of her taking him all the way to the base, holding him in a grip that somehow managed to make him even harder.

In response, Mels cried out, her nails biting into his back, her body jacking up against his own, her sex spasming clearly as she orgasmed.

"Oh, God," he groaned, crushing her to his chest as he started to move in the midst of her release.

He meant to go slowly. He really did.

But when she linked her legs around his ass and worked herself against him, something snapped. All at once he went ferocious on her, his hips swinging loose at the base of his spine, the urgency ratcheting up until he was positively pounding into her.

And God bless her, she was with him, every step of the way, wanting everything he had to give, taking him as he came—

His release shattered him sure as that explosion in the desert had—blowing him apart, sending him sky-high.

The difference was that instead of rocketing him into a hell on earth, it took him straight to heaven. . . .

As Mels felt Matthias's erection kick deeply inside of her, she held him tight, absorbing his orgasm, finding another of her own. Embracing him, she turned her face into his neck and shoulder, feeling the power in his flesh as his once broken body became whole again.

It was a . . . miracle.

There was no other word for it.

When she finally came back into her own head, she found him staring at her, his face grave . . . if not downright grim.

"I'm okay," she said with a smile. "You didn't hurt me."

He opened his mouth as if he were going to say something, but then he just kissed her softly.

He was still hard.

Rolling them over, he kept them joined. "I don't want this to end," he said gruffly.

Neither did she.

Moving quickly, they dealt with the particulars, getting the second of her friend's condoms into place.

This time, she was in charge.

And she wanted to straddle him.

As she settled into place over his hips, she planted her palms on his shoulders and started riding him, his arousal going in and out of her, turning up the heat again. As the tempo increased, they were together in it, lockstep, the momentum of the sex taking on a power of its own.

They came at the same time, his release going right into her, her sex milking him, the pleasure so acute and sustained, it was a kind of pain. . . .

And then, after what had seemed like a century, it was over.

Mels collapsed on him; then eased onto her side so they were lying together.

Staring into her eyes, he said, "You are incredible."

"Wrong pronoun."

He brushed a strand behind her ear. Then, with a gentle finger, he traced her face, as if he were memorizing it by touch.

"You're leaving in the morning, aren't you," she whispered with sudden dread.

His nod was slow and steady.

Mels closed her eyes and fell back against the pillows. Putting her forearm under her head, she stared at the ceiling.

Man . . . this hurt—

"I'm in love with you," he said quietly.

Her head jerked around. Matthias was still staring at her, those eyes level and penetrating, his harsh face dead serious.

For a moment of pure stupidity, she just wanted to slap him. He was pulling out of town for parts unknown, never to return, and he hit her with that?

Fuck. Him.

"I just wanted you to know."

"Before you leave," she muttered.

"Some things are worth saying."

She turned back to him and tucked her hands in—in the event they acted on that impulse. "If that's true, then why leave?"

"It's not up to me."

"So someone else is buying your bus ticket and forcing you on a Greyhound?" God, she sounded like a bitch. "Ah, hell . . . look, I don't want you to go. But you know that—so, we are where we are."

He loved her.

And as she looked into his face, her feelings were crystal-clear as well.

Reaching out, she put her hand on his cheek—and not in a slap. "What am I going to do without you?"

And P.S., how the hell had someone she'd just met come to mean this much? It wasn't like she was a teenager in the heat of the crush years, when any passing guy could become a tragedy of *Romeo and Juliet* proportions. Yet here she was, on the verge of tears because she had nearly no time left with him.

"Will I ever hear from you?" she asked.

His answer was to kiss her, and as he did, her eyes stung so badly she had to blink fast.

This time the sex was slow and gentle, but no less devastating than the passion had been: As he touched her, as he reentered her, as they moved as one, she told her brain to remember every single gasp and groan, each and every shift and sigh.

It was going to have to last for a lifetime.

Chapter Forty-four

Sitting buck naked on the dock at the boathouse, Jim took his cigarettes out of his jacket pocket with hands that shook. Same thing with his lighter. And putting the flame to the tip wasn't a coordination party either.

All the while, the sound of the Hudson lapping at the undersides of the empty slips crowded in on him, making him feel like there were bars on all four sides.

"She's not actually the key to this," Devina said from behind him.

Man, his hearing was just way too acute: Her zipper going up was like a scream in his head, and no one should ever take note of feet being slipped into stilettos.

"The reporter," the demon prompted, like she was looking for a reply. "Matthias is so far gone, nothing can save him."

Jim tapped his cig and watched the ash float off in the water.

Devina was right about one thing: She had managed to make

him feel worse than before. He was positively stained, inside and out—from his anger, from the sex, from the game.

Saviors were *not* supposed to be hopeless—but here he was, completely surrounded by an utter lack of optimism.

Devina's fancy-schmancy heels marched over and parked themselves in his peripheral vision, the bright blue alligator something-or-anothers burning his retinas.

He hadn't intended on fucking her.

But he had. Twice.

The clash had been of biblical proportions—and it showed. The rowboats that had been so carefully stacked up were all over the place, pushed out of whack when he'd shoved her face-first against them. The buoys were scattered around. A number of life preservers had been torn, their fluffy stuffing like blood on a battlefield.

Looked like a hurricane had come up the Hudson.

Maybe it had been three times?

The demon knelt down, her perfect lie of a face intruding on him. "Jim? You in there?"

He wasn't so sure about that.

"We're getting down to the end of this round," she said softly. "Maybe afterward, you and I can have a little vacation together? Go somewhere hot and make it hotter?"

"I'd rather die."

She smiled, truly smiled, as if all was well in her world. "Then it's a date."

The demon straightened, and his eyes followed her as she stood to her full height. So beautiful, so evil.

"You want me to leave the reporter alone?" she said. "Okay. I will. Because I think the game is already won—I was just belt-and-suspendering it with her. The truth about that woman? Matthias and his past are going to take care of her by themselves—after all, he's one of mine. He's a liar and a megalomaniac, and his choices are going to mow her right over, even if you try to sweet-talk him and ply him with morality—hell, even if you frame the argument for goodness in terms of her? You won't get the stains out of his soul, and his past deeds are going to come back to haunt him."

Jim took another drag on his cigarette.

"Just remember, we can do this again," she said with satisfaction. "When you need your exercise. Bye for now, enemy mine."

Devina disappeared into thin air, leaving him to the river's constant chatter and the chill of the night.

As he flicked his butt into the water, he thought about all the environmentalists who would be pissed off that he'd littered.

He merely fired up another.

Smoked.

Went back for a third.

As he lit Marlboro after Marlboro, he wasn't sure exactly how long he sat there with his nuts in the breeze, making smoke rings and being disgusted with himself. The reality was, however, that what had just gone down was so much worse than the stuff she'd tortured him with in her Well of Souls.

This had been voluntary. At least the prior time he'd been with her, it had been against his will.

Staring out of the boat slip at the river beyond, he watched the moonlight tickle the tops of the ripples in the water, the current, or maybe the night wind, creating just enough of a disturbance so that the illumination had something to play with.

It was so beautiful, even though the water was filthy from the spring rain runoff. Even though his mood was foul. Even though he hated himself and the game to the point where he was tempted to quit . . .

That light was pure grace on the water. . . .

Back when he'd accepted the role of savior, he'd never considered it would eat him alive. Hell, after having worked with and for Matthias for all those years in XOps, he had assumed he'd seen the worst of himself—and humanity.

He hadn't expected this low point.

And what he needed was something to believe in.

Something tangible, something greater even than fear for his mother's eternity—and his own.

Getting to his feet, he felt ancient as he went over to the two-sizes-too-small sweatpants he'd borrowed from Matthias. Devina had ripped them off his legs at some point, and they'd ended up underneath one of those damn rowboats. At least they hadn't gone into the river, though.

Picking up the wad, he grabbed the waistband and gave them a good shake to get them in put-on-able condition—

Something went flying out of the pocket.

And he knew what it was the instant he saw it—even in the darkness, he knew what it was.

He pulled the pants on as he went over and picked the thing up.

The folded-up newspaper article had landed a thin inch away from the open water of the slip, almost lost.

He didn't want to look at it. Had no interest in seeing that photograph he'd memorized. Didn't want to measure even one word of the text he knew by heart.

His hands had other ideas, though.

Next thing he knew, he was staring at Sissy's face, that beautiful, smart, young face. And as he couldn't look away, he told himself that he was captivated by the image because it was a symbol of everything he hated about Devina.

But it wasn't all that. Not completely.

Running his fingertips over the pixelated composite of light and dark pinpoints, he touched the delicate gold necklace he wore around his neck, the one given to him by Sissy's mother . . . and he thought of those moments he'd been with his girl, talking about his dog, trying to give her something to hold on to, something to believe in when she felt like nothing was ever going to get better. . . .

In a moment of vicious clarity, he realized that Devina was winning. In spite of the score being two to one, the shit she'd been pulling with those blondes had gotten to him, keeping the bitterness and rage about Sissy right in the forefront of his mind.

Excellent strategy.

That girl truly was his Achilles' heel.

Jim looked out to the river, to that light. Looked back at the printout.

Devina wasn't going to change. She was going to continue to exploit the weakness; it was, as she'd said, what she'd been designed to do.

So he was going to have to be different.

With a curse, he folded up the article and walked along the slip. At the far edge of it, out from under the boathouse's roof, he paused in the moonlight.

Grasping the article at the top, he started to rip the piece of paper in half, one hand drawing away from the other—

He didn't make it very far before he stopped.

"Damn it," he muttered. "Do it—just fucking do it!"

Except something was clogging the nerves to his appendages, the order from his brain diverted somewhere else.

Dragging a hand through his hair, he wanted to let Sissy go. He really did.

He actually prayed for it.

The only thing that came to him, however, was the reality that she was not just suffering down in that demon's living room. She was under Devina's control—and that meant she wasn't safe.

His enemy was capable of anything.

What he needed was to get Sissy out of there. . . .

Chapter
Forty-five

Mels woke up with a jerk, the darkness that surrounded her taking her back into the river and the water's suffocation—

The instant she saw the glowing strip across the way at floor level, reality returned. The hotel room. Matthias . . .

Rolling over to face him, she found him deep asleep, his chest under the duvet rising and falling slowly. He was on his back, his arms on the outside of the covers, his hands down by his sides. He looked like he was ready to get out of bed on an instant's notice.

Either that or as if he were lying in a coffin.

Happy thought.

God, what a night.

Thanks to her having made a quick trip down to the twenty-four-hour gift shop, the evening had passed the way their other one had, with episodes of erotic connection alternating with the kind of sleep that comes when you're passed out cold.

Well, except for the fact that they'd been able to go so much farther this time.

Abruptly, his eyes opened. "You okay?"

"How did you know I was awake?"

He shrugged one bare shoulder. "I don't really sleep."

"I guess so."

As Matthias shifted his eyes away and stared up at the ceiling, he was so still, it appeared as though he wasn't breathing—and that was when she knew for sure that they had been together for the last time. But like all that aerobic exercise had changed his mind?

Then again, it had been so much more than just sex, she thought. At least on her side. . . .

In the horrible silence that followed, she gave herself permission to feel the loss, and as if he knew exactly what she was thinking about, his hand found hers and squeezed.

"I'm going to take a quick shower," he said.

He leaned over and gave her a kiss that lingered, but then he was up on his feet so fast, she recoiled.

Talk about turning over a new leaf. It was as if he'd never had the limp.

Especially as he stalked through the darkness into the bathroom.

A second later, a light came on and then so did the shower.

A quick check of the hour told her it was seven o'clock.

Time to head home, have her own shower, and get dressed. With any luck, this would be a Pilates morning for her mother, and they could both be spared the walk of shame—not that Mels regretted the night. She just wasn't too happy this morning.

Except that was because things were over, not because she was sorry it happened.

Getting out of the warm bed, she went over and turned on the desk lamp—and remembered, joy of joys, that she had no underwear or real clothes.

God, that fall into the river seemed like it had happened to someone else—at least until she felt the aches in her ribs and her forearms from when she'd dragged herself out of the Hudson.

Glancing to the sound of the running water, she thought maybe she should join him—no, it might look like she was chicking out, trying to make a come-on in hopes of changing his mind.

She had her pride.

Although she was taking a pair of his boxers. No way she was going home in nothing but a raincoat.

Heading over to the bag Jim Heron had rifled through, she found two pairs of the things, and she took one, pulling them up her legs and onto her waist. They fit okay—and wait, there was another pair of warm-up pants in there, along with a couple of shirts.

She ended up having to roll the sweats over at the waistband, and the shirt swam on her, but everything was black, and as she slipped her shoes on and pulled the raincoat around her, she felt a lot less like a hooker.

Matthias was still in the shower.

It was tempting to sneak out and save them both the awkwardness, and, looking toward the door, she put her bag up on her shoulder. She could always write a note?

Nah. She refused to be a coward—

The muffled sound of her alarm went off in her purse.

Shoving her hand in deep, she rooted around, found the damn phone, and took it out. The familiar, annoying beeping made her skin crawl, but that was the point. Anything more user-friendly and she worried she'd sleep through it.

After she shut things off, she glanced back over at the open door of the bathroom.

The waiting wore on her, and she checked her voicemail to pass the time. There were three messages when she got into the system—

"Hi, this is Dan over at Caldwell Auto. We've been looking at your car, and to be honest with you, it's right on the edge of being totaled. A vehicle that age, with this kind of damage? We could fix it, but I can't guarantee it wouldn't lemon on you a week later. My advice is that you take the insurance money and buy something new. Give me a call. . . ."

For some reason, the idea that her car had died made her tear up.

Man, she needed to pull it together.

Message number two was from her hair salon, reminding her that she had an appointment coming up with Pablo.

Message number three was . . .

"Hey, this is Tony's friend? From over at the police department? Jason?" The guy's inflection turned it all into questions, as if he weren't sure of his own name. "Listen . . . I need to talk to you ASAP. That bullet you found? It's a match—that round was discharged from the same weapon that was used in the shooting down at the Marriott"—a chill started at the back of her neck and spread all over her body—"and that means you need to come in and talk to us. It's ten o'clock now and I need to get some sleep—but first thing tomorrow morning, I've got to disclose this and your . . ."

At that moment, the shower cut off in the bathroom.

Leaning to the side, she watched Matthias step out of the tub. He seemed so much bigger now, and as she looked down, she saw only faded scars on his lower body, nothing that would warrant self-consciousness. Or a limp.

Tony's friend was still talking as Matthias turned away to get the towel he'd left on the back of the toilet—

Mels nearly dropped her phone.

Covering his back, from the tops of his shoulders to below his waist, was a massive black-and-white tattoo of the Grim Reaper standing in a field of grave markers—and underneath it were dozens and dozens of hatch marks in an orderly row.

It was precisely like the one that Eric had shown her—

Get. Out. *Now.*

Mels bolted for the door, but didn't make it.

Just as she started to run, Matthias stepped out of the humid little room, right into her path.

Matthias had gone the shower route not because he particularly wanted to be clean, but because he'd had to scrub his aching head. He'd never been one for good-byes—although previously, that had been because he'd never really been emotionally involved with anybody.

Now, it was because the prospect of leaving Mels hurt like hell.

What did he say? How did he let her walk out the door?

Wrapping a towel around his waist, he walked out of the bathroom and—

Mels screeched to a halt in front of him, like she'd pulled short out of a dead run. Dressed in some of the clothes he'd gotten at the gift shop, she looked like she was being chased.

"Mels—"

"Get away from me." She shoved a hand in her purse, and before she took it out, he knew she was going for her gun.

Sure enough, that muzzle trained directly at the center of his chest.

He put his hands up, palms forward. "What's going on?"

"Nice tattoo—oh, and I just found out that you shot that man here in the hotel. The bullet matches."

"What bullet?"

"The one that I found outside that garage—when I came to see you the first time. You remember, don't you? Well, I gave the casing to someone who did a ballistics comparison—and your gun is the one that was used in that shooting."

Matthias closed his eyes. Shit, that shell must have been from Jim's gun, the one he'd taken, the one that, yeah, he'd used on the operative down in the basement hallway.

"Did you disappear the body from the morgue, too? I'm guessing that, given the ink you two share, you're connected—but don't bother giving me the details. I won't trust anything you say." Mels shook her head, disgust written not just in her face, but in her whole body. "It was lies, all of it—wasn't it. The amnesia . . . the limp—those damn scars, your *eye*." She cursed in a vile way. "Jesus Christ, it was a fucked-up contact lens, wasn't it—with some makeup to get the old injuries to look worse. Oh, God . . ." Now, she cringed. "The impotence, too, right? Guess you decided getting laid was worth the risk of exposure. Or did you just get lazy with the upkeep?"

As he died right in front of her, Matthias could only cross his arms over his chest and take what she gave him. He didn't blame her for the extrapolations: Miracles were inexplicable for a reason, and the conclusions she was jumping to, while they screwed him, would seem like the only possible explanations if he were in her shoes. . . .

When she finally stopped talking, he opened his mouth; then shut it when he realized that he had nothing of value to add. He'd hated lying to her—but she wasn't going to hear that.

Shit, she might as well have pulled that trigger. He sure as hell felt as if she'd mortally wounded him—but honestly, it was his own damn fault, all of this: Although patches of the past remained in a fog, he knew this was exactly the kind of reckoning that had been waiting for him with her.

And in the end, the only thing he could do was step aside and give her the way out—and maybe this was good. There was no way she was going to ever come looking for him now.

The instant he moved, Mels went for the door, all the while keeping that gun on him, and then just as she stepped into the hall, she glanced back.

In a dead voice, she whispered, "There's only one thing I don't understand. Why did you bother? What do I have that you want?"

Everything, he thought.

"So it was just a game, huh," she bit out. "Well, not sure what you thought the prize was—but I am telling you right now to never contact me again under any circumstances. Oh, and I'm calling the police station this minute and telling them everything I know about you. Although I have to wonder exactly how much that is."

And then she was gone, the door shutting automatically behind her.

Matthias closed his eyes and leaned back against the wall.

He'd known that leaving her was going to hurt—but like this? With her thinking he was a manipulator and a liar?

Then again, in his heart, he knew she was right. He'd always been a master liar.

A schemer.

A manipulator—

The headache came on hard and fast, and, as it turned out, it was the final one . . . not because he died, but because on that short-napped carpet of the hotel room, right at the foot of the door Mels had put to good use, everything came back to him—all of it.

From beginning to end, through all the evil in the middle, his memory returned with a roar, exploding the lid off of whatever had kept it down, filling the space between his ears, owning him.

It was ten thousand TVs in a room, all with the sound cranked up, the din so great it was a wonder people down on the street didn't hear the noise.

It was a tsunami that swept onto the shore, wiping clean these last few days of relative innocence with Mels, ruining the landscape he had created for himself with her, revealing the foul earth beneath the feelings he had found with her.

It was, in many ways, worse than the nightmare of Hell.

Because after he saw what he was, up close and in detail, with no shadows to obscure the ugliness, he knew whatever game he was caught in was not going to end well.

His soul was rotten to the core.

And he'd already learned that what you sowed was what you reaped.

Chapter Forty-six

When Mels got home, she took the longest shower of her life: After scrubbing her skin with a soapy washcloth, she stood under the spray until the hot water heater was empty and things got stone cold.

Stepping out and wrapping her flushed body in a towel, she thought she really shouldn't have told Matthias she was going to call the police. No doubt he'd already pulled out of that hotel room—although knowing how paranoid he'd always been, he probably would have done that anyway now that the lie was over.

At least she'd done the right thing. She'd called Detective de la Cruz from the taxi—at his home, no less. And she'd told him everything, even though she felt like she had shamed her father with the way she'd behaved.

At least de la Cruz was on it, and doing his job well: Matthias's room was going to get a visit imminently—probably already had—

Shoot. She really should have stayed put to make sure that Matthias met the police, but at the point when she'd left, she'd been focused on her personal safety.

Dear Lord, she felt dirty . . . absolutely filthy, and her emotions were another goddamn mess.

The irony, of course, was that the reporter in her was convinced she'd feel better if only she knew the why's: Why her? Why now?

What the hell had he really wanted?

Then again, maybe that approach was no more illuminating than asking an out-of-control bus for its thinking behind which pedestrian it had "chosen" to run over.

Going into her bedroom, she took more care than usual as she got dressed, and she also delayed things an extra fifteen minutes to do her hair with a curling iron—which was unheard-of.

Last time she'd taken that thing out had been for a friend's wedding, like, a year and a half ago.

Makeup seemed like a good idea, too, and she even threw some pumps on.

Bracing herself, she measured her reflection on the back of her closet door.

Shit. Still her.

Guess she'd been hoping to see someone else in the mirror, somebody who hadn't spent the night before screwing a stranger she hadn't known for more than a couple of days . . . who had turned out to be a violent criminal.

"Oh, God . . ."

Disgusted, she turned her back on herself, went downstairs, and started the coffee. She didn't make it to the cups in the cupboard, however. Instead, she got stalled at her chair at the kitchen table, even as the percolating got louder on the counter as the cycle finished up.

In the oppressive quiet of the house, her mind seemed to be obsessed with replaying The Matthias Movie, everything from that moment of impact outside the cemetery to the visit in the hospital afterward . . . from her tracking him down at that garage to the two of them at the hotel . . . from the first night to last night. . . .

She'd had inner doubts all along, and yup, look at how it had turned out.

"So stupid . . . so goddamn stupid."

Putting her head in her hands, she rubbed her temples with her thumbs, wondering how long it was going to take before she didn't blame herself for this mess.

Long time. Maybe forever.

Part of her just wanted to rewind time and return to that night when Dick had come to her desk and tap-danced through his prick routine. If only she had decided to leave before that, like at five o'clock with the other reporters, she could have avoided the letch-boss thing . . . and everything else that had followed.

If only . . .

As she sat in her mother's cheery kitchen, the minutes drained away, the sun shifting its position from warming her back to bathing the side of her face and body. And as it moved, so did the close-exam thing, the introspection shifting from just Matthias to other areas of her life, like her career, and what it had been like to live in this house, and how the last few years since her father's death had gone.

Looking at everything, it was clear she'd needed this wake-up call. She'd been so damned driven, and yet stuck in neutral: living at home, but not there for her mother; in mourning for her father—just not aware of it.

But seriously. If her life had required some recalibration, why couldn't she have just changed her hairstyle or gotten a dog or done something less nuclear than having a disastrous affair?

That possibly had legal implications.

Dropping her hands, she sat back and stared at the seat her

mother always used. All the sunlight streaming in through the window was heating up the wood, making it clear why the woman liked that place at the table.

Plus you could see every corner of the kitchen, in case there was something on the stove.

Frowning, Mels realized she'd chosen her father's chair, the one to her mom's left, the one that faced the hallway that led to the front door.

Growing up, she'd always been in the seat across from this one.

She'd stepped into her father's shoes in a lot of ways, hadn't she.

In fact . . . it might be possible that the real reason she'd quit her job down in Manhattan at the *Post* had been to come back here and be with her mom.

The more she thought about it, the more that felt like the truth. First, there had been her father's last words, his dying worries about his wife. And then after the funeral, her mother had been so very alone, lost in so many ways. Like any good daughter, and as she imagined her father would want, Mels had stepped in to fill the void . . . but the sacrifice had driven her mad—and made her resentful of her mother, her job at the *CCJ*, her life here in Caldwell.

Best of intentions. But not so great—or necessary—an outcome. No one had asked her to do what she had. Not her father or her mother. And as she looked around the kitchen, and the dining room, and out through the sliding glass doors to the porch and the garden . . . everything was in order.

Not because she had arranged for the upkeep, however: Her mom had taken care of it all.

Shaking her head, she wondered how this *pater familias* transformation had happened without her knowing it. Then again, was she really asking herself that after the crap with Matthias? Clearly, interpersonal stuff was not her forte—

The sound of keys in a lock was followed by the front door opening, and as light flared in the hall, her mother's diminutive form was spotlit from behind. She was carrying a yoga mat and talking on the phone as she shut herself in and came down the corridor.

"—oh, I know she did, and I really do believe the best of people—up until they prove me wrong. So, yes, I think you should cut this off and stop talking to her." Her mother paused to wave hello and put her things down on the counter by the refrigerator. Then she frowned, as if sensing all was not well in Mels-land. "Listen, Maria, may I call you back? Okay, thanks. Talk to you soon."

She ended the call and put the cell down next to her *Go Organic!* canvas bag. "Mels, what's wrong?"

Mels eased back and thought of her father doing the same thing. The chair had always creaked under his weight, but with her, it was silent.

"Can I ask you something really bizarre?" she said to her mother. "And please know I don't mean to offend you."

Her mom slowly sat down beside her. "Sure."

"Do you remember when Dad was still with us—how he used to sit here and pay bills?" Mels patted the surface of the wood in front of her. "With that checkbook open, the big one that had three checks a page? He'd sit here and write out the bills and put them in the envelopes and record everything in the registry."

"Oh, yes," her mother said sadly. "Every month. Like clockwork."

"He had those reading glasses—they'd fall to the end of his nose, and they'd annoy the crap out of him. And the entire time, he'd squint like his toes were in a vise."

"He hated the whole thing—he made sure it got done, though. Every month."

Mels cleared her throat. "How do you . . . I mean, you pay the bills here now. But where? When? I've never seen you write a check."

Her mother smiled a little. "Your father wanted to do everything by hand. He didn't trust banks—I used to think that monthly ritual was a physical expression of his suspicion of First National Bank and Trust. I'm not like that. I have everything from my car payment to the electric bill to my insurance on automatic deduction. My accounts are linked online—I look at them once a week and keep track of it all that way. Cuts down on stamps, paperwork, and visits to the mailbox. More efficient."

Mels felt surprise ripple through her—but come on. Her mother wasn't a child. "What about . . . like, the lawn care? Dad used to mow the grass, but who does it now?"

"Right after he died, I asked the neighbors how they handled it. Some have their husbands or their kids tackle the yard, and that obviously wasn't an option for me. I gave it a go a couple of times, but it was so much work, I knew it was better to pay someone. I went with a professional service, because I don't want to worry from week to week if it's getting done—plus they do a cleanup in the fall and the spring. Mels, is there something you're worried about?"

"Yeah, actually, there is." She smoothed the table again, running her palm over the place where her father had taken care of things his way. "I—ah, I'm concerned that I've spent the last few years trying to be Dad for you, and not only hasn't it worked—I haven't been very supportive on any level. And you've managed to take care of yourself quite nicely."

There was a long silence. "You know, I've wondered," her mother murmured, "why you stayed. You've been so unhappy here—and it's pretty clear you've resented me."

"Which is not your doing—and a bad call on my part, all the way around." Mels tapped the table. "I just . . . he would have wanted me to look after you. Or someone to."

"That was his way." She shook her head slowly. "He was always

old-fashioned, a real man's man with values that were very traditional. I loved him, so I let him love me the way he saw fit."

"But you didn't need it, did you."

"I needed him. I was very happy with him." A sad light came into
her eyes. "He was the type of man who had to be in control, and I
married him and had you when I was young. But I did grow up."

"Were there . . . problems about that?" God, that seemed so personal.

There was a long period of quiet. "I loved him, he loved me—at
the end of the day, nothing changed that."

"I'm so sorry."

"For what?"

"That he died and left you alone."

"I'm not alone. I have a life now that is rich and full with friends
and things I like to do. And what has worried me most about you
is that that doesn't seem to be happening for you. This is your time
to do what you want, succeed where you wish, choose your own
path. It's what I did with your father . . . and I was so glad I didn't
hesitate because he and I got shortchanged out of a good thirty
more years. You deserve the same the thing, with whoever or wherever or whatever you love."

Tears pricked. "I'm not sure why I haven't figured this all out
until now. I'm a reporter—you'd think I could get to the bottom of
my own life."

"Things are not always so easy and clear." Her mother reached
over and covered Mels's hand. "These last few years have been really hard. But I'm building my own place in this world . . . and I
think you need to do the same."

"You are so right." Mels brushed her cheeks and laughed a little.
"You know what I've been working on these last few months?"

"Tell me."

"An article on missing persons. I haven't gotten anywhere with it—after hours and hours at my desk, staring at the statistics, tracking down the sources, questioning and requestioning everything, I'm no closer than any of the other journalists to what the real story is."

"Maybe you'll find the answers eventually, though?"

Mels met her mother's eyes. "I think I should have been looking into the mirror, instead. It's going to sound weird, but . . . since he died, I've been missing in my own life. I don't know if that makes sense?"

"Of course it does. The two of you were peas in a pod—I'm sure you know this, but he was so proud of you."

"It's funny . . . growing up, I always wondered if he wouldn't have preferred a son."

"Oh, not at all. He wanted you. He used to say you were the perfect child for him. Nothing made him prouder and happier than you did, and that was among the main reasons I loved him so. That father/daughter bond? It's so important, and I should know. I was a daddy's girl—I wanted that for you, too, and you had it with him. I only wish it had been for longer."

"God, I love you, Mom." Mels jerked up from the chair and went around. Falling to her knees, she put her arms around the woman. "I love you so much."

As she felt herself get held in return, she thought that, of all the days when she needed this, today was it.

In the sunshine, in the kitchen, in the embrace of a mother she had never thought she would understand, she realized that her father wasn't the only awesome one in the family—and she had a terrible sense that if he hadn't died, this moment might never have happened.

Kind of made her think about that whole God-doesn't-close-a-door-without-opening-a-window thing.

Mels eased back and wiped under her eyes again. "Well. There you go."

Her mom smiled. "Your father used to say that."

"Was he as good to you as he was to me?"

"Every bit as wonderful. Your father is one in a million—and his death didn't change that. Never will."

Mels rose to her feet. "I, ah, I made coffee a while ago. Would you like some?"

"Yes, please."

When Mels turned away for the coffee pot and the cupboard, she thought at least all was not lost. As devastated as she was about Matthias, this gave her a measure of peace.

And set her to thinking about where she was at.

She might not have found all those missing persons, but she was through being lost in her own life.

Chapter
Forty-seven

Back downtown at the Marriott, Adrian had had a front row seat for the reporter's departure: sitting out in the corridor, he'd watched as the woman took off from Matthias's hotel room, her I'm-outta-here gait a pretty clear indication that she was not a happy camper.

Annnnd the gun in her hand was another dead giveaway.

Looked like he'd given up his sex life for nothing.

As she'd stepped into an elevator, Adrian went to jump to his feet—and for the first time in his life, he didn't go instant vertical.

His body just refused to work right, the pain in his leg joints slowing him down, his lack of depth perception creating a wonky balance problem—

"What the hell's wrong with you?"

Ad glanced across to the left. Jim had arrived in all his glory—or, in this case, all his grunge. The guy appeared to have been pulled through a rosebush ass-backward, his hair sticking out, his clothes wrinkled, the bags under his eyes big enough to pack a family vacation in.

The other angel froze the second their stares met. "What have you done."

Ad let the guy draw his own conclusions. The math was pretty simple—and hey, check it, Jim was getting the solution: His head slowly turned to the door to Matthias's room.

"He's whole?"

"You said she was the key—so I made it possible for him to get a little closer. So to speak."

Ad rubbed the nape of his neck and braced himself for a lecture, or maybe some fireworks. Frankly, he just didn't have the energy for any more drama.

"Are you okay?" Jim asked roughly.

"Yeah, just a little stiff—and the lack of depth perception can be overcome. I'll still be good to go on the field—"

"I don't give a shit about the fighting. I want to know if you're all right. Is it permanent?"

Adrian blinked. "Ah, probably."

"Jesus . . ." The guy looked back over at the hotel room door. "You really took one for the team."

The admiration and respect in the angel's voice made Ad stare at his combat boots. "Don't get all excited—it didn't work."

"What do you mean?"

"She left here about a minute and a half ago—and not to get some bagels and lox and a copy of the *Times*. Whatever happened in there was not all hearts-and-flowers wonderful."

"Shit." Jim cleared his throat. "Well, I talked with Devina. Told her to lay off the reporter."

"How'd that go?"

As the other angel crossed his arms over his chest and thinned out his mouth, Adrian thought, oh, fuck. . . .

"You were with her again, weren't you," he said in a dead voice.

Jim cleared his throat. "I was angry—so was she. It just . . . you know, happened."

"Well, guess that's one way of arguing. Who won?"

"Not a win/lose sitch."

Ad wasn't so sure about that. "Where's the bitch now?"

"I don't know."

As the guy glanced down at the elevator like he was worried about Matthias's female, Ad nodded. "Go check on Mels—I'll keep an eye on Prince Charming."

"I won't be far."

"Take your time. I got this." Unsheathing his crystal dagger, he held it up so that the transparent blade caught the light. "Trust me."

Jim hesitated. "Call if you need me."

"I won't, but I will."

Cue the poof! and Heron was gone.

Adrian limped to the door, rapped with his knuckles, and then opened the way in. Matthias was yanking some pants on, and he froze in midpull.

"I knocked," Ad said dryly.

The other guy finished the job, cranked the sweatpants' tie tight around his waist, and tucked in his Caldwell Red Wings T-shirt. "You're lucky I didn't shoot you."

Sure enough, the gun wasn't far, and Ad knew for a fact that it had been reloaded after the showdown in the forest. Still, it wasn't like the forty was capable of doing anything more than annoy him.

"You off to somewhere?" Ad asked.

Moving fast, the man sat down on the edge of the bed and shoved his feet into those black Nikes. "You always so good with doors?"

"I'm good with a lot of things."

Matthias paused. "You're limping, you know that?"

Ad shrugged. "Bad foot."

"Bullshit."

"I've said all I'm going to."

Matthias cursed as he got up to collect his wallet and wind-breaker. "Okay, fine. But we've got to leave—the cops are on the way. Or will be shortly."

"Why?"

"Mels is going to them right now—she figured out that Jim and I got busy in the basement here the other night. My memory's back, by the way."

"Everything?"

"Yup."

Shit. "Congratulations."

"Not really." The man was speaking quick and concisely. "Listen, Jim said I'm going to face a crossroads?"

Ad nodded. "What happened to your girl?"

"She figured out who I really was."

"That's so not going to help us."

"Well, the eye-opener helped her, and that's more important. I should never have been with the woman."

On that note, Matthias got quiet, and yeah, wow, you could practically smell the wood burning.

"I know what I have to do," he said after a moment. "It's the only way . . . to make things right. I know *exactly* what to do."

Ad let his head fall back in frustration. What this situation did *not* need was any more bright ideas.

"We've gotta blow this place," Matthias said, as he stalked to the door. "But first, a little breaking and entering on the way out."

"Isn't that an oxymoron?"

As the guy just walked into the hallway, Adrian cursed and snagged the cane from where it was by the television built-in thingy.

Turned out it was a good call—the old-man affect increased his speed. Hard to get used to needing the thing, however.

Not really his style.

As Matthias hit the emergency exit into the stairwell, and started descending the concrete steps, Mels's voice dogged him.

It was lies, all of it—wasn't it.

That one sentence, over and over again, like a repeating rifle—or a machine gun—until he prayed for the amnesia to come back.

The tragedy was that nothing around how he'd felt about her had been anything less than the God's honest truth. Same with the physical condition he'd been in, and his sense of where he'd been . . . and where he was in danger of returning.

But over the course of his life? Shit, yeah, there had been too many deceptions to count.

And that was what he was going to take care of.

With him leaving her as she had, and his memory now back in full force, there was no way he couldn't do something about the web of lies and evil he'd spun for so long.

This was indeed the reckoning he'd earned, and he was damn well going to pay the price . . . and do the right thing. Finally.

Keeping up the quick, silent pace down the stairwell, it dawned on him that his partner in crime, so to speak, was probably not making the kind of time he was. Which was so fucked-up. Glancing over his shoulder, he—

Matthias stopped dead and gripped the rail.

The bastard behind him was hovering about three inches over the stairs, ghosting above them like he had anti-gravity shoes on.

"What are you?" Matthias breathed.

Instantly, the man's combat boots went terra firma. "Nothing special."

"Bullshit."

"Aren't we running from the cops? Do you *really* want to do this now?"

Guy had a point, but there was a lot at stake. If only in the mental-health department. "Just answer me one thing. Which side are you on? And before you hit me with another round of 'no BFD,' I know where I've been—and I'm not talking about the Middle East."

"I'm on the side that thinks it's good."

"Which tells me nothing. Even the devil believes he's right."

"She's not."

"She, huh." As the guy shrugged like they were talking about sports . . . or cars . . . or the Thursday-night lineup on NBC, Matthias cursed softly. "So you know the devil, and you're just a normal guy. You assume all of my injuries, internal and otherwise, and you're nothing special."

The roommate lifted one shoulder again, and looked utterly unconcerned with whatever mind-fuck Matthias was rocking.

It was lies, all of it—wasn't it.

"You know," Matthias said roughly, "I've heard about the devil—that he—that *she* is a great liar."

"It's the only thing you can trust."

"Guess I got that in common with her."

"You do, but times change, don't they."

"How does Jim Heron fit into this?"

Adrian exhaled like he was ancient. "Worry about yourself, Matthias. That's the only advice I can give you—just do the right thing, even if it hurts."

Matthias focused on that cloudy eye—which had been his own just twelve hours ago. "Speaking from firsthand experience?"

"Not at all. Now, shouldn't we be running from the CPD?"

Abruptly, he thought about the night with Mels. Shit had ended so very badly, but the night . . . and everything that had had to do with her . . . had helped him find his soul. Without that, and without her, he would have just left Caldwell—and his past—behind.

"Thank you," Matthias murmured. "I owe you."

"I don't know what the fuck you're talking about."

Clearly, he was knocking on a door that was locked, deadbolted, chained, and barred. Fine. He knew how that was—gratitude could be harder to bear than pain.

At least he knew what to do. There was just one more thing. . . .

"Is Jim like you," he demanded.

The guy looked like he was so done with the talking, he was ready to scream, but tough shit.

"Tell me," Matthias barked. "I gotta have some kind of solid in this."

Adrian rubbed his jaw. "You can talk to Jim about that—when this is over, 'kay? Right now, my job is to keep you alive so that you can do the right thing when it comes along. I can't tell you how important this is. Just do the right damn thing for once in your miserable existence."

"Roger that," Matthias said, turning away and taking off once more.

Chapter
Forty-eight

Several blocks over from the Marriott, in the CCJ newsroom, Mels sat in her musical chair, rocking back and forth to the tune of "Yankee Doodle." Her e-mail account was up on her computer monitor, and periodically the auto send/receive coughed another couple of entries into her in-box. The screensaver came on at regular intervals, too, and each time the rainbow-colored bubbles appeared, she'd reach out, fuss the mouse, and keep things alive.

The only call she'd made since she'd come in had been to Tony's contact down in the CSI lab. She'd told him that she'd called Detective de la Cruz and made a statement about everything.

She'd been hoping the phone would ring at any minute with an update on the situation, but de la Cruz and his team were no doubt busy down at the hotel, searching an empty room.

Matthias was long gone—

"Psst."

Shaking herself, she glanced across the aisle. Tony was leaning forward in his seat with a Ding Dong in his palm, offering the little wheel of chemical, chocolaty glory like it was a diamond. "You look like you could use this."

"Thanks." She forced a smile—and thought, What the hell. Maybe a load of sugar and preservatives would wake her up out of this stupor. "Not myself today."

"I can tell. You've been sitting there staring at that screen for the last hour."

"Lot of e-mail to read."

"Then why haven't you been reading it?"

Popping the seal on the Hostess bomb and biting into the thing, the outer shell flaked and sent bits and pieces into her lap. Before they melted and fused at the molecular level with the fabric of her slacks, she picked them off and flicked them into the wastepaper basket.

Man, Ding Dongs tasted delicious.

Better munching through chemistry.

"Hey, listen, Tony . . . I know we've never really talked career stuff, but do you have an endgame with this paper? I mean, is this the place where you see yourself staying for the rest of your working life?"

Her buddy shrugged. "I don't think a lot about that shit. I just work on my articles, do my digging—I'm chill with the future. If this is all I have? I'm good." He grabbed a Ho Ho for himself and stripped off its wrapper. "But I've been waiting for you to pull out."

"From Caldwell? Really?"

"Yup." He took a bite. "You've never settled in. Made the contacts. Kept them going."

He was right, of course. And maybe that was why she hadn't really accomplished as much as she'd wanted to in the last couple of years. Yes, Dick was a prick and a confirmed member of the old boy club, but it was possible she'd been hiding behind that as an excuse for phoning things in.

"I think I want to go back to New York City." Actually, take out the "think," she realized with a jolt. "It's time."

Her mother was okay; Mels was the one who needed direction. And she had a feeling that would be "south."

"You're a damn good reporter." Tony took another bite. "And you're under-utilized here—I think Dick knows it."

"He and I have never gotten along."

"That's true of him and women, generally." Tony crushed the wrapper and tossed it. "So, what are you going to do? You got any in's down in Manhattan?"

Opening up her drawer, she took out a card she'd stuffed in there the day she'd moved to the desk. It read, PETER W. NEWCASTLE, FEATURES EDITOR—and had the iconic *New York Times* masthead right under his title.

Back in the day, she'd met Peter in and around Manhattan, and he was still at the *Times*. She'd seen his name just last Sunday.

"Yeah, I think I do," she murmured. "Hey, speaking of leaving, I have something I'd like to give you."

"Lunch, I hope?"

She laughed a little. "Tragically, no."

Kicking herself out of neutral, she opened up her e-file on all the research she'd done on those missing person cases. Staring at the words she'd typed, the tables she'd made, the references she'd listed, she couldn't help thinking that all this was what she'd been doing before the storm had rolled through her life.

Memories of Matthias rose like spikes breaking through skin, the pain making her short of breath.

Closing her eyes briefly, she told herself to get a grip.

"It's coming over e-mail," she said gruffly.

Tony snagged a Twinkie and swiveled in the direction of his computer screen.

A moment later, she heard him mutter under his breath and then he turned back around to her. "This is . . . incredible. Absolutely incredible—I've never seen . . . How long have you been gathering all this? And what's your angle? Who are your—wait, you aren't turning this over to me exclusively, are you?"

Mels smiled sadly and nodded. "Think of it as my going away present. You've been so generous with me ever since I started. And maybe you can get further with it than I could." She glanced at his screen, seeing all of the work she'd done. "I've been stalled out, but I have a feeling that it's going to be in good hands with you. If anyone can crack the truth behind those disappearances, it's you."

As Tony's eyes went even wider, she knew she'd done the right thing—for herself, for him . . . and most important, for all those missing boys out there, those souls that had somehow, inexplicably, disappeared into the Caldwell night.

Tony was going to find the answer. Somehow.

As Matthias strode down a carpeted hallway in the ground floor, employees-only part of the hotel, he walked with his head up and his arms swinging casually at his sides. Passing by open doors, he read the little plaques next to each one, and checked out various administrative, human resources, and accounting personnel, all of whom were working hard, talking on their phones, typing on their computers.

Busy, busy. Which was perfect if you were looking to infiltrate somewhere where you didn't belong. The key was walking with purpose, like an appointment was waiting for you, and making eye contact in a casual, bored manner. That combination, even more than a suit and tie, was critical: You didn't want to give any of the worker bees an excuse or opportunity to get off their asses and get in the way.

Thank God Adrian had agreed to hang in the lobby. Someone like him, with those piercings, was a billboard for Duck Out of Water in this situation.

As Matthias went along, he knew that sooner or later he was going to find what he was looking for: a vacant computer that was networked into the Marriott's big database. And what do you know, bingo presented itself three doors down in the form of an empty office with a full desk setup: The little plaque detailing who belonged in there had been slid out of its holder, and there were no personal effects on the desk, no coat hanging in the corner—no window, either. Better solution than he'd expected.

Slipping inside and closing the door, he thought it would have helped if he'd had access to the resources of XOps—nothing like a badge with your picture and an IT title on it to smooth over any inquiries. As it was, all he had was a loaded gun with a silencer.

Sitting in the cushiony leather office chair, part of him was very clear that everyone was expendable, that if anybody walked in while he was working, he was going to shoot them and drag the body under the desk.

But God, he prayed it didn't come to that for more reasons than one.

Bending down, he hit the switch on the CPU and cut the boot-up off before the inevitable password-protected sign-in screen flashed. Going in under the operating system's radar, he took control, scrambled the IP address, and jumped onto the World Wide Web.

The XOps computer system was a monolith set up by the best experts he'd been able to recruit, whether they'd been MIT graduates, fifteen-year-old arrogant little shits, or multinational hackers—and each and every one of those big brains had been silenced by means of leverage . . . or the cold embrace of the earth.

After all, the builders of your castle knew your secret escapes—

and he'd especially not wanted anyone in the organization to be aware of the hidden path he now took into the network.

Eventually, someone would probably discover he'd snuck in and out using a ghost admin account, but it would be weeks, months— maybe not ever—

He was in.

A quick check of the clock in the corner of the screen told him he had no more than sixty seconds before he ran the risk of being identified as a concurrent user.

He needed less than thirty.

Putting his hand in his pocket, he took out the SanDisk he'd bought on the way here from the gift shop. Punching the thing into the USB port in the front of the machine, he initiated a data download that was nuclear in its scope, but relatively self-contained in terms of bytes.

Not a lot of operatives, after all, and their missions were short and to the point.

And talk about intel—the files were the lynchpin of his self-protective exit strategy: he'd set up this comprehensive information cache, along with its auto-updating function, the moment the XOps computer systems had been put into service. It was just as important as the weapons and the cash he'd hidden in New York. And London. And Tangier. And Dubai. And Melbourne.

In his business, the emperor stayed on the throne only as long as he could hold on to his power—and you could never be sure when your base was going to erode.

In fact, the return of his memory told him all about how he'd guarded his influence, hoarded it, nurtured it, kept himself alive and in control . . . until he'd begun to stink from the filth of his deeds; until his soul—or what little of a one he'd had—had withered and died; until he'd become so emotionless he was practically an inanimate object; until he'd realized that death was the only way out, and better that he choose the time and the place.

Like in a desert, in front of a witness . . . with a bomb that he'd rigged to do the job.

Guess he hadn't been in control of everything, though, because Jim Heron hadn't left him where he'd lain and so he hadn't died according to schedule.

Without Heron's interference, though, he wouldn't have eventually met Mels.

And he wouldn't be using this information in the way he was going to.

This felt like the better outcome.

Except for the losing Mels part, that was.

Just before he signed out, an abiding curiosity got to him. With a quick shift, he pulled out of his shadow account and his little secret locker of information—and signed in for real, using an account he had set up for one of his administrators about six months ago.

It was still active. And the password hadn't been changed— which was stupid.

Going into the personnel database, he typed in a name and hit return.

In the center of the gray screen, a tiny hourglass spun slowly, and seemed to do that weightless rotation forever. In reality, it was probably less than a second or two. The data that flashed next was Jim Heron's profile, and Matthias quickly scanned the orderly notations.

He wasn't worried about this activity getting traced—and it would. Operatives were going to show up at this particular computer ASAP.

Naturally, they would know it was him, and they wouldn't be surprised.

The next profile he reviewed was his own, and he went back to Heron's again before he signed off. He wasn't sure exactly what was wrong, but something stuck with him, something that just wasn't right. No time to figure it out, however—at least not in this office.

Matthias jacked out and crushed the flashdrive in his fist. After shutting down the comp, he popped open the door, looked to the left and the right, and stepped into the hall. Walking off, he—

"Can I help you?" a female voice demanded.

He paused and turned around. "I'm looking for Human Resources? Am I in the right place?"

The woman was short and stocky, built on the lines of a dishwasher or maybe a file cabinet. She was dressed in a steel gray suit, too, and her hair was cut right at the jawline, like she felt as though she had to prove that she was all business, all the time.

"I'm the head of HR." Her eyes narrowed. "Who exactly are you here to see?"

"I'm applying for a waiter position in the restaurant? The front desk sent me here?"

"Oh for godsake." Ms. VP looked like she was going to boil over on the spot. "Again? I've told them not to refer you guys here."

"Yeah, I know—shouldn't I be meeting with the hospitality manager or something—"

"Take this hall here out to the lobby. Go past the restaurant— until you're almost at the fire exit. There's a door marked 'Office'— you're looking for Bobby."

Matthias smiled. "Thanks."

She wheeled away and started marching in the opposite direction, the muttering suggesting she was already on the phone with whoever she was about to bitch-dial.

Have fun with that, he thought as he strode out.

Chapter
Forty-nine

"You okay, big guy?" Jim asked as he carried Dog back up the stairs to the apartment over the garage.

The little man had been guarding the place all night, keeping everything as it should be, his eyes as fierce as his fur was not.

Up in the studio, Jim put the animal down and went over to the kitchen. "Just kibble this morning, sport. Sorry. But I'll bring you back a turkey club, 'kay?"

As Dog let out a chuff of agreement, Jim figured deli sandwiches were probably not the best diet, but life was too short not to enjoy something as simple as what you liked to eat. And Dog loved 'em.

Running water in the sink, he rinsed out a small red bowl and refilled it. Putting the thing on the floor next to a cup and a half of Eukanuba, he stepped back and let Dog sniff around, take a test bite, and settle into his breakfast.

With the meal in progress, Jim walked over to the door and

took out his cigarettes. Lighting up on the landing, he exhaled and braced one hand on the rail.

The reporter was at work; he'd checked on her as soon as he'd left the Marriott. And given that there was no sign of Devina anywhere, and the tracer spell remained up and rolling on both Matthias and the guy's female, he'd decided to head back here and make sure all was cool.

Now he wasn't sure what to do . . . except listen to Dog crunch.

Off in the distance, a truck traveled over the road on the far side of the meadow, going at a steady pace. Closer by, crows cawed to one another on the pineboughs. Behind him, Dog kept working his jaw.

Everything was so damned tranquil, he nearly jumped out of his skin.

It was on his second coffin nail that he realized he was waiting for Nigel to make an appearance. That British dandy always seemed to show up at critical times, and now felt like one: Jim couldn't believe what Ad had done. The self-sacrifice, the mission critical, the man-up. On some level, it was unfathomable.

Eddie would have been really proud of the guy.

But what were they going to do now? Jim still didn't know where the crossroads were, and Devina was undoubtedly getting up to something.

"Nigel—my man," he muttered on the exhale. "Where are you."

Instead of a royal visit, all he got was ashes to tap off the tip of his Marlboro, and he began to wonder if there hadn't been a trickle-down effect to Devina's getting her chain yanked by the Maker: Looked like the archangels were sitting back on this round as well.

Fair enough—

Just as he turned around, another vehicle came into view on the opposite side of the meadow. It was traveling fast—and it had a friend, a perfectly matched buddy.

Cops.

And what do you know, they were hanging a louie and shooting down the lane.

"We got company, Dog," he muttered, grinding out his butt in the ashtray he kept on the railing. "Come here, my man. Let's disappear together and watch the show."

As he ducked inside, the pair of squad cars tore right up to the double doors, dust rising from their wheels grinding to a halt on the pea gravel.

Naturally, his phone went off as the unis were getting out. With his animal under his arm, he answered the call softly and watched through the drapes.

"I'm busy, Ad."

"Where are you?"

"At the garage. And the CPD just showed up—make my day and tell me you got rid of the body?"

"We fish-tanked it, along with the car he came in. They aren't going to find a damn thing."

"So why are the cops here now?"

"I don't know—hold on." There was some muted conversation at that point. "Matthias is with me. He says it's the bullet Mels took when she came out to the garage—she had it analyzed, and of course it matches the casings in the basement of the Marriott. You can draw the conclusions from there."

"Great."

Now Ad's voice dropped to a whisper also. "By the way, your old boss is good with a computer."

"What's he up to?"

"I think he's going to blow the lid off of the whole XOps operations."

"He's doing *what*?" Jim nearly forgot to keep his voice low. "How do you know this?"

"He and I left the hotel room together, and on the way to the exit, he made a little detour into Toshiba territory. He's got a San-Disk with a lot of information on it—I was right behind him when he loaded up the damn thing."

What was he going to—

The reporter, Jim thought. He was going to give it to her, and tell her to do her job.

Man, talk about your one-eighties. Matthias had devoted his life to keeping XOps hidden. Had killed for it, tortured for it, turned on friends and allies for it. He'd bullied the White House and frightened worldwide leaders; he'd leveraged money and sex; he'd double-talked, double-crossed, and buried the quick and the dead.

And now he was letting it all go?

"We've done it," Jim breathed. "This is the crossroads."

"Looks like it." Ad's voice resumed normal volume. "Anywho, he's all worked up about you—he doesn't want you shanked and told me to call."

Which was another surprise. "Tell him thanks, I can take care of business here. Where's he going?"

"Won't say, and he wants privacy."

"Well, give it to him, but stick around."

"You got it, boss."

Jim hit *end* and scrubbed his face. It appeared as if he'd won the round . . . because the crossroads could be any number of things requiring a choice or a decision that revealed the quality of the soul in question.

And that man was giving up his seat of evil—not by stepping down, but by blowing the place the fuck up.

Jim would have spiked something at the goal line . . . but he didn't want to upset his visitors: Down below, the cops were sniffing around, checking those locked doors where the F-150, the Explorer, and the Harleys were kept. Their next move was to head for the stairs, and as they ascended, he was grateful that Dog stayed silent.

Knock. Knock.

"Caldwell Police," came the shout. "Anybody home?"

Knock. Knock.

"Caldwell Police."

One of the pair cupped his hands together and leaned into the glass, peering inside.

Jim raised his invisible palm and gave the guy a little wave just to be neighborly—but what he really wanted to do was flip his middle finger. This visit probably meant he and his boys needed to decamp—peace and quiet were going to be impossible to come by after this, particularly when the police followed up with his landlord.

But he had other problems at the moment

Especially as the police decided to throw civil rights out the window, and jimmied the lock.

"Mels Carmichael." Mels frowned. "Hello?"

When there was no answer, she hung up and checked the time. One o'clockish. Grabbing her coat, she got to her feet and gave Tony a wave.

As she left through the newsroom's front door, she wondered if she shouldn't have had her buddy get off his phone and come with her. Last time she'd done this, she'd nearly died.

Then again, she wasn't meeting Monty anywhere near the river. And how many people had kicked it in an urban Barnes & Noble?

Stepping over to the curb, she measured the traffic and the temperature, and decided to hoof it instead of take a cab: Monty wanted to convene at that same open-air mall where she'd met Mr.

Ballastics the day before, and it was only five blocks away—besides, maybe the walk would clear her head.

Not.

She spent the entire trip looking over her shoulder, wondering if she was being followed.

On the plus side, there was nothing like a good shot of paranoia to get someone over the afternoon hump. The stuff was better than a shot of espresso, and free.

The street mall was busy again, people out in the April sunshine, hustling between the shops and those chain restaurants where you could eat a huge plate of food as well as a dessert for fifteen bucks. The bookstore was at the far end, and when she walked in, she casually strolled through the stacks.

One good thing about getting out of Caldwell would be never having to deal with Monty and his stupid-ass, pseudo-spy crap again.

As instructed, she went to the back, passed the magazine section, mounted the three steps up into the Romance and Fiction area, and then headed farther down to Military.

Naturally. Because when you were pretending that you were sharing intel of national security-level importance, you didn't want to do it in the Health & Beauty section: A background of picture books of guns and wars were much more manly. Yup.

"You're here," came the hushed voice.

As she turned to Monty, she braced herself—but this was actually him. Same big forehead, same pinchy little mouth, right pair of sunglasses, which he kept on—because wearing something like that made you much less noticeable indoors. Another great plan.

God, her Ray-Bans . . . Matthias had kept them, hadn't he.

"So what have you got for me?" she said roughly, forcing herself to plug into the conversation.

It was so tough to concentrate. The blowup with Matthias had scrambled her so badly, anything that had gone on before it seemed like ancient history. But those two women were still dead, and she was determined to finish the story before she left town.

Monty took a book on WWII aircraft off the shelf and idly flipped through the thing. "You know the victim who was found on the library steps? My pictures match what was on her stomach."

"Her abdomen was marked as well?"

"Yup."

"Well, that's interesting." And highly suspicious. "But they still don't match the first victim's actual body—which is the problem."

"Don't you think that's curious, though? Two dead women with identical inscriptions in their skin, in the same place on the belly— and they were killed in the same way."

"Are you sure you want me to extrapolate from that."

"Excuse me?"

"Well, at least one conclusion is a little disturbing. Maybe you're the killer."

His head turned around so fast, his sunglasses wobbled on his nose. "What the hell are you talking about?"

"Let's look at things from the beginning. The true "first" victim was the one with those markings who was found in the quarry. She's blond, she's young, and she's got her throat slit. Victim number two is a prostitute who colors her hair, blows it out straight, and has her throat slit. Third one? Color. Blowout. The same method of death. And here you are, in the middle of all this, showing up with a photograph of number two with markings superimposed on the abdomen—just like numbers one and three. Now, this second dead girl is a prostitute—perfect place to start if you want to be a copycat in real life. You hire her, kill her, except you get interrupted before you can put the marks were they need to go. You take the pictures, Photoshop them, and show me because you need someone to see your work—someone other than your good self."

He snapped the book shut and took off the glasses. His eyes were dead serious. "Not at all what happened."

"Then how do you explain what you gave me?"

"Someone tampered with her. I'm telling you."

"No offense, but bullshit. Scars don't disappear from skin."

The instant the words came out of her mouth, she thought of Matthias—and then reminded herself that there was no magic in the world. There was, however, plenty of makeup. She'd used it on her own bruises. So had he.

Monty jutted forward on his hips. "I'm not feeding you any more information. I had something you might like to know, but you can go to hell—and give up your day job. I can make it so no one talks to you about so much as the fucking weather."

Mels closed her eyes and bit her tongue.

The truth was, she didn't actually think Monty killed anyone. Egomaniacs were not necessarily murderers—and she'd rolled out that soliloquy because she was tired of being jerked around.

After a moment, she said, "I'm sorry. You're right. . . ." Ego stroke, ego stroke, apology . . . girl eyes. "I didn't mean to go overboard and offend you."

"You need to learn how things are done," Monty grumbled.

"Clearly." Oh, teach me, big boy—blech. "So . . . what else do you have for me?"

He didn't answer her in a hurry, and she had to invest some more smooth-over effort. Eventually, however, he came back around.

"Someone brought in a bullet casing that matches the ones found in the Marriott basement."

Mels lifted her brows. "Really."

"Yup. It's a confidential source, apparently—but CSI established that it was indeed from the gun used in that murder. And here's the bizarre thing. The owner's name that was given over? A dead man by the name of Jim Heron."

Okay, she could *not* believe the guy was feeding her her own damned story.

Monty leaned in. "The question is, how does the gun of a dead guy end up shooting someone in a hotel a good week or more after he died?"

"Someone took the weapon," she said flatly. "And used it."

Monty shrugged. "They're sending officers over to Heron's last known address right now to find out more. And I don't need to tell you that any link to that disappeared body at the Marriott is significant."

"True. . . ." Hell, at least she knew she'd made a difference. And she'd had to bring Jim Heron in on it when she'd talked to de la Cruz: In spite of the fact that the guy had saved her life—twice—the bottom line was that a criminal was a criminal, and obstruction of justice was not just a felony; it was, in her view, a moral outrage.

"Maybe I'll let you know what comes of it," Monty said. "It depends."

"On what?"

"Whether or not I'm still pissed off at you."

As he sauntered away, she cursed and wanted to kick the stack of books next to her. Way to handle a source: by accusing him of murder.

Note to self—save the insults for *after* she got the information.

Although really, what had he given her?

Bracing her elbow in front of a three-volume set on Allied flight paths, she leaned into her hand and cursed—

"Don't turn around."

As he stood behind Mels, Matthias knew he'd better talk fast. She wasn't going to want to breathe the same air he did, and she was exactly the kind of woman who would walk away—or worse.

"I know you don't want to see me—"

"Or talk to you," she gritted out.

"But I have something to give you—"

"Don't want it." Moreover, given by her stiff shoulders, she was probably considering throwing a punch. "I don't want *anything* from you."

Leaning in, he put the SanDisk on the shelf at her eye level and slid the thing into the range of her peripheral vision.

Keeping his fingertip on the black bullet, he said, "You believe that I shot at that man. So believe what's in this." He tapped the plastic casing. "It's the whole story."

"An autobiography of lies? I don't read fiction."

"Not fiction." He tapped the thing again. "It's the whole truth—everything I did, everything I hid."

Her head slowly turned toward the bookcases, and he drank in her profile: The sight of her cut right through him, slicing him to the bone, and he wanted to touch her, pull her back against him, put his face in her hair and smell her.

Instead, he moved the flashdrive even closer. "It's all in here. And I'm giving it to you."

"Why."

"Because after you go through it, after you verify the information—and I know you will—you'll have to believe what I'm saying to you now. When it came to you, and being with you, I always told the truth—that was real, the only real I've ever had. I'm leaving now, and I had to tell you this before I go—"

"Goddamn you, I don't want your confession, and I will *never* believe you about *anything*—"

"Take this. Open it up. The file directory is easy to navigate." He stepped back. "One caveat—do not review the files on a networked computer with access to the Internet. Go laptop—with no Web. It's safest that way."

Her head went back and forth. "You're crazy if you think I—"

"You want the story of a lifetime? You got it." Matthias cleared his throat. "Bear in mind, however, that the information in those files is explosive, so choose wisely who you share it with."

"I'm not looking at it."

"You will. You have to. For everyone's sake, please just open the files."

Matthias lifted his hand and held it above her hair, which had been left down and been loosely curled. Passing his palm downward, as if he were stroking the silky lengths, he then dropped his arm . . . and disappeared into the store.

XOps wasn't going to come after Mels: Part of what he'd built into the organization was a self-destruct protocol. If there was ever an information data dump to the press, everyone was going to scatter, disavow knowledge, and disappear into the populace of whatever country they wanted to settle in.

After all, killers who had their murders come to light were not incented to confess and take their sentencings like good little children. If they stuck together, stood strong, or—and this was the most important piece—retaliated for exposure, they risked being put away for life, or executed for capital crimes against humanity.

Besides, if they were of a mind to lash out at having had their lifestyle taken away, they'd target the whistle-blower, *not* the reporter.

Matthias's gut told him it was going to be okay—and he'd never been wrong when he was this certain. Ever.

He did not leave the store.

Calling on his years of training and experience, he made himself look like he was just another schlub with a baseball cap pulled down low, a hoodie up to his neck, and a book in front of his face.

In fact, he was a professional assassin who left no footprints, no trace, no mark of his ever having been in the store.

He kept his eye on Mels.

Especially as she palmed that SanDisk.

Standing in the Military section, Mels grabbed the flashdrive, the hard plastic casing cutting into her palm. She hated the sound of his voice, and more than that, she utterly despised the way her body seemed to recognize him, even as her mind was all about the epithets.

"Screw you, Matthias. You can take this and—"

She wheeled around, half a mind to throw the thing in his face.

He was gone.

Jogging around the floor-to-ceiling bookcase, she looked down the aisle in front of her . . . the stacks to the left and the right . . . the people milling through the store.

"Goddamn you . . ."

Mels marched all over, searching the Fiction section; then the lower level by the magazines, and even further on to the checkout area. Matthias was nowhere to be seen, no matter where she went or what she looked at. Hell, for all she knew, he'd taken off through a staff-only door.

Hitting the exit, she stepped out into the pale sunlight and shielded her eyes, measuring the crowds.

When it came to you, and being with you, I always told the truth—that was real, the only real I've ever had.

Okay, right, the healthy thing to do was throw his little parting gift in the trash and walk away from the drama to focus on something that actually mattered—like what she was going to do with the rest of her life or wrapping up that article on the dead women.

For all she knew, he'd just downloaded a bunch of eighties ballads off iTunes.

Left with a whole lot of nothing doing at the mall, Mels strode back to the CCJ offices, pushed her way inside the newsroom, and stopped as the chaos enveloped her. So familiar, the sounds of phones ringing and voices muttering and feet hitting the concrete floor as people paced by their desks or went back and forth to the kitchen for more coffee.

She was going to miss this place . . .

Holy crap—she was actually going to leave.

The irrevocable decision settled onto her shoulders not as a weighty burden, but more like a grounding that felt right. And God, she hung on to the positive sensation because, at the moment, she really needed something that didn't feel like an epic failure.

That run-in with Matthias had taken the wind out of her sure as if she'd been knocked in the chest.

Walking over to her desk, she sat in her chair and took a stab at writing her resignation letter. The wording came out stiff and formal, but like there was another option? After massaging the text around for a while, and redoing the beginning, she saved the thing without printing it out. There was stuff yet to wrap up here, and Dick was just the kind of prick to take her two weeks' notice and shove it down her throat by telling her to leave right away.

Besides, it was probably better to know where she was going first. In this economy, no one just walked out of a job.

Easing back in her chair, she stared at her computer screen again.

Hard to say how long it was before she took the SanDisk out of her pocket. Could have been ten minutes. Fifty. An hour and a half.

Rolling it around in her palm, she eventually eased down on the white slide, and extended the silver metal plug-in.

Leaning forward, she went to put it into the USB port . . . and stopped just short of pushing it home.

Getting up, she put her purse on her shoulder and went across the aisle to Tony's partition. "I'm taking off for the day—just on follow-up. If anyone's looking for me, tell them to hit my cell?"

"You got it," he said as his own desk phone rang. "Tony DiSanto—hey, yeah, I was waiting to hear back from you. . . ."

As he waved at her and fell into his conversation, she remembered she still didn't have a car.

Outside, it took some time to get a cab, and of course, four in the afternoon was close enough to rush hour so that her taxi got stuck in the congestion on the Northway. When she finally got home, her mom was out, and as she checked the calendar on the wall and found that it was bingo night, she wondered why she hadn't noticed all the entries in the little boxes before. Bridge, Pilates, yoga, volunteering at the church, manning the help desk at

St. Francis in the pediatrics department, lunches and dinners with the girls . . .

Glancing around the kitchen, at least she knew that after she left, her mother wasn't going to be alone.

Mels grabbed a raspberry Snapple out of the fridge and went upstairs, the wooden steps creaking in the same way they always had. Up in her room, she closed the door and turned to her closet.

For some reason, she felt like she should get out her mismatched suitcases and start packing.

But instead of starting that job way prematurely, she looked over at her desk. Her old laptop was sitting on the same stretch of painted wood she'd done her homework on when she'd been in middle school and high school.

Going over, she sat down in the spindly chair and took out the SanDisk.

Before she plugged it in, she reached around the back of the laptop and disengaged the modem wire. Then she logged on and disabled Wi-Fi.

"I've got to be out of my mind."

She shoved the flashdrive in and the AutoPlay pop-up appeared in the center of the screen. Out of the options for Removable Disk (E:) she chose "Open folder to view files."

"What the . . . hell?"

The file directory was so big, she had to scroll down. Word documents. PDFs. Excel spreadsheets. The titles were alphanumeric codes that were clearly part of an organizational system, but they made no sense to her.

Picking one at random, she double-clicked, and frowned, pivoting into the screen.

The data appeared to be . . . dossiers of men, with their pictures, names, dates of birth, height, weight, eye and hair color, medical details, training certifications, and assignments—God, the assignments. Arranged by date, and with notes about countries and targets . . . and exterminations.

"Oh, my God . . ."

Shifting back to the directory, she opened another file, which seemed to detail sums of money, huge sums of money . . . and another, coded one about contacts in Washington, D.C., and the "favors" these individuals had asked . . . and still more about recruitment and training . . .

You want the story of a lifetime? You got it.

As the daylight dimmed and night came over Caldwell, she sat at her childhood desk and read everything.

Eventually, she returned to the dossiers, and this time, she took it slowly.

In a way, the men were all the same, their faces and ethnicities blending into one archetype of aggression and effectiveness. And if these assignments listed were true, she'd read about the deaths, some of which had been defined to the international public as "natural causes" or "accidents" or "counter-insurgent attacks." Other targets she thought were still alive . . . but perhaps that was just a case of the worldwide news machine not yet catching up with reality?

Was it possible this was legit?

Sitting back, she took a drink from her now room-temperature Snapple, and tried on for size the concept that maybe, just maybe, this was real.

Okay, assuming it was, Matthias's paranoia didn't seem unjustified . . . and it would also explain why he'd been on the run the night she'd hit him with her car. Also might explain why the identity he'd had was someone else's—and the reason that even with his amnesia, he'd had sensed that the house at the address on his driver's license hadn't been his own.

And maybe this was what was behind him killing that man

down in the basement of the Marriott. If Matthias had been part of this organization—and this level of access seemed to suggest he most certainly was—then it made sense if he were on his way out of it that someone would be sent to kill him.

And he'd have to defend himself . . .

Going through the dossiers a third time, she noted that each one had a red, green, or orange check by the name—

Jim Heron was among the men. Which somehow wasn't a surprise.

And he had an orange marking. Which, assuming the traffic-light connection was correct, meant he wasn't alive, but he wasn't dead either.

Interesting.

Continuing on through the listings, she gasped. About seven men down, she found a red-marked name with the notation, *Caldwell, New York*, RECLAIMED and the date of the night before last.

It was the dead guy. From the Marriott.

Who Matthias had shot.

And look . . . here was another. An orange mark by the name, last contact in Caldwell, New York, twenty-four hours ago.

What did she want to bet that he was a second man sent for Matthias?

Mels took another hit of the Snapple and grimaced at the sickly sweet taste. As her heart started to beat hard, she knew it wasn't from the caffeine.

What if it had been real, she thought again. All of it . . .

Going back to the directory, she carefully reviewed the other files again and started to piece together the structure of the organization, including its recruiting strategy and the way its funds flow worked. There was nothing about where its headquarters were, or what kind of administrative support they had, or exactly how its "clients" knew to contact them.

Was this organization affiliated with the government? Was it private sector?

She grabbed a pen and scribbled some notes on a pad.

Given the identities of the targets that had been effectively eliminated, she was struck with a chilling sense that this shadow organization—which had no logo, no title even, on any of the documents—went very high up. Those who had been taken out were largely political figures overseas, suggesting an international agenda far too broad-based to be generated by a private citizen, a common-interest group, or even a large, multi-national corporation.

This was the business of a whole nation.

And with her knowledge of current events over the last three years, it was pretty clear that the exterminations forwarded America's position across the globe.

Tapping her pen on the desk, she thought of other special ops groups, like the Navy SEALs, for example—or the Rangers. Those men were heroes, legitimate soldiers who functioned within rules of engagement.

This network of killers was completely outside of that.

The final spreadsheet was probably the most chilling one: a list of all the missions over the previous decade—and the dead, including a column for collateral damage.

Not a lot of that. Not much at all. And no women or children—at least, not that were listed.

Considering how this operation worked, she had a feeling the latter was not the result of any moral objection, but rather out of a directive to stay under the radar.

And again, for the men who had been killed . . . she knew ninety percent of the names, and they were evil . . . pure evil, the kind who slaughtered their own citizens or headed up brutal regimes or set in motion events of horrific proportions.

She imagined that the few she didn't recognize were of the same ilk.

This group of exterminators had done good work in a bad way, she supposed: Hard to argue that their efforts weren't justified, given the résumés of the targets.

It was like her father's ethos on a global scale . . .

Mels returned once more to the dossiers.

Matthias was nowhere to be found in the pictures or the names.

But she had a chilling suspicion as to the why.

He was the basis of it all, the driver. Wasn't he.

When it came to you, and being with you, I always told the truth—that was real, the only real I've ever had.

Rubbing her face, she cursed into her palms.

He had given her this to prove himself—and as much as she wanted to find some lie in and among the files, some fiction that revealed itself in contradictions among the nitty-gritty, too much of it was verifiable when it came to current events. She'd seen the articles, the newscasts, the commentaries around these deaths for herself over the years.

This was real. . . .

This *was* the story of a lifetime.

Chapter Fifty-one

Across the street from Mels's house, Matthias stood in the lee of a large maple, arms crossed over his chest, feet planted a hip's distance apart.

He could see her in the upstairs dormer, at her desk, her head bent, her brows down hard in the light shining from the ceiling above her. From time to time she eased back in whatever chair she was sitting in and stared straight ahead—then she returned to her laptop.

She was going through everything.

His job was done.

So why didn't he feel at peace? Surely this was his prove-it-or-lose-it crossroads, this confession through her that was going to go out to the world? On that single flashdrive, he'd undone his years of work, sending his organization into a free fall that was going to wipe it out: The operatives would scatter for cover. The politicians would go ultra-earnest and disavow all knowledge. A congressional or senatorial special committee would be convened. And at the end of countless taxpayer dollars and months of inquiry, the matter would be closed.

And then another arm of the operation would be started by someone else: Dirty work was still going to be sought by this otherwise lawful nation, because sometimes you had to sink to the lower level of your enemies and play ball in their sewer.

That was reality.

So why the hell was he not, at this very moment, dragging himself to Manhattan, getting his cache, and hitting the road for parts and countries unknown?

It wasn't Mels.

Leaving her was the death of him in a lot of ways, but he was okay with that. His disappearing was the right thing for her, and that was all that mattered—even though he was going to miss her for every heartbeat between now and when he actually died and stayed that way.

And it wasn't his conscience. He didn't feel the need to turn himself in just so his enemies could find him and kill him in a prison. His only chance of survival was out in the real world—and it wasn't like the constant hiding was going to be a party.

That shit was just a movable set of bars.

He was going to pay for the rest of his life for what he'd done.

So what the *hell* was his problem?

Abruptly, a scene in the desert came to him, the recollection of him and Jim in that crude hut, the sand under his operative's feet . . . the bomb under his own.

Matthias hadn't remembered anything after the explosion, not the horrible pain he must have been in, not the miles through the dunes or the Jeep that Isaac Rothe had come in or that first, endless night after he'd blown himself apart. But he knew what had happened a little while afterward: Jim had come to his bedside and threatened to expose what he'd nearly done to himself.

He had granted Jim his freedom from XOps then, giving the man a pass to get out.

The only one.

And then, after two years, their paths had crossed once more, up in Boston. In contrast to what had happened on the other side of the planet, that slice of the recent past was still unclear to him, the precise ins and outs of what had gone on fuzzy, even as the rest of his life was clear as a bell—

At the end of the block, a man turned the corner at a lazy pace and entered into the pool of light beneath a lamppost. He was walking a dog, a large dog, and he was dressed in some kind of suit . . . an odd suit, something that looked old-fashioned—

It was the man from the Marriott's restaurant.

Matthias put his hand into his pocket and settled his palm on the butt of the gun he'd gotten from Jim.

When you were in the situation he was, just-in-case was the only way of thinking.

The man came closer, going out of the reach of the illumination briefly before reentering into the lit skirt of the next streetlamp.

The dog was a wolfhound, an Irish wolfhound.

And as the pair passed, the man looked at Matthias with eyes that seemed to glow. "Good evening, sir," he said in an English voice.

As Mr. Dapper kept going, Matthias frowned. There was something off, something wrong. . . .

The guy didn't throw a shadow, he realized. Except how could that be?

Matthias quickly looked up to Mels's window. She was okay, still sitting there at her desk, reading about him—and when she dialed her phone and put it to her ear, he wondered who she was calling.

Time to go.

It was his theme song with her, wasn't it.

He glanced back, expecting to see the man and the regal beast. They were gone.

Okay, he was losing his ever-loving mind.

Turning away, he walked over to his rental car and took out the key with its little laminated tag. As he opened the door, Jim Heron was still on his mind, almost as if the guy had been placed there, like a cognitive billboard.

Matthias got in, locked the doors, and started the engine. Doing a three-sixty with his eyes, he double-checked that there was no one around, making sure that dog and the Englishman hadn't decided to magically reappear—

At that moment, a sedan turned in off the main road and traveled at a slow pace right to the driveway of Mels's place. The garage door went up, and a tidy-looking woman got out and went inside, pausing to hit the button to reclose the panels.

Mels was not alone.

This was good.

Matthias hit the gas and took off, thinking about the information, the challenge, the opportunity he'd given her. The good-bye that he hoped, maybe over time, would recast their short tenure together in her mind.

He was an evil man, and she had brought the only good out in him he'd ever had. Perhaps she would believe that someday. After all the truth was ugly, but hopefully it had served a purpose—

Matthias jerked in the driver's seat, shock flooding through him as the last thing he'd looked at before signing off on that desktop at the Marriott came back to him: his profile, his live profile, his current one that had not been included, on purpose, in his cache of exit strategy intel—

Jesus Christ.

That made no fucking sense.

As far as XOps knew, he was *dead*—it had been right there, so blatant he hadn't paid any attention to the red check by his picture.

So why the hell had they sent an operative to Caldwell for him?

He hit the brakes for a stoplight at the very moment it all became clear. "Oh . . . *shit.*"

The first operative had come to the Marriott. The second had shown up at Jim's place at that garage. And in both cases, everyone had reasonably assumed the assassins had been sent for Matthias.

Except he wasn't the target.

Jim Heron was.

The man's dossier had been marked orange, which meant his death hadn't been confirmed in person when he had "died" in Caldwell. So as far as the organization was concerned—and they were right—Heron was living and breathing.

And they were going after him.

The first rule of XOps always had been no loose strings. And there had been a number of people who had disapproved of Matthias's letting the man go—and now that he was out of the picure?

Heron was fair fucking game.

Chapter
Fifty-two

It wasn't that Jim couldn't appreciate the thoroughness, but come *on*. The CPD had shown up in the early afternoon, and it was now close to nine at night and the boys in blue were still hanging around.

The initial breaking-and-entering had just led to a walk-through. The real fun and games had come when they'd called the landlord— who, after he'd been informed his tenant had died well over a week ago, came at once and gave them permission to search the property in a legit way.

Funny, the old guy had still been wearing a traditional butler's uniform—and still looked like he should have been in a home instead of marching up and down stairs and offering everyone "refreshments." But he'd been very gracious, and opened up all manner of doors—except for one.

Even he hadn't been able to crack the crawl space where Eddie was kept. Then again, the spell that guarded that compartment had turned its panels into those of a bank vault.

When the cops had wrapped up their preliminary stem-to-stern, they hadn't found much. No weapons, because Jim had collected them all. No laptop because it was under his armpit. A couple of casings out in front from his playing target practice—but they already had one of those. Cigarette butts in an ashtray and some food in the fridge—big whoop.

Annnnd then it was time for round two, with the nitpicks arriving with their fingerprinting brushes and their big-ass Scotch tape, and the photographer snapping everywhere, inside and out. Finally, the yellow police tape had been run around and nailed into a tree on either side of the pea gravel. Kibitzing. Followed by a couple more exterior photographs.

Finally they were pulling out—and at least it hadn't been a total waste. Halfway through the penetration, as it were, Jim had sneaked off with the computer and his phone and made arrangements to rent another place in Caldwell.

There were advantages to having kept a couple of his home-grown aliases alive—and he and his three boys sure as shit couldn't stay here anymore.

As the last squad car took off and the CSI van pulled out, Jim put Dog down. "I thought they were never going to fucking leave."

The animal chuffed in agreement and sank into a big stretch, even though he'd hardly been traumatized: He'd slept soundly on Jim's arm, draped boneless as a waiter's cloth. Now, however, he wanted out.

Jim took a piss first, though. And texted Adrian that the coast was clear.

Opening the door to the outside stairs, he broke the nice official seal the CPD had put on things. "Oops."

Carrying Dog down to the ground floor, he let the furry little guy do his thing in his favorite stretch of bushes.

Just as the animal trotted back and Jim started walking him

back up the staircase, a car came tearing along the main road at the far side of the meadow, going at a dead run and skidding onto the lane that led to the garage's front door.

Matthias was behind the wheel.

Jim could sense the imprint clear as day. And Ad was with him, as instructed—had been all along, providing a stream of text updates: apparently, the angel had trailed the guy from a meeting with Mels at a Barnes & Noble downtown to a car rental place where Matthias had gotten himself a shiny new Ford product . . . to outside that reporter's home, as if the guy were doing a final check-in.

Certainly appeared as though Matthias had followed through on the XOps data dump, giving over the keys to Pandora's box to his woman.

So . . . what the hell? If that was the crossroads—and it seemed logical it could be—at any moment the man should get subsumed into Heaven, the win complete. Instead, he was pedal to the metal, coming here?

Unless the reporter had to follow through before it counted?

No, that was her will, not his—and Matthias was the focus. What he did, his actions and choices, was the issue—Jim had learned that one in the initial round with the guy: When Matthias had pulled the trigger on that gun, with the intention of killing Isaac Rothe, that had been enough to condemn him—the fact that the kid hadn't died had not been dispositive.

Intent had been the key.

Jim put Dog inside and jogged back down the stairs, wondering what the twist was.

The driver's-side door opened before the car was in park—probably not a good sign.

Matthias jumped out and ducked under the police tape. "We were wrong."

"I'm sorry?"

"The operatives were coming for you. They think I died—I saw it in my file. And XOps doesn't waste time on the dead, unless they're reclaiming them."

Jim frowned. He'd assumed the organization believed he was taking a dirt nap as well. "They think I'm still breathing?"

"I went into the system, and it's right in your dossier—status unconfirmed."

"But you came to check on me."

Matthias frowned like he was fighting with his memory. "I did?"

Well, that explained why the XOps record read as it had.

Matthias slashed his hand through the air like the particulars were the least of their problems. "Look, the assassins only came when we were together, and that first one may have seen me, but he was dead before he could pass the intel along. Think about it— they were coming for you the whole time."

So what, Jim thought. It wasn't as if they could kill him.

And then it dawned on him. "So what are you doing here? I thought you were leaving town?"

The man looked around, searching the shadows. "I wanted to make sure you knew so you'd watch your back."

Jim shook his head slowly in disbelief. The old Matthias? This conversation never would have happened. Self-interest had been the name of the game.

"I always watch my back," Jim said softly. "You should know that."

"I guess I figure I owe you."

"That's not like you."

"Whatever, I just don't want you waking up dead one morning." The man's eyes kept roving, his vision clear, thanks to Adrian— who was hovering in the background, an invisible guard. "You saved my life a couple of years ago, and I didn't think it was a favor.

Now? It gave me . . . a priceless few days that are worth every torture I'm going to wind up with soon enough."

"You sound so sure of that."

"You're part of this game—or whatever it is. You have to be. So you know where I've been. And as for XOps, in the next couple of days, maybe a week, everything is going to be over—you'll know when it happens. Everyone will know. If I were you, I'd go into deep hiding and stay that way."

Okay, this was all great, but where were the crossroads . . . ?

"You came here just to tell me this?" Jim said.

"Some things you've got to do yourself. And you . . . matter. I can lose myself—that's fine. Hell, that's inevitable. But I'm not living with your death on my conscience. Not if I can do something to prevent it."

Jim blinked, and was surprised to find some of the perma-pressure on his chest lifted a little.

God, he hadn't expected to get emotional. Hadn't thought that was possible anymore.

Matthias took a deep breath. "And I'd stay if I could, but I can't. I've got to get moving—and besides, I know you have good backup. That roommate of yours is a hell of a fighter—"

Another car made the turn onto the lane and came flying toward the garage.

"What is this, a fucking convention," Jim muttered. Except then he sensed who it was.

Not the cops. Not an operative.

"I think your girl is here," he said to Matthias softly.

As the headlights of her mother's car hit the garage in the woods, Mels's hands tightened on the steering wheel.

Matthias was standing next to a sedan with Missouri license

plates—clearly, a rental. At his side, Jim Heron loomed like a sentry.

Neither seemed particularly happy to see her, and tough shit with that.

Skidding to a halt on the far side of the police tape, she cut the engine and got out, marching up to the men.

In the tense moment before she spoke, she noticed for no good reason that the night sky was spectacular, glowing clouds streaking across the heavens, forming a shifting patchwork over the stars and the bright moon.

"I need to talk to you," she said gruffly. "Alone."

Matthias turned to Jim and spoke quietly; then the other man stepped away. The whole time, Matthias was looking at her face as if he'd never expected to see her again, his eyes roaming, drinking her in.

Mels fought the urge to do the same. God, she still felt a pull toward him and that was not just nuts; it was suicidal.

Crossing her arms over her breasts, she kicked up her chin. "Guess you avoided the cops—and intend to keep doing so."

"I told you I was leaving." His voice was rough. "What are you doing here?"

"I read through those files. Didn't you think I'd have some questions?"

"None you'd ask of me."

"Who better to go to than the primary source."

As he met her eyes, his stare was steady and focused, like he was a man with nothing to hide. "It's self-explanatory—"

"It was your baby, wasn't it." She nodded in Heron's direction. "You ran them all—you recruited them, told them what to do, kept control of the entire organization."

"So you think I should go to jail."

"Well, yeah. Although if what I saw is true, you did the world a service." She stalled out briefly. "To be honest . . . I'm stunned that you gave it all to me."

"I meant what I said." He dropped his voice. "I need you to believe that what I had with you was the truth—I can't . . . I can't live with the idea that you think I lied about that. And as for that operative at the Marriott—he was sent to kill, and it was a case of either we took him out or he completed his mission. We had no choice."

"You and Jim Heron?"

"Yes."

"Did you take the body?"

"No, we did not—but reclamation of remains is standard operating procedure for XOps. Someone else took care of that."

"XOps is the name, huh."

"It has no name, but that's what we call it."

"Some of the men were marked with an orange strike—what does that mean?" She pointed to Jim. "Like he was."

"In those cases, there has been some intel suggesting a mortal event, but the body has not been claimed or otherwise visually confirmed."

"Jim is certainly alive and well."

"He is."

A stretch of silence followed, and Mels thought back to being against the man's body, the two of them moving together under the sheets—so close, heart-to-heart, until the whole world didn't exist, the power and combustion between them sweeping everything away.

"What can I say to help you with this," he whispered. "What can I do."

"Tell me where you're going."

"I can't."

"Or you'd have to kill me, isn't that the line."

"Never. Not you."

Cue another stall-out, and in the tense quiet, she retraced the steps she'd taken to come out here: As soon as she'd finished looking at all the files on that flashdrive, the urge to confront him had taken hold. A quick dial into her contacts at the CPD had indicated he hadn't been arrested and there were no leads on his whereabouts. In the end, she'd decided to drive out here, because Jim Heron was the only contact she had.

And now here she was, speechless.

She wanted to yell at Matthias, as if his past had been lived solely to screw her.

She wanted to rail against the whole course of their . . . God, it wasn't even a relationship, was it. More like a collision that had involved so much more than just her car.

She wanted to throw her arms around him . . . because, looking in his face, she sensed that it could be true . . . the things he'd given her on the SanDisk—as well as the things they'd been to each other. So much in this situation was bizarre, but the feelings . . . could they have been real?

"What now," she demanded hoarsely, mostly to herself.

"As in?"

"I have a feeling, even if I called the cops again right now, that you'd get away."

He inclined his head. "I would."

"So what are you going to do for the rest of your life? Run?"

"Evade death. Until it finds me and sends me to Hell. And both are going to happen."

A chill went up her spine, tingling in the nape of her neck, making her hyper-aware of everything from the pine scent in the air to the coolness of the night to those lazy, traveling clouds overhead.

Matthias seemed sad to the point of agony. "Mels, I need you to know that I didn't have a clue what to do. The amnesia was real, and when things started coming to me, I kept them from you because . . . that expression on your face in that hotel room this morning was something I never wanted to see—and I knew it was coming. I knew it was inevitable. The thing was, there was no good news in any of my memories—no goodness, either. But with you, I was different." He dragged a hand through his hair and touched beside his eye, running his fingertips around the faded scars. "This I can't explain. I just can't—but it wasn't makeup and contacts. And that is the God's honest. The same's true about the impotence. I didn't lie about that."

Shit. He struck her as so open, everything about him seemingly bared to her.

Except, wasn't that what good liars did? They made themselves appear to be speaking the gospel—and they had a way of figuring out what would work with whoever was in front of them, what approach, what combination of affect and vocabulary would be successful.

Good liars were so much more than fib makers. They were self-ish seducers with agendas.

"I can't believe you," she said roughly.

"And I don't blame you. It is, however, the truth. My reckoning is coming for me—one way or the other the past is going to catch up with me, and I'm at peace with that. I was lucky—I got sent back to set things right, to give you what I did so you can expose the whole organization. That's the only way I can make amends, and it's also going to get you what you want—the story that can make an entire career. In the end, we'll both have what we deserve."

Funny, but her work had never seemed less important.

"You know what is still bothering me?" she said numbly. "I've never understood why I fell so hard for you—that's bothered me all along. I just can't find the reasoning, I mean, why a man I didn't know, who didn't even know himself? But you pursued me, didn't you—and you get what you want. So be honest with me now, why did you do it? Why . . . me."

"For the simplest reason there is."

"And that is?"

He was quiet for so long, she thought he wasn't going to answer her. Except then he said in a cracked voice, "I fell in love with you. I am a monster—it's true. But I opened my eyes in that hospital and the second I saw you . . . everything changed. I went after you . . . because I am in love."

Mels exhaled and closed her eyes, the pain in her chest taking her breath away. "Oh . . . God—"

"No!"

Her lids flew open as Matthias hollered, and then everything went into slow motion.

With a powerful shove from him, she went flying, her body cast aside as something whistled by her ear and pinged off the side of the garage.

A *bullet*.

Mels hit the pea gravel and slid along the drive. Scrambling to stop her momentum, she clawed at the loose ground cover as she rolled onto her back.

And saw everything.

Just as the moon broke free of the clouds, and silvery white light rained down on the night landscape, Matthias heaved his whole body up into the air, the trajectory putting him directly in front of Jim Heron.

Mels shouted out, but it was too late.

The illumination from the heavens spotlit him as he put his chest in the way of the second shot . . . that had clearly been meant for the other man.

She would never forget Matthias's face.

As he was mortally struck, his eyes were not trained on the one who was firing or the one he was saving. They were looking to the light from above, and he was . . . at peace.

As if his final act put him at ease all the way to his soul.

Mels reached out, as if she could stop him, or catch him, or re-wind time—but the end had come for him, and, God, it seemed like he had expected it.

Perhaps even welcomed it.

She screamed, the shrill sound peeling out of her throat. "Matthias . . . !"

His body landed in a heap, and the fact that he didn't try to brace himself against the impact was testament to how badly he was struck.

Tears sprang to her eyes as she tried to crawl over to him—

But she was held in place by invisible hands.

Chapter Fifty-three

Ultimately, it had been the moonlight that had shown the way.

As Matthias had stood and talked with Mels, he had kept his eyes steadily on her, because it was crucial that she believe him, and he knew he wasn't getting another chance. Indeed, he had never spoken more truthful words, in spite of the fact that some of them sounded crazy, and in so many ways, his life would be complete only if by some miracle she could believe what he was saying.

And then he had had the chance to tell her he loved her. To her face.

It was more than he had hoped for or deserved.

Except as he did, the moon peeked through the clouds, throwing shadows onto the ground, shadows of trees, branches, cars . . . people.

Including the operative in black who had crept up to the edge of the forest.

And was lifting his gun and leveling it across the driveway.

Matthias's first move was to get Mels out of the line of fire, and as she hit the fine gravel, he heard the first shot strike the garage. The second discharge was going to be deadly—but not to her.

Jim was standing unprotected by the rental car, as obvious a target as a goddamn dartboard.

Matthias reacted in an instant, throwing himself in the way of the second shot, becoming a human shield to protect the other man. Sailing through the air, he somehow timed the jump and the trajectory perfectly.

As he felt the bullet break into his sternum and strike his heart, he thought, Well . . . here it was.

His final moment on earth.

And it felt right, so right. He had done such ugliness, such evil, over the course of decades, but at least he was ending on a high note, a right note—giving Jim enough time to out his gun and pick off the assassin.

Which he would do. Heron was one of the best. Always had been.

He was going to take care of business, him and that deadly roommate.

And Mels had heard the truth, even if she couldn't believe it.

In the brief, rushing weightlessness as Matthias returned to earth, his eyes went to the sky above. He was going back into the pit of Hell, so he figured he might as well enjoy the view of Heaven one last time—

God, that moon, that beautiful, shining moon with its pure white light that bathed all parts of this drama—

The gravel drive jumped up and grabbed him. As he landed, his vision grew preternaturally clear so that he saw what he had known would happen: Jim palming his forty, waiting one breath, then two . . . and when the shooter popped his head out to check the carnage, Heron pulled the trigger and picked the other man off, nailing him in the cranium, blowing him back flat.

It was a crack shot that could only have been made by an expert.

And it meant that Mels was safe.

Lying flat on his back on the ground, Matthias turned his head to his woman. She was fighting against some kind of hold on her, her arms stretched out as if she were trying to reach him.

The second Jim yelled, "Clear!" she broke free of whatever had been keeping her stuck and scrambled over.

Matthias felt her take his hand, and as he looked up into her face, she was more beautiful than the moon.

He smiled at her, and then saw that she was crying. "No," he groaned. "No, you're fine—"

"Get an ambulance," she shouted.

It was too late, but he appreciated the thought.

Funny, shouldn't he feel pain? He was dying; he knew that by the way his breathing was getting difficult. But there was no agony, not even discomfort. Instead, he felt giddy, his brain buzzing.

On the verge of death, he was totally alive.

He squeezed her hand. "I love you. . . ."

"Don't even think about it," she barked.

"It's how . . . I feel. . . ."

"No, the dying thing. You are *not* dying on me." She jerked her head up. "Call nine-one-one!"

"Mels—Mels, look at me." When she did, he smiled in spite of the knowledge of where he was going to end up. "Just—let me see you. . . . You're so beautiful. . . ."

"Damn you, Matthias—"

"Yes, I am." Damned, that was. "Listen to me—no, just listen. I want you to wear your seat belt . . . wear it . . . promise me—"

"Screw you, stay with me and make me."

"Wear . . . it. . . ."

"Don't leave me," she moaned. "Not now, not when . . . I'm so confused . . ."

"*Wear it.*"

Turned out those were his two last words, and she was the final thing he saw: An abrupt suffocation took over, his cells starving for what they weren't going to get, the chaos jamming his brain, stealing from him the last moments he had with her.

And then it was done.

Vision gone, body still, senses of taste and smell finished.

He still had his hearing, though.

Mels's voice wrapped around him. "Stay with me. . . ."

God, he wanted to; he truly did.

That was not, however, going to be his destiny.

As the operative dropped to the forest floor like a side of beef, Jim lowered his gun, ready to kick his own ass. He and Adrian had been so wrapped up in the drama in front of them, neither one had paid any attention to the assassin creeping in through the forest.

Then again, if they had intervened . . . Shit, who could have ever guessed Matthias would take a bullet for someone?

"Adrian, get out there," Jim hissed.

Ad nodded and disappeared. Seconds later, the angel sounded an all-clear from the periphery.

"Call nine-one-one!" Mels said from where she was crouched, holding Matthias's hand.

This was the real crossroads, Jim thought. And Matthias had passed.

They had *won*—

Mels jerked up and glared at him. "We need an ambulance—"

From up above, a shaft of light pierced the sky, shining a hundred times brighter than the moon's illumination: It was Matthias's

reclamation, the rays pouring down from the heavens like a waterfall, eclipsing his body where it lay.

For a moment, Jim just watched the process, the shimmering
echo of Matthias's body pulled up in the centrifuge, drawn from
the flesh, headed for the Manse of Souls.

He had done it.

The motherfucker had *done it.*

That moment when Matthias had chosen someone else's life
over his own, when he had thrown himself into the path of that
bullet—even though Jim wouldn't have been affected—was the crossroads and the free will . . . and the victory.

"He's dying!" The sound of Mels's voice ripped him back into
focus. "He's—"

"Dead," Jim said grimly, lifting his hand in goodbye to his
old . . . friend, he supposed.

"No, he is not!"

Refocusing, Jim went over and got down on his haunches. "I'm
sorry, but he's gone."

The woman snapped out a hand and grabbed Jim's shirt, her
face that of a tiger, teeth bared, eyes gleaming. "He is *not* dead."

She dropped her hold and went for her own phone—

Jim snagged the thing out of her hands. "He's gone—I'm so
sorry, but he's not with us anymore. And you need to get out of
here—"

"What the hell are you talking about! Give me my goddamn
phone!"

"Mels—"

She launched herself at him, and he let her go, let her get her
energy and anger out as she struck him with her fists. Eventually,
he stilled her by turning her around and holding her back against
him, just so she didn't rip one of his eyes out.

When she finally quieted, she was breathing hard, and sobbing.

"He's gone," Jim said roughly. "And I'm really sorry. I'm so damned sorry for you. But you've got to listen to me. You have to leave—you do *not* want to be a part of this. He told me what he gave you—so I know you get it when I say it's not safe for you to be involved in what's going to happen next. Go home and get cracking on the information—that's how you'll be safe. As soon as you blow the cover and the story's out in the open, the organization will crumble. But until then, it's business as usual, and that means you're exposed. Go home. Do your work—and do it *fast*."

The woman sagged against his forearms and just hung there, loose in his hold, her head tilted in the direction of Matthias's body.

"You know I'm right," Jim said gently. "And I'll take good care of him. I promise."

Abruptly, Adrian stepped out from the tree line. "You'll never believe who I just ran into. Nigel."

Jim frowned. "I didn't sense him."

"Neither did I. But he was here."

To keep Devina away? he wondered. Or maybe that was the real reason he and Adrian hadn't sensed the assassin's approach?

"Is he gone?"

"Yup. Didn't say anything. Just gave me a wave and disappeared."

Okay, the why's and wherefore's of his boss were not what was important right now. "Ad, I want you to drive her home."

"Roger that."

"Mels?" Jim turned her around. "You *have* to go. It's not safe for you. Go and do what you can."

"He can't be gone. . . ."

"He is. You know he is. Trust me, he'll be treated good. Now go on . . . let Adrian take you home so you're safe. I can't have both of you dying on me."

Mels allowed Jim to lead her over to the car she'd arrived in, and after he opened the passenger-side door, he settled her in the seat. Given her docile act, it was pretty damn clear that shock had taken over—so they had to move quick, before she snapped out of it and put up another fight.

Before he shut her in, he leaned down. "There's someone you need to talk to. Isaac Rothe—he's one of us. You can find him through Childe with an E in Boston. Tell him that Jim Heron sent you, okay?"

She nodded, but he wasn't sure she'd really heard him.

Except suddenly she reached out and squeezed his hand. "Please don't . . . leave him somewhere anonymous. I mean . . ."

"I'll take care of him properly. I swear to you."

Looking into her eyes, Jim passed a hand over her face, sending her some peace to comfort her in her sadness.

Oh, man . . . he could feel the love she had for Matthias, and he ached for her. Was grateful for her, too. After all, what was the old adage? The love of a good woman . . .

It made all the difference, didn't it.

He had been right: Matthias had been the soul, but she had been the key.

"I swear to you," he said again. "Now go and do what's right."

Shutting the door, he banged on the roof and Ad backed the car out, doing a K-turn at the end of the drive and heading off.

Left alone, Jim pivoted around and looked for Nigel, but the archangel was nowhere to be seen or sensed. There was just the forest . . . and the two dead bodies on the gravel.

Matthias had gone to Heaven.

Wonder if the fucker was surprised? Then again, he'd made everything right on his way to the exit, and he'd done the ultimate— sacrificed himself for someone else.

On the scales of justice, he had a lot to make up for, but mere moments ago, he had given it all for another. . . .

As Jim went over to his old boss's body, he couldn't believe how far the man had come. Then again, Hell was clearly a transformative experience. And so was love.

Kneeling down, Jim said softly, "If you had told me we'd be here . . . I never would have believed it."

Truth really was stranger than fiction.

Jim rubbed his face and let himself fall back until he was sitting on his ass beside the man who had defined things for him for so long. In the silence, he became acutely aware of his breathing, of the way the air entered his nose cool, and came out his mouth warm.

He passed his palm over his face once more. Did it another time.

Overhead, the moon made another appearance, light raining down on the scene until he had to shut his eyes. For some reason, he didn't want to see anything of this moment, just couldn't bear it.

He had won the round, sure—but Matthias was still gone, and that struck him as a loss, and resonated deep.

And Adrian was still suffering. And Eddie was still gone. And him?

He was empty. So very empty—as if those orgasms he'd had with Devina had flushed the last part of his soul out.

Except he needed to pull it together—he had to get rid of the bodies.

Glancing over at the operative, he didn't give a shit where he stuffed the remains. His old boss, on the other hand, gave him a brain cramp. Where could he take Matthias? After all, it was a gift to the departed to treat what they had left behind with dignity—even as their souls soared free, it was important. And the man had saved his life . . . at least as far as Matthias had known.

Guess they were even—

Abruptly, a summoning came from up above, Nigel and his band of dandies calling him heavenward so he could see the flag he'd earned fly at the top of the great wall—along with the other two.

No, he thought. He wasn't going.

Fuck them and the game.

Shutting down the draw, he kept himself stuck on *terra firma*—to hell with the archangels, to hell with Devina, to hell with the Maker.

He wasn't playing right now. Maybe in a minute, an hour, a day, he would come back online, but at this moment? Fuck 'em all.

He was going to take care of his dead in the only way he could. That was all he knew.

With a curse, he forced himself to shift to the side and push his arms under Matthias's knees and shoulders. As he began to lift, Jim felt as dead as the other man—and knew it made no sense. He was now three up in the war. One more win and he could close this bizarre chapter in his life down and move along.

He should have been celebrating—

Matthias jerked wildly and drew in a huge breath of air.

"What the fuck!" Jim hollered.

And dropped the man like a bag of mulch.

Chapter Fifty-four

After her "chauffeur" parked her mother's car in the garage, Mels just sat in the passenger seat, staring straight ahead at the garden tools that had dust on them. "You can go now," she heard herself say.

She didn't look at the man, and prayed he left fast.

When he didn't move, she stated calmly, "If you don't get out of this car right now, I'm going to scream until I shatter the windshield. And I don't think either of us needs to go through that sort of thing. Do you?"

"He was a good guy."

Mels closed her eyes and slowly curled her arms around herself. She had thought that losing her father would be the greatest pain she would ever have to endure.

Maybe this just seemed worse because it was fresh?

"Matthias is going to be okay," the guy said.

"He's dead."

"And he's all right."

God, Mels really wanted to cry, just weep like crazy. But she felt frozen inside.

"Look at me," the man said. When she didn't, he put a gentle finger under her chin and shifted her head around—even as she refused to meet his eyes. "I'm not supposed to share certain kinds of intel, but I think you need something to keep you going tonight. Believe me, I know how that is."

"There's nothing you can say—"

"Your father's in the place where Matthias's going. They're both okay—"

"How can you be so cruel—"

"—where they are—"

"Pine Grove Cemetery is *not* okay!"

He just shook his head. "They're at eternal rest, and it's got nothing to do with where their bodies are buried. And you'll see them again, but not for a long while."

Finally meeting his stare, she—

With a gasp, Mels focused on his eyes . . . especially the one that looked as Matthias's had. *Precisely* as Matthias's had. And there were scars on his face he hadn't had before—right where Matthias had had them.

It was as if the man had lifted all of the injuries directly out of Matthias's flesh.

With a trembling hand, Mels reached up to touch his face, but he inched back, keeping away from the contact.

"It was true," she mumbled. "Matthias didn't fake the healing or the damage."

"Be at peace," the man said in a warping voice that seemed to be in her mind instead of coming through her ears. "You don't need to worry about either of them. They're safe."

At that moment, she knew in her heart what he was.

What Jim Heron was, too.

She had seen the truth in the mirror at the Marriott, and she was seeing it again now.

"You're an angel," she whispered in awe.

Her words seemed to snap him out of the connection, and he pulled away sharply. "Nah, just someone passing through your life."

Bullshit, she thought.

Abruptly, the man got out, shut the driver's-side door, and initiated the garage door to close . . . and then between one blink and the next, he was gone.

Mels wrenched her head over her shoulder, searching behind the car as the panels were trundling shut. Jumping out, she went to call his name. Except . . .

"You're still here—I can sense it."

No answer. No reveal—

"Mels?"

She whipped around. There, in the doorway that led into the kitchen, her mother was a dark silhouette in a pool of light.

Mels ran to her, tripping over her own feet, nearly losing her balance. When she got to her mother, she threw herself at the other woman.

"Mels? What's wrong? You're shaking—oh, my God, Mels . . ."

"I'm sorry—I'm sorry—"

Her mother held her up off the floor. "Mels? What are you sorry for? What's wrong—"

The tears came and didn't stop, everything breaking open, those years of keeping it together shattering like a mirror, a thousand cracks webbing out until she splintered completely.

Her mother was there to hold her as she fell apart.

And to think . . . she'd always believed she was the strong one?

Chapter Fifty-five

"That *hurt*, you son of a bitch."

Jim nearly lost his mind as he looked down at his old boss, who was—surprise!—alive and kicking.

One and only one thought went through his mind: "Do *not* tell me we're going for a round three with you."

As Matthias sat up and rubbed the back of his noggin, he shot a glare upward. "You dropped me on my head."

"You're dead!"

"Oh, and that's an excuse?" The guy stood up and brushed the pea gravel from the seat of his pants. "P.S., I found out what you are."

Jim started patting his pockets. "In need of a cigarette. Yeah, I am."

"You're an angel."

"Am I?" When he found the pack of Marlboros, he was tempted to take all ten that were left, put them in his mouth, and light them together. "Do I look like one?"

"I met with your Maker."

Jim froze with his Bic halfway to his lips.

"That's right." Matthias looked a little smug. "He says 'hi,' by the way—and he likes the turkey subs. Not sure what that means?"

"Excuse me?"

Matthias shrugged. "No clue on that one. But I met him—and I think he likes you. He told me about your game. Good luck with that, by the way—"

Jim presented his palm for review—directly in front of Matthias's face. "Stop. What the fuck are you doing here?"

Matthias walked around in a little circle like he was choosing his words, or maybe replaying a conversation in his mind. "Well, here's the thing, it's not that I don't trust you, but . . . she's my girl. I have to keep her safe. This is the only way."

"Only way how?"

Matthias pounded his chest with his fist. "I'm back in the saddle again, my friend. Okay, not *that* saddle—"

"This doesn't make any sense—"

"It's a simple case of free will. I went up there." He looked to the sky and frowned, as if he weren't entirely sure how all this had happened to him. "There was this massive castle thing—even had a moat in front of the entrance? An Englishman was waiting for me at the fortified doors, at the far end of this plank walkway. I'd seen him before, actually—at the Marriott? And then walking a dog? Anyway, I guess I understood, without being told, that all I had to do was walk across the bridge over the water and I was in forever."

The words dried up at that point, Matthias's brows going down hard, his eyes training on the ground.

"Annnnnnnd?" Jim bit out on the exhale.

"I couldn't do it. I knew if I crossed over there was no going back—I mean, I couldn't believe where I was. It was awesome, but . . . not for me."

"Let me get this straight. You're volunteering to go to Hell?"

"Not at all. The Maker came from out of nowhere and we talked. In the end, I just gave up one version of the place for another that was so much better. For me? Heaven is with that woman, and I'm going to spend the rest of my life trying to prove it to her—even though there's no guarantees about . . . well, shit, so much on that one. But I'm clear on the fact that I want to give it a shot."

"This can't be right."

"What can I say? The Maker's a fan of free will—maybe because if people make good choices, it affirms His creation? I don't know."

Jim got right up in the guy's grille, a strange fury driving him. "This is bullshit—if you get to pick, why doesn't everyone just stay with the ones they love?"

Like his mother.

Like his Sissy, for godsakes?

Man, he was too fucking tired of being jerked around by this game.

"People do come back from the dead," Matthias said. "Happens all the time."

"Not everyone." Not his dead. This was such bull*shit*.

"I got lucky. Look, if you have a problem with it, go talk to Him."

Jim stalked around, smoking, cursing—to the point where he nearly gave the dead operative's body a kick just because he could.

"Jim?" Matthias said slowly. "What's going on in that head of yours, my man."

At that moment, the solution presented itself, something that Nigel had said in the beginning of the round returning to him, taking root, and sprouting into a plan that was so heretical, it gave him pause even in his anger. But then he remembered things that Matthias had told him about the down below—and looked into the other man's face, his living, breathing, like-he'd-never-been-shot face.

The violent heat in Jim's gut was utterly familiar, the same force that had led him to fuck Devina, the same burn that sometimes took over and made him cruel, the same shit that had brought him to his first killings—of the men who had taken his mother's life.

This was the devil in him, he thought, this fury that had flared . . . and would soon settle into a cold determination that was going to change the shape of the game.

But goddamn it, as Matthias had said, some things you have to do yourself.

"Listen, Jim, how about we get rid of this body, and then go looking for the car he came in? I could really use a set of wheels that's not a rental, and with some work, I could locate the GPS on it and get rid of the thing."

"Yeah," Jim said offhandedly. "Sure."

"Are you okay?"

Nope. "Yeah." He stamped his cigarette butt out on the heel of his boot. "Sure."

Chapter
Fifty-six

The dawn's peachy rays were filtering through the forest and creating long shadows by the time Jim and Matthias accomplished their night's work.

Which had involved so much more than just getting rid of the stiff.

As Jim lit up the last of his cigarettes, he double-checked that two of the Harleys were secure in the bed of the F-150. It was a tight squeeze, but they weren't leaving Eddie's ride behind.

He was going to drive them out. Matthias was on Ad's bike. Adrian was taking the Explorer.

Because that was where Eddie had been packed.

"We ready?" Matthias asked.

When Jim gave the nod, the man put a pair of Ray-Bans on, jump-started the Harley, and pumped some extra gas into the motor, the growl rising and falling in the quiet early morning.

The flotilla left with Jim in front, and oh, what a shame, he split the police tape as he pulled out of the garage, the grille of the truck ripping it apart.

Sorry, CPD.

But at least they were leaving Matthias's rental behind so the unis had something tangible to get excited about.

Hitting the main road, he went north at an easy speed. They were going to travel around the city for quite a while, just making sure their tail was clean. Then at ten a.m., they were pulling into their new HQ.

Long night—and it felt good to sit on his ass for a while. Packing up the garage's studio hadn't been the issue; he didn't have a lot of personal shit. It had been dealing with the operative. The good news was that Ad had known right where to take the guy—a sinkhole in the mountains in which his buddy had been previously dropped like an anchor.

It was better that way. XOps was probably not going to care in the not-too-distant future, but in the interim, they could busy themselves finding the pair of bodies and feel good about themselves.

On the way out to the sinkhole site, they'd discovered the requisite sedan at the side of the road close to where number one had parked his ride—but Jim had talked Matthias out of using that vehicle. They were going to give the truck to his old boss as soon as they got to the new safe house and unpacked. Safer than trying to find the GPS on the unmarked, and license plates could be bought cheap if you knew where to go—

Jim's stomach let out a howl so loud even Dog, who was curled up in the passenger seat, lifted his head.

"Yeah, sorry—bet you need some food, too," he said gruffly. "Like maybe a turkey sub—right, Dog?"

As he glanced across the seat, the "animal" met his stare evenly, those almond-shaped brown eyes unblinking. Then one of those shaggy little paws lifted and grabbed at the air between them—like he was putting in an order for two—no, three hoagies.

So the Maker was with him, Jim thought. And had been all along.

Wonder what the big guy was going to think of his next move.

Going by Dog's grave face, Jim wondered if He knew already.

"Sorry," he muttered. "But some things you have to take care of yourself. . . ."

By the time the digital clock read nine fifty-four, Jim was pulling into the driveway of their new Casa d'Angel, and as the Explorer and the Harley came in behind him, someone whistled in appreciation.

Which was clearly a statement of irony.

"This place looks haunted," Matthias said as he cut the bike's engine.

"It's cheap and out of the way," Jim groused through his open window.

And however ugly it was, he didn't sense Devina anywhere around the place.

Picking up Dog, he got out from behind the wheel to find even Adrian looking a little surprised—which, considering what was on the angel's plate, was really saying something.

"I thought Rent-A-Wreck only did cars," the guy muttered.

Okay, fine, the bastard had a point. But who the hell else was going to rent to a shady character like Jim? Without asking for references?

And wreck was right: The mansion was cast in a palette of gray, everything from the cupolas on the third floor, to the stone porches at ground level, to the cockeyed shutters in between, painted with grisaille technique. Hell, even the vines that snaked up its flanks and crowded its huge front door were without leaves, the skeletal roots like an infection that had sprung from the black earth and was spreading.

The land that the thing was on covered some twenty-five acres, a ragged meadow running out in all directions to a thin tree line.

Off in the distance, other mammoth houses could be dimly seen—none of which was in a decrepit condition.

Bet the neighbors loved this place.

"Does it have running water?" Ad asked.

"Yeah. And electricity."

"Will miracles never cease."

Jim walked over to the mailbox. When he went to open the flap door, the thing fell off the hinges into his hand. "Here's the key."

"You mean they bother to lock this POS up?"

When he'd made the call on the property during the police raid, the owner had seemed stunned, as if she'd never expected to rent the house out. While they'd talked, he'd been concerned that she'd ask for references and he might not be able to hypnotize her over the phone, but she hadn't gone there. All she cared about was the security deposit, first and last month's rent, and an electronic debit—and he'd been more than happy to fall in line with all that: An exchange of account details later, and she was going to leave the key in the mailbox. Which she had.

Boom. Done.

Jim walked up the flagstone path to the front entrance, his boots making no sound, as if the slate were eating up his footfalls. Dog didn't follow him. Neither did the two men.

Scaredy-cats, all of them.

The key was not your humdrum Schlage variety—the thing was made of old brass and had a shaft thick as a finger. He expected to have to force it into the lock and then fight with the mechanism . . . but it went in like butter and opened smoothly.

Almost as if the house wanted him inside.

He expected the interior to be covered with cobwebs and dusty sheets, like an old-fashioned Abbott & Costello movie. Instead, the grand foyer was wilted, but clean, the scuffed floors and faded wallpaper and musty antiques testifying to a wealth that had been long lost.

Over to the left, there was a drawing room, and behind that, what looked like a living room. Dining room was to the right. Massive staircase straight ahead. And underneath the twin sets of steps, a solarium that opened out to the terraces behind the house.

Glancing upward, he thought, Yeah, this footprint could generate the eight bedrooms that had been advertised.

He twisted around, and looked through the open door. "Are you boys coming in? Or have you not finished pissing in your pants yet?"

Bitching. Whining. His name taken in vain.

Whatever.

"Bring some shit with you, wouldja," he called out.

Clomping through to the back of the house, he found a kitchen that was out of the forties, and a backyard that went on forever.

Must have been some kind of mansion in its heyday—

As the slow, rhythmic gonging of a grandfather clock started to ring out, he wondered where the damn thing was.

One, two, three, four . . .

Idly, he counted the measure of hours as he went back out to the front and looked around for the big daddy in charge of keeping time.

Eight . . . nine . . .

Frowning, Jim headed over to the base of the stairs and ascended, thinking the clock had to be on the big flat landing, halfway between the floors.

It wasn't.

Ten.

Just as his freak meter went off, Adrian and Matthias brought a load in, their voices echoing around the house.

Instead of going to help them, Jim went up farther on the steps, heading for the second story foyer.

Eleven.

He put his combat boot on the final step.

Twelve.

Not up there, either—at least, not that he could find. All he saw were open doors that framed the boxy space, the bedrooms clustered around an Oriental rug and sitting area the size of the garage's entire studio apartment—

Thirteen.

Or had that one just been in his imagination?

Rubbing the back of his neck, he contemplated calling the whole thing off. But that was a bullshit, pussy move—and the clock had *not* struck one hour too much.

Period.

Shaking his head, he jogged back to the first floor. "I gotta go," he told the guys.

Adrian didn't reply, and didn't look happy. Which suggested the angel might have guessed the destination. And what do you know, the guy muttered a quick, "Be careful."

Matthias put down a laundry hamper full of dirty—no, wait, clean?—clothes. "I'm not going to be here for long."

Jim felt a pull in the center of his chest, like someone had fisted his heart for a split second. "Yeah. Okay."

"I'm not going to see you again, am I?"

"No, you're not. That's the way it works."

"Just like an XOps operation, huh. You go in, do the job, get out."

"Something like that." Even now, after the round, Jim hadn't told Matthias exactly how things worked—and the guy hadn't asked, either. But his old boss wasn't stupid.

The two of them stared at each other for the longest time, until Jim felt like he couldn't stand the tension.

"Good luck with your girl," Jim said.

"Back at you with . . ." The guy looked around. "Whatever the hell you're doing here."

"Thanks, man."

Matthias cleared his throat. "I still owe you."

"Nah. After last night, we're even."

Matthias stuck out his hand, and Jim clasped it tight. Funny, they had met on a handshake, back when they'd started XOps training together, neither of them having a clue what they were in for. Same thing now, except this was a goodbye, not a hello.

"If you need me—" Matthias started.

"Just take care of yourself."

They embraced at that point, one of those hard-muscled, manly-man, chest-to-chest numbers that lasted only long enough for them to pound the crap out of each other's shoulder. And then they separated.

Jim didn't say good-bye. He just turned away . . . and disappeared himself.

Down below, in the depths of Hell, Devina sat upon her worktable, her rotting legs dangling off the end, her head down, her clawed hands gripping the edge of the wood so tightly, they sank in past the stained surface to the meat.

She had violated the rules—and lost.

She had tried to play by the rules—and lost.

One more win and Jim had wrapped up the game.

The embarrassment was nearly worse than the specter of not prevailing in the war: She had always prided herself on her ability to get under the skin of the Maker's flawed creations—and Jim should have been no different. In fact, after they'd fucked at the boathouse, she'd been overjoyed, feeling like she was making progress with her man, and certain that she'd was going to win with Matthias.

Instead, that fucker had chosen badly. And for crissakes, who could have guessed that? The sorry bastard had been a good boy for so long, his penchant for calculated violence such an example to others. Then at the last minute, he pussied out? Because of a chick?

What. The. Fuck.

And the worst thing? Devina hadn't been able to do a thing about it: She had gone to the final scene, concerned by his gesture to that reporter, ready to interject herself at the most critical juncture—only to find Nigel standing guard like some kind of morally justified mastiff.

There had been no way to get at the situation with that archangel in the cocksucking bushes. And Jim, damn him to hell, was continuing to betray her with the way he was influencing these souls.

At this rate, she was going to lose—

Devina lifted her head, a shot of energy ringing her internal bell.

Jim, she thought.

Uh-huh, yeah, right, she was letting him down here. The last thing she was in the mood for was him parading his win around.

Ignoring the signaling, she stayed where she was, even her OCD symptoms held at bay by a crushing sense of defeat.

What was she going to do—

"Oh, for fuck's sake." She glared up at the distant circle of gloom at the very top of her well. "Will you give it a rest, Heron? I don't want to see you."

The signal only got louder, more insistent.

Maybe something was wrong?

How fun would that be.

Abruptly, she changed into her suit of flesh, the one that he had so enjoyed ejaculating into the other evening. Her hair was perfect, as always, but she checked it with her hands anyway.

Staying right where she was, she allowed him entrance, his presence electrifying her the moment he got in range and appeared in his physical form.

Interesting . . . there was no triumph in his face, no ha-ha!, no macho swagger thanks to his victory.

He stood before her, unbowed, but not shitting on her parade, either.

Devina narrowed her eyes. "You haven't come to gloat?"

"I wouldn't waste my time on that."

No, he probably wouldn't. She would have, though—guess that part of him took after Nigel's side.

"So why are you here?" She hopped off the table and walked in a slow circle around him. "I'm not in the mood to fuck."

"Neither am I."

"So . . . ?"

"I'm here to strike a deal."

She laughed in his face—considered spitting in it, too, for that matter. "We've done that once already, and in case you haven't forgotten, you didn't keep your side of the bargain."

"I will now."

"How do I know that—and who says I'm interested."

"You're interested."

She stopped in front of the table and put her hand on it in an effort to remind him of how she'd had him there. "I doubt it."

The angel brought his arm out from behind his back, and in his hand, on a short pole . . . was a victory flag.

Devina's brows lifted. "Taken up sewing, have you."

He waved the thing idly. "I have something you need. You have something I want."

The demon stopped breathing—even though she didn't require the inhale/exhale thing to survive. Was he actually suggesting . . . he would *give* her one of his wins?

Well, it was in the rules, she thought. At least technically. That victory was his property . . . and she supposed that he could assign it to her, if he so chose.

"Does Nigel know what you're doing?" she said softly.

"I'm not talking about him. This is between you and me."

Ah, so the archangel had thrown a fit—or didn't know yet.

And if this worked, it would make the score two to two, instead of one to three. Whole different ball game.

The demon started to smile. "Tell me, my love . . . just what is it you want?"

Even though she knew.

Well, well, well, wasn't the game really going to get interesting now. And it looked as if her therapist had been right: It was possible, with enough exposure, to rewire one's brain—or somebody else's—to produce a given reaction.

All that hair color might have been worth it.

Just like the L'Oréal ad said.

Devina slinked her way over to her lover, her sex blooming in the tense quiet. "Tell me, Jim, and I'll think about it. But I would like to hear you say the words."

It was a while before he answered her.

And then he spoke, loud and clear. "I want Sissy."

Epilogue

Three weeks later . . .

"Are you ready?"

As Mels nodded, she squinted into the noonday sun. Putting her hand up to shield her eyes, she said, "I can't wait."

Redd's Garage & Service was the kind of place her father would have gone to, an auto-body repair and mechanics shop that was full of old-school types who had tattoos they'd gotten in the Army, grease on their faces, and wrenches instead of computers to do the work.

And unlike Caldwell Auto, they had seen Fi-Fi worth saving.

Mels's old Civic was backed out to the kind of fanfare that *West Coast Choppers* revealed their masterpieces with.

Then again, Mels's ancient set of wheels, back in working order, was a miracle: Somehow the team here had gotten her into shape again.

"Oh, look at her!" Mels walked over as the mechanic got out from behind the wheel. "It's . . . well, it truly is a miracle."

That was the only word that kept coming to her: Her steady and sure car had been resurrected out of its catastrophic injuries and was once more on the road.

Frankly, she felt a kinship with the Civic. She had been through a crash, had pulled herself back together, and was about to hit the road. With Fi-Fi's help, of course.

"Thank you so much," she murmured, blinking fast.

A quick signature on some paperwork, and then she was sitting in the driver's seat, running her hands around the wheel. Parts of the dash had had to be replaced because of the air bag deployment, and Fi-Fi smelled different—a little like clean oil. But she sounded the same and she felt the same.

Mels briefly closed her eyes as that familiar pain came back.

Then she opened them, reached over to her left hip, and drew the seat belt across her lap. After clicking the thing home, she put the engine in drive and eased out into traffic.

The previous three weeks had been . . . illuminating. Scary. Lonely. Affirming.

And her solace, apart from work, had been writing it all down . . . everything from stories about her father to details about the man she'd fallen in love with, to the aftermath.

Well, part of the aftermath, at least.

Hopping onto the highway, she allowed the other cars to set her speed as opposed to rushing around them impatiently. And she stopped at a deli on the way home, because it was a little past lunchtime and she was exhausted and starving from packing up her room and putting everything she owned into a little U-Haul trailer.

She wasn't due in Manhattan until the following morning, so maybe when she got back to the house she'd take a nap in the sunroom.

Funny, she'd been doing that a lot lately, stretching out on that sofa that looked out over the garden, her head buttressed on a pillow, her legs crossed at the ankles, a throw blanket pulled up to her pelvis.

She had a lot of sleep to catch up on.

Right after Matthias had died in front of her, she hadn't slept for days, her mind spinning with a ferocity that made her feel like she was going insane. She'd been obsessed with replaying the whole thing over and over, from the impact outside the cemetery to Matthias taking that bullet in front of the garage. From seeing him in the hospital to sharing his bed. From her suspicions rising to their falling once again.

To the SanDisk.

As she came to a slowdown around a stretch of construction, she glanced at the radio. Bracing herself, she leaned in and turned the knob—

"—explosive investigation conducted by the *New York Times* into a shadow organization that, for decades, has been operating under the nation's radar, conducting assignments at home and abroad—"

She turned the thing off.

Staring out over her pristine new hood, she tightened her grip on the wheel.

After three days of not sleeping and thinking over her options, she'd put a call in to her contact at the *Times* and driven down to meet him face-to-face.

When she'd turned the flashdrive—and the name of Isaac Rothe—over to Peter Newcastle, her only caveats had been that he not ask her where she got it, and that he not attempt to follow up with her in any way—because she had nothing to add.

The story had finally broken the morning before, on the front page of a paper with the resources, the balls and the worldwide reach to do the information justice. And the fallout was already beginning, government agencies up in arms, senators and congressmen addressing cameras and microphones with outrage, the president scheduled to do a Q & A with Brian Williams at nine this evening.

In the end, she'd decided to give the story of a lifetime to someone else for two reasons: one, she valued her own life too much to roll the dice that there wouldn't be retaliation; and two, if she reported it under her own byline, that meant she'd used Matthias, that he hadn't been anything more than a source to her, that she'd helped when she had not out of the goodness of her heart, but because she'd been following a story.

It was kind of in the same vein of his having given her the intel to prove he'd been truthful—she passed it on to someone else so nobody could ever say that she hadn't loved him.

Not that anyone knew about him.

At all, as it were. There had been nothing in the paper about his death—or his body. And when she'd gone back to the garage in the middle of her seventy-two-hour period of crazy-crazies, all she'd walked into was a police scene that had turned hot again.

Gone, gone, gone. The vehicles, the personal affects, any signs of inhabitation.

Jim Heron, and his friend, had disappeared.

End of the trail.

It was strange—she had started sleeping again the night after she'd gotten back from the trip to Manhattan to meet with Peter. Which was how she'd known she'd done the right thing with the flashdrive . . .

She had not expected to hear from the man again.

Except then, three days prior to the big story's release, he'd called to let her know the massive article was coming out—and to offer her a job. He'd said that wanted someone with her kind of tenacity and focus to come in at the junior level—and she'd stopped him right there, explaining that a source had given her the files as is; she'd done nothing to compile, organize, or format the information.

"But you got to the source, didn't you."

Well, yes. And had her heart broken in the process.

In the end, she'd accepted the offer. She wasn't stupid—and she was ready to get back to hard work and start pulling long hours again. Maybe it would help with pain management. . . .

God, she missed Matthias.

Or rather, what they might have had.

Because he had told the truth. About everything.

Pulling into her mom's driveway, Mels parked Fi-Fi behind the U-Haul and left the window down, because the day was clear as a bell, without any rain in sight.

She ate half her deli sandwich at the counter, drank a ginger ale, and cleaned up just in case her mom returned from her camping trip on Lake George early.

Couch?

Why, yes, please . . . thank you.

Stepping out into the slate-floored sunroom, she popped the sliders and felt the warmth rush in. It was seventy-five in the sun, and the air smelled like fresh-cut grass, because the lawn men had come that morning.

The sofa was perfectly soft and cozy, and as she lay down, she took that blanket and SOP'd it, pulling it over her legs. Settling back, she glanced around at the potted plants on the little tables and the rocker and the fat armchair in the corner. So familiar, so safe.

She wasn't aware of shutting her eyes or falling asleep . . . but a little later, the strangest noise woke her.

A scratching.

Jerking awake, she lifted her head off the cushions. On the far side of the screen, there was a little mutt of a dog, his fur standing straight up at all angles, his head cocked, his eyes kind under bushy eyebrows.

Mels sat up. "Well . . . hello, there."

The animal pawed again, but carefully, like he didn't want to damage the screen.

"Ah . . . we're not a dog house, I'm afraid." They'd never done the pet thing. "Are you lost?"

She expected him to run off when she approached, but he just stayed at the door, dropping his butt to the ground, as if that were the polite thing to do.

The moment she slid the screen back, he shot in and wagged in a circle at her feet.

Crouching down, she tried to find his collar or a tag or something—

"Hi."

Mels froze.

Then she turned so fast to the screen door that she fell over.

Standing there, in the sunlight, between the jambs was . . . Matthias.

Mels grabbed on to her own throat and started breathing hard.

He lifted a hand. "I . . . ah . . . yeah, hi . . ."

As he stuttered, she decided it had finally happened. Instead of getting better, her brain had snapped free of reality completely—

Wait, wait, wait, this had to be a dream.

Right? This was just a dream—she'd fallen asleep on the couch and was imagining that that which she had wanted to happen was actually occurring.

His voice sounded so perfect in her ears: "I know I said I wouldn't come back, but I thought maybe, now that the story was out, you might see me."

"You're dead."

"No." He lifted his foot like he was going to walk in, and then stopped. "Can I come in?"

She nodded numbly—because like there was another response?

And in the dream, he was as he had been, tall, harsh faced, intense. He wasn't limping, though, and his eyes and scars were as they had been just as he had left her.

After that angel had taken them from him.

Matthias leaned back against the jamb. "I was surprised you gave the story to someone else."

Well, what do you know, her subconscious was up on current affairs. "It was the right thing to do. The safer choice."

"Yeah, I—"

"I love you." Now it was his turn to jerk in shock. "Sorry, but I have to tell you. I'm going to wake up from this soon enough, and I'd kick myself if I didn't actually say it to you once. Even if it's only in my dreams."

His eyes shut as if he were absorbing a physical blow.

"I know what the angel did to you," she explained. "You know, about your sight and things. So I know you didn't lie to me about that. Or how you felt. And to be honest, that's the only thing that's gotten me through this."

Eventually, his lids rose up. "This isn't a dream."

"Of course it is."

"I'm alive, Mels. I'm here for good."

"Uh-huh." What else would he say in her made-up construct of reality? "I just want you to know that I understand why you did what you did, and I'm really glad you came forward with all that stuff about XOps. You did the right thing—wrapped it all up in a good way. So Hell can't be where you went. Right?"

Matthias came over to her, kneeling down on the bright green Astroturf rug that was supposed to look like a patch of grass in the middle of the flagstone.

"This isn't a dream." He reached out with a shaking hand and touched her face. "Trust me."

"That's exactly what I would want you to say," she murmured, grasping his wrist and holding him in place. "Oh, God . . ."

As she breathed him in, her broken heart hurt so badly that she couldn't bear the pain—because she knew she was going to come out of this soon, and it would be over, and she would have to go back to a world where she missed him like crazy, where things that should have been said hadn't been, where what might have been could never be.

Lonely place. Cold place.

"Come here," he said, pulling her into his chest.

She went willingly and rested against him, hearing a vital heartbeat beneath his sternum. And Matthias began to speak to her, telling her again how it was all real, his voice low and raspy, like he was struggling with his own emotions.

When a cold, wet nose bumped under her arm, she drew back. "Well, hello, little man."

"I see you've met Dog," Matthias said.

"Is he yours?"

"He's everyone's."

Huh? "He just showed up here. Right before you did."

"That's because he cares about you. And . . . is there any chance you have any food in the house he could eat? I think he's hungry."

"Just half my sandwich."

The little dog curled into a sit and wagged his tail as if he understood every word—and wouldn't mind taking one for the team and polishing off whatever she'd left uneaten.

On some level, she couldn't believe they were speaking so nicely and normally about deli meat, but in dreams, weird things happened—

"Oh, hello! Who's your friend?"

Mels jumped and looked up to the doorway into the kitchen:

Her mom was standing there with luggage hanging off her shoulder, a sunburn on her nose, and a smile on her face.

"Mom?"

"I came home a little early." The bags dropped and her hair was smoothed. "Aren't you going to introduce us?"

Abruptly, her father's voice came back to her, telling her she didn't need to believe in something for it to be real.

Mels's skin began to prickle from head to foot as she looked back and forth between her mother and her . . . well, whatever he was.

As an awkward silence sprang up, she took Matthias's hand and squeezed as hard as she could. Until he went, *"Ouch."*

And that was when she knew.

This . . . was not a dream.

Okay, Matthias had never expected to meet any woman's parents—and certainly not like this . . . with the female he loved thinking he was a figment of her imagination, and her mother standing in a doorway like she didn't know whether to come in again and give it another go—or disappear altogether.

Before things grew even weirder, he shifted Mels out of his arms and got to his feet. Straightening his Hanes T-shirt, he wished he didn't look like a homeless man, except that's what he was. Rootless, but clean-shaven, at least.

For the past three weeks, he'd been staying in hotels in the area, keeping an eye on Mels, watching her from a distance to make sure she was okay. And she had been.

Which was not to say there hadn't been some surprises. All those mornings she'd gone into the newsroom, he'd assumed she was working on the story, but no. After that one trip to Manhattan—and of course he'd followed her down there and segued to raid his secured stash for cash and supplies—she had stuck to home base in more than one sense.

It wasn't until the story broke the day before that he realized she hadn't reported it herself.

Somehow, it made him love her even more.

He walked over and stuck his hand out to her mom. "Ah . . . I'm Matt. A friend of Mels's."

Her mother was nothing like her, shorter, more delicate, with salt-and-pepper hair and bright green eyes—but absolutely lovely . . . and with a brisk handshake that absolutely made him think of the woman's daughter.

"I'm Helen. I'm so glad to meet you." And going by the way her eyes were shining, that was the truth. "Are you staying for dinner?"

He looked at Mels. When she seemed incapable of answering, he figured, Why the hell not. "Yes, ma'am. If you two will have me."

"Oh, wonderful!" Helen clapped her hands together, and then bent down to the pile of scruffy fur that had come over to welcome her into her own home. "Is this your dog?"

"He's everyone's," he and Mels answered together.

"Well, he's welcome, too—yes, you are, yes, you are, what a good boy." After proper love was shown, Helen glanced over. "I'll head out and get us some burgers to do up on the grill. It's going to be a fantastic, warm night, and we should take advantage of it while it's here!"

On that note, the woman turned on her heels, grabbed her keys, and left—like maybe she knew there was some talking that needed to be done away from any third parties.

Dogs excluded.

Mels just stared up at him as he turned to her. "You're really back?"

He nodded. "Yeah."

"I watched you die."

He took a deep breath. He'd spent a lot of time wondering how to explain it all, and then decided that if he got the chance, he was going to be vague. No reason for her to think he was lying—or mentally ill.

"It looked that way, yeah."

"Have you been in the hospital? Where did you go?"

"Jim took care of me."

"I thought that meant he buried your body."

In time, he thought, he'd explain everything. But his woman looked as if her mind was cramping up. So, yeah, hitting her with an I've-been-to-Heaven-and-met-God was probably not the best idea.

"Not the way it played out." He crouched down. "Let's just say, I was saved. In the end . . . I was saved and all I could think of was coming back to you."

Tears spilled out of her eyes and onto her cheeks. "I didn't think I'd ever see you again."

"I'm here. So will you let me kiss you now?"

She reached for him by way of answer, her arms linking around his neck, her mouth finding his, the two of them coming together as one.

And it was better than Heaven.

In fact, if he hadn't thought it would lead to difficult conversations with the neighbors, he would have taken her right then and there—but there would be time for that sort of thing when there was more privacy.

God willing.

Easing back, he brushed her hair behind her ears. "There's one thing you have to know—I'm not going to give myself up."

"To authorities?"

"If I do, I'll get killed in jail. Maybe it's by an operative, maybe an old enemy—but I . . . I've already done my time in a prison. I've paid my dues."

That stint in Hell had been just as he deserved, and though on earth the stay might have been measured in days, down below it had been an eternity, a life sentence carried out.

"And I vow to you, no more lying, no more deceit, nothing. I'll pack groceries for a living, I'll be a meter maid, I'll . . . I don't know what. But I'll figure something out, and it's going to be honest."

Mels studied his face, then ran her hand over his cheek to his jaw. "If you're at peace, I'm at peace," she murmured. "Who am I to judge? And it's funny, my father would have liked your way of doing business. I'm not saying it's okay, it's just . . . you've always been good for me, and maybe it makes me selfish, but that's what matters. Well, that and you did right by coming forward and exposing everything."

"That part of my life is over. Forever." Thanks in large part to her . . . and to Jim Heron . . . he just didn't have that evil in him anymore.

As she started to smile, Matthias kissed her again, lingering on her mouth, holding the curves of her body tight.

"I love you," he said.

His woman returned the words against his lips and he drank them in, drank all of this in, the salvation, the relief, the sheer joy of being with her. And he thought also of Jim Heron, and how much he owed the guy.

He wasn't going to see the man again; he knew it in his bones. And that was . . . okay. Everything was okay as long as he had Mels—

A yap brought their heads up and around.

Dog had gone into the kitchen and was sitting by the refrigerator, one paw in the air.

Just as well, Matthias thought. He was a heartbeat away from ripping Mels's clothes off.

As they got to their feet and went into the kitchen, he asked, "Any chance that sandwich is turkey?"

"As a matter of fact, yes."

Matthias leaned in and kissed his woman. "Perfect. Dog loves that."

"Then he can have every bit that's left, and anything else that's in the fridge."

As they opened the door, the animal circled their feet, tail going, limp not slowing him or dimming his enthusiasm in the slightest.

Matthias kissed his woman once more.

Then they got down on their knees and took care of the little guy, feeding the sandwich piece by piece . . . together.

After all, it was the least he could do, Matthias thought. Considering God had given him everything he'd asked for . . . and couldn't live without.